D0103705

"Terrific new novel . . . Andrew Taylor has long been in the top rank of British crime writers, never disappointing, particularly strong on depth of characterisation and moody atmosphere. In *Bleeding Heart Square* he excels himself."

—*The Times*

"Moody, delightful . . . The period details are pitch perfect."

## PRAISE FOR *THE FOUR LAST THINGS*

"A surefire thriller to take your mind off those winter blues . . ."

"Every parent's nightmare."

"A finely crafted story of suspense . . . His ingredients are doubt, guilt, and moral ambiguity, intermingling with the more usual trappings of crime detection. It is a book which can be read at more than one level. The appetite for the remaining two of the trilogy is firmly whetted."

## PRAISE FOR *THE JUDGEMENT OF STRANGERS*

"Taylor cloaks all the horrid doings in prose as stately and deliberate as Dorothy Sayers's . . . A superior village mystery that whets the appetite for the promised third volume."

"The second part of Andrew Taylor's Roth Trilogy, which is being written in reverse order as a way of exploring the creation of a psychopath and, perhaps, the roots of evil . . . Andrew Taylor has set himself a huge task . . . the first two [novels in the trilogy] work well, throwing light forward and backwards on to the characters and their behaviour."

—*The Times Literary Supplement*

"Nostalgic setting, contemporary surprises."

—Frances Fyfield, *The Sunday Mail*

## PRAISE FOR *THE OFFICE OF THE DEAD*

"With all due deference to its heavenly virtues, this is a hellishly good novel."

—Frances Fyfield, *The Sunday Express*

"Deals, in the quietest and most civilised way, with abominable suffering . . . It is in the domestic sphere that Andrew Taylor triumphs [in] this highly sinister piece of work."

—*The Times Literary Supplement*

"Quietly compelling."

—*The Sunday Telegraph*

# The
# JUDGEMENT
# of
# STRANGERS

# JUDGEMENT

# STRANGERS

## ANDREW TAYLOR

HYPERION

NEW YORK

ISBN: 978-1-4013-2262-5

Hyperion books are available for special promotions, premiums, or corporate training. For details contact Michael Rentas, Proprietary Markets, Hyperion, 77 West 66th Street, 12th floor, New York, New York 10023, or call 212-456-0133.

*Design by Ralph Fowler / rlfdesign*

FIRST HYPERION EDITION

*For Val and Bill*

## AUTHOR'S NOTE

*The Judgement of Strangers* is the second novel in the Roth Trilogy, which deals, layer by layer, with the linked histories of the Appleyards and the Byfields. Each book may be read on its own as a self-contained story. The three novels are also designed to work together, though they may be read in any order.

The first novel, *The Four Last Things*, is set in London in the middle of the 1990s. The third novel, *The Office of the Dead*, is set in the cathedral city of Rosington over a decade before the events described in *The Judgement of Strangers*.

*"Cursed is he that perverteth the judgement of the stranger, the fatherless, and widow."*

—FROM THE SERVICE OF COMMINATION,
IN THE OFFICE FOR ASH WEDNESDAY IN
*THE BOOK OF COMMON PRAYER.*

*"The Manor of Roth is not mentioned in the Domesday Book . . ."*

—AUDREY OLIPHANT, *THE HISTORY OF ROTH*
(RICHMOND, PRIVATELY PRINTED 1969), P.1.

*Then darkness descended; and whispers defiled*
*The judgement of stranger, and widow, and child . . .*

.   .   .

*With flames to the flesh, with brands to the burning,*
*As incense to heav'n the soul is returning*

—FROM "THE JUDGEMENT OF STRANGERS"
BY THE REVEREND FRANCIS ST. J. YOULGREAVE
IN *THE FOUR LAST THINGS*
(GASSET & LODE, LONDON, 1896)

# Chapter One

WE FOUND THE MUTILATED CORPSE of Lord Peter in the early evening of Thursday the 13th August, 1970. He was the first victim of a train of events which began toward the end of the previous summer when I met Vanessa Forde—or even before that, with Audrey Oliphant and *The History of Roth*.

Every parish has its Audrey Oliphant—often several of them; their lives revolve around the parish church, and in one sense the Church of England revolves around them. It was inevitable that she should be a regular visitor at the Vicarage, and it shamed me that I did not always welcome her as warmly as I should have done. It also irritated me that the Tudor Cottage cat treated the Vicarage as his second home, braving the traffic on the main road to get there.

"Miss Oliphant practically lives here," said my daughter Rosemary at the end of one particularly lengthy visit. "And if she doesn't come herself she sends her cat instead."

"She does an awful lot for us," I pointed out. "And for the parish."

"Dear Father. You try and find the best in everyone, don't you?" Rosemary looked up at me and smiled. "I just wish she would leave us alone. It's much nicer when it's just the two of us."

Audrey was in her late forties and unmarried. She had

lived in Roth all her life. Her house, Tudor Cottage, was on the green—on the north side between Malik's Minimarket and the Queen's Head. Its front garden, the size of a large bedspread, was protected from the pavement by a row of iron railings. Beside the gate there was a notice, freshly painted each year:

YE OLDE TUDOR TEA ROOM
(Est. 1931)
PROPRIETOR: MISS A. M. OLIPHANT
Telephone: Roth 6269
Morning Coffee — Light Meals — Cream Teas
Parties By Appointment

I had known the place for ten years, and in that time trade, though never brisk, had steadily diminished. This gave Audrey ample opportunity to read enormous quantities of detective novels and to throw herself into the affairs of the parish.

One evening in the spring of 1969, she appeared without warning on my doorstep.

"I've just had the most wonderful idea."

"Really?"

"I'm not interrupting anything, am I?" she asked, initiating a ritual exchange of courtesies, a secular versicle and response.

"Not at all."

"Are you sure?"

"Nothing that can't wait." I owed her this polite fiction. "I was about to have a break."

I took her into the sitting room and, making a virtue from

necessity, offered sherry. Audrey was a small woman, rather plump, with a face whose features seemed squashed; it was as though her skull, while still malleable, had been compressed in a vise—thus the face would have been splendidly in proportion if the eyes and the cheekbones and the corners of the mouth had not been quite so close together.

She took a sip of sherry, allowing the wine to linger in her mouth before she swallowed it. "I was in the library this afternoon and some schoolchildren came in to ask Mrs. Finch if she had any books on local history. And it turns out that there's a certain amount on neighboring towns and villages. But very little on Roth itself."

She paused for another sip. I lit a cigarette, guessing what was coming.

"Then it came to me in a flash." Her heavy jowls quivered with excitement. "Why not write a history of Roth? I'm sure lots of people would like to read one. And nowadays so many people are living here who have no idea what the *real* Roth is like."

"What an interesting idea. You must let me know if there is anything I can do. The parish records, perhaps? I wonder if Lady Youlgreave might have some useful material. She—"

"I'm so glad," Audrey interrupted. "I hoped you'd want to help. Actually, a collaboration was what I had in mind. It seemed to me that we would be ideally suited."

"I wouldn't say—"

"Besides," she rushed on, "the history of the village can't be separated from the history of the church and the parish. We could even have a chapter on famous inhabitants of the past. Francis Youlgreave, for example. What do you think?"

"I'm not sure how much use I'd be. After all, you're the one with the local knowledge. Then there's the question of time . . ."

I watched the excitement draining from Audrey's face like water from a bath. I felt ashamed of myself and also irritated with her. Why did she insist on calling Roth a village? It was a suburb of London, similar in all essentials to a dozen others. Most of its inhabitants had their real lives elsewhere. In Roth they merely serviced their bodily needs, watched television and on Sundays played golf or cleaned their Ford Cortinas.

"I quite understand." Audrey stared at her empty glass. "Just an idea."

"I wonder," I went on, trying to lessen the guilt that crept over me, "would it be a help if I were to glance through your first draft?"

She looked up, her face glowing. "Yes, please."

The decision was made. If Audrey had not decided to write her history of Roth, none of what followed might have happened. It is tempting to blame her—to blame anyone but myself. But fate has a way of finding its agents: if Audrey had not volunteered to be the handmaid of Providence, then someone else would have come forward.

Audrey completed her little book early in August 1969. In a flutter of excitement, she brought me the manuscript, which was written almost illegibly in pencil. It was mercifully short, largely because Roth had relatively little history. Since the Middle Ages, the parish had been overshadowed by its larger neighbors. It was too far from the Thames, and later too far from the railway.

Still, to judge from the old photographs which Audrey had

found, Roth had been a pretty place, and remarkably un-spoiled, despite the fact that it was only thirteen miles from Charing Cross. All that had changed in the 1930s, when the Jubilee Reservoir was built: seven hundred acres of the par-ish, including the northern part of the village itself, were drowned beneath seven billion gallons of water, sacrificed to assuage the endless thirst of the inhabitants of London.

I soon discovered that Audrey's spelling and grammar were shaky. The text consisted of a patchwork of speculations—*Who knows? Perhaps Henry VIII stayed at the Old Manor House on his way to Hampton Court*—and quotations lifted, often inaccurately, from books she had found in the library. I persuaded her to have the manuscript typed, and managed—diplomatically, I hoped—to arrange for the typist quietly to incorporate some of my corrections. I then went through the typed draft with Audrey and revised it once more. By now it was early September.

"We must find a publisher," Audrey said.

"Perhaps you could have it privately printed?"

"But I am sure it would interest readers all over the coun-try," she said. "In many ways the story of Roth is the story of England."

"In a sense, yes, but—"

"And, David," she interrupted. "I want all the royalties to go to the restoration fund. Every last penny. So we must find a proper publisher who will pay us lots of money. Why don't you come to supper tomorrow and we'll discuss it? I'd like to cook you a meal to say thank you for all the work you've done." She tapped me playfully on the arm. "You look as if you need a good feed."

"Unfortunately I can't manage tomorrow. The Trasks have asked me to dinner. Some other time, perhaps."

"Some other time," she echoed.

I was relieved that the Trasks had given me such an impregnable excuse. As a consequence of my accepting their invitation, two people died, a third went to prison, and a fourth was admitted to a hospital for the insane.

## *Chapter Two*

THE TRASKS LIVED IN a rambling Victorian rectory cheek by jowl with a rambling Victorian church. I knew from past visits that both the church and the house were warm and welcoming. Ronald did a very good job. His congregations were considerably larger than average.

I parked on the graveled forecourt in front of the house. Two other cars were already there: an Austin Cambridge and a dark-green Daimler. The front door opened before I had reached it. Ronald beamed at me. I was wearing my clerical suit and a dog collar, but he was in mufti—rather a good dark suit, which made him look slimmer than he was, and a striped tie. He was shorter than me but much broader, and he gave the impression of never walking when he could trot. This evening, everything about him sparkled, from his black shoes to his fair hair. Aftershave wafted out to meet me.

"David!" He clapped me on the shoulder and drew me into the house. "Good to see you. Come and meet the others."

The hall was full of flowers and smelled strongly of polish. Ronald led me into the drawing room, which was at the back of the house. It was a warm evening. The French windows were open and a knot of people was standing on the terrace beyond.

Cynthia Trask came forward to greet me. She was square and trim, like her brother, and she wore a severe blue dress like a uniform. While Ronald fetched me a glass of sherry, she steered me toward the other guests.

I knew one of the couples—Victor and Mary Thurston. Thurston had made a great deal of money selling cabin cruisers for use on the river, and now he and his wife "served the community" as they liked to put it, which meant sitting on a variety of committees; she preferred philanthropic causes and he concentrated on political ones. Thurston was a councillor and, now that he was on the Planning Committee, wielded considerable power.

I had not met the other couple before—they turned out to be the headmaster of one of the local grammar schools and his wife; she was one of Ronald's churchwardens.

The first thing I noticed about the fifth guest was her hair, which was curly and the color of glossy chestnuts. As she turned toward me, the evening sun swung behind her, giving her head a nimbus of flame. She was wearing a long dress of thin cotton, with full sleeves and a ruffled neck. For an instant, the setting sun made her dress almost transparent. Her body darkened. I saw the inside of her legs up to her crotch. The dress might as well have been invisible.

"Here we are, David." Ronald was at my elbow with a glass of sherry. "Vanessa, I don't think you know David Byfield. David, this is Vanessa Forde."

We shook hands. I was momentarily unnerved by the sudden lust I felt. This was a familiar problem. Over the years I had learned to ride the feeling as a surfer rides a wave, until its force diminished. One way to avoid wallowing in sensation was to concentrate on observation. In a few seconds I had noticed that Vanessa had a pleasant face, attractive rather than beautiful, with a high color and curving nose.

"Let me get you another drink." Ronald snatched the empty glass from Vanessa's hand. "Gin and lemon?"

She nodded, smiling. Ronald darted toward the drinks trolley, which was just inside the drawing room. There was something very boyish about him that evening. At times I glimpsed the adolescent he must once have been; and if I am honest, I should add that I preferred what I glimpsed to the senior churchman he had now become.

I offered Vanessa a cigarette. She accepted, bending forward to receive a light. I saw that she wore a wedding ring. For an instant, I smelled her perfume. It reminded me of one my wife used to wear. We spoke simultaneously, diving into the conversation like swimmers at the start of a race.

"Do you live locally?"

"Do you have a parish—?"

We smiled at each other and any awkwardness dissolved.

"After you, Mrs. Forde."

"Vanessa, please. To answer your question, I live in Richmond."

I noticed that she had said I rather than we. "And to answer yours, I'm the vicar of Roth."

"Oh yes."

"Do you know Roth, then?"

"A little." She stared up at me and smiled. "Does that surprise you?"

I smiled back. "Its identity tends to get swamped by its neighbors. A lot of people think the name is familiar but have no idea where it is."

"I went there a few years ago to see the church. Rather an interesting one. You've got that medieval panel painting over the chancel, haven't you? The Last Judgement?"

"That's right. With scenes from the life of Christ underneath."

"One gin and lemon coming up," said Ronald, materializing at Vanessa's elbow and handing her the glass with a flourish. He had a similar glass in his own hand, which he raised. "Chin-chin." He beamed at me. "David, I know Cynthia wanted to have a word with you about Rosemary."

"My daughter," I explained to Vanessa.

"Our niece dropped in last week," Ronald went on. "She left school at the end of last term and she brought over a trunk of stuff for us to dispose of. Clothes, I suppose. I think there's a lacrosse stick, too. Cynthia wondered if anything might come in useful for Rosemary."

I smiled and thanked him. There was a time when I would have objected to being on the receiving end of the Trasks' philanthropy. Now I knew better. Pride is a luxury and children become increasingly expensive as they grow older. At this moment Cynthia reached us, bearing bowls of peanuts and olives.

"Did I hear Rosemary's name?" she asked. "Such a delightful girl. How's she liking school now?"

"Much better, I think." I turned to Vanessa. "When Rosemary first went away, she disliked it very much." In fact, she had twice tried to run away. "But she seems to have settled down in the last year."

"She will be taking her A levels next summer," said Cynthia, with a hint of interrogation in her voice, indicating that this was an inspired guess rather than a statement of fact.

She detached me from Vanessa and Ronald and talked to

me for a moment or two about Rosemary. We decided—or rather Cynthia decided—that she would send Ronald over with the trunk during the next week or so. Anything we did not want for Rosemary could go to our next jumble sale. Having settled the matter, she steered me away from Vanessa and Ronald, who were talking together at the far end of the terrace, and skilfully inserted me into a conversation between Victor Thurston and the headmaster's wife.

I did not get another opportunity to talk to Vanessa for some time. While we were on the terrace I glanced once or twice in the direction of her and Ronald, still talking, their faces intent. At one point I noticed her shaking her head.

Eventually we went through to the dining room, and Cynthia steered us to our places at the round table. Vanessa was diametrically opposite me. There was a substantial flower arrangement in the middle of the table, so I caught only the occasional glimpse of her. I was sitting between Cynthia and the headmaster's wife.

Ronald said grace. The meal which followed was uncharacteristically elaborate. Melon with Parma ham gave way to *coq au vin*. Ronald, usually the most careful of hosts, kept refilling our glasses with an unfortunate Portuguese rosé. The headmaster's wife tried delicately to interrogate me about Ronald. It soon became clear that she knew the Trasks rather better than I did. At last she gave up and spoke across me to Cynthia.

"My dear, this is wonderful. How on earth do you manage to prepare a meal like this and go out to work?"

"I only work in the mornings. I find there's ample time if one is sufficiently organized."

"I didn't know you had a job," I said.

"I work for Vanessa. I'm her secretary, really. Jolly interesting."

I wondered whether that explained the special effort the Trasks were making. Was Cynthia hoping for promotion?

"I suppose you spend most of your time dealing with authors and so on," said the headmaster's wife. "It must be marvelous. Do you have lots of bestsellers?"

Cynthia shook her head. "We tend to do fairly specialized non-fiction titles. Actually, I think Royston and Forde's out-and-out bestseller was something called *Great Engines of the 1920s.*"

Ronald and Thurston talked to Vanessa for much of the meal. When we left the table, Mary Thurston seized her husband's arm as if to re-establish her claim to him. Ronald went to the kitchen to make coffee.

"Ronald bought a machine when he was in Italy last year," Cynthia explained to the rest of us. "He does like to use it when we have guests. Too complicated for me, I'm afraid." She added as an afterthought, "Super coffee."

We went back to the drawing room to wait for it. Vanessa came over to me.

"I don't suppose you could give me another cigarette, could you? I've mislaid mine. So silly." She smiled up at me. Even then I think I knew that Vanessa was never silly. She was many things, but not that. She sat down on the sofa and waved to me to join her.

"Are you in Ronald's—whatever it is?—area?"

"He's my archdeacon, yes. So in a sense he's my immediate boss."

I did not want to talk about Ronald. He and I did not get on badly—not then—but we had little in common, and both of us knew it.

"Cynthia tells me you're a publisher."

She squeezed her eyes together for an instant, as though smoke had irritated them. "By default."

"I'm sorry?"

"It was my husband's firm." She stared down at her cigarette. "He founded it with a friend from Oxford. It never made much money for either of them, but he loved it."

"I didn't realize. I'm sorry."

"I—I assumed Ronald might have mentioned it to you. No reason why you should know. Charles died three years ago. A brain tumor. One of those ghastly things that come out of a clear blue sky. I've taken over his part in the business. Needs must, really. I needed a job."

"Do you enjoy it?"

She nodded. "I'd always helped Charles on the editorial side. Now I'm learning a great deal about production." She smiled toward Cynthia, who was embroiled with the headmaster's wife. "Cynthia keeps me in order."

"At dinner Cynthia said she thought *Great Engines of the 1920s* was your bestselling book."

"She's perfectly right. Though I have my hopes of *The English Cottage Garden*. It's been selling very steadily since it came out last year." She drew on her cigarette. "In fact, our real bestseller in terms of copies sold is probably one of our town guides. The Oxford one. We do quite a lot of that sort of thing—that's where the bread and butter comes from."

At that moment, Ronald appeared in the doorway bearing a large silver tray. "Coffee, everybody," he announced in a voice like a fanfare. "Sorry to keep you waiting." He advanced into the room, his eyes searching for Vanessa.

"One of my parishioners has written a book," I said to her.

Vanessa looked warily at me. "What sort of book?"

"It's a history of the parish. Not really a book. I'd say it's about ten thousand words."

"How interesting."

She glanced at me again, and I think a spark of shared amusement passed between us. She knew how to say one thing and mean another.

"She's looking for a publisher."

"Sugar, Vanessa?" boomed Ronald. "Cream?"

"In my experience, most authors are." She smiled up at Ronald. "Just a dash of cream, please, Ronnie."

*Ronnie?*

"She believes it might appeal to readers all over the country," I continued. "Not just to those who know Roth."

"The happy few?"

I smiled. It was a novelty to have someone talk to me as a person rather than as a priest. "Could you recommend a publisher she could send it to?" I stared at the curve of her arm and noticed the almost invisible golden hairs that grew on the skin. "Someone who would have a look at the book and give a professional opinion. I imagine you haven't got the time to look at stray typescripts yourself."

"Vanessa's always looking at stray typescripts," Ronald said, and laughed. "Or looking *for* them."

"I might be able to spare five minutes," she said to me, her voice deadpan.

Once again, she glanced at me, and once again the spark of amusement danced between us.

"Brandy, anyone?" Ronald inquired. "Or what about a liqueur?"

For the rest of the evening Vanessa talked mainly to Ronald, Cynthia and Victor Thurston. I was the first to leave.

*Chapter Three*

THE FOLLOWING MONDAY, I looked up Royston and Forde in the directory and phoned Vanessa at her office. Cynthia Trask answered the phone. Oddly enough this took me by surprise. I had completely forgotten that she worked there.

"Good morning, Cynthia. This is David Byfield."

"Hello, David."

After a short pause I said, "Thank you so much for Friday."

"Not at all. Ronald and I enjoyed it."

I wondered if I should have sent flowers or something. "I don't know if Vanessa mentioned it, but one of my parishioners has written a book. She volunteered to have a look at it."

"I'll see if she's engaged," Cynthia said.

A moment later, Vanessa came on the line. She was brisk with me, her voice sounding much sharper on the telephone. She was busy most of the day, she was afraid, but might I be free for lunch? Ninety minutes later, we were sitting opposite each other in a café near Richmond Bridge.

The long, clinging dress she had worn at the Trasks' on Friday had given her a voluptuous appearance. Now she was another woman, dressed in a dark suit, and with her hair pulled back: slimmer, sharper and harder.

The typescript of *The History of Roth* was in a large, brown envelope on the table between us. I had picked it up from Audrey on my way to Richmond. ("So kind of you, David. I'm so grateful.")

Vanessa did not touch the envelope. She picked at her sandwich. A silence lay between us, and as it grew longer I felt increasingly desolate. The friendly intimacy that had flourished so briefly between us on Friday evening was gone. I found it all too easy, on the other hand, to think of her as a desirable woman. I had been a fool to come here. I was wasting her time and mine. I should have sent the typescript in the post.

"Do you visit many churches?" I asked, to make conversation. "You mentioned our panel paintings on Friday."

Vanessa fiddled with one of the crumbs on her plate. "Not really. I wanted to see Roth because of the connection with Francis Youlgreave."

"The poet?" My voice sounded unnaturally loud. "He's buried in the vault under the chancel."

"He deserves a few paragraphs in here." Vanessa tapped the envelope containing the typescript. "Quite a sensational character, by all accounts."

"Audrey does mention him, but she's very circumspect about what she says."

"Why?"

"There's a member of the family still living in Roth. I think her husband was the poet's great-nephew. Audrey didn't want to give people the wrong idea about him."

"Defile their judgement, as it were." Vanessa smiled across the table at me. Then she quoted two lines from the poem that had found its way into several anthologies. It was usually the only poem of his that anyone had read.

> *"Then darkness descended; and whispers defiled*
> *The judgement of stranger, and widow, and child."*

"Just so."

"Does anyone remember him in the village?"

"Roth isn't that sort of place. There aren't that many people left who lived there before the last war. And Francis Youlgreave died before the First World War. Have you a particular reason for asking?"

She shrugged. "I read quite a lot of his verse when I was up at Oxford. Not a very good poet, to be frank—all those jog-trot rhythms can be rather wearing. But he was interesting more for what he was and for who he knew than for what he wrote."

"Not a very nice man, by all accounts. Unbalanced."

"Yes, but rather fascinating." She looked at her watch. "I'm awfully sorry, David, but I've got to rush."

I concealed my disappointment. I paid the bill and walked with her back to the office where I had left my car.

"Would you like to telephone me tomorrow?" she asked. "I should have had time to look at the book by then."

"Of course. At the office?"

"I'll probably read it at home, actually."

"What time would suit you?"

"About seven?"

She gave me her number. We said goodbye and I drove back to Roth, feeling profoundly dissatisfied. I had made a fool of myself in more ways than one. I had expected more, much more, from my lunch with Vanessa—though quite what, I did not know. I was aware, too, that there was something absurd in a middle-aged widower acting in the way that I was doing. It was clear that she saw me as an acquaintance and that by looking at the typescript she was merely doing me—and Audrey—a good turn from the kindness of her heart.

Still, I thought, at least I had a reason to telephone Vanessa tomorrow evening.

In the event, however, I did not telephone Vanessa on Tuesday evening. This was because on Tuesday afternoon I received an unexpected and unpleasant visit from Cynthia Trask.

*Chapter Four*

CYNTHIA ARRIVED without warning in the late afternoon.

"I hope I'm not disturbing you," she said briskly. "But I happened to be passing, and I thought this might be a good opportunity to drop in those odds and ends from my niece."

In the back of her Mini Traveler were two suitcases and a faded army kitbag containing the lacrosse stick and other sporting impedimenta. I carried them into the house and called Rosemary, who was reading in her room. She did not appear to hear.

"I won't disturb her, if you don't mind," I said. "She's working quite hard this holiday. Would you like some tea?" It would have been churlish not to offer Cynthia tea but I was mildly surprised that she so readily accepted. She followed me into the kitchen which, like the rest of the house, was cramped, characterless and modern.

"Anything I can do to help?"

"Everything's under control, thank you."

"This is the first time I've been inside the new vicarage. You must be so relieved."

"It's certainly easier to keep warm and clean than the old one was."

It was partly due to Ronald's influence that the old vicarage—a large, gracious and completely impractical Queen

Anne house—had been demolished last year. The new vicarage was a four-bedroomed, centrally heated box. Its garden occupied the site of the old tennis court and vegetable garden. The rest of the old garden and the site of the old house itself now contained a curving cul-de-sac and six more boxes, each rather more spacious than the new vicarage.

"Of course, you didn't really need all that space. You and Rosemary must have felt you were camping in a barrack."

"Rather an elegant barrack," I said. "Do you take sugar?"

I carried the tea tray into the sitting room. Having a stranger in your home makes you see it with fresh eyes, and the result is rarely reassuring. I imagined that Cynthia was taking in the shabby furniture, the cobwebs in the corner of the ceiling and the unswept grate.

"Much cozier," Cynthia said approvingly, as though she herself were responsible for this. "Do you have someone who comes in to do for you?"

I nodded, resenting the catechism. "One of my parishioners acts as a sort of housekeeper." I handed Cynthia a cup of tea. "Your house is pretty big," I said, trying to change the subject, "but it always seems very homely."

She smiled wistfully. "Yes, I've enjoyed living there."

"Are you moving?"

"Almost certainly."

"How wonderful." I felt a sudden stab of envy. "You must be very proud of Ronald."

Cynthia frowned. "Proud?"

"I assumed you meant he's been offered preferment. Well deserved, I'm sure."

Cynthia flushed. She was sitting, pink and foursquare in

my own armchair. "No, I didn't mean preferment. I meant that, when Ronald marries, I shall naturally move out. It will be time to make a home of my own. It wouldn't be fair to any of us if I stayed."

"I didn't realize that he *was* getting married." I guessed that Cynthia and her brother had shared a house for nearly twenty years, for I remembered hearing that Ronald's first wife had died soon after their marriage. I wondered how Cynthia felt at the prospect of being uprooted from her home. "I hope they will be very happy."

"There hasn't been a formal announcement yet. They haven't sorted out the timing. I know Ronald nearly said something on Friday evening, but they decided it would be better to wait."

A suspicion mushroomed in my mind. Suddenly everything began to make sense.

"They are ideally suited," Cynthia was saying, talking rapidly. "And Vanessa has been so lost since Charles died. She's the sort of woman who really needs a husband."

"Yes. Yes, of course."

Cynthia put down her cup and saucer and looked at her watch. "Heavens, is that the time? I really must be going."

I took Cynthia out to her car. I think I said the right things about the charitable donation she had brought. I asked whether she would like me to return the suitcases, though I cannot remember what she replied.

At last she drove away. I trudged back into the house and took the tea tray into the kitchen. I was being childish, I told myself. I had not even realized that I was entertaining foolish hopes about Vanessa Forde until Cynthia had made it so clear that my prospects were hopeless. I had been celibate now for ten years—at first from necessity and later by choice—and there was no reason why I should not remain celibate for the rest of my life.

That afternoon some very unworthy thoughts passed through my mind. Jealousy and frustrated lust are an unsettling combination. I respected Ronald Trask, or rather I respected some of his achievements. One day he would probably be a bishop. I did not find that easy to accept. It was a shock to discover that I found even less palatable the thought that he and Vanessa would soon be married.

Sex apart, I had liked what I had seen of Vanessa. Ronald was a bore. A worthy bore, but still a bore. Vanessa deserved someone better. But of course there was nothing I could do about it. In any case, if Ronald and Vanessa chose to marry, it was nothing to do with me.

It was one thing to frame these rational arguments; it was quite another to accept them emotionally. I went into my study and tried to write a letter to my godson, Michael Appleyard. That proved too difficult. I turned to the parish accounts, which were even worse. Always, in the back of my mind, were the interlocking figures of Ronald and Vanessa. Physically interlocking, I mean. It was as if I were trapped in a cinema with a film I did not want to see on the screen.

Time crept on. Rosemary was still working in her room. At six-thirty I decided to go over to the church and say the Evening Office. Then I would ring Vanessa about Audrey's book. I went into the hall.

"Rosemary?"

She did not answer. I went upstairs and tapped on the door

of her room. Her room was uncluttered. Even as a young child she had had a formidable ability to organize her surroundings. She was sitting at her table with a pile of books in front of her and a pen in her hand. She glanced at me, her eyes vague.

"Is it suppertime already?"

"No—not yet. I'm going over to church for a while. Not for long."

"OK."

"You'll be all right, my dear?"

She gave me a condescending smile, which said, *Of course I'll be all right. I'm not a baby.* "I'll start supper in about fifteen minutes."

"Thank you."

Rosemary let her eyes drift back to her book. I envied her serenity. I wanted to say something to her but, as so often, I could not find the words. Instead I closed the door softly behind me, went downstairs and let myself out of the house and into the evening sunlight.

The Vicarage was next to the churchyard, separated from it by a high wall of crumbling eighteenth-century brick. I walked through the little garden to our private gate, a relic of the old house, which gave access from the grounds of the Vicarage to the churchyard. As I opened the gate the church was suddenly revealed, framed in the archway.

Most of the exterior of the St. Mary Magdalene was of brick, and in this light it looked particularly lovely: the older bricks of the sixteenth-century rebuilding had weathered to a mauve color, while the eighteenth-century work was a contrasting russet; and together the colors made the church glow and gently vibrate against the blue of the sky. Housemartins darted around the tower.

I closed the gate behind me. Traffic rumbled a few yards to the left on the main road and there was a powerful smell of diesel fumes in the air. I caught sight of a shadow flickering through the grass near the gate to the road. I was just in time to see Audrey's cat slipping behind a gravestone.

I walked slowly around the east end to the south door on the other side. On my way I passed the steps leading down to the Youlgreave vault beneath the chancel. The iron gate was rusting and the steps were cracked and overgrown with weeds. No one had been interred there for almost fifty years. The last Youlgreave to die, Sir George, had been killed in the Pacific in 1944, and his body had been buried at sea. I noticed there were gray feathers scattered on the bottom step, immediately in front of the iron gate, where no weeds grew. I wondered if Audrey's cat was in the habit of dismembering his kills there.

I went into the porch. The door was unlocked—I left the church open during the day, though after two robberies I now locked it at night. Inside, the air smelled of polish, flowers and—very faintly—of incense, which I used two or three times a year. The church was small, almost cozy, with a two-bay nave and a low chancel. Above the chancel arch were the panel paintings, their colors murky; the pictures looked as if they were wreathed in smoke. I walked slowly to my stall in the choir. I sat down and began to say the Evening Office.

Usually the building itself had a calming effect on me, but not this evening. At times I found my mind drifting away from the words of the office and had to force myself to concentrate. Afterward I simply sat there and stared at the memorial tablets on the wall opposite me. It was as though my will had abdicated.

Vanessa and Ronald, I thought over and over again. I wondered if I would be invited to the wedding and, if so, whether I should accept. By that time, perhaps it would no longer matter. I was aware, of course, that I was making too much of this. On the basis of two short meetings, I could hardly claim to have become deeply attached to Vanessa. The real problem was that, quite unintentionally, she had aroused my own long-suppressed needs. At the bottom of my unhappiness was a feeling of profound dissatisfaction with myself.

Time passed. Slowly the light slipped away from the interior of the church. It was by no means dark—merely less bright than it had been before. The memorial tablets were made of pale marble that gleamed among the shadows. Gradually there crept up on me the feeling that I was being watched.

I stared with increasing concentration at the tablet directly in front of me, which belonged to Francis Youlgreave, the poor, mad poet-priest. Everything led back to Vanessa. How odd that she should be interested in him. I remembered the lines that she had quoted to me at lunchtime. I could not recall the words exactly, something about darkness, I thought, and about whispers that defiled the judgement.

*Defiled.* It suddenly seemed to me that I was irredeemably defiled, not just by the events of the last few days, but by the active choice of someone or something outside me.

At that moment, I heard laughter.

It was a high, faint sound, like the rustle of paper or a whistle without a tune. I thought of wind among the leaves, of beating wings and long beaks, of geese I had seen as a boy flying high above Essex mudflats. Sadness swept over me. I fought it, but it turned to desolation and then to something darker.

"No. Stop. Please stop."

I was on my feet. The paralysis had dissolved. I stumbled down the church. The sound followed me. I put my hands over my ears but I could not block it out. The church was no longer a place of peace. I had turned it into a mockery of its former self. *Defiled*. I had defiled the church even as I had defiled myself.

I struggled with the latch of the south door. I was in such a state that it seemed to me that someone on the other side was holding it down. At last I wrenched it up and pulled at the door. I almost fell into the porch beyond.

Something moved on my right. Audrey's cat, I thought for a split second, her wretched, bloody cat. Then I realized that I was wrong: that a person was sitting on the bench in the corner by the church notice board. I had a confused impression of pale clothing and a golden blur like a halo at the head. Then the figure stood up.

"Hello, Father," said my daughter Rosemary. Her voice changed, filling with concern. "What's wrong?"

# Chapter Five

A T HALF PAST NINE the following morning there was a ring on the doorbell. I was alone in the house. Rosemary had caught the bus to Staines to go shopping. I had managed to shave, but the only breakfast I had been able to face was a cigarette and a cup of coffee.

I found Audrey hovering on the doorstep, her body poised as if ready to dart into the hall at the slightest encouragement. I kept my hand on the door and tried to twist my mouth into a smile.

"Sorry to disturb you, David. I just wondered what the verdict was."

"What verdict?"

"You're teasing me," she said in an arch voice. "The verdict on the book, of course."

"I'm so sorry." Indeed I was, though not for the reasons Audrey assumed. "I've not been able to talk to Mrs. Forde about it yet."

She stuck out her lower lip, which was already pinched and protuberant, and increased her resemblance to a disappointed child. "I thought you were going to phone her yesterday evening."

"Yes, I'd hoped to, but—but there was a difficulty."

"Oh. I see."

"I'll try to talk to her today." I smiled, trying to soften the effect of my words. "I'll phone you as soon as I hear some-thing, shall I?"

"Yes, please." She turned to go. She had taken only a couple of steps toward the road when she stopped and turned back to me. "David?"

"Yes?"

"Thank you for all you're doing."

My conscience twisted uncomfortably. Audrey smiled and walked away. I went back to my study and stared at the papers on my desk. Concentration demanded too much effort. I had slept badly, with dreams that hovered near the frontier of nightmare but did not actually cross it. One of them had been set in a version of Rosington, where Rosemary and I had lived before we came to Roth—when my wife Janet was still alive. I had not dreamed of Rosington for years. Vanessa had unsettled me, breached the defenses I had built up so laboriously. (And I had been all too willing to have them breached.)

Audrey's visit reminded me that I still had the problem of contacting Vanessa. I should have phoned her, as arranged, the previous evening, but I had spent much longer in the church than I had intended. By the time I had returned to the Vicarage the last thing I had wanted to do was talk to any-one, let alone Vanessa. I had persuaded myself without much trouble that it was too late to phone.

On the other hand, I could not run away from Vanessa for-ever, or at least not until I had sorted out the business of Audrey's wretched book. I did not want to phone her at the of-fice, however, because that would mean having to run the gauntlet of Cynthia. I remembered that Cynthia worked only in the mornings. In that case, I thought, I would phone Vanessa this afternoon.

Now that I had made the decision, I felt slightly happier. I returned to the accounts I had abandoned the previous evening. But I had not got very far when there was another ring at the doorbell. I swore under my breath as I went into the hall. I opened the door. There was Vanessa herself.

I stared at her, fighting a rising tide of disbelief. She was wearing her dark suit and she had the envelope containing Audrey's typescript clamped to her chest.

"Hello, David."

"Vanessa—do come in."

"I'm not interrupting anything, am I?"

"Only the accounts. And I was about to make some coffee, in any case. But I hope you haven't come all this way to bring me back the book?"

She shook her head. "I had to visit a bookshop in Staines this morning. I'm on my way back."

She followed me into the hall, and I led her through to the sitting room.

"I'm sorry I didn't phone yesterday evening."

"That's all right." She looked out of the window, not at me. "I didn't expect you to phone me back so late."

"I'm sorry?"

She turned from the window and looked at me. "Didn't you get my message?"

"What message?"

"I phoned last night. I had another phone call, and I—I thought you might not have been able to get through. I left a message saying I'd phoned."

"I didn't receive it." I thought of Rosemary waiting for me in the porch of the church. "You must have spoken to my daughter. I expect it slipped her mind."

She smiled. "Young people have more important things to think about than relaying phone messages."

"Yes." I did not know what to say next. I knew I should make the coffee, but I did not want to leave Vanessa. I cleared my throat. "I saw Cynthia yesterday afternoon. She brought those things round for Rosemary."

"I know. She told me . . . I think she may have misled you about something."

I stared at her. We were still standing in the middle of the room.

Vanessa picked at a piece of fluff on her sleeve. "I believe she gave you to understand that Ronnie and I are engaged."

I nodded.

"Well, that's not true. Not exactly."

I patted the pockets of my jacket, looking for the cigarettes I had left in the study. "There's no need to tell me this. It's none of my business."

"Cynthia and Ronnie were very good to me when Charles died."

"I'm sure they were."

"You don't understand. When something like that happens you feel empty. And you can become very dependent on those who help you. Emotionally, I mean."

"I do understand," I said. "Only too well."

"I'm sorry." She bit her lip. "Ronnie told me about your wife."

"It's all right. It was a long time ago."

"One gets so wrapped up in oneself."

"I know."

"Listen, two weeks ago, Ronnie asked me to marry him. I didn't say yes, but I didn't say no, either. I said I needed time. But he thought I was eventually going to say yes. To be perfectly honest, *I* thought I was going to say yes. In a way I felt that he deserved it. And I'm fond of him . . . Besides, I don't like living on my own."

"I see. Won't you sit down?"

I was not sure whether she was talking to me as a man or as a priest—a not uncommon problem in the Anglican Church. When we sat down, somehow we both chose the sofa. This had a low seat—uncomfortably low for me. It caused Vanessa's skirt to ride up several inches above the knees. The sight was distracting. She snapped open her handbag and produced a packet of cigarettes, which she offered to me. I found some matches in my pocket. Lighting the cigarettes brought us very close together. There was now no doubt about it: as far as I was concerned, the man was well in ascendancy over the priest.

"Ronnie hoped to announce our engagement on Friday evening," she continued. "I think that's why he wanted the dinner party—to show me off. I didn't want that." She blew out a plume of smoke like an angry dragon. "I didn't *like* it, either. It made me feel like a trophy or something. And then this morning, Cynthia told me she'd been to see you, told me what she'd said. I was furious. I'm *not* engaged to Ronnie. In any case, it's nothing to do with her."

"No doubt she meant well," I said, automatically clinging to the saving grace of good intentions.

"We all mean well," Vanessa snapped back. "Sometimes that's not enough."

We smoked in silence for a moment. I glanced at her stockinged legs, dark and gleaming, and quickly looked away. She fiddled with her cigarette, rolling it between finger and thumb.

"The book," I said, my voice a little hoarse. "What did you think of it?"

"Yes." She seized the envelope as if it were a life belt. "There's a good deal of interesting material in it. Particularly if you know Roth well. But I'm afraid it's not really suitable for us."

"Is it worth our trying elsewhere?"

"Frankly, no. I don't think any trade publisher would want it. It's not a book for the general market."

"Too short," I said slowly, "and too specialized. And not exactly scholarly, either."

She smiled. "Not exactly. If the author wants to see it in print, she'll probably have to pay for the privilege."

"I thought you might say that."

"She'll probably blame my lack of acumen," Vanessa went on cheerfully. "A lot of authors appear to believe that there are no bad books, only bad publishers."

"So what would you advise?"

"There's no point in raising her hopes. Just say that I don't think it's a commercial proposition, and that I advised investigating the cost of having it privately printed. She could sell it in the church, in local shops. Perhaps there's a local history society which would contribute toward the costs."

"Is there a printer you could recommend?"

"You could try us, if you like. We have our own printing works. We could certainly give you a quotation."

"Really? That would be very kind."

Simultaneously we turned to look at one another. At that moment there was a sudden movement at the window. Both our heads jerked toward it as if tugged by invisible strings, as if we were both conscious of having done something wrong. I felt a spurt of anger against the intruder who had broken in on our privacy. Audrey's cat was on the sill, butting his nose against the glass.

Vanessa said, "Is that—is that *yours*?"

"No—he belongs to Audrey, in fact—the person who wrote the book."

"Oh." She looked relieved. "My mother was afraid of cats. She was always going on about how unsanitary they were. How they brought germs into the house, as well as the things they caught." She glanced sideways at me. "Do you think these things can be hereditary?"

"Phobias?"

"Oh, it's not a phobia. I just don't particularly like them. In fact, that one's rather dapper. It looks as though he's wearing evening dress."

She was right. The cat was black, except for a triangular patch of white at the throat and more white on the paws. As we watched, he opened his mouth, a pink-and-white cavern, and meowed, the sound reaching us through the open fanlight of the window.

"He's called Lord Peter," I said.

"Why?"

"As in Dorothy L. Sayers. Audrey reads a lot of detective

stories. His predecessor was called Poirot. And before him, there were two others—before my time: one was called Brown after Father Brown, and the first of the line was Sherlock."

"I can't say I have much time for detective stories."

"Nor do I."

I repressed the uncharitable memory of the time that Audrey had lent me Sayers's *The Nine Tailors*, on the grounds that it was not only great literature but also contained a wonderfully convincing portrait of a vicar. I stood up, went to the window and waved at Lord Peter, trying to shoo him away. I did not dislike cats in general, but I disliked this one. His constant intrusions irritated me, and I blamed him for the strong feline stench in my garage. Ignoring my wave, he meowed once more. It occurred to me that I felt about Lord Peter as I often felt about Audrey: that she was ceaselessly trying to encroach on our privacy at the Vicarage.

"David?"

I turned back to Vanessa, ripe and lovely, looking up at me from the sofa. "What is it?"

"To go back to—to Ronnie. It's just—it's just that I'm not sure I'm the right person to marry a clergyman."

"Why?"

"I'm not a regular churchgoer. I don't even know if I believe in God."

"It doesn't matter," I said, knowing that it did, though not perhaps in the way she thought. "In any case, belief in God comes in many forms."

"But his parish, the bishop—"

"I am sure Ronald thought of all that. I don't mean to pry, but surely it came up when he asked you to marry him?"

She nodded. "He said that God would find a way."

There was a silence. Lord Peter rubbed his furry body against the glass and I wanted to throw the ashtray at him. I felt a rush of anger toward Ronald, joining the other emotions which were swirling around the sitting room. If I stayed here, they would suck me down.

I moved to the door. "I'll make the coffee. I won't be a moment."

I slipped out of the room without giving her time to answer. In the hall I discovered that my forehead was damp with sweat. The house seemed airless, a redbrick coffin with too few windows. I went into the kitchen and opened the back door. While I was waiting for the kettle to boil I stared at my shrunken garden.

It was then that the idea slithered like a snake into my mind, showing itself openly for the first time: if anyone was going to marry Vanessa Forde, why shouldn't it be me?

*Chapter Six*

V ANESSA DID NOT LINGER over coffee. It was as if she were suddenly desperate to leave. We made no arrangement to see each other again. During the afternoon, I called at Tudor Cottage and relayed her opinion of *The History of Roth* to its author. Audrey's reaction surprised me.

"But what do *you* think, David?"

"I think Vanessa's opinion is worth taking seriously. After all, it's her job. And it's true that *The History of Roth* is rather short for a book."

"Perhaps she's right. Perhaps it would be simpler to have it privately printed. And then we wouldn't have to share the profits with the publisher. I wonder how much it would cost?"

"I don't know."

"Would you mind asking Mrs. Forde on my behalf? I'd feel a little awkward doing it myself. I haven't even met her."

Audrey continued to play the unwitting Cupid. After discussing the pros and cons exhaustively with me, she entrusted Royston and Forde with the job of printing *The History of Roth*. Audrey asked me to—in her words—"see it through the press" for her. The typescript provided a reason for Vanessa and me to see each other without commitment on the one hand or guilt on the other; she was doing her job and I was helping a friend. We spent several evenings editing the book, and several more proofreading it. Usually we worked at her flat.

Vanessa cooked me meals on two occasions. Once I took her out to a restaurant in Richmond to repay her hospitality. I remember a candle in a wax-covered Chianti bottle, its flame doubled and dancing in her eyes, a red-and-white checked tablecloth and plates of gently steaming spaghetti bolognese.

"It's a shame there's not more material about Francis Youlgreave," she said on that evening. "And why's Audrey so keen to avoid giving offense?"

*Because she's a prude and a snob.* I said, "When she was growing up, the Youlgreaves were the local grandees."

"So you had to treat even their black sheep with respect? That may have been true once, but does she need to be so coy now?"

I shrugged. "It's her book, I suppose."

"I've been rereading Francis's poems. He'd be an interesting subject for a PhD. Or even a biography. Now that *would* be commercial."

"Warts and all?"

Vanessa grinned across the table. "If you took away the warts, you wouldn't have much left. Nothing interesting, anyway."

There was no element of deception about our meetings. Vanessa never mentioned Ronald, and nor did I. I assumed that an engagement was no longer on the cards. The Trasks knew that Vanessa and I were working together on *The History of Roth*. What Cynthia thought about it, I did not know; but Ronald took it in his stride.

"And how's the book coming along?" he asked me at one of the committee meetings he so frequently convened. He smiled, and his white teeth twinkled at me. "Vanessa's told me all about it. I'm grateful, actually. She's seeing another clergyman in a secular context, as it were. It's so easy for lay people to assume we're all dog collars and pious sentiments."

When two people work together toward a shared goal, it can create a powerful sense of intimacy. Vanessa and I did not hurry, and at least the little book benefited from the attention we lavished on it. It was a happy time because we discovered that many of our tastes coincided—books, paintings, humor. Being a parish priest can be a lonely job, and her friendship became precious to me. Two months later, by the middle of November 1969, I decided to ask Vanessa to marry me.

It was not a decision I reached hastily, or rashly. It seemed to me that there was a host of reasons in favor. Vanessa was an intelligent and cultivated woman, a pleasure to be with. I was lonely. Rosemary would benefit from having an older woman in the family. The Vicarage needed the warmth Vanessa could bring to it. The wife of a parish priest can act as her husband's eyes and ears. Last but not least, I urgently wanted to go to bed with Vanessa.

I was very calm. How things had altered, I thought smugly, since I had last considered marriage. Before proposing to Vanessa, I discussed my intentions with my spiritual director, Peter Hudson. He was an old friend who had helped me cope in those dark days after I left Rosington.

Peter was a few years older than I and was now a suffragan

bishop in the neighboring diocese of Oxford. At that time, he lived in Reading, which meant I could easily drive over and see him.

The Hudsons had a modern house on an estate. Peter's wife June welcomed me with a kiss, gave each of us a cup of coffee and shooed us upstairs to his little study. The atmosphere was foggy with pipe smoke.

"You're looking well," he said to me. "Better than I've seen you for some time."

"I'm feeling better."

"What do you want to talk about?"

"I'm thinking of getting married again."

Peter was in the act of lighting his pipe. He cocked an eye at me through the smoke. "I see."

"Her name's Vanessa Forde. She's a widow, and a partner in a small publishing company in Richmond. She's thirty-nine."

Smoke billowed from the pipe, but Peter said nothing. He was a small, sturdily built man who carried too much surplus fat. His plump face was soft-skinned and relatively unlined, with heavy eyebrows sprouting anarchically like twin tangles of barbed wire. He was the only person in the world who knew how ill suited I was to celibacy.

"Tell me more."

I told him how I had met Vanessa and how working on *The History of Roth* had brought us together. I outlined my reasons for asking her to marry me.

"I realize it must seem selfish of me," I said, "but I know she doesn't want to marry Ronald. And I honestly think I could make her happy. And she could make me happy, for that matter."

"Do you love her?"

"Of course I do. I'm not pretending it's a grand passion—I'm middle-aged, for heaven's sake. But there's love, nonetheless, and liking, shared interests, affection—"

"And sexual attraction, at least on your side."

"Yes—and why not? Surely that's one of the purposes of marriage?"

"You're not allowing that to warp your judgment? Ten years is a long time. The pressure can build up."

I thought of Peter's comfortable wife and wondered briefly if the pressure had ever built up in their marriage. "I'm making allowances for that."

We sat in silence for a moment. The sound of the television filtered up the stairs.

"Other things worry me," he said at last. "It seems that there's a very real danger that this will cause trouble between you and Ronald Trask."

"She and Ronald were never engaged."

"That's not the point, David."

"He misunderstood the situation completely. One could even argue that he took advantage of her emotional vulnerability after Charles's death. Unconsciously, of course."

"Unlike you?"

"I'm not proposing to take advantage of her. Any more than she'd be taking advantage of me. Besides, Vanessa's husband died three years ago. Plenty of time to get back on to an even keel."

"Your wife died more than ten years ago. Do you feel you were on an even keel after three years?"

"That was different."

"I see."

"Ronald will understand," I said with an optimism I did not feel. "I'll make every effort to talk to him. I wouldn't want to let the problem fester, naturally."

"Do you think it's possible to build happiness on the unhappiness of others?"

"Is that worse than making all three of us unhappy?"

Peter nodded, not conceding the point but merely passing on to the next difficulty. "And there's the consideration that if a priest marries, he should choose someone who shares his beliefs. Otherwise it can put an intolerable strain on the marriage."

"Vanessa was confirmed in her teens. She's not an atheist or anything like that. She's simply not a committed churchgoer." I drew in a deep breath. "Quite apart from anything else, I think that this may be a way of bringing her back to the Church."

"I shall pray that you're right."

"You don't sound very hopeful."

"It's merely that, if I were you, I'd tread very carefully. In my experience, a priest should be a husband to his wife. If he tries to be a priest as well, it can cause difficulties. It's like a doctor treating his own family. There are two sets of priorities, and they can conflict."

"I take your point. I wouldn't be heavy-handed about it. But Vanessa's the sort of person who might well appreciate the more intellectual side of postwar theology. Tillich, Bultmann, Bonhoeffer—people like that. They could offer her a way back. I doubt if she's even read *Honest to God*. I know you and I don't altogether see eye to eye with—"

"David?"

"Sorry. I'm rambling, aren't I?"

"Have you discussed the idea with Rosemary?"

"Not yet." I hesitated, knowing Peter was waiting for more. "All right. I suppose I'm putting it off. I could have mentioned it when she was home at half-term."

"You've obviously made up your mind that you're going to ask Vanessa to marry you," he said slowly. "Very well. But in that case, I think you should tell Rosemary as soon as possible. She's bound to feel upset. And if she hears the news from somebody else, think how much more damaging it will be."

"You're right, of course."

"You may even find Rosemary's jealous."

I smiled. "Surely not."

Even as I spoke I remembered the evening in September when I experienced that unpleasant, dreamlike state in church: the sense of being defiled; the wings of geese flying over the mudflats of an estuary. On the same evening Vanessa had phoned the Vicarage and left a message for me with Rosemary. I had never discovered why Rosemary had failed to pass on the message. I wondered now if she really had forgotten. But what other reason could there be?

The following evening I went to Vanessa's flat in Richmond. She led me into the living room. A parcel was lying on the coffee table.

"The book's ready," she told me. "I've brought advance copies for you and Audrey."

"Damn the book," I said. "Will you marry me?"

She frowned, staring up at me. "I don't know."

"You don't want to?"

"It's not that. But I'm not sure I'd be right for you."

"You would. I'm sure."

"But I'd be no good as a vicar's wife. I just don't have the credentials. I don't *want* to have them."

"I don't want to marry a potential vicar's wife." I touched her arm and saw her eyes flicker, as if I had given her a tiny electric shock. But she did not move away. "I want to marry *you*."

We stood there for a moment. She shivered. I slipped my arm around her and kissed her cheek. I felt as clumsy as a teenager with his first girl. She pulled away. Hands on hips, she glared at me with mock anger.

"If I'd known this wretched book would lead to . . ."

"Will you marry me? Will you?"

"All right." Her face broke into a smile. "As long as I don't have to be a vicar's wife. I ought to get that in writing."

I put my arms around her and we kissed. My body reacted with predictable enthusiasm. I wondered how on earth I could restrain myself from going further until we were married.

Afterward, Vanessa brought out a bottle of Cognac, and we drank a toast to our future. Like teenagers, we sat side by side on the sofa, holding hands and talking almost in whispers, as though there were a danger that someone might overhear and envy our happiness.

"I can't believe you've agreed," I said.

"*I* can't understand how you've managed to stay single for

so long. You're far too good-looking to be a clergyman, let alone an unmarried one." She stared at me, then giggled. "You're blushing."

"I'm not used to receiving compliments from beautiful women."

Simultaneously we picked up our glasses. I think we were both a little embarrassed. The small talk of lovers is difficult when you're out of practice.

Vanessa cradled the glass in her hand. "You've made me realize how lonely I've been," she said slowly. "I've had more fun with you in the last two months than I've had in the last three years put together."

"Fun?"

Her fingers tightened on mine. "When you're living on your own, there doesn't seem much point in having fun. Or a sense of humor. Or going out for a meal. Didn't you find that?"

*Didn't*, not *don't*. "Yes. But surely Ronald—"

"Ronnie's kind. He's a good man. I like him. I trust him. I'm grateful to him. I almost married him. But he isn't much fun."

"I don't know if I am, either," I felt obliged to say. "Not on a day-to-day basis."

"We'll see about that." She turned her head to look at me. "You know what I really love about you? You make me feel it's possible to *change*."

My inclination was to announce our engagement at once. It gave me great joy, and I wanted to share it. Vanessa, however, thought we should keep it to ourselves until we had told Ronald and Rosemary.

Her delay in telling Ronald almost drove me frantic. I could not feel that she was truly engaged to me until she had made it clear to Ronald that she would never be engaged to him. She did not tell him until ten days after she had agreed to marry me. They went out to lunch, in the Italian restaurant where we had talked about the warts of Francis Youlgreave.

Vanessa did not tell me what they said to each other and I did not ask. But the next time I saw Ronald, which was at a diocesan meeting, he was cool to the point of frostiness. He did not mention Vanessa and nor did I. I had told Peter that I would talk to Ronald, but when it came to the point I could not think of anything to say. He was businesslike and polite, but I sensed that any friendship he had felt for me had evaporated.

His sister Cynthia was less restrained. I had been up to London one afternoon, and I met her by chance at Waterloo Station on my way back home. We saw each other at the same time. We were walking across the station concourse and our paths were due to converge in a few seconds. Her chin went up and her mouth snapped shut. She veered away. After a few paces, she changed her mind and swung back toward me.

"Good afternoon, Cynthia. How are you?"

She put her face close to mine. Her cheeks had flushed a dark red. "I think what you did was despicable. Taking advantage." There were tears in her eyes. "I hope you pay for it."

She turned away and, head down, plowed into a crowd of commuters and vanished from my sight. I told myself that she was being unreasonable: that the fact of the matter was that Vanessa had chosen to marry me of her own free will; and there was no element of deception about it.

*Chapter Seven*

THE ROUND OF PARISH WORK continued. Normally I would have welcomed much of this. Week by week, the rhythm of the church services made a familiar context for my life, a public counterpart to my private prayers. Weddings, baptisms and funerals punctuated the pattern.

There was satisfaction in the sense that one was carrying on a tradition that had developed over nearly two thousand years; that, through the rituals of the church, one was building a bridge between now and eternity. Less satisfying was the pastoral side of parish work—the schools and old people's homes, visiting the sick, sitting on the innumerable committees that a parish priest cannot avoid.

At that time Roth Park, once the big house of the village, was still an old people's home. The Bramleys, who owned it, were running it down, which meant that their guests were growing older, fewer and more decrepit. Their policy had an indirect effect on me. There was a run of deaths at Roth Park in those winter months of 1969–70, which became cumulatively depressing. Sometimes, when I walked or drove up to the house, I felt as though I were being sucked toward a dark vacuum, a sort of spiritual black hole.

Rosemary came back from school for the Christmas holidays. She had changed once again. Boarding school had that effect: each time she came home she was a stranger. I was biased, of course, but to me it seemed that she was becoming increasingly good-looking, developing into one of those classic English beauties, with fair hair, blue eyes, a high brow and regular features.

On her first evening home, I told her about Vanessa while we were washing up after supper. While I was speaking I could not see her face because her head was bent over the cutlery drawer. Afterward she said nothing. She stacked the spoons neatly in the drawer, one inside the other.

"Well?" I said.

"I hope . . ." She paused. "I hope you'll be happy."

"Thank you, my dear."

Her words were formal, even stilted, but they were better than I had feared.

"When will you get married?"

"After Easter. Before you go back to school. Talking of which, Vanessa and I were wondering if you would like to transfer to somewhere nearer for your last year in the sixth form. So you could be a day girl."

"*No.*"

"It's entirely up to you. You may well feel it would be less upheaval to stay where you are. Where you are used to your teachers, among your own friends, and so on."

Rosemary gathered a pile of plates and crouched beside a cupboard. One by one, with metronomic regularity, she put them away. I still could not see her face.

"Rosie," I said. "I know this isn't easy for you. It's been just the two of us for a very long time, hasn't it?"

She said nothing.

"But Vanessa's not going to be some sort of wicked

stepmother. Nothing's going to change between you and me. Really, darling."

Still she did not speak. I crouched beside her and put a hand on her shoulder. "So?" I prompted. "What do you think?"

At last she looked at me. To my horror, I saw that her eyes had filled with tears. Her face was red. For a moment she was ugly. The tea towel slipped from her hands and fell to the floor.

"What does it matter?" she said. "We'll end up doing what you want. We always do."

Christmas came and went. Vanessa and I announced our engagement, causing a flurry of smiles and whispers among my congregation. We also agreed on a date for our wedding—the first Saturday after Easter, shortly before Rosemary would be due to return to school for the summer term.

"Couldn't we make it sooner?" I said to Vanessa when we were discussing the timing.

"I think we're rushing things as it is."

I ran my eyes over her. Desire can produce a sensation like hunger, an emptiness that cries out to be filled. "I wish we didn't have to wait. I'd like to feast on you. Does that sound absurd?"

She smiled at me and touched my hand. "By the way, I had a chat with Rosemary. It was fine—she seemed very pleased for us."

"I'm so glad."

" 'I do hope you and Father will be very happy.' That's what she said." Vanessa frowned. "Does she always call you 'Father?' It sounds so formal."

"Her choice, as far as I remember. She always did, right from the start."

"Is it because you're a priest? She's very interested in the trappings of religion, isn't she?"

"It must be because of growing up in the odor of sanctity."

Vanessa laughed. "I thought clergymen weren't meant to make jokes about religion."

"Why not? God gave us a sense of humor."

"To go back to Rosemary: she's agreed to be maid of honor."

The wedding was going to be in Richmond, and Peter Hudson had agreed to officiate. The only other people we invited were two of Vanessa's Oxford friends and a couple called the Appleyards, whom I had known since my days at Rosington. Early in the New Year, Vanessa and I spent a day with the Appleyards.

"They seemed quite normal," she said to me as I drove her back to Richmond. "Not a dog collar in sight. Have you known them long?"

"For years. Henry rented a room from us when we were living in Rosington."

"So they knew Janet?"

"Yes."

We drove in silence for a moment. I had told Vanessa about Janet, my first wife. Not everything, of course, but everything that mattered to Vanessa and me.

"Michael's nice," she went on. "How old is he?"

"Coming up to eleven, I think."

"You're fond of him, aren't you?"

"Yes." After a pause I added, "He's my godson," though that did not explain why I liked him. Michael and I rarely had much to say to each other, but we had been comfortable in each other's company ever since he was a toddler.

"Do they ever come to Roth?"

"Occasionally."

"We must ask them to stay."

I glanced at her and smiled. "I'd like that."

She smiled back. "It's odd, isn't it? It's not just us getting married. It's our friends and relations as well."

In January, Rosemary went back to school. Vanessa spent the following Saturday with me. Now that we had the house to ourselves, we wanted to plan what changes would have to be made when Vanessa moved in; we had thought it would be tactless to do this while Rosemary was there. After lunch, the doorbell rang. I was not surprised to find Audrey Oliphant on the doorstep.

She wore a heavy tweed suit, rather too small for her, and a semi-transparent plastic mac, which gave her an ill-defined, almost ghostly appearance.

"So sorry to disturb you," she said. "I wondered if you'd seen Lord Peter recently."

Vanessa came out of the kitchen and said hello.

"Lord Peter—my cat," Audrey explained to her. "Such a worry. He treats the Vicarage as his second home."

I leaned nonchalantly against the door, preventing her from stepping into the hall. "I'm afraid we haven't seen him."

"The kettle's on," Vanessa said. "Would you like a cup?"

Audrey slipped past me and followed her into the kitchen. "Lord Peter has to cross the main road to get here. The traffic's getting worse and worse, especially since they started work on the motorway."

"Cats are very good at looking after themselves," Vanessa said.

"I hope I'm not disturbing you." No doubt accidentally, Audrey tried to insinuate a hint of indecency, the faintest wiggle of the eyebrows, into this possibility. "I'm sure you were in the middle of something."

"Nothing that wasn't going to wait until after tea," Vanessa said. "How's the book selling?"

"Splendidly, thank you. We sold sixty-three copies over Christmas. I knew people would like it."

"Why don't you take Audrey's coat?" Vanessa suggested to me.

"People like to know about their own village," Audrey continued, allowing me to peel her plastic mac away from her. "I know there have been changes, but Roth really is a village still."

Changes? A village? I thought of the huge reservoir to the north, of the projected motorway through the southern part of the parish, and of the sea of suburban houses that lapped around the green. I carried the tea tray into the sitting room.

"There's not much of it left," Vanessa said. "The village, I mean."

Audrey stared at Vanessa. "Oh, you're quite wrong. Let me show you." She beckoned Vanessa toward the window, which looked out over the drive, the road and the green. "*That's* the village." She nodded to her left, toward the houses of Vicarage Drive. "Here and on the left: the Vicarage and its garden. And then on our right is St. Mary Magdalene, and beyond that the gates to Roth Park and the river. If you cross the stone bridge and carry on down the road, we'll come to the Old Manor House, where Lady Youlgreave lives."

"I must take you to meet Lady Youlgreave," I said to Vanessa, attempting to divert the flow. "In a sense she's my employer."

It was no use. Audrey had now turned toward the green and was pointing at Malik's Minimarket, which stood just beside the main road at the western end of the north side of the green.

"That was the village forge when I was a girl." She laughed, a high and irritating sound. Her voice acquired a faint sing-song cadence. "Of course, it's changed a bit since then, but haven't we all? And beside it is my little home, Tudor Cottage. (I was born there, you know, on the second floor. The window on the left.) Then there's the Queen's Head. I think part of their cellars are even older than Tudor Cottage."

We all stared at the Queen's Head, a building that had been modernized so many times in the last hundred years that it had lost all trace of its original character. The pub now had a restaurant which served steaks, chips and cheap wine. At the weekend, the disco in the basement attracted young people from miles around, and there were regular complaints— usually from Audrey—about the noise.

"The bus shelter wasn't there when I was a girl," Audrey went on. "We had a much nicer one, with a thatched roof."

The bus shelter stood on the green itself, opposite the pub. It was a malodorous cavern, whose main use was as the wet-weather headquarters of the teenagers who lived on the Manor Farm council estate.

"And of course Manor Farm Lane has seen one or two changes as well." Audrey pointed at the road to the council estate which went off at the northeast corner of the green and winced theatrically. "We used to have picnics by the stream beyond the barn," she murmured in a confidential voice. "Just over there. Wonderful wild flowers in the spring."

The barn was long gone, and the stream had been culverted over. Yet she gave the impression that for her they were still vivid, in a way that the council estate was not. For her the past inhabited the present and gave it meaning.

The finger moved on to the east side of the green, to a nondescript row of villas from the 1930s, defiantly suburban, to the library and the ramshackle church hall. "There was a lovely line of sixteenth- and seventeenth-century cottages over there."

Vanessa's eyes met mine. I opened my mouth, but I was too late. Audrey's head had swiveled round to the south side, to the four detached Edwardian houses whose gardens ran down to the Rowan behind them. Two of them had been cut up into flats; one was leased as offices; and the fourth was where Dr. Vintner lived with his family and had his surgery.

"A retired colonel in the Bengal Lancers used to live in the one at the far end. There was a nice solicitor in Number Two. And the lady in Number Three was some sort of cousin of the Youlgreaves."

Black fur streaked along the windowsill. A paw tapped the glass. Lord Peter had come to join us.

"Oh look!" Audrey said. "Isn't he clever?" She bent down, bringing her head level with Lord Peter's. "You knew Mummy was coming to look for you, didn't you? So you came to find Mummy instead."

# Chapter Eight

In FEBRUARY, Lady Youlgreave demanded to see Vanessa. She invited us to have a glass of sherry with her after church on Sunday.

When I told Vanessa, her face brightened. "Oh good."

"I wish she'd chosen some other time." Sunday was my busiest day.

"Do you want to see if we can rearrange it?"

"It would be diplomatic to go," I said. "No sense in upsetting her."

"I'll take you out to lunch afterward. As a reward."

"Why are you so keen to meet her?"

"Not exactly keen. Just interested."

"Because of the connection with Francis Youlgreave?"

Vanessa nodded. "It's not every day you have a chance to meet the surviving family of a dead poet." She glanced at me, her face mischievous. "Or for that matter the man responsible for the care of his earthly remains."

"No doubt that was the only reason you wanted to marry me?"

"Beggars can't be choosers. Anyway, I want to meet Lady Youlgreave for her own sake. Isn't she your boss?"

The old woman was the patron of the living, which meant that on the departure of one incumbent she had the right to nominate the next. The practice was a quaint survival from the days when such patronage had been a convenient way to provide financially for younger sons. In practice, such private patrons usually delegated the choice to the bishop. But Lady Youlgreave had chosen to exercise the right when she nominated me. An ancient possessiveness lingered. Though she rarely came to church, I had heard her refer to me on more than one occasion as "my vicar."

On Sunday, swathed in coats, Vanessa and I left the Vicarage. We walked arm in arm past the railings of the church and crossed the mouth of the drive to Roth Park. The big wrought-iron gates had stood open for as long as anyone could remember. Each gate contained the letter Y within an oval frame. On the top of the left-hand gatepost was a stone fist brandishing a dagger, the crest of the Youlgreaves. On the right-hand gatepost there was nothing but an iron spike.

"What happened to the other dagger?" Vanessa asked.

"According to Audrey, some teddy boys pulled it down on New Year's Eve. Before my time."

Vanessa stopped, staring up the drive, a broad strip of grass and weeds separating two ruts of mud and gravel, running into a tunnel of trees which needed pollarding. The house could not be seen from the road.

"It looks so mournful," she said.

"The Bramleys haven't spent much money on the place. I'm told they're trying to sell it."

"Is there much land left?"

"Just the strip along the drive, plus a bit near the house. Most of it was sold off for housing."

"Sometimes it all seems so pointless. Spending all that time and money on a place like that."

I glanced at the gates. "How old are they, do you think?"

"Turn of the century? Obviously made to last for generations."

"Designed to impress. And the implication was that the house and the park would be in your descendants' hands forever and ever."

"That's what's so sad," Vanessa said. "They were building for eternity, and seventy years later eternity came to an end."

"Eternity was even shorter than that. The Youlgreaves had to sell up in the nineteen-thirties."

"I remember. It was in Audrey's book. And they hadn't been here for very long, had they? Not in dynastic terms."

We walked across the bridge. A lorry traveling north from the gravel pits splashed mud on my overcoat. Vanessa peered down at the muddy waters beneath. The Rowan was no more than a stream, but at this point, though shallow, it was relatively wide.

We came to the Old Manor House, a long low building separated from the road by a line of posts linked by chains. This side of the house had a two-story frontage with six bays. The windows were large and Georgian. At some point the facade had been rendered and painted a pale greeny-blue, now fading and flaking with age. There were darker stains on the walls where rainwater had cascaded out of the broken guttering.

Between the posts and the house was a circular lawn, around which ran the drive. The grass was long and lank, and there were drifts of leaves against the house. Weeds sprouted through the cracks of the tarmac. In the middle of the lawn was a wooden bird table, beneath which sat Lord Peter, waiting. Hearing our footsteps, the cat glanced toward us and moved away without hurrying. He slithered through the bars of the gate at the side of the house and slid out of sight behind the dustbins.

"That cat's everywhere," Vanessa said. "Don't you find it sinister?"

I glanced at her. "No. Why?"

"No reason." She looked away. "Is that someone waving from the window? The one at the end?"

An arm was waving slowly behind the ground-floor window to the far left. We walked toward the front door.

"How do you feel about dogs, by the way?"

"Fine. Why?"

"Lady Youlgreave has two of them."

I tried the handle of the front door. It was locked. There was a burst of barking from the other side. I felt Vanessa recoil.

"It's all right. They're tied up. We'll have to go round to the back."

We walked down the side of the house, past the dustbins and into the yard at the rear. There was no sign of Lord Peter. The spare key was hidden under an upturned flowerpot beside the door.

"A little obvious, isn't it?" Vanessa said. "It's the first place anyone would look."

We let ourselves into a scullery which led through an evil-smelling kitchen toward the sound of barking in the hall.

Beauty and Beast were attached by their leads to the newel post at the foot of the stairs. Beauty was an Alsatian, so old she could hardly stand up, and almost blind. Beast was a dachshund, even older, though she retained more of her faculties. She, too, had her problems in the shape of a sausage-shaped tumor that dangled from her belly almost to the floor. When she waddled along, it was as though she had five legs. When I had first come to Roth, the dogs and their owner had been much more active, and one often met the three of them marching along the footpaths that criss-crossed what was left of Roth Park. Now their lives had contracted. The dogs were no longer capable of guarding or attacking. They ate, slept, defecated and barked.

"This way," I said to Vanessa, raising my voice to make her hear above the din.

She wrinkled her nose and mouthed, "Does it always smell this bad?"

I nodded. Doris Potter, who was one of my regular communicants, came in twice a day during the week, and an agency nurse covered the weekends. But they were unable to do much more than look after Lady Youlgreave herself.

The hall was T-shaped, with the stairs at the rear. I led the way into the right-hand arm of the T. I tapped on a door at the end of the corridor.

"Come in, David." The voice was high-pitched like a child's.

The room had once been a dining room. When I had first come to Roth, Lady Youlgreave had asked me to dinner, and we had eaten by candlelight, facing each other across the huge mahogany table. Then as now, most of the furniture was Victorian, and designed for a larger room. We had eaten food which came out of tins and we drank a bottle of claret which should have been opened five years earlier.

For an instant, I saw the room afresh, as if through Vanessa's eyes. I noticed the thick gray cobwebs around the cornices, a bird's nest among the ashes in the grate, and the dust on every horizontal surface. Time had drained most of the color and substance from the Turkish carpet, leaving a ghostly presence on the floor. The walls were crowded with oil paintings, none of them particularly old and most of them worth less than their heavy gilt frames. The exception was the Sargent over the fireplace: it showed a large, red-faced man in tweeds, Lady Youlgreave's father-in-law, standing beside the Rowan with his large red house in the background and a springer spaniel at his feet.

Our hostess was sitting in an easy chair beside the window. This was where she usually passed her days. She spent her nights in the room next door, which had once been her husband's study; she no longer used the upstairs. She had a blanket draped over her lap and a side table beside the chair. An aluminum walker stood within arm's reach. There were books on the side table, and also a lined pad on a clipboard. On a low stool within reach of the chair was a metal box with its lid open.

For a moment, Lady Youlgreave stared at us as we hesitated in the doorway. It was as though she had forgotten what we were doing here. The dogs were still barking behind us, but with less conviction than before.

"Shut the door and take off your coats," she said. "Put them down. Doesn't matter where."

Lady Youlgreave had been a small woman to begin with, and now old age had made her even smaller. Dark eyes peered up at us from deep sockets. She was wearing a dress of some stiff material with a high collar; the dress was too large for her now, and her head poked out of the folds of the collar like a tortoise's from its shell.

"Well," she said. "This is a surprise."

"I'd like to introduce Vanessa Forde, my fiancée. Vanessa, this is Lady Youlgreave."

"How do you do. Pull up one of those chairs and sit down where I can see you."

I arranged two of the dining chairs for Vanessa and myself. The three of us sat in a little semi-circle in front of the window. Vanessa was nearest the box, and I noticed her glancing into its open mouth.

Lady Youlgreave studied Vanessa with unabashed curiosity. "So. If you ask me, David's luckier than he deserves."

Vanessa smiled and politely shook her head.

"My cleaning woman tells me you're a publisher."

"Yes—by accident really."

"I dare say you'll be giving it up when you marry."

"No." Vanessa glanced at me. "It's my job. In any case, the income will be important."

Lady Youlgreave squeezed her lips together. Then she relaxed them and said, "In my day, a husband supported a wife."

"I suppose I've grown used to supporting myself."

"And a wife supported her husband in other ways. Made a home for him." Unexpectedly, she laughed, a bubbling hiss from the back of her throat. "And in the case of a vicar's wife, she usually ran the parish as well. You'll have plenty to do here without going out to work."

"It's up to Vanessa, of course," I said. "By the way, how are you feeling?"

"Awful. That damned doctor keeps giving me new medicines, but all they do is bung me up and give me bad dreams." She waved a brown, twisted hand at the box on the stool. "I dreamed about that last night. I dreamed I found a dead bird inside. A goose. Told the girl I wanted it roasted for lunch. Then I saw it was crawling with maggots." There was another laugh. "That'll teach me to go rummaging through the past."

"Is that what you've been doing?" Vanessa asked. "In there?"

"I have to do something. I never realized you can be tired and in pain and bored—all at the same time. The girl told me that the Oliphant woman had written a history of Roth. So I made her buy me a copy. Not as bad as I thought it was going to be." She glared at me. "I suppose you had a hand in it."

"Vanessa and I edited it, yes, and Vanessa saw it through the press."

"Thought so. Anyway, it made me curious. I knew there was a lot of rubbish up in the attic. Papers, and so on. George had them put up there when we moved from the other house. Said he was going to write the family history. God knows why. Literature wasn't his line at all. Didn't know one end of a pen from another. Anyway, he never had the opportunity. So all the rubbish just stayed up there."

Vanessa leaned forward. "Do you think you might write something yourself?"

Lady Youlgreave held up her right hand. "With fingers like this?" She let the hand drop on her lap. "Besides, what does it matter? It's all over with. They're all dead and buried. Who cares what they did or why they did it?"

She stared out of the window at the bird table. I wondered

if the morphine was affecting her mind. James Vintner had told me that he had increased the dose recently. Like the house and the dogs, their owner was sliding into decay.

I said, "Vanessa's read quite a lot of Francis Youlgreave's verse."

"I've got a copy of *The Four Last Things*," Vanessa said. "The one with 'The Judgement of Strangers' in it."

Lady Youlgreave stared at her for a moment. "There were two other collections, *The Tongues of Angels* and *Last Poems*. He published *Last Poems* when he was still up at Oxford. Silly man. So pretentious." Her eyes moved to me. "Pass me that book," she demanded. "The black one on the corner of the table."

I handed her a quarto-sized hardback notebook. The seconds ticked by while she opened it and tried to find the page she wanted. Vanessa and I looked at each other. Inside the notebook I saw yellowing paper, unlined and flecked with damp, covered with erratic lines of handwriting in brown ink.

"There," Lady Youlgreave said at last, placing the open notebook on her side table and turning it so it was the right way up for Vanessa and me. "Read that."

The handwriting was a mass of blots and corrections. Two lines leaped out at me, however, because they were the only ones which had no alterations or blemishes:

> *Then darkness descended; and whispers defiled*
> *The judgement of stranger, and widow, and child.*

"Is that *his* writing?" Vanessa asked, her voice strained.
Lady Youlgreave nodded. "This is a volume of his journal.

March eighteen-ninety-four, while he was still in London." The lips twisted. "He was the vicar of St. Michael's in Beauclerk Place. I think this was the first draft." She looked up at us, at our eager faces, then slowly closed the book. "According to this journal, it was a command performance."

Vanessa raised her eyebrows. "I don't understand."

Lady Youlgreave drew the book toward her and clasped it on her lap. "He wrote the first half of the first draft in a frenzy of inspiration in the early hours of the morning. He had just had an angelic visitation. He believed that the angel had told him to write the poem." Once more her lips curled and she looked from me to Vanessa. "He was intoxicated at the time, of course. He had been smoking opium earlier that evening. He used to patronize an establishment in Leicester Square." Her head swayed on her neck. "An establishment which seems to have catered for a variety of tastes."

"Are there many of his journals?" asked Vanessa. "Or manuscripts of his poems? Or letters?"

"Quite a few. I've not had time to go through everything yet."

"As you know, I'm a publisher. I can't help wondering if you might have the material for a biography of Francis Youlgreave there."

"Very likely. For example, his journal gives a very different view of the Rosington scandal. From the horse's mouth, as it were." Her lips twisted and she made a hissing sound. "The trouble is, this particular horse isn't always a reliable witness. George's father used to say—but I mustn't keep you waiting like this. You haven't had any sherry yet. I'm sure we've got some somewhere."

"It doesn't matter," I said.

"The girl will know. She's late. She should be bringing me my lunch."

The heavy eyelids, like dough-colored rubber, drooped over the eyes. The fingers twitched, but did not relax their hold of Francis Youlgreave's journal.

"I think perhaps we'd better be going," I said. "Leave you to your lunch."

"You can give me my medicine first." The eyes were fully open again and suddenly alert. "It's the bottle on the mantel-piece."

I hesitated. "Are you sure it's the right time?"

"I always have it before lunch," she snapped. "That's what Dr. Vintner said. It's before lunch, isn't it? And the girl's late. She's supposed to be bringing me my lunch."

There was a clean glass and a spoon beside the bottle on the mantelpiece. I measured out a dose and gave her the glass. She clasped it in both hands and drank it at once. She sat back, still cradling the glass. A dribble of liquid ran down her chin.

"I'll leave a note," I said. "Just to say that you've had your medicine."

"But there's no need to write a note. I'll tell Doris myself."

"It won't be Doris," I said. "It's the weekend, so it's the nurse who'll come in."

"Silly woman. Thinks I'm deaf. Thinks I'm senile. Any-way, I told you: I'll tell her myself."

I could be obstinate, too. I scribbled a few words in pencil on a page torn from my diary and left it under the bottle for the nurse. Lady Youlgreave barely acknowledged us when we said goodbye. But when we were almost at the door, she stirred.

"Come and see me again soon," she commanded. "Both of you. Perhaps you'd like to look at some of Uncle Francis's things. He was very interested in sex, you know." She made a hissing noise again, her way of expressing mirth. "Just like you, David."

# Chapter Nine

V ANESSA AND I WERE MARRIED on a rainy Saturday in
April. Henry Appleyard was my best man. Michael
gave us a present, a battered but beautiful seventeenth-
century French edition of *Ecclesiasticus*; according to the
bookplate it had once been part of the library of Rosington
Theological College.

"It was his own idea," his mother whispered to me. "His
own money, too. Quite a coincidence—Rosington, I mean."

"I hope it wasn't expensive."

"Five shillings. He found it in a junk shop."

"We've been very lucky with presents," Vanessa said. "Rosemary gave us a gorgeous coffee pot. Denbigh ware."

It was only then that I realized Rosemary was listening
intently to the conversation. Later I noticed her examining
the book, flicking through the pages as if they irritated her.

Vanessa and I flew to Italy the same afternoon. She had
arranged it all, including the *pensione* in Florence where we
were to stay. I had assumed that if we had a honeymoon at all
it would be in England. But Florence had been Vanessa's idea,
and she was so excited about it that I did not have the heart
to try to change her mind. Her plan had support from an unexpected quarter: when I told Peter Hudson, he said, "She's
right. Get right away from everything. You owe it to each
other."

·  ·  ·

It was raining in Florence, too. Not that it mattered. I wouldn't have cared if the city had been buried beneath a pall of snow.

We had dinner in a little restaurant. Vanessa was looking alluring in a dark dress which set off her hair. We talked more about Rosemary than ourselves. I found myself glancing surreptitiously at my watch. I did not eat much, though I drank more than my fair share of the wine.

While we talked, I allowed my imagination to run free for the first time in ten years. I felt like a schoolboy at the end of term, or a convict coming to the end of his sentence.

As the meal progressed, we talked less. An awkwardness settled between us. My thoughts scurried to and fro as though I were running a fever. Once or twice, Vanessa looked at me and seemed about to say something.

The waiter asked if we would like coffee. I wanted to go back to our room, but Vanessa ordered coffee, with brandies to go with it. When the drinks came, she drank half her brandy in a few seconds.

"David, I have to admit I feel a bit nervous."

I leaned forward to light her cigarette. "Why?"

"About tonight."

For a moment, neither of us spoke.

"We'll get used to it," I said. "I dare say we'll both find it strange." The urgency was building up inside me. I touched Vanessa's hand. "Dearest—you know, there's no reason why it needn't be enjoyable as well."

She ran her finger around the rim of her glass. "Charles didn't seem—he didn't want it very much. I don't know why.

Of course, it happened quite a lot when we were first married, but then it tailed off."

"You don't have to tell me this."

"I want to explain. Charles used to stay up reading until all hours and often I was asleep when he came to bed. There just never seemed to be much opportunity."

"Darling," I said, "don't worry."

Her mouth twitched. "It'll be all right on the night, will it?"

"It will be. And then it will get better and better. Shall I get the bill?"

We walked back—sedately, arm in arm—to our *pensione*. There was a part of me that wanted to make love to her there and then: to pull her into an alley, push her up against a wall and tear my way into her clothes; and all the while the rain would patter on our heads and shoulders, the lamplight would glitter in the puddles, and the snarls and honks of the traffic would make a savage, distant music.

At the *pensione*, we collected our key and went upstairs. I locked the door behind us. I turned to find her standing in the middle of the room with her arms by her side.

"Vanessa." My voice sounded like a stranger's. "You're lovely."

I took off my jacket and dropped it on a chair. I went to her, put my hands on her shoulders, stooped and kissed her gently on the lips. Her lips moved beneath mine. I took off her coat and let it fall to the floor. I nibbled the side of her neck. My fingers found the fastening of her dress. I peeled it away from her. She stood there in her underwear, revealed and vulnerable. Her arms tightened around my neck.

"I'm cold. Can we get into bed?"

I was a little disappointed: I had looked forward for months to slowly removing her clothes, to touching as much of her body as I could with my mouth. But all that could wait. She allowed me to help her quickly out of the rest of her clothes. She scrambled into bed and watched me as I quickly undressed. My excitement was obvious.

"My handbag. I've got a cap."

"I've got a condom." I dropped my wallet on the bedside table and slithered into bed beside her.

There was goose flesh on her arm. It was hard to move much because she was holding me so tightly. The restraint somehow increased my excitement. I kissed her hair frantically.

"I want you," I muttered. "Let me come in."

She released her hold. I rolled over and found the condom in my wallet. My fingers were twice as clumsy as usual. At last I extracted the condom from its foil wrapper and rolled it over my penis. Vanessa was lying on her back, her legs slightly apart, watching me. There was a noise like surf in my ears.

"Now, darling," I said. "Now, now."

I climbed on top of her, using my knees to spread her legs wider. I abandoned all attempts at subtlety. I wanted one thing and I wanted it now. Vanessa stared up at me and put her hands on my shoulders. Her face was very serious. I lowered myself and thrust hard into her. She gasped and tried to writhe away but now my hands were on her shoulders and she could not move. I cried out, a groan that had been building up inside me for ten years. And then, with embarrassing rapidity, it was all over.

Trembling, I lay like a dead weight on top of her. In a moment, my trembling turned to sobs.

Once again her arms tightened around me. "Hush now. It's all right. It's over."

It wasn't over, not for either of us, and it wasn't all right. Two hours later, I wanted her again. We were still awake, talking about the future. Vanessa agreed with me that it would obviously take time before we were sexually in tune with each other. That was to be expected. The second time everything happened more slowly. She lay there while I explored the hollows and curves of her body with my mouth. She let me do whatever I wanted, and I did.

"Dearest David," she murmured, not once but many times.

After I had come again, I asked if there was anything I could do for her, and she said no, not this time. She went into the little bathroom. I lit a cigarette and listened to the rustle of running water. When she came back, she was wearing her nightdress and her face was pink and scrubbed. Soon we turned out the light and settled down for sleep. I rested my arm over her. I felt her hand take mine.

"How was it?" I asked. "Was it very painful?"

"I'm a little sore."

"I'm sorry. I should have—"

"It doesn't matter. I want to make you happy."

"You do."

We were in Florence for seven days. We looked at pictures, listened to music and sat in cafés. And we made love. Each night she lay there and allowed me to do whatever I wanted; and I did. On the seventh night I found her crying in the bathroom.

"Darling, what's wrong?"

She lifted her tear-stained face to me, a sight which I found curiously erotic. "It's nothing. I'm tired, that's all."

"Tell me."

"It's a little painful. Sore."

I smiled. "So am I, as a matter of fact. Not used to the exercise. I dare say we'll soon toughen up. It's like walking without shoes. One needs practice."

She tried to smile, but it didn't quite come off. "And my breasts are rather painful too. I think my period is due."

"We needn't do anything tonight," I said, my disappointment temporarily swamped by my desire to be kind.

We sat in bed reading. She was the first to turn out the light. The evening felt incomplete. I lay on my back and stared up into the darkness.

"Vanessa?" I said softly. "Are you awake?"

"Yes."

"How do you feel about making love when you have a period?" It had suddenly occurred to me that it might be several days before we had an opportunity to do it again. "I should say that I don't mind it, myself."

"Actually, it's very painful for me. I have heavy periods. I'm sorry."

"Not to worry," I said; I turned and put my arm around her. "It doesn't matter. Sleep well. God bless."

As usual, her hand gripped mine. I lay there, my penis as erect as a guardsman on parade, listening to the sound of her breathing.

*Chapter Ten*

AFTER OUR RETURN FROM ITALY, Vanessa and I slipped into the new routine of our shared lives. We were even happy, in a fragmentary fashion, as humans are happy. Though what was in store was rooted in ourselves—in our personalities and our histories—we had no inkling of what was coming. As humans do, we kept secrets from ourselves, and from each other.

Toward the end of May, Peter and June Hudson came to supper. They were our first real guests. The meal was something of a celebration. Peter had been offered preferment. Though there had been no official announcement, he was to be the next Bishop of Rosington.

"It's a terrifying prospect," June said placidly. "No more lurking in the background for me. No more communing with the kitchen sink. I shall have to be a proper Mrs. Bishop and shake hands with the County."

"You could be a Mrs. Proudie," Vanessa suggested. "Rule your husband's diocese with a rod of iron."

"It sounds quite attractive." She smiled at her husband. "I'm sure Peter wouldn't mind. It would give the little woman something to do."

The news unsettled me. I was not jealous of Peter's preferment, though in the past I might have been. But inevitably the prospect of his going to Rosington awakened memories.

After the meal, June and Vanessa took their coffee into the sitting room while Peter and I washed up.

"When will you go to Rosington?" I asked.

"In the autumn. October, probably. I shall take a month off in August and try to prepare myself."

I squirted a Z of washing-up liquid into a baking dish. "I'll miss you. And June."

"You and Vanessa must come and visit. At least there'll be plenty of space."

"I don't know. Going back isn't always such a good idea."

"Sometimes staying away is a worse one."

"Damn it, Peter. You don't make it easy, do you?"

He dried a glass with the precision he brought to everything. We worked in silence for a moment. It was a muggy evening and suddenly I felt desperate for air. I opened the back door to put out the rubbish. Lord Peter streaked into the kitchen.

Had I been by myself, I would have shouted at him. But I did not want Peter—my friend, not the cat—to think me more unbalanced than he already did. When I returned from the dustbin, I found that the two Peters had formed a mutual admiration society.

"I didn't know you liked cats."

"Oh yes. Is this one yours?"

"It belongs to one of my parishioners."

The cat purred. Peter, who was crouching beside it with a pipe in his mouth, glanced up at me. "You don't like either of them very much?"

"She's a good woman. A churchwarden."

"Is that an answer?"

"It's all you're going to get."

"I shall miss our regular meetings."

"So shall I."

"When I go to Rosington, you'll need a new spiritual director."

"I suppose so."

"A change will do you good." Peter's voice was suddenly stern, and the cat wriggled away from him. "Perhaps we know each other too well. A new spiritual director may be more useful to you."

"I'd rather continue with you."

"It just wouldn't be practical. We shall be too far away from each other. You need to see someone regularly. Don't you agree?"

"Yes. If you say so." My voice sounded sullen, almost petulant.

"I do say so. Like one of those high-performance engines, you need constant tuning." He smiled at me. "Otherwise you break down."

*Chapter Eleven*

I F IT HADN'T BEEN FOR SEX, or rather the lack of it, Vanessa and I would probably still be married. There was real friendship between us, and much tenderness. We filled some of the empty corners in each other's lives. A semidetached marriage? Perhaps. If so, the arrangement suited us both. Vanessa had her job, I had mine.

One of the things I loved most was her sense of humor, which was so dry that at times I barely noticed it. On one occasion she almost reduced Audrey to tears—of rage—by suggesting that we invited the pop group that played on Saturday nights at the Queen's Head to perform at Evensong. "It would encourage young people to come to church, don't you think?"

On another occasion, one afternoon early in August, Vanessa and I were in our little library on the green. Vanessa took her books to the issue desk, to be stamped by Mrs. Finch, the librarian. Audrey was hovering like a buzzard poised to strike in front of the section devoted to detective stories.

"I'd also like to make a reservation for a book that's coming out in the autumn," Vanessa said in a clear, carrying voice. "*The Female Eunuch* by Germaine Greer."

I glanced up in time to see a look of outrage flash between Mrs. Finch and Audrey.

Mrs. Finch closed the last of Vanessa's library books, placed it on top of the others and pushed the pile across the issue desk. She jabbed the book cards into the tickets; the cardboard buckled and creased under the strain. She directed her venom at inanimate objects because by and large she was too timid to direct it at people.

While Vanessa was filling in the reservation card, I joined her at the issue desk to have my own books stamped. Audrey swooped on us; today her color was high, perhaps because of the heat. "So glad I caught you," she said, her eyes flicking from me to Vanessa. "I wanted a word about the fete."

I did not dare look at Vanessa. The annual church fete was a delicate subject. It was held in my garden on the last Saturday in August. Audrey had organized it for the past nine years. Although she would almost certainly have resisted any attempt to relieve her of the responsibility, she felt organizing the church fete was properly the job of the vicar's wife. She had made this quite clear to both Vanessa and me in a number of indirect ways in the past few weeks.

Vanessa, on the other hand, was determined not to act as my unpaid curate in this capacity or in any other, and I respected her for the decision. We had agreed on this before our marriage. She had a demanding and full-time job of her own, and had little enough spare time as it was: I could not expect her suddenly to take on more work, even if she had wanted to.

This year we had another problem to deal with. This was the suburbs, so many of our patrons came in cars. In recent years, the Bramleys had allowed us to use their paddock, a field which lay immediately behind the church and the Vicarage, as a car park. Unfortunately, they had suddenly left Roth Park at the beginning of June. They had sold the house and grounds without telling anyone. Bills had not been paid. There were rumors—relayed by Audrey—that litigation was pending.

The new owner of Roth Park had not yet moved in, so we had not been able to ask whether we could have the paddock. It would not be easy to find an alternative.

"Time's beginning to gallop," Audrey told us. "We really must put our thinking caps on."

"Perhaps they could park in Manor Farm Lane," I suggested.

"But they'd have to walk miles. Besides, it's not a very safe place to leave cars. We have to face it: without the paddock, we're hamstrung. I even rang the estate agents. But they were most unhelpful."

"We've still got several weeks. And if the worst comes to the worst, perhaps we can do without a car park."

"Quite impossible," Audrey snapped. "If people can't park their cars, they simply won't come."

It wasn't what she said—it was the way in which she said it. Her tone was almost vindictive. In the silence, Audrey looked from Vanessa to me. Audrey's face was moist and pink. Mrs. Finch studied us all from her ringside seat from behind the issue desk. The library was very quiet. A wasp with a long yellow-and-black tail flew through the open doors into the library and settled on the edge of the metal rubbish bin. Trucks ground their way down the main road. The heat was oppressive.

Audrey snorted, making a sound like steam squirting from a valve, relieving the pressure of her invisible boiler. She turned and dropped the novels she was carrying on to the trolley for returned books.

"I've got a headache," she said. "Not that any of you need concern yourselves about it. I shall go home and rest."

Mrs. Finch and Vanessa began to speak at once.

"My mother always said that a cold flannel and a darkened room . . ." began Mrs. Finch.

Vanessa said, "I'm so sorry. Is there anything we . . . ?"

Both women stopped talking in mid-sentence because Audrey clearly wasn't listening, and had no intention of listening. She walked very quickly out of the library. I noticed that her dress was stained with sweat under the armpits. In a moment, the doorway was empty. I stared through it at the green beyond, at the main road, the tower of the church and the oaks of Roth Park. I heard the faint but unmistakable sound of a wolf whistle. I wondered if one of the youths were baiting Audrey as she scurried around the green to the sanctuary of Tudor Cottage.

"That'll be one shilling, Mrs. Byfield." Mrs. Finch held out her hand for the reservation card. "Five pence. We'll do our best, of course, but I can't guarantee anything. The stock editor decides which books we buy. He may not think this is suitable."

Vanessa smiled at Mrs. Finch and gallantly resisted the temptation to reply. A moment later, she and I walked back along the south side of the green toward the Vicarage.

"Is Audrey often like that?" she asked.

"She gets very involved with the fete." I felt I had to explain

Audrey to Vanessa, even to apologize for her. "It's the high point of the year for her."

"I wonder why." Vanessa glanced up at me. "Tell me, is she normally so irritable?"

I felt uncomfortable. "She did seem a little tetchy."

"I wonder how old she is. Getting on for fifty? Do you think she might be going through the menopause?"

"I suppose it's possible. Why?"

"It would explain a great deal."

"Yes." I was in fact unclear what the change of life could mean for a woman. I put on speed, as if trying to walk away from this faintly unsavory topic. "But was she really acting so unusually? She did say she had a headache."

"David." Vanessa put a hand on my arm, forcing me to stop and look at her. "You've known Audrey for so long that I don't think you realize how odd she is."

"Surely not."

We moved on to the main road. We waited for a gap in the traffic.

"I'd better look in on her this evening," I said. "See how she is."

"I wouldn't. Fuel to feed the flame."

"Flame? Don't be silly."

In silence, we crossed the road and went into the drive of the Vicarage.

"It's not that I *want* to see her this evening," I went on, wondering if Vanessa might conceivably be jealous. "People like Audrey are part of my job."

Vanessa thrust her key into the lock of the front door. "You sometimes sound such a *prig*."

I stared at her. This was the nearest we had ever come to a quarrel. It was the first time that either of us had spoken critically to the other.

Vanessa pushed open the door. The telephone was ringing in the study. When I picked up the receiver, the news I heard pushed both Audrey's problems and my squabble with Vanessa into the background.

*Chapter Twelve*

W HEN I WAS A CHILD I had a jigsaw with nearly a
thousand pieces, intricately shaped. Some of them
had been cut into the shapes of objects which were entirely
unrelated to the subject of the picture.

I remember a cocktail glass lying on its side in the blue of
the sky, and a stork standing upside down in the foliage of an
oak tree. A rifle with a telescopic sight was concealed in a
door. Not that I knew that it was a door at the outset, or that
the stork was in an oak tree. The point about the jigsaw was
that a picture had not been supplied with it. Only by assembling the pieces could one discover what the subject was.
Since much of the picture consisted of sky, trees, grass and
road, it was not until a relatively late stage in the assembly
that you realized that the jigsaw showed a Pickwickian stage-
coach drawing up outside a country inn with a thatched roof.

The analogy may seem labored, but something very similar happened in Roth during 1970. One by one, the pieces
dropped into place. My marriage to Vanessa, for example.
*The History of Roth*. The preparations for the fete. The sudden
departure of the Bramleys from Roth Park. Peter Hudson's
preferment. Lord Peter's inability to stay away from the Vicarage. Lady Youlgreave's belated interest in her husband's
relations. Vanessa's long-standing interest in the poetry of
Francis Youlgreave.

All these and more. Slowly the picture—or rather its components—came together. And one of the pieces was my godson Michael.

The telephone call on that August afternoon was from Henry Appleyard. He had been offered the chance of a lucrative four-week lecture tour in the United States, filling in for a speaker who had canceled at the last moment.

"I'm flying out the day after tomorrow, from Heathrow," he said. "I wondered if I could look in for lunch?"

"Of course you can. When's your flight?"

"In the evening."

"Are all of you coming?"

"Just me, I'm afraid."

The organizers had offered to pay his wife's travel expenses as well, I gathered, but she had to stay to look after Michael.

"Can't you leave him with someone?"

"It's such short notice. His schoolfriends are all on holiday, too."

"He could stay with us. If he wouldn't find us too dull."

"It's too much of an imposition."

"Why? He's my godson. But would he be lonely?"

"I wouldn't worry about that. He's quite a self-contained boy."

"Rosemary will be home in a few days, so at least he'd have someone nearer his own age. And our doctor has a boy of eleven."

"It still seems too much to ask."

"Why don't I have a word with Vanessa and phone you back?"

Henry agreed. I put down the phone and went into the kitchen to talk to Vanessa. She listened in silence, but when I had finished she smiled.

"That's a wonderful idea."

"I'm glad you like it. But why the enthusiasm?"

"It'll make it easier when Rosemary comes home. For her as well as me." She touched my arm, and I knew our squabble was over. "Besides, you'd like it, wouldn't you?"

Two days later the Appleyards arrived for lunch.

"I'm sorry this is such short notice," Henry said as we were smoking a cigarette in the drive.

"It doesn't matter. Michael's welcome. I'm glad Vanessa's here. For his sake, I mean."

Henry started to say something but stopped, because the front door opened and Michael himself came out to join us. The boy was now eleven years old, fair-haired and slim. He stood close to Henry. They didn't know what to say to each other.

At that moment a dark-blue car drove slowly down the main road toward the bridge over the Rowan. It had a long bonnet and a small cockpit. It looked more like a spacecraft than a car. The windows were of tinted glass and I could make out only the vague shape of two people inside. It slowed, signaled right and turned into the drive of Roth Park.

"Cor," said Michael, his face showing animation for the first time since he had arrived. "An E-type Jaguar."

Another piece of the jigsaw had arrived.

That evening I telephoned Audrey to see if she was all right. I had not seen her since her outburst in the library. When she answered the phone, her voice sounded weak.

"Just a headache," she said. "I'll be fine in a day or two. Rest is the best medicine. That's what Dr. Vintner said."

"You've been to see him?"

"He came to me, actually. I wasn't up to going out."

I felt guilty, as perhaps she had intended me to feel. "Is there anything we can do?"

"No. I'll be fine. Well, actually there is one thing. Apparently the new people have moved into Roth Park. You could go and ask them about the paddock. I'd feel so much happier if that were settled. It'd be a weight off my mind."

I remembered the Jaguar. "When did they move in?"

"Today at some point. Mr. Malik told Charlene when he brought the groceries round this afternoon. They've opened an account with him. Their name is Clifford."

"Are they a family?"

"Mr. Malik's only met a young man so far. Perhaps he's the son."

I promised I would go to see them in the morning. A moment later, I rang off and went to join the others in the sitting room. Michael had lost that frozen look his face had worn since his parents left. He was talking to Vanessa about his school. They both looked up as I came in. I allowed myself to be drawn into a game of Hearts with them. I hadn't played cards for years. To my surprise I enjoyed it.

The next morning I walked up to Roth Park. Vanessa was at work, and we had arranged for Michael to spend the day with the doctor's son, Brian. I had not been to Roth Park since May, when the last of the Bramleys' patients had moved to another nursing home. Privately I had never had much time for Mr. and Mrs. Bramley, a red-faced and loud-voiced couple who, I suspected, bullied their patients.

It was another fine day. With a copy of the parish magazine under my arm, I strolled down the road, past the church. The traffic was still heavy. In the last thirty or forty years, houses had mushroomed like a fungus along the highways and byways of Roth. The fungus had spread away from the highways and byways and devoured the fields between them. All the occupants of these new houses appeared to own at least one car.

I turned into the drive. On the right was the south wall of the churchyard. To the left, the turbid waters of the Rowan were visible through a screen of branches, nettles and leaves. It was mid-morning and already very warm. It was too hot to hurry.

I was not in the best of moods. I had wanted to make love the previous evening, but when I came to bed Vanessa was asleep. Or rather—I uncharitably wondered—she was pretending to be asleep.

After about sixty yards, the drive dived into a belt of oak trees. It was cooler here, and I lingered. At the time this felt an indulgence. Now, when I look back, it seems as though I were clinging to my state of innocence. A track went off to the right, following the west side of the churchyard; it passed through the paddock behind the Vicarage garden, which we hoped to use as our fete car park, and ran north-west toward the drowned farmlands beneath the Jubilee Reservoir.

I walked on. Once past the oaks, the park opened out. To the south was the Rowan, now a silver streak, lent enchantment by distance. Beyond it, housing estates covered what had once been pastureland south of the river. On the right were the roofs of another housing estate south of the reservoir, encroaching on the grounds from the north.

The drive, which had been moving away from the river, changed direction and swung toward it in a long, leisurely leftward loop around the base of a small hill. There, sheltered by the hill and facing south, was Roth Park itself.

Looked at with an unbiased eye, the house was not a pretty sight. Thanks to Audrey's book, I now knew that the great fire of 1874 had destroyed most of a late-seventeenth-century mansion. The owner of the estate, Alfred Youlgreave, had built a plain, ugly, redbrick box on the same site with an incongruous Italianate tower attached to the west end.

As the house came into view, two things happened. First, I had the sensation, rightly or wrongly, that I was being watched, that behind one of the many blank windows was a face. I had an impression of stealth, even malice. I knew, of course, that it was more than possible that I was entirely mistaken about this—that the sensation had no external correlation whatsoever; that I was merely projecting my inner difficulties on to the outside world. That did not make the experience less unpleasant.

The other feeling was, if anything, even more powerful. I wanted to run away. I wanted to turn and scurry down the drive as fast as I could. It was not, strictly speaking, a premonition. It was in no sense a warning. I was simply scared. I did not know why. All I knew was that I wanted to run away.

But I did not. I had spent most of my life learning how to restrain my feelings. Besides, I remember thinking, think how odd it would look if there were a watcher: if he or she saw a middle-aged clergyman in a linen jacket hesitating in front of the house and then leaving at a gallop. Our dignity is very precious to almost all of us; and fear of losing face is a more powerful source of motivation than many people imagine.

I walked toward the house. There was an overgrown shrubbery on the right. Outside the house, marooned in a sea of weed-strewn gravel, was a large stone urn stained with yellow lichen. On the plinth—again, according to Audrey—was a plaque commemorating a visit that Queen Adelaide had paid to the Youlgreaves' predecessors in 1839. I paused by the urn, pretending to examine the worn lettering. I really wanted a chance to look more closely at the house.

I could see no one at any of the windows, but that proved nothing. The building was not as imposing as it looked from a distance. Several slates were missing from the roof at the eastern end. A length of guttering had detached itself and was hanging at an angle. There was a large canopy sheltering the front door, a wrought-iron porte-cochère supported by rusting cast-iron pillars, which gave the house the appearance of a provincial railway station.

Parked beneath the canopy was the Cliffords' E-type Jaguar, the car which had aroused Michael's admiration. I marched up the shallow steps to the front door and tugged the bell pull. It was impossible to tell what effect, if any, this had. I noted with irritation that my fingers had left smudges of sweat on the pale-blue cover of the parish magazine.

No one answered the door. I rang the bell again. I waited. Still, nothing happened. I did not know whether to be relieved or irritated. I moved away from the door and walked a few paces down the drive. It felt like a retreat. I didn't like the idea that I might be running away from something. Then I heard music.

I stopped to listen. It was faint enough to make it difficult to hear. Some sort of pop music, I thought; and suddenly I guessed where the Cliffords were. It was a fine morning, their first in their new home. They were probably in the garden.

I was familiar with the layout of the place from my years of visiting the Bramleys and their patients. I followed a path that led through the shrubbery at the side of the house to the croquet lawn below the terrace on the east front. The lawn was now a mass of knee-high grass and weeds. On the terrace, some four feet above it, were two people in deckchairs, with a small, blue transistor radio between them. A male voice was croaking against a background of discordant, rhythmic music. I walked on to the lawn and raised my Panama hat.

"Good morning. I hope I'm not disturbing you. My name is David Byfield."

Two faces, blank as masks, turned toward me; astonishment wipes away much of a person's outward individuality. If the Demon King had appeared before them in a puff of smoke, the effect would have been much the same.

The moment of astonishment dissolved. A young man switched off the radio and stood up. He was skinny, his figure emphasized by the fitted denim shirt and the hip-hugging bell-bottomed jeans. He had a beaky nose and bright, pale-blue eyes. His hair was thick and fair, with more than a hint of ginger, and it curled down to his shoulders. A hippy, I thought, or the next best thing. But I had to admit that the long hair suited him.

"Good morning. What can we do for you?"

I took a step forward. "First, I'd like to welcome you to Roth. I'm the vicar."

The man dropped the cigarette he was holding into the bush of lavender which sprawled out of an urn at the edge of the terrace. "The church at the gates?" He came down the steps to the lawn and held out his hand. "I'm Toby Clifford. How do you do?"

We shook hands. I realized that he was a little older than I had thought at first—perhaps in his middle or late twenties.

"This is my sister Joanna." Toby turned back to her. "Jo, come and say hello to the vicar."

I looked up at the terrace. There was a flurry of limbs in the other deckchair. A young woman stood up. She wore a baggy T-shirt which came halfway down her thighs and—I could hardly help noticing as she scrambled out of the deckchair—green knickers. Short hair framed a triangular face.

"The vicar," she said and giggled. "Sorry. Shouldn't laugh. Not funny."

I held out my hand. "It's the dog collar. It often has that effect on people."

Her eyes widened with surprise. I guessed she was a year or two younger than her brother.

"Would you like some coffee?" Toby said. "We were just going to make some."

"Thank you. If it's not too much trouble."

Toby tapped Joanna's shoulder. She trailed through the French windows into the house. Toby settled me in one of the deckchairs and went to fetch a third. He sat down cautiously.

"I don't trust these chairs," he said. "We found them in the old stables. They look as if they came out of the ark."

"I brought you a parish magazine."

"Thank you. You must put us down for a regular copy."

We chatted for a few minutes. Toby's appearance was misleading, I decided: he had decent manners and knew how to keep a conversation going—indeed, he was rather better at it than me. While we talked, I wondered how best to introduce the subject of his parents. Did they or did they not exist?

"Who'd have thought it could be so quiet on the edge of London?" Toby said. At that moment, a jet roared low across the sky toward Heathrow Airport. He snorted with amusement. "Some of the time, anyway."

"What are your plans for the house?" I asked. "By modern standards, it's pretty big."

He looked at me, a swift, assessing glance that was at variance with his earlier smiles, his light conversation and the way he sprawled so casually in the deckchair. "In the long run, I'm not sure. But in the short term, Jo and I need somewhere to live. And we both like having lots of space." He leaned toward me and lowered his voice. "Between ourselves, Jo needs a little peace and quiet. She's not been well."

I abandoned subtlety. "So it's just the two of you?"

Toby nodded.

At that moment Joanna returned, carrying a tray with three mugs of coffee, a half-used bottle of milk and a packet of sugar. She was still wearing the T-shirt, but she had pulled on a pair of jeans. Soon the three of us were sitting in a row facing the overgrown lawn, each with a mug in one hand and a cigarette in the other.

"God, I'm hot," Joanna said.

"It'll be better when we've got the swimming pool fixed," Toby said. "A man's coming round tomorrow."

"Will it be difficult?" I asked. "I don't think the Bramleys have used it for years."

"I can't swim," Jo said.

Toby waved his cigarette impatiently. "You'll soon learn. Having a pool in your back garden makes all the difference."

"Talking of your back garden," I said, "I have a favor to ask."

Toby smiled but said nothing.

"It's the church fete. The Bramleys used to let us borrow your paddock as our car park. I wondered if you might be kind enough to do the same."

"A paddock?" Joanna giggled. "We've got a *paddock*?"

"I've never known horses to be kept there," I said. "I imagine the name goes back to a time before the Bramleys. It's the field beside the churchyard."

Toby nodded. "When is this fete?"

"The last Saturday in August."

"I don't see why you shouldn't. It'd be a pleasure. Wouldn't it, Jo?"

His sister said nothing.

Soon afterward, I levered myself out of the deckchair and said goodbye. Toby ushered me through the shrubbery and back to the drive. On the fringe of the shrubbery, though, I turned back, intending to wave at Joanna. She was still sitting in her deckchair. She was staring at me with great concentration, her face not so much sullen as serious. She did not wave at me and I did not wave at her.

I had taken only a few steps down the drive when I realized that my Panama hat was still beside the deckchair I had been sitting in. I went back through the shrubbery. Toby was speaking in a soft, pleasant voice. I could only just make out what he was saying.

"You've got to pull yourself together, Jo. We want the natives to like us."

She said something inaudible in reply.

"You'll do as I say," he said. "You're not in fucking Chelsea now."

*Chapter Thirteen*

I COULD HAVE TELEPHONED Audrey with the good news about the paddock, but I decided that it would be better to go and see her. I could spare twenty minutes. I tended to forget that she was a person and treat her as a convenience.

The front door of Tudor Cottage stood open. Inside was a square hall several feet below the ground level outside. The place was cool, even on a warm day in August. The smell of damp lingered beneath the scent of the potpourri in the bowl on the oak table. The ground floor of the cottage was almost entirely given over to the café. The long room on the left of the hall, which stretched the depth of the house, was the tea room itself. The kitchen was at the back of the house, overlooking the walled garden where, on fine days, they put out tables and chairs. On the right was the small paneled room which Audrey used as an office.

I looked into the tea room. At the table in the window, two women with three toddlers in tow were talking in shrill voices. Judging by the bags around them, they had done their shopping at Malik's Minimarket. Charlene Potter was sitting by the till, listlessly polishing a selection of the numerous horse brasses which hung around the fireplace and dangled from the beams. She was a fat girl, with wiry yellow hair, a spotty complexion, and a mouthful of gray fillings. She looked up as I came in and smiled. She had one of the warmest smiles I had ever known, the sort that makes you feel that the person smiling is actually pleased to see you. The two women and the three toddlers stopped talking and stared at me.

"If you want Miss Oliphant," Charlene said, "she's in the office."

"Thank you. By the way, how's your father?"

Again, the smile flashed out. "He's got himself a job. Working down the gravel pits. Like a new man."

"Give him and your mother my best wishes."

Charlene's mother Doris was a regular communicant, which was one reason why Audrey had offered her this job. The other reason was that Charlene's mother helped to look after Lady Youlgreave. The family lived on the council estate and Audrey had entertained grave doubts about Charlene's suitability. But her mother's piety, the Youlgreave connection and the absence of other candidates had tipped the scales in her favor.

I tapped on the office door and Audrey called me to come in. She was sitting at a roll-top desk and turning the pages of a red exercise book. When she saw me, her face colored. With sudden violence, she shut the book, snatched off her glasses, pushed back her chair.

"David—how nice. I'll get Charlene to bring coffee."

"Not on my account, please. I've just had some with the Cliffords."

"What are they like?"

"Very pleasant; and they say we can use the paddock."

Audrey wanted more than this. I told her what I knew. She would like Toby, I guessed, despite his louche appearance, but I was less sure how she would react to Joanna.

"It's a very respectable surname," she remarked when I had finished.

I wondered if Audrey were fantasizing aristocratic connections for the new inhabitants of Roth Park.

"Roth Park—a private house again," she went on. "I can hardly believe it. It really could make a difference to the village. To the whole feel of the place."

The two women and their children were leaving, and the sounds of their voices penetrated from the hall.

Audrey winced. "There'll be crumbs all over the floor. And the last time those two were in, I found jam all over one of the chairs." A wistful expression settled on her face. "It would be so pleasant to have some *nice* customers."

"Are you feeling all right now?"

She put her hand to her forehead. "A slight migraine. I don't think this heat agrees with me. And then there were the louts last night."

"The louts?"

"A whole gang of them in the bus shelter. I could see them quite plainly from my sitting room window. Smoking and drinking. They had a girl in there, too. I closed the windows, but I could still hear them. And then . . ." Her voice trailed away, her cheeks were pinker than before. "I hardly like to mention it. I—I noticed a puddle spreading across the floor. It looked black in the streetlamp." The flush deepened in color. "And suddenly, I realized that one of them must be urinating."

"They hadn't spilled their drink?"

"Oh no. Sometimes that bus shelter smells like a public lavatory. Anyway, I telephoned the police and frankly they weren't very helpful. They said they'd send someone down, but if they did, I didn't see them. Sometimes I despair at this place. I just don't know what the village is coming to."

I stayed with Audrey for a few minutes, trying to calm her down. At one point I thought I caught a whiff of alcohol on her breath, which surprised me. I knew she sometimes had a sherry before lunch, but it was not yet midday. I tried to distract her by steering her thoughts toward the church fete. James Vintner had offered to do a barbecue for us. Audrey was instinctively against innovation, but James had persuaded her into agreeing on principle. By the time I left her, she was in a happier frame of mind.

Charlene intercepted me in the hall.

"Do you think she's all right?" she asked.

"Why?"

Charlene led the way outside and said in a low voice, "Seems a bit hot and bothered, I suppose. Them kids last night upset her. And Lord Peter wasn't in for breakfast, and that always upsets her."

"He'll be all right. That cat always lands on his feet."

"I'm not worried about the cat," Charlene said. "I'm worried about Miss Oliphant."

# Chapter Fourteen

I N THE LATE AFTERNOON, my daughter Rosemary came home. Since the end of term she had been staying on the Isle of Wight with the family of a schoolfriend.

Vanessa was still at work, but Michael had returned from the Vintners', so I took him with me to meet Rosemary. He and Brian seemed to have enjoyed each other's company—they had arranged to go to the cinema the following afternoon. I had a vague hope that Michael and Rosemary would entertain each other. I should have realized that there might not be much common ground between a seventeen-year-old girl and an eleven-year-old boy. Especially, perhaps, between this girl and this boy.

There was little conversation on the drive back from the station. Rosemary sat beside me; she was grave-faced and beautiful, and she answered my questions with a series of monosyllables. She was not rude: it was merely that she had withdrawn into a private place inside herself. I knew that because I was inclined to do the same thing myself when under stress. I thought that I knew the reason: her A level results were due in a few days' time.

Michael was sitting in the back. Every now and then I glanced at him in the rear-view mirror. He was always staring out of the window.

Rosemary was beside me in the front of the car. She opened

her bag, produced a small mirror and examined her face. Her absorption excluded me—excluded everyone but herself. I glanced in the rear-view mirror at Michael's face, as rapt as Rosemary's. For them both, I was no more than a mechanical contrivance driving the car. Each of them might have been alone in the world.

We reached Roth and parked in the drive of the Vicarage. Vanessa's car was not there—she had promised to leave work early, in honor of Rosemary's return, but she was unlikely to reach Roth before 6:30 p.m. Rosemary glided into the house. A moment later, I heard the bathroom door closing. Michael helped me carry in the luggage. The boy looked at a loose end so I suggested he put the kettle on.

I went back outside to lock the car. My heart lurched when I saw a familiar figure waving vigorously at me from the other side of the stream of traffic. Audrey darted across the road and scurried into the Vicarage drive.

"I've got them," she announced. "I really have."

"Who have you got?"

"Those louts, those wretched louts. Someone had to blow the whistle. Give them half a chance and they would try to get away with murder."

My mind filled with an improbable image of one of those overgrown children running berserk waving an axe. "But what have they been doing?"

"What they always do." Audrey's face was now a dark red verging on purple. "They're no better than animals. When the Queen's Head closed at lunchtime, a whole group of them trooped into the bus shelter. I knew what they were up to. Filthy, degenerate beasts."

"Audrey, why don't you come inside and sit down? We were just about to make some tea."

"I won't tell you what I found in there this morning. Too horrible. They're no better than animals."

I wondered what she meant. A contraceptive? Excrement?

"Anyway, they were in there this afternoon, and I happened to see a police car turn into Vicarage Drive. Aha, I thought, I'll settle your hash. So I popped out there and made the two policemen come with me to the bus shelter. You should have seen the faces of those hooligans. There were five of them. Two of them were girls, would you believe? I told the police I wanted to have them prosecuted to the full rigor of the law."

"But what were they doing?"

Audrey waved her hand. "Smoking. Drinking. You could tell where it was going. That sort of person is only interested in one thing." Audrey's face suddenly changed, as though an invisible sponge had wiped away the anger and the agitation. "Why, Rosemary. How lovely to see you. I didn't realize you were coming home today."

When I went to lock the church that evening, I found a surprise waiting for me. It was not late—a little after seven o'clock. I had left Vanessa preparing supper in the kitchen, with Michael sitting at the table peeling potatoes. Rosemary was having a bath, and had been for some time.

I let myself into the churchyard by the garden gate. The sky was gray, and a breeze ruffled the long grass among the graves. I walked round the east end of the church to the south door. Before locking it, I went inside to check that the church was empty.

It was as well that I did. A figure was standing in the chancel.

I cleared my throat. "Good evening."

The figure turned and I saw that it was Joanna Clifford. I walked up the church to join her. Her arms were folded across her breasts as though she felt cold. She was looking at the floor.

"It's all right," she mumbled, "me coming in here?"

"Of course it is. This is your church."

"I must be going. Toby will be wondering where I am."

I remembered what Toby had said about Joanna having been ill. I walked with her to the door. When I had met her that morning, I had taken away an impression of sullenness. Now I thought she was more likely to be shy than sullen. I opened the door for her and followed her into the porch.

"Where were you living before?"

"We had a flat just off the King's Road." Joanna watched me locking the door. "It's so quiet here."

I turned to face her, and for the first time I noticed her eyes. I was standing quite close to her, in the archway dividing the porch from the churchyard. For an instant her eyes reminded me of sunlit seawater trapped in a rock pool. They were not large but their color was unusual: a mottled greeny-brown, their vividness accentuated by small pupils, and by a black rim which separated the irises from the whites. She was smaller than Vanessa, the top of her head barely above my shoulders.

"I must get back," she said.

"You must have a lot to do."

She looked up at me, her eyes startled. "What do you mean?"

"It's always a busy time, isn't it? Moving into a new home."

"Oh—that. Yes. Well, goodbye."

She darted away from me toward the small gate in the west wall of the churchyard, which led directly into the grounds of Roth Park. I watched her go. What an awkward child, I thought—except she wasn't a child at all: she was probably well into her twenties.

I walked slowly home. All evening, the memory of Joanna Clifford stuck on the back of my mind like a burr on the back of my jacket.

At Vanessa's suggestion, we tried to make Rosemary's first meal at home something of a celebration: we ate Coronation Chicken and drank a bottle of white Burgundy. Michael had half a glass of wine and became sufficiently relaxed to tell us an interminable joke involving an Englishman, a Scotsman and an Irishman.

Part way through the meal, Vanessa said, "You'll never guess who phoned me today."

Michael and I looked expectantly at her. Rosemary stared at her plate.

"Lady Youlgreave's cleaner. Mrs. Potter, isn't it? She phoned the office this morning. Lady Youlgreave wants me to go and see her."

"Why?" I asked.

"To talk about Francis Youlgreave. She said something about wanting to get the family papers catalogued. And she wondered if I was serious about wanting to publish a biography of Great-Uncle Francis."

"Are you?"

"Oh yes. As long as there really is new material. That notebook she showed us looked promising. If I could find the time, I wouldn't mind writing it myself."

"Who would want to read about him?" Rosemary said. "Most people have never heard of him." She stared challengingly around the table. "It's not as if he was a real poet, after all."

"I've heard of him," Michael said.

We all looked at him, and he blushed.

"What have you heard?" Vanessa asked.

"He was mad. He preached a sermon about how there should be women priests. And he used to cut up animals and things."

"You *are* well informed," Vanessa said. "How did you learn all that?"

"Dad told me. There was something in the paper about the Methodists having women ministers, and Dad said it would soon be the Church of England's turn. And Mum laughed, and said it was just like Francis Youlgreave said it should be. So I asked who Francis Youlgreave was."

"He used to cut up animals?" Rosemary said. "I never knew that. Did he do it here?"

"Mainly in Rosington," I said abruptly. "He was a very sick man. He had delusions. This business about women priests was one of them. Another was some sort of mumbo jumbo about blood sacrifices."

"Plenty of classical precedents," Vanessa said. "And Old Testament ones, too, for that matter."

"Why?" Michael said. "What were blood sacrifices *for*?"

"In those days, people thought the gods liked them—they were sort of presents to the gods, I suppose." I did not want to get too involved in this subject. "The idea was that if the gods liked your present, they'd be nice to you."

"Or they'd be nasty to your enemies," Rosemary added. "Which came to much the same thing."

"But that was the Old Testament," Michael said. "Francis Youlgreave was quite modern."

"He was mentally ill," I said. "He was—"

"Mad," Rosemary interrupted. "Or maybe a genius. 'Great wits are sure to madness near alli'd,' " she added smugly. "Dryden. *Absalom and Achitophel*."

There was a stunned silence. And into that silence came the ringing of the telephone.

"Oh *no*," said Vanessa to me. "I wish they'd leave you alone. Just for an evening."

I pushed back my chair and went into the study. Perhaps the wine had loosened Vanessa's tongue, as it had Michael's. I picked up the phone.

It was Audrey Oliphant and she stumbled over her words as though someone were shaking her as she was speaking. Lord Peter still had not come home and someone had thrown a stone through the window of her office at Tudor Cottage.

# Chapter Fifteen

THE NEXT MORNING there was a postcard from Peter and June Hudson. They were looking at ruins in Crete, eating olives, and swimming every day. "Rosington," Peter wrote, "seems very far away. See you on the 9th September." That was the date for me to meet my new spiritual director, an Anglican monk who lived in Ascot. ("Absolutely ruthless," Peter had told me on the telephone. "Just what you need.")

Vanessa had arranged to see Lady Youlgreave in the morning. I asked if she would mind my coming with her.

"Why do you want to see her?"

"No particular reason. I like to pop in from time to time, and I thought it would be nice if we could do it together."

Vanessa said nothing. I caught a sudden glimpse of the darkness that lay beneath the friendly harmony between us. Perhaps Peter had been right: I had taken advantage of her vulnerability. Need and love are so curiously and inextricably entwined.

When we reached the Old Manor House, there was a Harrods van parked outside the front door. Lady Youlgreave never shopped at Malik's Minimarket. She had everything she needed, from lavatory paper to sherry, sent down by weekly delivery from Harrods. If Doris wasn't there, the driver let himself in with the key hidden near the back door.

Today the front door stood open. Beauty and Beast barked

at us, but more half-heartedly than usual, perhaps because the man from Harrods had already exhausted them. Before I could ring the bell, Doris, Charlene's mother, came into the hall with the delivery man. She was a small woman with a gentle face and an overweight body encased in a shiny, pale-blue nylon overall. She came to the Old Manor House twice a day, morning and evening, trying to care for an obstinate old woman who should have been in a nursing home and a decaying house the size of a small hotel.

"Hello, Vicar. Mrs. Byfield. Wasn't expecting you both."

"It's not inconvenient?" I asked.

"Oh no. The more the merrier. Could you find your own way? I'm up to my ears this morning. It'd be wonderful if you could keep her occupied for a while."

The dogs were quiet now. Beast even wagged her tail as we passed her. Vanessa and I went along the corridor to the dining room. Lady Youlgreave was in her usual chair, her head bowed over an old letter. She seemed to have aged by as many years in the few weeks since I had last seen her.

"Ah, David." She gave the impression she'd last seen me five minutes earlier. "And who's this?"

"Vanessa Byfield," Vanessa said. "Do you remember? You asked Doris to ring me at work yesterday, to talk about Francis Youlgreave."

Lady Youlgreave's fingers plucked at the blanket over her legs. "Silly man. Thought he'd raised the dead. Thought he talked to them, and they talked to him."

"Who did he talk to?" I asked.

She gave no sign that she had heard me. "Sometimes they told him to write his poems, like the angels did. One of them made him preach that sermon, the one about the women priests. Then afterward they hounded him out of his job—not the dead, of course, the living; though they're all dead now. So's he. He came back here to die."

"Here?" Vanessa said. "In this house?"

Lady Youlgreave shook her head. "No. Roth Park. He had the room at the top of the tower."

"How did he die?"

"Jumped out of his window. Thought he could fly." The old woman's hand gestured feebly toward the black metal box beside her chair. "There's something in there about it. The last entry in his journal. An angel had come for him and was going to carry him up to God." Her mouth twisted into a grin. "In a manner of speaking, I suppose that's exactly what happened."

"But he went down rather than up," Vanessa said.

Lady Youlgreave stared at her. Then she grasped the joke and cackled. I pulled up the chairs we had used last time. Vanessa and I sat down. The medicine bottle was still on the mantelpiece. Outside the window two blackbirds were pecking at something on the bird table. The front door slammed and the blackbirds flew away. The delivery man's shoes crunched across the gravel. A moment later, the Harrods van pulled into the main road.

Vanessa leaned forward. "Do you still want me to look at his papers?"

The old woman nodded.

"If you like, I could catalog them for you, and then you could decide what you'd like done with them. If there's enough material for a biography, I'm sure we could find a suitable author."

Lady Youlgreave snorted. "How my father-in-law would have hated it. A book about Uncle Francis." She threw a glance at the Sargent over the fireplace. "Such a conventional man. He wouldn't have minded if Francis had been a bishop. But a mad poet—that was quite different."

"So you'd like me to go ahead?"

The old woman stared at the bird table. "If you like."

Vanessa moistened her lips. "There's no time like the present." She looked at me. "I'm sure David wouldn't mind bringing the car round. We could take the box away now."

"Oh no." Lady Youlgreave huddled more deeply into her chair, as if trying to retract into herself. "The papers must stay here. Everything must stay here. I may want to look at them. You must read them here. In this room. Where I can see you."

There was a silence. Outside, the blackbirds had returned to the bird table; one of them pecked and the other gave off a thread of melody.

I said, "Are you sure you wouldn't find that rather a disturbance? You could let Vanessa take away just one or two things at a time. I'm sure she'd take the greatest care of them and she could tell you exactly what she finds in them, too."

"Yes, of course." Vanessa sat back, smiling, but her hands were knotted together on her lap. "That's the best way to do it, isn't it?"

There was a look of yearning on my wife's face, a look that was almost sexual in its intensity.

"If you want to read them, you must do it here."

The wizened face settled into a barely human mask. Nothing moved in the hot, stuffy room with its smell of old age. It was as if all three of us were holding our breath. Even the blackbird was silent. The bird table was empty.

"I'm tired now. David, I want you to give me my medicine. It's on the mantelpiece, with a spoon."

Lady Youlgreave agreed to let Vanessa begin looking through the papers on Saturday morning; and Vanessa had to be content with that. We left soon afterward—Vanessa to go to her office in Richmond, and I to carry on with my work.

"I suppose she wants the company," Vanessa said as we walked back to the Vicarage. "But it's going to be very inconvenient."

In the afternoon, Lord Peter turned up. He appeared on the windowsill of the Vicarage sitting room. I was not at home at the time. Rosemary was, however, and she phoned Audrey with the good news. Audrey came over at once with the cat basket. Lord Peter, who had been lured into the sitting room with the help of a saucer of cream, protested violently when Audrey put him in his cat basket. He left two parallel scratches on her left forearm.

I knew about the scratches because Audrey showed them to me. They were in some way meritorious—a sign of Lord Peter's intrepid personality, perhaps, or of Audrey's willingness to suffer torments, if necessary, for the wellbeing of her pet.

The incident had an unexpected consequence. Audrey was fulsomely grateful to Rosemary. To hear Audrey speak, you would think Rosemary had saved Lord Peter, at considerable personal cost, from a terrible fate. She asked Rosemary to tea the following afternoon, ostensibly to see how well Lord Peter had recovered from his trying experience. To my surprise, Rosemary accepted. She appeared to enjoy the experience. A few days later, she went over to Tudor Cottage again for coffee.

I was pleased. In the past, Rosemary had considered Audrey as an irritation. But now a sort of friendship seemed to be developing between the two of them. Vanessa said they would be company for each other; she thought Rosemary was trying to develop emotional independence from me, on the whole a healthy sign. Vanessa had a weakness for amateur psychology.

Gradually, the four of us at the Vicarage fell into a routine. Vanessa went into the office every day, but somehow managed to find time to buy the ingredients for and to prepare our evening meal. Rosemary and I usually organized something at lunchtime—sandwiches, perhaps, or soup.

Rosemary retreated to her bedroom for hours at a time, where she worked and listened to music that jarred on me. After the summer she was going back to school for one more term to sit the Oxford entrance exam. In the evenings we sometimes talked about her reading, and I helped her with her Latin. I enjoyed these sessions—intellectually our minds worked in a remarkably similar way.

"I wish you could coach me for Oxford," she said on one occasion when we were alone in the sitting room. "I'm sure I'd do much better than at school."

"I wish I could, too."

"I wish—" she began.

Then the door opened, and Michael and Vanessa came in.

"He *did* do something here," Michael announced.

Bewildered, I looked at him. "Who did?"

"Francis Youlgreave."

"I was just telling Michael," Vanessa explained. "Lady Youlgreave showed me a letter."

"It was a cat." Like many small boys, Michael took an uncomplicated pleasure in past bloodshed. "He cut it up. But they didn't put him in prison for it. I suppose it was just an animal, so it didn't matter too much."

"The family hushed it up," Vanessa said. "It was just before he died. It happened in Carter's Meadow, wherever that is. I imagine it's covered with houses by now."

"Carter's Meadow?" Rosemary stood and began to gather up her books. "No, it's still there. It's a field on the other side of Roth Park."

"We came to see if you wanted to play cards," Vanessa said.

Rosemary raised her eyebrows. "Cards? I'm afraid I haven't got time for things like that."

She went upstairs to her room. Vanessa, Michael and I played Hearts.

Later, in our bedroom, I whispered to Vanessa during one of our nightly conferences, "Was it wise to tell Michael about the cat?"

"Meat and drink to him. Small boys like that sort of thing." She looked at me. "He's having a surprisingly good time here, isn't he?"

"Thanks to Brian Vintner. A friend of his own age makes all the difference."

"And he's much more relaxed with us than he was."

"But not with Rosemary. And she's not very pleasant to him. Do you think I should have a word with her?"

"I wouldn't."

"Why not?"

"Rosemary's having an awful time. I don't think you realize. She's had you to herself all these years, and now I've come along and pinched you. Added to that, she's worried about her exams. And on top of everything else, we've got Michael in the house. It's obvious you're fond of him, and he's fond of you. So he gets treated as the baby of the family, and we can't even spoil Rosemary."

"That doesn't make sense—"

"It's not a matter of logic," Vanessa hissed. "We're talking about people. You expect everyone to be too rational."

"Do you mind?"

"Mind what? You expecting others to be rational?"

"All these people in the house. The lack of privacy."

Vanessa stared at me. She was sitting up in bed, with her auburn hair brushed down on to the shoulders of her cotton nightdress. She looked very attractive.

"Me?" she said at last. "At present, I'm just trying to keep the peace, and trying to survive."

I wanted her to expand on this, but she wouldn't. Instead, she said she was tired and turned out her light.

During this time I kept out of Audrey's way as much as possible. I had no wish to be drawn into the arrangements for the fete. Besides, I told myself, I was so busy that I had to be careful how I used my time.

To my relief, her feud with the adolescents of the council estate seemed to have died a natural death. No prosecutions resulted from the raid on the bus shelter; the police let the youths off with a caution. Audrey had the broken glass in her window replaced and assumed a martyred expression whenever the incident was mentioned.

All this was a lull. But the storm—or rather the series of storms—was about to break over our heads. The lull ended on Thursday the 13th August, the day of Vanessa's party.

It was Vanessa's party in the sense that it was her idea. She felt that it would be polite to welcome the Cliffords to Roth, and to return the hospitality they had given me the previous week. It would also be a way of signaling our gratitude for the loan of the paddock. We invited Audrey, so we could discuss the practicalities of the fete with them, and several other parishioners, including the Vintners. James and Mary were involved in the fete, and Brian would be company for Michael.

We asked Rosemary if there was anyone she would like to invite, but she said that there wasn't. I remember her coiling a strand of blonde hair around her finger and saying, "But I don't know anyone in Roth."

Vanessa had another reason for wanting to get to know the Cliffords: "I'll want to have a good look over the house at some point," she told me as we were going to bed on Wednesday night. "There are lots of references to it in the Youlgreave papers. And to the grounds. I'd especially like to see Francis's room in the tower."

"Isn't that rather morbid?"

"Not at all."

"But what would you do in his room? Look for scratches on the windowsill?"

She stared at me, ready to snap. "Listen, the more I see of those papers, the more I want to do the biography myself. Francis really was interesting. He came from an Establishment background, and yet he lived on the margins of society. He did all the things the Victorians weren't meant to do. And even this business about women priests strikes a modern chord. Perhaps Rosemary was right—perhaps in some ways he wasn't as mad as people thought."

"The ordination of women is theologically unsound. It was then, and it is now, whatever the Methodists think."

She shrugged away my interruption. "If only the old lady would let me take away the papers and look at them properly."

"When are you going there next?"

"Tomorrow afternoon. I'm taking the afternoon off work because of the party. If you do some of the shopping, I should be able to fit in an hour or two with the papers after lunch." She picked up a pencil and a notepad from the bedside table. "I'd better make a list of what we need to get."

Vanessa's party on the 13th August: that was the day when we passed the point of no return, though we did not realize it at the time.

# Chapter Sixteen

T HURSDAY STARTED BADLY.

After breakfast, Rosemary went to the study to phone the school. It was the day her results were due. She was so long that eventually I went into the hall and eavesdropped at the study door. There was nothing to hear except the ticking of the clock on the wall and the rumble of traffic. I knocked and opened the door.

Rosemary was sitting at my desk, staring at the bookcase on the opposite wall. Her eyes flicked toward me and then back to the bookcase. Her face was pale.

"Are you all right?"

She nodded.

"Did you get through to the school?"

Another nod.

"Have the results come?"

She moistened her lips. "Yes."

"And?"

She said nothing. I put my arm around her shoulders. She pulled away.

"What did you get?"

"Bs in Latin and History. An A in English."

"That's marvelous." I kissed the top of her head. "I'm very proud of you."

She pushed me away and stood up. "There must have been a mistake. There should have been three As."

"But you don't need them. Your results are excellent. You—"

"I wanted three As," she said. "I *deserved* three As."

"But, Rosie—"

"*Don't* call me that."

She walked quickly out of the room. The front door slammed.

Rosemary returned before midday. To my relief she seemed to have come to terms with her results. I gave her a check as a present, and Vanessa gave her another when she arrived at lunchtime.

"Please don't tell people unless they ask," Rosemary said as we were eating. "I don't want everyone to make a fuss."

After lunch we separated. Vanessa walked down to the Old Manor House. Rosemary went up to her room. Michael went to the library. I drove into Staines to do the shopping.

In the off-license, I bumped into Victor Thurston; I had not seen him since that evening nearly a year ago when we had dined together at the Trasks' and I had met Vanessa for the first time. Because of the fondness for committees he shared with his wife, he was often mentioned in the local paper. I came up to the counter with two bottles of sherry, one of gin and one of lemonade to find him in the process of ordering three cases of Moët & Chandon. He turned and saw me. He had a rubbery face with features always on the move.

"Hello," he said. "We've met, haven't we?" He raised his eyebrows in a combative way, as though I had denied this.

"Yes, it was—"

"I remember. At Ronnie and Cynthia Trask's last year."

"That's it. September."

"And how are you and Vanessa getting on?" If I hadn't been wearing a dog collar, I think Thurston would have dug me in the ribs. "She's adjusted to the life of the manse, has she? Ha ha."

I smiled dutifully. I tried and failed to remember the name of his wife. For a moment we had a labored conversation about the Trasks.

Then Thurston said, "You live at Roth, don't you? I gather there are changes in the air."

"What do you mean?"

"I was talking to a chap who was thinking of buying a house there. Off the record, as it were. It was only a few weeks ago. Young fellow."

"Toby Clifford?"

"That's the one. Bit too hairy for my liking, but seemed a nice enough young chap under the thatch."

"He and his sister have moved into Roth Park—that's the big house behind the church."

"So I dare say you've heard his plans," Thurston said. "Could bring a few changes."

I nodded.

Thurston went on, "Of course, schemes like that need a good deal of money. Many a slip between cup and lip, eh? And then there's the Planning Committee. He was only sounding me out on an informal basis. At first sight I couldn't see any objection myself. But the planning officer may think otherwise, and you can never be quite sure which way some members of the committee are going to jump."

Neither of us wanted to prolong the conversation—we had little to say to each other. But as I drove home, I puzzled over his remarks about Roth Park. Toby had given me to understand that he and Joanna intended to treat the house as their home. He had not mentioned any development of the site. But from what Thurston had said, Toby had been investigating the possibility before they even moved in. Perhaps he was merely looking to the future. Thurston had made it clear that Toby had not made a formal application for planning permission.

When I got back to the Vicarage, Michael was hoovering the sitting room. Vanessa, who had cut short her researches at the Old Manor House, was assembling cocktail snacks in the kitchen.

She pecked me on the cheek. "Mary Vintner phoned. They've cried off. James's got to cover for his partner this evening, and she's got a stinking cold."

"It solves the problem of not having enough armchairs."

"Could you check there's ice in the fridge? And we may need to get some more tonic from Malik's."

"How was Lady Youlgreave?"

"Slightly more loopy than usual, I'm afraid. I wonder how long she's going to last. There aren't any children, are there?"

I was refilling the ice tray at the sink. "No."

"So who will inherit the papers when she does die?"

"I've no idea."

"It's a worry. Do you know, I found a letter from Oscar Wilde today. It's so frustrating. And I was just about to look at another packet of letters when Lady Youlgreave got worried about the bird table."

"The bird table?"

"The one she can see from her window. There were a couple

of crows on it who were frightening away the smaller birds. She'd got out a pair of opera glasses, trying to work out what was interesting them. She wanted me to go and find out. But when I did go out, there wasn't much left. Looked like a bit of bone or something. Quite fresh—there was blood as well."

"On the bird table? Isn't that a bit odd?"

Vanessa shook her head. "I imagine one of the birds brought it. Or perhaps Doris put it out. The trouble was, by the time I'd done that, Lady Youlgreave had had enough. The poor thing finds it very tiring having me there. All she really wants is her medicine and some peace and quiet. That and no pain." She glanced at me, the knife in her hand poised over a slab of Cheddar. "I wish we didn't have to get old. It's so dreary."

I put the ice tray into the freezing compartment of the refrigerator and closed the door. "Where's Rosemary?"

"She went to see Audrey."

"Heaven knows what they find to talk about."

At that moment, the phone began to ring yet again.

"I'm sometimes tempted to cut the wires," Vanessa said. "Don't people realize that you occasionally need five minutes' peace?"

It was the secretary of the Parochial Church Council. His wife had gone down with flu so they would be unable to come this evening. I went back to the kitchen to tell Vanessa.

"Oh well," she said. "In some ways, the fewer the better. It will give us more chance to get to know the Cliffords."

"Audrey will be there."

"I'm sure she will. She'll be waiting on the doorstep on the stroke of half past six."

As it happened, though, Vanessa was wrong. Rosemary

returned home at teatime with the news that Lord Peter was missing again. Audrey was very worried and had set off on a tour of the neighborhood in search of him. She had asked Rosemary to warn us that she might be late, and to apologize on her behalf.

Neither Vanessa nor I was disposed to take this latest disappearance very seriously. Vanessa murmured that she could quite understand the cat's wanting an occasional break from his mistress's company.

At a quarter to seven, the E-type bringing our sole surviving guests pulled up outside the front door of the Vicarage. I heard Vanessa suck in her breath as Toby got out of the car. He was wearing very tight bell-bottomed trousers and a white shirt without a collar. Joanna climbed awkwardly out of the passenger seat, exposing almost all of her bare legs. She wore a short, crumpled green dress which looked as if it were made of silk. We went out to meet them.

"If I hadn't known better," Toby told Vanessa as they shook hands, "I'd have said that you and Rosemary were sisters."

The tips of Vanessa's ears went pink, the way they did when someone paid her a compliment. Then it was Rosemary's turn. I heard him asking which university she went to. We went into the house. Michael was hesitating in the hall. I introduced him to the Cliffords. Michael's eyes drifted out toward the E-type in the drive.

"You can look inside her, if you want," Toby said, following the direction of his gaze. "It's not locked."

"Really? Thanks."

"You should try the driving seat. It's fantastically well designed."

I wished that Michael would look at me as he looked at Toby. We left the boy with the car and went into the sitting room, where I poured drinks. Toby chatted with Vanessa and Rosemary. Joanna sat down in an armchair and asked for gin and tonic. As I gave it to her, she leaned forward and the neck of her dress gaped open. I could not help noticing that she was not wearing a bra.

"Thank you," she said, looking up at me.

Her face distracted me. She looked pinched and worried; and the whites of her eyes were bloodshot.

"Are you feeling all right?" I murmured, too low for the others to hear.

"It's OK," she said equally softly. "It's OK here."

Her eyes met mine. I was about to say something when Toby appeared at Joanna's shoulder. "Have you got your cigarettes, Jo? I must have left mine at home."

She delved into her bag, a gaudy object made of leather patches and fastened with a drawstring, and produced a packet of Rothmans.

"I bumped into Victor Thurston this afternoon," I said to Toby.

For an instant the skin tightened at the corners of his eyes, as though a bright light had unexpectedly shone into them. "Oh yes. Nice chap. I've only met him the once. I went to see him just before we exchanged contracts on this place. The estate agent thought it might be a good idea."

"He seemed to think you were considering developing the place."

Toby played it exactly right—relaxed, smiling, with every appearance of frankness: "Well, in the long term, anything's possible. Just a case of knowing what one's options are. As I say, the estate agent practically bullied me into it."

"If you did develop Roth Park, what might you do?"

"I did wonder about turning it into a hotel. There's lots of room. And it's not a bad location, either. Heathrow Airport only a few miles away. There'll soon be two motorways within easy reach. And of course London's on the doorstep."

"The house and grounds might appeal to the Americans," Vanessa suggested. "Feed their fantasies about the English aristocracy. And you could offer culture, too."

"Francis Youlgreave?"

She smiled at him, and he smiled back; it was like watching an evenly matched game of tennis. "You've obviously done your research," she said.

"I bought a copy of *The History of Roth* from Mr. Malik."

"To go back to Francis Youlgreave: I'm researching his life at present. I wondered if you'd mind me looking over the house some time. I've never seen it."

Toby spread out his hands. "Whenever you want. In fact, Jo and I were thinking about holding a little housewarming party after the fete. Do you think that's a good idea? You could have the Grand Tour while you're there, if you liked. We should be more or less straight by then. At present we're rather at sixes and sevens."

The conversation moved on to the fete and the proposed party. Time passed quickly, and I was aware that I was drinking more than I usually did.

At a quarter to eight, Toby glanced at his watch. "Is that the time? We'd better get going."

"Michael's still in your car," Vanessa said, peering out of

the window. "He's sitting behind the wheel and looking very serious. Having a whale of a time, I think."

"You could take him for a drive, Toby," Joanna suggested suddenly. "I'll walk home. It's not exactly far."

Toby glanced at her and then at Vanessa and me. "I'd be happy to—if it wouldn't upset your plans for the evening."

"I'm sure Michael would love it," Vanessa said. "But can you spare the time?"

"Oh, we wouldn't be long. Twenty minutes or so. Would that be OK?"

By now we had all moved into the hall. I opened the front door. A diversion was approaching in the shape of Audrey, who was walking very quickly over the gravel. Her face was pink and shiny; she was not wearing a hat, and her hair hung raggedly down over her left ear.

"Hello," I said. "Has Lord Peter turned up?"

She shook her head. "I've looked everywhere. But I found this."

She held up a thin green strap with a small brass medallion attached to it.

"What is it?" Vanessa asked.

Audrey took a deep breath. Her chest was pumping up and down. "It's Lord Peter's collar," she said between gasps. "It was in the bus shelter. I phoned the police but—but they weren't very helpful."

The evening broke up quickly after that. Vanessa and Rosemary took Audrey into the sitting room. Rosemary sat with her while Vanessa made her some tea. Meanwhile, Toby took Michael for a drive, as originally arranged; it seemed the best thing for all concerned.

"Will you be all right?" Toby asked Joanna before he left.

"Of course I shall. It's only a few hundred yards."

"You'll cut off quite a bit if you go through the gate in the garden and then through the churchyard," I said. "I'll show you."

My motives were mixed. To be frank, I was glad of the chance to leave Audrey with Vanessa and Rosemary. And common politeness required that I show Joanna the way to the gate. I took her down the path at the side of the house and into the garden at the back. We walked in silence across the lawn to the gate in the wall of the churchyard. I opened it for her.

"If you follow the path round the church, go past the south door, then you come to the little gate in the paddock. The one you used the other day."

Joanna stopped under the archway and looked up at me. I looked into the shifting green depths of her eyes and thought how beautiful they were; and another part of my mind smugly congratulated myself on the fact that my appreciation was purely aesthetic.

"Can I talk to you?" she said suddenly.

"Of course you can." I had been half expecting this. "That's what I'm here for."

Unexpectedly, she giggled. "A sort of agony uncle?"

I smiled back. "Sort of."

"Will you walk with me a little way?"

I followed her into the churchyard and shut the gate behind us.

"It's strange here," she said. "I miss the noise of the city. There were always people around where we lived—day or night. But here, apart from the main road and the planes, most of the time it's dead."

We passed the east end of the church and the flight of steps leading down to the vault under the chancel.

"It's not town," she went on, "and it's not country, either. It's not *real*."

"That's the trouble with suburbs," I said. "They feel like the middle of nowhere. But one gets used to them."

She glanced at me, and for the first time I saw her smile. She stopped suddenly. We were beside the south porch. It was quiet, as if the churchyard had slipped away from the suburbs and returned to the country it had left behind. I distinctly remember hearing a bee in the rosebush that grew in the southwest angle between the porch and the church.

"Do you believe in ghosts?" She looked up at me and then past me. Suddenly her eyes widened. Her expression changed as completely as though a mask had been dropped over her face. She clutched my arm.

"What is it?"

"Look. In the porch." She had difficulty forcing the words out. "Beside the door."

I stepped under the archway into the porch. Immediately before me was the heavy door into the nave of the church, great oak planks bleached with age. To the left of this was the board we used for parish notices.

Someone had given it a new use. Dangling in front of it was a ragged mass of black fur. I stared at it and felt my stomach churning in disgust. There were patches of white and red among the black.

I remembered Joanna. I swung around. She was still staring

at the obscenity in the porch. I put my arm over her shoulder and she pushed her head into my chest. She was shaking. I tightened my grip around her. She was trying to say something.

"What?"

She lifted her head and said, "Why would someone do a thing like that?"

She pushed her head into my chest again. Absently, I lowered my head to smell her hair. Dear God, I even felt, on some level, a stirring of sexual excitement. It was too long since Vanessa and I had made love.

Joanna's question remained unanswered, and terrible in its implications. Why would anyone want to slaughter Lord Peter and display his body at the door of my church?

# Chapter Seventeen

IT SEEMED TO ME that the younger of the two policemen was looking at Vanessa with an interest that went some way beyond the purely professional. His name was Franklyn. He was a thin, sallow-skinned constable with thick eyebrows; he seemed barely old enough to have left school. I guessed that Vanessa was aware of his gaze because she turned slightly in her chair and crossed her legs, impeding his view.

"So," Sergeant Clough said wearily to Audrey. "Let me see if I've got this right."

We were in the living room amid the debris of our little party. The two policemen had arrived in their patrol car forty-five minutes after Vanessa had first dialed 999. Sergeant Clough had a tanned, knobbly skull which made me think of an unwashed potato. He asked most of the questions while Franklyn took notes. Audrey was sitting opposite Clough in the big armchair by the fireplace, hunched like a frightened child over her second glass of brandy. Her face was sheet-white and her hair was still awry; she had resisted Vanessa's suggestion that she have a rest upstairs.

"The last time you saw your cat was yesterday evening?" the sergeant went on.

Audrey's face crumpled. "I do try to keep him in at night, but it's so difficult, especially in summer."

Clough cleared his throat. "No need to blame yourself, miss. Now, when exactly did you last see him?"

"He had his supper, a nice bit of fish, about seven-thirty. I saw him dozing in the chair at about half past eight. He must have slipped out of the kitchen window downstairs. It could have been any time after then. You could ask Mr. and Mrs. Malik, of course, and see if they—"

"Yes, Miss Oliphant, and you realized he was missing this morning, when he didn't come back for breakfast?"

"I wasn't worried at first, or not that worried. He often went off on his own. He was such an adventurous cat. It was such a worry because of the road. There's always a lot of cars on it, and vans and lorries, even at night. I started looking seriously for him at about five o'clock. I went all over the village, calling him. I was just about to come over to the Vicarage—Mr. and Mrs. Byfield had asked me over—when I had a brainwave. The bus shelter."

She looked triumphantly at the sergeant, who stared back.

"I should have thought of it at once," she went on. "Don't you see? It's obvious. They blamed me for calling out the police the other week."

"Who did?"

"The vandals. They even threw that stone through my window. I phoned the police station and told you all about it. Surely you remember?"

Clough said, "I think one of my colleagues handled the case. So you looked in the bus shelter, because the kids go there, and you thought they might have taken your cat out of revenge. Is that it?"

"The bus shelter was empty," Audrey said, ignoring his

question. "They were all guzzling beer in the pub. And on the floor, under the bench, I found that." With a dramatic gesture, she pointed at the thin, green leather strap on the coffee table in front of the sofa. "Proof positive, Sergeant."

Franklyn scribbled briefly in his notebook and glanced at Vanessa. Clough scratched his left kneecap.

"How could they?" Audrey burst out. "Lord Peter never harmed a soul."

Clough blinked. "Who, miss?"

"My cat," she snapped. A flush rose in her cheeks. "It makes me feel quite ill."

Vanessa leaned forward and put her hand on the arm of Audrey's chair. "He may have died in a road accident. Perhaps someone found the body."

"The postmortem will tell us," Audrey said. "I hope that's what happened. He wouldn't have felt as much pain. And he wouldn't have been so upset—he always trusted people, you see." She stared at Clough. "How soon will you hold the postmortem?"

"Ah—we don't usually hold postmortems on animals, Miss Oliphant. I tell you what, though. We'll take him down for you. Then you can bury him, nice and decent—in your back garden, perhaps."

"But I want to find out how he died."

The sergeant gently rubbed a finger over his knee, as if caressing an itch. "I suppose you could ask a vet to have a look at him."

"But it's *evidence*, Sergeant. It may well be important to your investigation to know how Lord Peter died."

"I think if you want a postmortem, miss, a vet is your best

bet." He glanced out of the window. "Look, if we're going to get him down, I suggest we do it now, rather than later. I mean, anyone might see him. Could give some old lady a nasty shock, eh?" He stood up and stretched. "Mr. Byfield—would you happen to have a cardboard box or something of that sort we could use?"

I went into the kitchen. Rosemary was sitting at the table eating a strawberry yogurt and apparently absorbed in Sartre's *Nausea*, in a French edition. She looked up as I came in.

"How's it going in there?"

"Audrey's still in quite a state. Understandably enough. They want a cardboard box to put the cat in."

Rosemary pushed back her chair. "There are some in the garage."

She went through the utility room and opened the connecting door to the garage. As she was rummaging in there, Vanessa came into the kitchen.

"I'll put the kettle on. We could all do with a cup of tea."

"Have you got something we could wrap the body in?" I asked.

"What?"

"To use as a shroud."

Vanessa blinked. "There's an old pillow case under the sink. I was going to cut it up for dusters." She filled the kettle and plugged it in. "You make it sound as if Lord Peter's going to have a state funeral." Her voice wobbled. "Is there a section in the Prayer Book to meet the contingency? 'The Order for the Burial of Murdered Pets?' "

I put my arm around her. She leaned against me, only to pull sharply away when Rosemary returned with a box that had once contained tins of cocoa.

"The coffin," Rosemary announced.

I found the pillow case under the sink and took it and the box into the sitting room. Audrey and the two policemen seemed not to have moved since I left.

Clough stood up quickly. "Right. We'll go and sort it out. Frankie, you can carry the box."

Franklyn scrambled up and took the box and pillow case from me.

Clough turned to Audrey. "I'd be inclined to go home now, if I were you. Maybe Mrs. Byfield will take you over."

"I can't do that. Not until Lord Peter—"

"I'm afraid there's nothing you can do now. The best thing is to go home, have a nice sweet cup of tea, get into bed and have a nice sleep. Have you got any sleeping tablets or something like that?"

Audrey shook her head violently.

"Maybe you should ring your GP. Or perhaps Mrs. Byfield could do it for you. You've had a shock, you know."

"I don't want a doctor." Audrey scowled at him and then remembered her manners. "Thank you."

"It's up to you."

"I want the culprits caught."

"Culprits? So there's more than one, you think."

"Those louts always go round in gangs."

Clough sighed. "We don't know it was them."

"Who else could it have been?"

He shrugged and said nothing. An uncomfortable silence hung in the air. Franklyn cast a longing glance at the door. Vanessa came back into the room.

"How many for tea?"

Franklyn and Clough declined. Audrey said she wouldn't mind another glass of brandy, but was persuaded to try tea instead. Clough asked if he could have a word with me on the way out. We went into the drive, where Franklyn collected a torch and a pair of rubber gloves from the car. While we were walking around to the gate to the churchyard, Clough stuck a briar pipe in his mouth and lit it with a gas lighter whose flame was like a flare.

"Has anything like this happened before, sir?"

"Mutilated cats?"

"Not just that. Every now and then we get someone who's been reading too many Dennis Wheatley novels."

"Satanism?"

"Whatever you want to call it. Witchcraft. Mumbo jumbo. Raising the devil. Usually it's just an excuse for naughty sex in fancy dress. Sometimes it gets nasty, though."

"No. To the best of my knowledge, there's been nothing like this before. Not here."

"Sure?"

"Quite sure. I think I would have noticed."

"Did you have a good look at the cat?"

"No." I had not wanted to. "Enough to see it had been cut open."

"More than that. Its head's missing."

"*What?*"

"Let me know if you come across it, eh?" Clough clicked his lighter and a tongue of flame licked the bowl of his pipe. "Do you lock the church?"

"Only at night."

"It might be wise to consider locking it during the day as well. There's some sick people around these days."

"There always have been."

"I wouldn't take it personally," he went on. "Probably any old church would have done." He tapped his head. "Just another passing nutter, eh? Oh—by the way: who was the young lady you were with when you found the cat?"

"Her name's Joanna Clifford. Do you need to talk to her? She lives near here."

"Where?"

"She and her brother have just moved into Roth Park. You know it? The big house behind the church. They had been having a drink with us and I had been showing her a short cut home through the churchyard."

"Her brother? Would that be Toby Clifford?"

"That's right. Do you know him?"

Clough paused to relight his pipe. "Oh—someone mentioned there were new people up at Roth Park."

We walked on to the south porch. The light was fading fast. The bricks in the porch glowed palely in the dusk.

"You get it down, Frankie," Clough said. "I'll hold the torch."

"Oh, *Sarge*."

"Get on with it, lad." In a stage whisper, he added to me, "Privilege of rank, eh?"

Franklyn gave Clough the torch and pulled on the gloves. The beam leaped into the porch, a stripe of light across the stone floor, and slid up to the notice board on the left of the door. Lord Peter was no longer there. Clough puffed smoke into the evening air.

"We've only been gone half an hour," Franklyn said, his voice aggrieved, as if Lord Peter's absence were a personal insult.

Clough let the torch beam drop to the floor. He gave a whistle of relief. There was a huddle of black fur in the corner, partly concealed by a cast-iron umbrella stand.

"Thought we'd lost him for a moment," he said. "That would have been a turn-up for the books."

"The case of the vanishing pussy," Franklyn suggested, as he stepped forward with the box and the pillow case. "Whoops."

"How did he fall?" I said.

Clough stepped into the porch. The beam zigzagged across the notice board, then down to the cat. Franklyn bent down and lifted the tail. A piece of string was still attached to it.

"Simple enough." Clough let the torch slide up the wall to the hook from which the notice board hung. "One end of the string was tied to the hook, and the other to the cat. Obviously they weren't very good at knots."

"Probably not a boy scout, then?" Franklyn said.

"Aren't you going to photograph it?" I asked. "Or at least examine it?"

"We've seen all we need to see, sir," Clough said. "There's a limit to what we can do in cases like this. It's a question of resources."

I shrugged, knowing from his tone of voice that I had irritated him. We watched Franklyn stuffing the body into the pillow case and dropping shroud and corpse into the box. He closed the flaps with a flourish.

"You'd better have a look here in the morning, sir," he said to me. "There may be a bit of blood or something. I dare say you'll want to clean up."

The police drove away soon afterward. Vanessa and I took

Audrey back to Tudor Cottage. The brandy and the shock were having their effect: we had to support her, one on each side. She would not let Vanessa help her into bed, but she accepted one of my sleeping tablets.

"What have you done with Lord Peter?" she asked me.

"He's in the garage."

"I shall bury him in the garden. After the postmortem."

"I'm not sure the police—"

"I'll pay to have it done. Then they'll see I'm right. Why are the police so *stupid*?" She put her hand to her temple. "My head hurts."

Vanessa and I walked back to the Vicarage. Laughter and music poured through the open doors of the Queen's Head, and the river of traffic still flowed on the main road.

"Do you think she's serious about the postmortem idea?" Vanessa asked.

"Audrey's always serious."

A light shone in the window of the spare bedroom. Michael was still awake. We found Rosemary in the sitting room, still reading *Nausea*.

"How is she?"

"Audrey?" Vanessa said. "Still in a state. Understandably."

"It's horrible." Rosemary looked at me. "I just don't understand why people do things like that."

I touched her shoulder. "None of us does. Not really."

While Vanessa was making tea, I went up to see Michael. He was already in bed, sitting in blue-and-white striped pajamas, with his hair neatly brushed, reading a book. He glanced up at me but said nothing. I thought he looked worried.

"What are you reading?"

He held up the book, a paperback in the green-and-white Penguin crime livery. "*The Adventures of Sherlock Holmes*. It was in the bookcase."

"You must be finding it rather dull here."

Michael smiled at me and shook his head.

"And I'm afraid this evening can't have been much fun. Did you manage to get something to eat?"

"Aunt Vanessa made me a sandwich."

"Good. This business with the cat—you mustn't let it upset you."

"It's not upsetting," Michael said. "It's interesting."

Vanessa and I did not get a chance to talk privately until we were in bed.

"So what do you think?" Vanessa whispered. "Is it personal?"

"The police seem to think it's most likely someone mentally unbalanced. Probably any church would have done. St. Mary Magdalene just happened to be the first they noticed."

"And any cat? It's perfectly possible that Audrey's right. She's really upset some of those kids from the council estate."

"I hope you're wrong."

She snorted in exasperation. "You have to at least consider the possibility that I'm not. And there's two other things you ought to think about. The first one is Francis Youlgreave."

I picked a feather out of the eiderdown. "Surely what he did isn't common knowledge?"

"You'd be surprised. It's the sort of thing that people re-member if they remember nothing else about a person. After all, you remembered it."

"But it doesn't really narrow the field much," I pointed out. "And I don't think it's enough to establish a connection."

"And then there's the other thing. Do you remember I told you about the crows pecking something on Lady Youl-greave's bird table?"

I stared at her. "Surely not. You're not implying—?"

"Why not? The cat's head had to go somewhere. What if someone put it on the bird table? It would be one way of ram-ming home a connection with Francis Youlgreave."

"But why?"

"How should I know?" Vanessa picked up her book. "Isn't that more your province than mine?"

I glanced at her, trying to tell if she was being serious. Her sense of humor could be so very dry. She settled her glasses on her nose and opened the book, her own copy of Youl-greave's *The Four Last Things*. It struck me that I was only beginning to discover the real Vanessa. I was like one of those nineteenth-century explorers traveling up a river into the heart of an unknown continent and glimpsing a vast, un-charted interior, more mysterious with every passing mile.

"I don't follow," I said at last. "What's my province?"

"Evil, of course, what did you think I meant?"

# Chapter Eighteen

T HE NEXT PROBLEM came from an unexpected direction. I was working in the study the following afternoon when the telephone rang.

"David, it's Ronald Trask." The voice was abrupt to the point of rudeness. "What's this Cynthia tells me about an outbreak of Satanism at St. Mary Magdalene?"

He used the word *Satanism* like a cudgel. I took a deep breath and tried to persuade myself that Ronald was only doing his duty. An archdeacon used to be known as the bishop's eye. Such matters came within his province.

"We don't know it's Satanism. I think it's unwise to jump to conclusions. It may just have been a teenage prank which got out of hand."

"A prank? A cat beheaded in your own parish church?"

"It wasn't beheaded in the church. We found the body hanging from a hook in the porch."

"That's not the point, in any case."

"Then what is?"

"That this could be a public relations disaster." Ronald lowered his voice, as if he were afraid of being overheard. "Not just for the church. For you personally."

There was a pause. Vanessa had gone into the office this morning. She must have mentioned the events of last night to Cynthia, who had evidently lost no time in relaying the news to her brother. Anger stirred inside me. Ronald might have a right to interfere, but not in this heavy-handed way.

"There's just a chance we can nip this in the bud," he went on. "I think the best thing to do is to ring Victor Thurston."

"I don't see any need to bring Thurston into this. It's nothing to do with him. In any case, I think I'd prefer to handle it in my own way."

Ronald sighed, expressing irritation rather than recording sorrow. "Let me spell it out for you. This is just the sort of story that the more sensational elements of the press will leap at. First, it's August, the silly season. They're hungry for material. Secondly, anything that smacks of devil worship sells newspapers. It's regrettable, but it's a fact of life. Third, Cynthia tells me there's local color in the shape of that damned poet, the priest who dabbled in Satanism. Youlgreave—the one Vanessa's so keen on. And finally, once the hacks start digging, heaven knows what they might come up with. How will you feel if they connect you with that business in Rosington? How will Vanessa feel?"

I was so surprised that for an instant I forgot to breathe. I sucked in a mouthful of air. I had not even realized that Ronald knew about Rosington. He had never mentioned it. In that same instant there rushed over me the crushing knowledge of my own naivety. Of course he knew. Probably every active Christian in this part of the diocese fancied that they knew all about it. One of the less desirable qualities of the Church of England is that it is a nest of gossip.

"Listen to me, David." His voice was gentler now, almost pleading. "You'll get an army of journalists on your doorstep.

You'll probably have coachloads of sightseers coming to gawp at the church. You may even get copycat incidents."

I said nothing. It was true that devil-worshipers tended to be unimaginative. By and large, evil is banal; imagination is not a quality it nurtures, so repetition is common. Into my mind came an image of gray mudflats, silver streaks of water and a gray sky; and far above me I heard the sound of wings. The hand holding the telephone receiver was slippery with sweat, and my armpits prickled. Evil causes led to evil effects which themselves became causes of further evil. Could you ever hope to end the consequences, or would they stretch through the centuries from past and future?

I tried to focus on Ronald, sensible and safe. I imagined him sitting at his polished desk, surrounded by serried ranks of dusted books; I gave him a silver vase full of white rose-buds; no clutter on the desk, just a blotter, a notepad and perhaps a file containing letters to be answered. And there was Ronald, impeccable in his suit and clerical collar, the very picture of a senior clergyman in waiting for a bishopric.

It wasn't good enough. The beating of the wings was growing gradually louder. My mouth was parched.

The wall, I thought, the wall beside his desk. No book-shelves there. A crucifix. A plain wooden crucifix. No body on it, but there would be a rush cross, left over from Palm Sunday, tucked behind the crossbar. I thought so hard about the crucifix that I could visualize the color of the varnish and the grain of the wood.

"David? I'm trying to *help*."

Ronald was sane, I told myself. Ronald was good. Recognizing that was hard, too. He was doing his best to do his Christian duty, according to his lights. I had stolen the woman he had thought of as his future wife. He had every reason to dislike me, even hate me. Yet he was going out of his way to help me—or perhaps Vanessa. I might not enjoy his assumption of authority and superior knowledge, but that was a relatively minor matter.

"Are you still there, David?"

"Yes. I was thinking. Why should all this reach the papers in the first place?"

"Through the local rag, of course. They'll be in regular contact with the police. Fortunately, Victor Thurston's on the board of the *Courier* group. I'll have a word with him tonight." Ronald sounded cheerful now, delighted to have his hands on the reins. "He has some useful contacts with the police, too, through the Masons. Don't worry. We'll do our best to smooth things over."

There was another pause in our conversation. There was only one thing to say and in the end I made myself say it. "Thank you."

The trick with Lady Youlgreave was to catch her at her lucid times. Her body was a battlefield: old age, pain, decay, a cocktail of medicines and an almost willful reluctance to die fought each other, changing sides frequently, forming shifting alliances.

The morphine encouraged her mind to drift. Often she was confused about the day of the week, occasionally the year and, on at least one occasion, the century. Time is a slippery notion, a set of assumptions she found it increasingly difficult to grasp.

She was at her best in the late mornings and the early

evenings. I left the Vicarage at 5 p.m. on Friday, shortly after the phone call from Ronald Trask. I was restless, tired of my own company. Doing anything was better than doing nothing.

I called upstairs to Rosemary but there was no answer. I went into the garden. Michael was playing patience on the grass in the shade of an old apple tree that had survived Ronald's restless desire to modernize my house and garden. There was a deckchair on the lawn, with *Nausea* on the seat. The afternoon had been sunny, but now the sky was beginning to cloud over, and there was a clinging dampness in the air that presaged rain.

"I'm just going out for a while," I told Michael. "I shouldn't be more than half an hour. Will you be all right on your own? I'm sure the Vintners wouldn't mind if—"

"No. I'll be fine."

"I'll be at the Old Manor House if anyone needs me."

"OK."

"Is Rosemary upstairs?"

"I think she went for a walk. She was here until about five minutes ago."

"Aunt Vanessa should be home between half past five and six."

"OK."

He smiled at me and returned to his game. I walked down the road, over the bridge and turned into the forecourt in front of the Old Manor House. The bird table stood at a slight angle from the perpendicular at the center of the scrubby lawn. I went over to it. It was a simple affair—a small wooden tray nailed to a stake, obviously home-made. The surface of the wood was cracked and covered with a patina of dirt from the weather and traffic. I found no trace of the blood and bone which Vanessa had seen, and which had so excited the crows.

I bent down and looked at the grass below the table. I felt ridiculous, like a schoolboy looking for clues, for cigarette ash or strands of hair. I abandoned the search, walked on to the door and rang the bell. The dogs barked. Doris answered the door.

"Hello, Vicar."

"Is Lady Youlgreave well enough for visitors?"

"She'll be glad to see you. Just had her tea and that always gives her a bit of a lift. Which means she wants to talk. And I just don't have time to listen."

I followed her into the gloom of the hall. Beauty was tethered to the newel post and did not bother to get up. She thumped her tail on the floor. Beast, trailing her tumor, waddled toward me and sniffed my shoes.

"You should have more help," I said to Doris. "Either that or Lady Youlgreave should go into a home."

Doris shook her head. "She doesn't like strangers in the house. And if you talk to her about going into a home, she starts crying."

"It's not fair to you."

"I cope. Dr. Vintner is in and out, and that helps. And then there's the nurse from the Fishguard Agency at weekends. Not that they're much use."

"Even so—"

"She wants to die in her own home," Doris interrupted. "So why shouldn't she?"

There wasn't any answer to that, or rather, none that Doris would accept. I wondered how much Lady Youlgreave paid her.

"I hear your husband has a new job." I wished I could remember the man's name.

"About time, too," she said. "If there was an Olympic gold medal for sitting on your backside in front of the telly, Ted would be in the running for it."

Beast slobbered over my shoe. She looked up at me with imploring eyes. What did she want? Everything to be all right again? For herself and Beauty and her mistress to be young?

"You go and see her, then," Doris said, deciding it was time to dismiss me. "I'll go and make her bed again. Can you find your own way? Otherwise I'll get caught as well."

Lady Youlgreave was nodding over a book when I went in. She looked up with a start.

"David? Is that you?"

"Yes. How are you today?"

"The same as always. Where's the girl? It's time for my medicine."

"Soon. Doris will be here soon."

I wasn't sure if she had heard me. She closed the book slowly—a thin volume bound in green leather with gilt lettering on the spine. Then she said, "She's late. She's always late. If she doesn't get her skates on, I'll sack her."

I knew better than to argue. "Doris is making your bed."

"How odd."

"Why?"

"Beds are made in the morning. Everyone knows that. Is it the morning?"

"No." I looked at my watch. "It's a quarter past five in the evening. Friday evening." I noticed that Lady Youlgreave was still looking expectantly at me, a worried frown on her face. "Friday, August the fourteenth." She was still frowning, so I added, "Nineteen-seventy."

"Oh. Where's your wife? Not been in today. Or has she?"

"No. Vanessa's at work."

"Never thought you'd get married again. Poor old Oliphant. Bet it made her squirm." Lady Youlgreave paused, and her lips moved as though she were chewing something. A thread of saliva ran from the corner of her mouth, as though marking the passage of a tiny snail. "Could have liked you myself, once. Silly business, don't you think?"

"What is?"

"Sex. Best thing about growing old: not having to worry about sex." The little eyes peered at me and looked away. "You should stop Vanessa wasting her time on Uncle Francis."

"I can't do that. I'm not her master."

"You should put your foot down."

I could imagine Vanessa's response if I tried to do such a foolish thing. "What's wrong with Francis, anyway? I thought you wanted Vanessa to go through the papers."

"I didn't realize what he was like. Not then." Lady Youlgreave tapped the book on her lap. "Nasty mind. And getting worse. Do you know why he started killing those animals?"

I said nothing.

"I think you do." She sighed. "This was his last book."

"*The Voice of Angels*?"

"More like devils. There's one poem called 'The Children of Heracles.' Disgusting. He must have had an evil mind to make up something like that."

I would have liked to take the book and glance at the poem, but her fingers had locked themselves around the covers. "It's part of a Greek myth."

"So Heracles really did kill his children? He really chopped them up?"

"As far as I can remember, Zeus's wife, Hera, hated Heracles, and one night she put a spell on him. In his sleep, he lashed out with his sword, dreaming that he was killing imaginary enemies. Then he woke up and he saw that he'd killed his own children."

"And chopped them up." Lady Youlgreave snuffled, a sound that might have expressed mirth. "*He* did that, too."

"Francis?" I smiled. "Not children, though."

"How do you know?" She stared up at me. "There's a lot you don't know."

She opened the book and seemed to become absorbed in a poem. I waited for a moment. Vanessa had warned me that these mood swings were becoming more frequent and more pronounced.

I cleared my throat. "Vanessa told me about your bird table. About the meat or whatever it was that the crows were pecking at. I don't suppose you got a good look at it, did you? With your opera glasses?"

She raised her head once more and I realized at once that I was not forgiven or forgotten. "I said there's a lot you don't know, David. Even about your own family."

"What do you mean?"

"I saw the whole thing. I'm not blind." The irises of her eyes were mud-brown pools, the pupils almost invisible. "It was in a paper bag."

"What was?"

"Whatever it was. A little head?"

"So you saw who put it there?"

"I told you. I'm not blind." She sniffed. Her eyes misted with tears. "I don't understand. Why don't I understand? Is it late? My watch has stopped. What's the time?"

The door opened and Doris came in. "How about a nice drink before bed, love? A nice cup of cocoa?"

"Medicine." Lady Youlgreave brightened. "It's time for my medicine."

"Not quite, dear. I've put it all out on your bedside table, like usual. You can have the first one when you get into bed." Doris looked at me. "You'll want to be getting home, I expect, Vicar. I saw Mrs. Byfield's car go by."

*Chapter Nineteen*

S HE RUSHED OUT of the drive of Roth Park, her arms outstretched toward me.

"Father! Wait!"

I stopped. Rain was drifting from a gray sky. Rosemary
propped herself against one of the gateposts. She was out of
breath and bursting with life. Even when wearing jeans and a
white shirt which had once belonged to me, she somehow
contrived to look elegant.

"I found something. You'd better come and see."

"What is it?"

She shook her head. "Come with me." She seized my arm
and gave it a little tug. "Please."

I allowed her to draw me into the drive. "Why all the mystery?"

"Not a mystery."

She led me past the churchyard and into the grove of oaks.
Instead of continuing down the drive toward the house, she
turned right on to the footpath which led into the paddock we
hoped to use for the fete's car park. It was raining harder,
now, and I suggested going back for an umbrella. But Rosemary urged me on.

On the far side of the paddock, the footpath split into two—
one branch continuing north toward a cluster of council
houses and the Jubilee Reservoir, the other cutting westward

across a patch of waste ground in a direction roughly parallel to the drive. The land had been part of the demesne of Roth Park, and was owned by the Cliffords.

"Where are we going?" I asked.

She looked back, her eyes gleaming and her face full of color. "Carter's Meadow. Look—there's the way in."

We followed the path to a five-bar gate made of rusting tubular steel, wired permanently closed. Rosemary and I climbed over. Nowadays Carter's Meadow was a no man's land sandwiched between the ruined formal gardens of Roth Park and the housing estate. Like so many places on the fringes of cities, it was permanently dirty: even the weeds were grubby.

Rosemary led me past an abandoned car to a small spinney, a self-seeded clump of straggly trees and saplings. A track zigzagged through ash and birch, brambles and nettles. She plunged into it. I wondered what she had been doing here. Smoking? Meeting a boy? The air smelled rank, as though the spinney were a large animal beginning to decay. We came out on the far side of it.

She stopped abruptly, wiping rain from her face. "There." She pointed to the ground beside a dead elder tree on the edge of the spinney. "Look at that."

I followed the direction of her finger. An empty bottle leaned against the tree. The grass at the foot of the tree was stained a rusty brown.

"*Look*," she repeated, stabbing the air with her finger. "Don't you see what must have happened here?"

I hitched my trousers and crouched down. The grass was dry. The bottle had contained a cider called Autumn Gold. The label was fresh. The bottle might have been left there yesterday. Cigarette ends lay in various stages of decay between the blades of grass. There was sadness in this place.

"It's blood," Rosemary said. "Father, it's blood, isn't it?"

"I think so."

I picked up the bottle between finger and thumb. Underneath was a tuft of black hair.

"This is where they did it," Rosemary said. "You can buy that cider in Malik's Minimarket. Did you know?"

I wished she had not found this. It meant nothing but trouble. We could not be sure that the stain was dried blood, let alone that it and the fur came from Lord Peter. But I would have to tell the police, who would not want to hear. I would also have to tell Audrey, and the discovery would feed her forensic fantasies—and incidentally serve to confirm her belief that the youths from the council estate were responsible. And why did Rosemary have to be the one to find it?

"What were you doing here?" My voice was sharper than I had intended.

"I wanted a walk."

"Here?"

"If you follow the path you get to the river. It's pretty."

Pretty? I had not been this way for years. I had a vague memory of a tangle of trees on boggy ground, through which meandered the Rowan, scarcely more than a stream. But teenagers had different standards of beauty from adults. I looked at Rosemary and suddenly remembered my adolescent self finding a perverse satisfaction from reading Auden in the shell of a burned-out house: I had sat on a pile of rubble bright with rosebay willowherb and smoked illicit cigarettes.

I stood up. The rain was falling more heavily now. The trees gave us partial shelter but I did not want to stay here any longer than necessary. There was poison in this place, and I felt it seeping into me.

"Do you think they cut up Lord Peter here?" Rosemary asked.

"It's possible. But we mustn't jump to conclusions."

"This is where Francis Youlgreave cut up a cat, isn't it?"

"So they say. Come on."

"But we'll get soaked."

I glanced at her. Her eyes met mine. Her face was calm and beautiful. *My daughter.* I wanted to believe that truth was beauty, and beauty truth. But what if Keats was wrong and beauty did not have a moral dimension? What if beauty told lies? Rosemary had told lies in the past. But she had been too young to know better. Children only gradually become moral beings. I pushed aside the memory.

I walked quickly away from the shelter of the trees. I felt better in the open. Rosemary followed me. Did she not feel the atmosphere of the place? There was a growl of thunder. The rain sluiced out of the sky. Water ran down my neck and soaked through the shoulders of my jacket. *Wash me clean.* Would it wash away the evidence—and, if so, was that a good thing, for fear of what the evidence might reveal?

Rosemary took my arm again—unusual for her, because she tended not to touch me very much. "Are you OK?"

"Fine. We'd better go home and get dry."

"You'll ring the police?"

"Yes."

She nuzzled against me, as if trying to push me into action.

"If we cut through the Cliffords' garden we can get up to the drive. It'll be quicker than going back the way we came."

I followed her. It was easier than arguing about whether or not we should trespass. In a way I was grateful that she had taken charge. I was not usually indecisive. Indeed, I tend to go the other way, sometimes to the point of arrogance. But at that moment I could no more make a choice than I could play a note on a violin with slackened strings. The poison under the trees was working at me, sapping my will.

The poison had other effects. Rosemary led the way—she seemed to know it, and I did not. We walked along the line of a straggling hedgerow toward a dark-green mass of trees and shrubs. The rain plastered her hair to her head and her clothes to her body. I could not see her face—just her figure, and the lilting sway of her bottom as she walked. I felt a stirring of desire, just as I had when I put my arms around Joanna the previous evening. But this was far worse. Rosemary was my daughter. *What is happening to me?* Nausea mingled with my desire. I stared at the ground. It was so long since Vanessa and I had made love.

"Lord have mercy," I muttered. "Lord have mercy."

She could not have heard me, but she turned. "I'm *soaking*," she said happily.

We came to a barbed-wire fence which separated the strip of wasteland from the belt of trees and bushes. The wire was rusting and some of the posts were either missing or leaning.

Rosemary picked up one of the posts, leaving a gap nearly three feet high between the ground and the lowest strand of wire. "I'll hold it for you."

I crawled underneath. It was clear that people had been through the fence at this point before, and I suspected that Rosemary had been one of them. I felt ridiculous: a middle-aged clergyman dragged back to adolescence. Rosemary scrambled after me. I had never been here before, but I guessed that we were in what had once been part of the garden of Roth Park. The belt of trees was dominated by a big copper beech. Among the tangle of seedlings were other, older plants—rhododendrons and laurels; the remains of a yew hedge; and the long carcass of a fallen Douglas fir.

"This way," Rosemary urged, the rainwater streaming down her cheeks. She smiled brilliantly. "Follow me."

We picked our way through the undergrowth and passed under the canopy of the copper beech. Despite the cover from the branches, the rain was still pounding down. Suddenly the trees thinned and the rain increased in intensity. I caught sight of the chimneys and upper windows of the house. I realized where we were.

A few paces ahead of me, Rosemary stopped. She turned back to me. The rain poured over her. "Oh *no*," she hissed. "How embarrassing."

The ground shelved. Before us was what had once been a sunken rose garden surrounded by stone walls. Now it contained a kidney-shaped depression made of concrete, filled not with water but with dead leaves. A springboard still arched over what had once been the deep end, its coconut matting slimy with rain. A pavement of stone flags ran around the pool. There were benches set at intervals in the wall, and halfway down one of the longer sides was a wooden structure with a pitched roof and a little verandah running along the front. Sitting in a director's chair on the verandah was Toby Clifford, smoking a long, white cigarette.

He saw us a few seconds after we saw him. He waved. "Come and get out of the rain," he called.

We picked our way around the edge of the pool toward the building, a combination of changing room and summer house. Toby was wearing jeans and a loose cotton top with embroidery around the neck, and his feet were bare; he looked more like a hippy than ever. He stubbed out his cigarette, even though it was only partly smoked, and threw it into the bushes. There was another chair on the verandah. He unfolded it with a flourish. Rosemary was first up the steps. He bowed from the waist, waving her into the chair.

"I'm sorry," I began. "We were walking across Carter's Meadow, and it began to rain hard."

"So you thought you'd look for shelter. Jolly good idea. Have a seat."

"I'm afraid we're trespassing—"

"You're welcome." Toby perched on the rail. "I'll run up to the house and get an umbrella and a couple of towels."

"There's no need."

"You mustn't catch cold."

Rosemary said, "I'm not cold. I'm *boiling*."

We both looked at her—sitting back in the chair, smiling—almost laughing—at us. She was bedraggled but as beautiful as ever, almost as if the rain had colluded with her and brought out another aspect of her beauty: nature meant her to be drenched and glistening. Her shirt was plastered to her body, marking the outlines of her thin bra, through which poked the outlines of her erect nipples. Now my emotions shifted to another mode, and I wanted to cover her up, to shield her body from the eyes of a strange man. There was a half smile on Toby's face.

"You mustn't let us put you to any trouble," I said. "When the rain slackens off, we'll be on our way."

"It's no trouble. Nice to have an opportunity to return your hospitality. How's Miss—Miss Oliphant, is it? Jo told me about the business with the cat."

"She's taking it—"

"That's why we came out," Rosemary interrupted. "We found some blood."

"Blood?" He stared at her. "Where?"

"In Carter's Meadow. You know, the field beyond your garden. It's part of the park, isn't it?"

"Not exactly—but what do you mean, some blood?"

"There's a place under one of the trees . . . Father found some fur as well."

Toby whistled.

"It may be where they cut off the cat's head," Rosemary said, her voice prim. "We shall have to tell the police."

"You can phone from here, if you like." Toby was talking to Rosemary, not me. "It's nearer. And then I could run you home in the car."

She nodded. "Thank you."

"Do you think the police will do anything about it?"

"I don't know. But one has to try. Poor Audrey."

I noticed that at some point in the last few days Rosemary had stopped calling Audrey "Miss Oliphant."

Toby stood up. "You stay there. I'll fetch the umbrella."

"There's no point," Rosemary said. "We're both soaked as it is."

Toby stared at her again, and they exchanged smiles. "OK.

We'll run through the rain instead." Then he remembered me. "But I can bring back the umbrella for you, David."

"No need, thanks. But I may not run. Walking's more my style, these days."

The two of them ran ahead—darting up the steps behind the pavilion and tearing ragged tracks through the long grass of the croquet lawn. I followed them up to the terrace where I had had coffee with Toby and Joanna. Sexual desire had sensitized me to the presence of desire in others. It was quite clear that Rosemary was attracted to Toby, and that he was attracted to her.

The two of them entered the house through one of the French windows that opened on to the terrace. "Jo!" I heard Toby call. "Visitors!"

I went after them. The room beyond was large, light and well proportioned, a double cube at least twenty-five feet long. As well as two pairs of French windows on to the terrace, there were two tall windows looking out on the drive. In the Bramleys' time this had been the residents' lounge.

"I'm afraid it's still a bit of a mess." Toby grinned at Rosemary. "Any time you want a job as a housekeeper, you have only to ask."

I hesitated just inside the door, aware that a puddle was rapidly forming around my feet.

"Come on in," Toby said. "A little water won't hurt the place."

The size of the room dwarfed its contents—G-Plan furniture, two easy chairs, a mattress, several tea chests and a roll of carpet. Beside the empty fireplace was a record player—a series of expensive-looking boxes linked by wires—and several cartons of long-playing records. Ghostly traces of the Bramleys remained—pale patches marking the sites of pictures and furniture. There were cigarettes and whiskey on the mantelpiece. Propped against the wall behind them was a large mirror with an ornate gilded frame and a long crack running diagonally down the glass. Our footsteps were loud on the bare floor and left trails of wet prints across the boards.

Toby was at the door. "Let's find some towels, shall we? This way."

He led us into a short corridor which ran down to the central hall by the front door. I had been here often enough in the Bramleys' day, but now the place felt and looked like a different house. The clutter of wheelchairs had gone from the foot of the stairs. The carpets, pictures, and shabby furniture had departed, and so had the smell of powder, perfume, disinfectant and old age. I was aware of empty rooms around and above us, of the cellars beneath our feet, of silent, enclosed spaces, of damp, musty smells.

In the hall, the emptiness stretched up to a skylight like a glass tent on the roof of the house. The panes were cracked and stained with bird droppings. To our right, a pitch-pine staircase divided in two at mezzanine level and ran up to a galleried landing.

"Damn," Toby said. "There's a leak. I'm not surprised."

A puddle had already gathered on the black-and-white tiles of the floor. *Plop—plop—plop*. I watched a silver drop describe what looked like a curving path from skylight to floor, where it shattered.

"Jo," Toby called, and his voice bounced up the stairwell. "Jo, where are you?"

I heard feet pattering along the landing above our heads. Not pattering: bare feet thudding on bare boards. Suddenly the footsteps stopped and Joanna's pale face appeared twenty feet above us, hanging over the rail of the banisters.

"What is it?" She sounded out of breath.

"We need towels," Toby said. "David and Rosemary were caught in the storm, and so was I. There are clean ones in that room by the bathroom. Inside the blue trunk."

The head vanished. A moment later Joanna came down the stairs with an armful of towels. She was wearing a dark-blue halter-neck T-shirt, which clung to her body, and a long wrap-around skirt. Her feet were grubby, and the toenails were decorated with green nail varnish, much chipped. She handed around the towels. When she came to me, she raised her head. Our eyes, met, and I saw that her eyelids were puffy.

Toby toweled himself vigorously. "I'm sure that Jo could find something for Rosemary to change into. As for you, David, I could see what—"

"There's no need," Rosemary interrupted. "Thank you. I'm quite warm. I'll soon dry out."

"I'm all right as well," I said to Toby.

He grinned. "To be perfectly honest, I'm not sure I've got anything that would fit you."

"Hadn't you better ring the police, Father?" Rosemary suggested.

"The police?" Joanna's face was stiff like a mask, the green eyes murky. "What's happened?"

"We found some fur and something that might be blood on

the waste ground near your garden," I said. "We think it may have something to do with that business last night."

"The cat?" She hugged herself and, still staring up at me, murmured, "That's horrible."

"There's a phone along here, David," Toby said from the other side of the hall.

I smiled in what I hoped was a reassuring fashion at Joanna and followed Toby into a small room facing the front of the house. The Bramleys had used it as an office. It was furnished with a scarred dining table, a pair of kitchen chairs and a row of empty shelves screwed to the wall. On the table was an ashtray and a telephone.

Toby left me alone. I rang the operator, who put me through to the police station. I asked for Sergeant Clough, and after a few minutes he came on the line. I told him what Rosemary and I had discovered.

"Well, that's very interesting." There was a pause, filled with a click followed by a hissing noise: Clough was lighting his pipe. "I'll make a note of it. No sign of the cat's head, I suppose?"

"No." I wondered whether to tell him about Vanessa's theory but decided against. It was a safe bet that Clough would not be interested in speculations about Lady Youlgreave's bird table. "Aren't you going to send someone out to look at the place?"

"In an ideal world, yes. But we're very stretched at present, Mr. Byfield, very stretched." Another pause, another click, another hiss. "We have to allocate resources as we think best. We do have one or two slightly more important cases than this business with the cat. And—if you don't mind me speaking plainly—we can't even be sure that what you and your daughter found has any bearing on it. I can't help feeling my inspector would say it was all a bit of a wild-goose chase. I'm sorry, sir, but you know how it is."

I agreed that I knew how it was, though of course I didn't. I didn't much like Clough, but I had to admit, if only to myself, that the man probably knew what he was talking about.

"But let us know if anything else turns up, Mr. Byfield. No harm in it, is there, and you never know."

We said goodbye politely and I went to find the others. They were waiting in the big room with the French windows. Rosemary and Toby were kneeling on the floor and leafing through a box of long-playing records. Joanna was by the fireplace with a cigarette in her hand, staring in the mirror at my reflection in the doorway.

"Are the police coming?" she asked.

"No."

Rosemary looked up, her face flushed. "Why ever not?"

"They don't think it sufficiently important."

She stood up. "That's terrible. Of course it's important." She turned her head sharply to look at Toby, and her hair lifted from her shoulders. "Don't you agree?"

"Policemen aren't like other people," he said. "Their minds are mysterious."

"But it could be a vital clue," Rosemary persisted, talking not to me but to Toby. "Did you know that Audrey is going to pay the vet to do a postmortem?"

He shook his head. "You said there was a tuft of fur?"

Rosemary nodded.

"If they put that under a microscope," he went on, "they'd be able to match it up with the hair of the cat. Well, I expect they could, anyway." His eyebrows shot up. "Modern science is wonderful. I suppose we'd better go and fetch it."

"Now?" Rosemary said.

"The sooner the better." He flashed a glance at me and then a smile at Rosemary. "Otherwise we'll dry out and then get wet again. And if we leave it, anything might happen. The rain could wash it away. Or . . ." He paused and licked his lips. "Or the person who did it might come back to tidy up."

"We must go. It's only fair to Audrey." Rosemary looked at me. "Don't you agree?"

Before I could answer, Toby said, "It can do no harm, at least, can it? And who knows, it might actually do some good."

I looked at the mirror, but Joanna had turned her head so I could no longer see the reflection of her face. "Surely you'll wait until the rain has stopped, at least?"

"Better not," Toby said. "Anyway, Rosemary and I can take an umbrella. Why don't you stay and have some tea with Joanna?"

Rosemary pushed a strand of damp hair from her cheek like a cat grooming her face with a paw. "No point in us all getting wet."

The two of them were already at the door. I sensed Rosemary's excitement. I had never seen her like this before. Her body was taut, and in every movement there was an awareness of its possible effect on Toby.

He threw a glance at his sister. "You'll be OK?"

It seemed a strange question. Why should she not be all right in her own home in the company of a middle-aged priest?

Jo nodded, dropping her cigarette end in the empty grate.

"On second thoughts," Toby went on, "it's a bit late for tea—must be after six. Why don't you see if David would like a drink?"

Then he and Rosemary were gone. I heard their footsteps in the corridor. Toby said something and Rosemary laughed in reply, a quick, high, gasping laugh. A door slammed in the distance. The big room filled with silence. The only sound was the patter of the rain. Joanna stared down at her hands and flexed her fingers. Automatically, I fumbled in my pocket for cigarettes. The packet was damp but the contents were dry.

"What would you like to drink?" Joanna said, without looking at me.

"Nothing just now, thanks."

She looked up at me and smiled, which transformed her face, filling it with warmth and charm. "You won't mind watching me, will you?"

I shook my head, smiling, and lit a cigarette. She fetched a glass from the cupboard by the fireplace and poured herself an inch of whiskey from the bottle on the mantelpiece. And I watched.

"Let's sit down," she suggested.

She led the way to the nearer French window, the one we had not used when we came in from the terrace. Two arm-chairs faced each other on either side, standing on bare floorboards. An upturned tea chest between them served as a table. Joanna sat down and, holding the glass in both hands, sipped. Color filled her face. The skirt parted. I watched as the triangular gap extended, riding up her legs to an inch above the knee. I looked away; I remembered who I was and where I was; I remembered Vanessa.

I sat smoking, staring outside at the rain pounding down on the flagstones of the terrace, sending up a fine, gray spray. Beyond the terrace, the long grass of the lawn swayed and bowed beneath the onslaught; and the trees of the garden rustled and trembled in agitation.

"Can I have a cigarette?" she asked. "I've finished mine."

I gave her a Players No 6. When I bent down to light it for her, for a moment our faces were very close. Her eyes were outlined in kohl, and she wore a faint but insistent perfume which made me think of Oriental spices. There was a fine, fair down on her cheek; and I knew that if I touched it it would be softer than anything in the world. I hastily straightened up and blew out the match.

"Do you believe in ghosts?" she said.

Joanna had a talent for catching me off guard. I stared at the hissing curtain of rain and wondered if the question had anything to do with our truncated conversation the previous evening, when she had hinted at difficulties just before we found Lord Peter's body.

"I don't know about ghosts," I said at last, "but I certainly believe that there are phenomena which don't fit into the accepted scheme of things."

She leaned forward in her chair. "Like what?"

"Any parish priest comes across odd events which can't be explained. People tend to call us out when there's a hint of the supernatural."

"Like plumbers? To deal with spiritual leaks?"

"In a way."

"Can *you* explain them?"

I shook my head. "It's not like that. It's perfectly possible that there are rational explanations for everything we now class as paranormal. But we simply haven't stumbled on them yet. In the meantime, the church can sometimes help people come to terms with their existence, if only because theology at least recognizes the existence of the supernatural. And the average scientist doesn't. It's a curious truth that modern materialism is far more dogmatic about its beliefs than modern theology . . ."

I broke off, aware that I was beginning to lecture Joanna. The truth was that she was making me nervous, and I was taking refuge in my classroom manner—just as I had with every woman who had ever attracted me; it is chillingly easy to repeat our mistakes. I glanced at her sitting opposite me, hunched over the glass in her hands, with a cigarette smoldering between her fingers. The harsh gray light revealed every detail of her without flattery; and I liked what I saw.

"I'm wasting your time," she said abruptly. "But I don't know who else to talk to about it."

"Of course you're not wasting my time. Do you believe you've seen a ghost?"

Joanna half shrugged, half shivered; her body moved fluidly as water flexes to contain a ripple. "Not *seen*, exactly. But I've heard things."

"Has Toby, too?"

She shook her head. "It was the night before last. I—I don't sleep well. You know the tower at the end of the house? My room's there, the one below the top. I was going to have the top one but I didn't like the atmosphere, and Toby thought it smelled of dry rot. Anyway, I was lying in bed and I heard a man walking. At least, I think I heard him. A man in the room above me. To and fro, to and fro."

"What did you do?"

"Nothing. I locked the door and covered my head with the bedclothes. After a while the noise stopped. Or maybe I dozed off . . . You'll think I'm a coward. I suppose I am."

"It's not cowardly to be afraid. Did you tell Toby in the morning?"

She stubbed out her cigarette, stabbing it in the ashtray. "He said I was imagining things." She bit her lip. "I don't know—maybe I was. I made him fetch the key and we went upstairs together, to the top room. There was nothing there, of course. Just an empty room."

I waited, looking at the rain.

"You don't believe me," she burst out. "You're just like Toby."

"I believe you."

She stared hard at me, as though trying to read in my face whether or not to trust me. At length she said, "Do you think rooms can have emotions? That they can be happy or sad?"

I remembered my uncomfortable experience in the chancel of St. Mary Magdalene the previous summer, the evening when Rosemary had failed to pass on a message for me from Vanessa. "I'm not sure whether places have atmospheres or whether we project our emotions on to them and create an atmosphere."

She looked disappointed. "The room was unhappy," she said flatly. "I don't know—maybe someone had been unhappy there. Toby said that poet used to sleep there—Vanessa told him. Or maybe it was me: maybe it was me who was unhappy."

I waited for a moment, listening to the rain and looking at Joanna, whose head was bowed over her lap. Her neck and shoulders were bare and I would have liked to stroke them, for stroking is the simplest and the oldest way to bring comfort.

"Joanna," I said slowly. "Would it help if—"

There was a rapping on the window. Joanna and I both looked up sharply. For an instant I felt a shaft of shame, as though I had been surprised in a guilty secret.

Standing on the terrace on the other side of the window were Toby and Rosemary, both of them streaked with rain, despite the umbrella which Toby carried. In his other hand was a nylon shopping bag containing what looked like a bottle. Rosemary, her blue eyes glowing, was even wetter than she had been before, her hair dark with water, plastered in tendrils over her skull. She held up what looked like a tobacco tin, tapped it with her finger and mouthed through the glass: "We've got it."

Joanna smiled at Toby and made as if to open the window. He shook his head and pointed along the terrace: it was as clear as if he had spoken the words that he did not want to come in by the French windows because they were too wet. Then he and Rosemary had gone, and all we could see through the French windows was the gray sky and the green, rainswept garden.

"I was beginning to think they'd got lost," I said to Joanna.

In the distance, a door slammed and Rosemary laughed. Joanna looked up. There was no trace of a smile left on her face.

"*Please*, David," she whispered. "I need to talk to you without Toby knowing."

Chapter Twenty

RAIN SLUICED DOWN the windscreen and thrummed on the long bonnet of the Jaguar. The car rolled over the gravel of the Vicarage drive and pulled up outside the front door. There were lights in some of the windows, earlier than usual because of the gloom.

"Have you got time for a drink?" Rosemary asked from the tiny back seat, sounding a good ten years older than she really was, apart from a quiver on the last word.

"That's very kind." Toby turned, including me in the conversation. "Are you sure I wouldn't be in the way?"

"Not at all," I said, as I had to say.

The three of us struggled out of the car. Toby produced a black umbrella and held it over Rosemary and myself as we stumbled to the front door: it was a courteous gesture, but not one that kept much rain from us. I unlocked the front door and the three of us fell into the hall. Vanessa opened the kitchen door. Michael was behind her, sitting at the table with a plate in front of him.

"I was about to send out a search party," she said, smiling. "Hello, Toby. Have you rescued them?"

"Yes, he has," said Rosemary, still aspiring to a precarious adult dignity. "And now we're going to reward him with a drink."

Vanessa's eyes sought mine and found no objection there.

"Of course. Come into the sitting room. David, you and Rosemary look as if you need a change of clothes."

Rosemary began to say something and then stopped. "Back in a moment," she said and then, flushing, she galloped upstairs with uncharacteristic clumsiness.

"You'd better have this," Toby said to me, holding out the nylon shopping bag which contained the tobacco tin and the empty cider bottle.

"What's that?" Vanessa asked.

Toby grinned at her. "Clues."

I explained briefly to Vanessa and then went upstairs. While I was changing, I heard a Niagara of rushing water from the bathroom. I went downstairs and poked my head in the kitchen. Michael was working his way through an enormous bowl of apple crumble.

"Everything all right?"

The boy's mouth was full, so he nodded.

"We'll be in the sitting room. Come and join us if you like."

Michael swallowed. "Thank you." He loaded his spoon with another mouthful of crumble. I shut the kitchen door. How did one talk to children? Something about Michael encouraged one to treat him as more grownup than in fact he was: his stillness, perhaps, his wary eyes and his slow, grave smile.

I went into the sitting room. Vanessa was laughing at something that Toby had said, genuine, unforced amusement with her head thrown back. It was a long time since I had seen her so eager to be pleased.

"We're having gin and tonic," she said to me, "so I poured you one, too."

I sat down and took a long swallow of my drink.

"Vanessa's been telling me about her book," Toby said. "Wonderful stuff. I can't wait for my signed copy."

Vanessa flushed. "There's a long way to go before that happens."

There were footsteps on the stairs and Rosemary came in. In her short time upstairs she had managed to transform herself. It looked as if she had bathed and washed her hair. She had changed into a short turquoise needlecord skirt and a tight, long-sleeved T-shirt. On her wrist were silver bangles, and she brought in a powerful cloud of perfume.

"I could murder a gin and tonic," she said in an airy voice.

"I beg your pardon—" I began.

Vanessa was already on her feet. "I'll get it, shall I?" she said to no one in particular. As she turned toward the drinks trolley, her face averted from everyone in the room except me, she glared, wordlessly telling me not to interfere.

"I like your bracelets," Toby said. "Jo's looking for some like that."

"It's a Moroccan *semaine*," Rosemary explained. "One bangle for each day of the week."

While she was speaking, I watched Vanessa pour a teaspoonful of gin into a long glass and top it up with tonic water. She gave the glass to Rosemary, who raised it and said, "Cheers." If I had not known better, I would have thought Rosemary was already a little tipsy. But people can intoxicate you as well as alcohol.

Vanessa sat down beside me on the sofa. "By the way, there was a message for you while you were out. Doris phoned."

"But I saw her this evening at Lady Youlgreave's."

"This was after you left. The old lady wants you to come and see her on Monday morning."

"It sounds like an order," I said, trying to make a joke of it, though Lady Youlgreave's occasional outbreaks of imperiousness irritated me profoundly. "Did Doris say why?"

Vanessa hesitated. "It's about the bird table, apparently. Lady Youlgreave wants to tell you—ah—who was feeding the birds."

It was clear what Vanessa meant. She was a discreet and diplomatic woman, in many ways an ideal clergyman's wife—ironically enough. Rosemary was asking Toby a question about the fuel consumption of his Jaguar, no mean achievement considering she had never shown any interest in cars before.

"Has she told Doris who it was?" I murmured.

Vanessa shook her head. "Doris sounded quite put out."

"I've no idea how much juice she uses." Toby wrinkled his eyebrows in a way that I suspected women might find attractive. "I just like driving the thing. What goes on under the bonnet is an enormous mystery to me." Turning to Vanessa, he went on, "Talking of mysteries, I wanted to ask you something about our poet. I feel quite possessive about him, you know—because he lived in the house."

"And died," Rosemary pointed out in a cool voice.

"And died." Toby flashed a grin at her, then turned back to Vanessa. "Jo found a copy of that poem of his—'The Judgement of Strangers'—in an anthology she's got. I read it last night and I just couldn't make head or tail of it. What's it meant to be about? What does the title mean?"

"No one's quite sure," Vanessa said. "I hope to find out

when Lady Youlgreave lets me examine the relevant part of the journals. It's generally taken to be a medieval trial scene. With a woman in the dock who's being accused of everything from heresy to murder. And finally she's condemned and burned at the stake."

"A bit like Shaw's *St. Joan*?" said Toby, sounding like a bright undergraduate in a tutorial.

"In a way. But it's a narrative poem, remember, rather than drama. Like Keats's 'Eve of St. Agnes' or Browning's 'Abt Vogler.' Youlgreave goes all mystical at the drop of a hat, and there's a rather unpleasant theme of defilement running through it. The idea that when judgment is perverted, then everything falls apart. But it's hard to know for certain. Francis is almost willfully obscure."

"He probably found the title in *The Book of Common Prayer*," I said.

Vanessa's face sharpened; she was a scholar *manqué*, a sort of intellectual terrier—wasted as a provincial publisher. "Where?"

"I think it's in the Service of Commination. I'll see if I can find it."

I went to the study to fetch a Prayer Book. When I came back, a moment later, Rosemary was on her feet. She emptied her glass and put it down on the table. "I'll leave you to it," she said. "I'd better go and do some work." She slipped out, shutting the door behind her.

"She's working very hard at present," Vanessa said, as if apologizing for the abruptness of Rosemary's departure. "Oxbridge entrance, next term. But you wouldn't think this was her summer holiday, would you?"

"Here it is, 'A COMMINATION OR DENOUNCING OF GOD'S ANGER AND JUDGMENTS AGAINST SINNERS.' There's a list of curses. Rather like the Ten Commandments. 'Cursed is he that perverteth the judgement of the stranger, the fatherless, and widow.' "

"Where does it actually come from?" Vanessa asked.

"It might be from one of the Ash Wednesday services of the Middle Ages. But originally it probably comes from the Old Testament. I can look it up, if you like."

"Please." Vanessa smiled at Toby. "You must find this rather tedious."

"Not at all," he said politely. "But do remember to tell me what the poem means when you find out."

"I'm looking forward to seeing the house, too—especially Francis Youlgreave's room. How are you getting on with the swimming pool?"

"They could have it ready by next week." Toby glanced out of the window. "All we need is the weather for it."

He finished his drink. Vanessa offered him another, but he shook his head. "I really should be going, thank you. I don't like leaving Joanna alone for too long." Despite his words, he stayed in his chair, looking from Vanessa to me. "Actually, there's something I wanted to tell you," he said slowly. "And this might be a good moment. You remember that I mentioned that Joanna hasn't been well? Well, in fact, the trouble was mainly psychological. Our mother died—it was an overdose, actually—and poor Jo was the one who found the body."

"I'm so sorry," Vanessa said, "for you both."

He smiled at her. "Afterward, she had a sort of nervous

breakdown." He hesitated. "Obviously, it's not something she generally likes known. But I thought I'd better mention it. If only in case she sometimes acts a little strangely. So you'll know why." He looked at his watch. "I really must go."

Vanessa and I saw him out. In the hall, I called upstairs to tell Rosemary that Toby was leaving but there was no answer.

Behind Toby's back, Vanessa mouthed a single word: *sulking*.

"Don't bother," Toby said. "I don't want to break her concentration."

We watched him skipping like a dancer through the rain to the shelter of the E-type. The Jaguar's engine roared. As the car slipped out of our drive, Vanessa said, "It's not a car, is it? It's a phallic symbol on wheels."

## Chapter Twenty-One

AS THE EVENING PROGRESSED, the storm slackened to a steady downpour. It was surprisingly cold for August.

After Toby had driven away, I went into the study and, without turning on the light, dialed the familiar number of Tudor Cottage. The phone rang on and on. I stared out at the village green. There was less traffic than usual and hardly any pedestrians. The car park of the Queen's Head was almost empty.

The tea room would have closed several hours ago. Audrey must have been out. I wondered idly what could have taken her away from the warmth and shelter of her home on a night like this. It did not occur to me to worry about her. In the end, I replaced the receiver. The news about Rosemary's unpleasant discovery this afternoon could wait.

The next day, Saturday, the doorbell rang while we were still having breakfast. Vanessa raised her eyes to the ceiling. Rosemary pushed back her chair and went to answer the door. I heard an excited voice and footsteps; then Audrey burst into the kitchen. She seemed somehow larger and pinker than before, as though she were on the verge of erupting from her clothes like a chick from its shell.

"Well!" she announced, stopping in the kitchen doorway. "I was right."

Vanessa gave me what old-fashioned novelists used to call a speaking look. This one said, loud and clear: *Can't your bloody parishioners leave us alone even at breakfast time?*

I abandoned my toast and stood up. "Shall we go in the study? Perhaps a cup of coffee—?"

Rosemary's face, bright and feverish, appeared at Audrey's shoulder. "What do you mean? How were you right?"

"I saw the vet last night. He confirmed what I've said all along." Audrey sniffed. "Lord Peter was beheaded. The good news is that the poor darling was . . . was dead before those terrible things were done to him. The vet said his spine was broken, almost certainly by a car going over him, and that's probably what killed him. He may not even have known what was happening." Audrey's voice faltered. "If only that was all that had happened. I think I could have accepted that."

Michael was staring in fascination at Audrey. I took a step toward her, hoping to shoo her into the study. She stood her ground.

"He was beheaded some time after death," Audrey went on, her voice sounding unexpectedly triumphant. "It was no accident, Mr. Giles was sure of that. It was almost certainly some sort of saw, definitely something with a serrated edge, like a hacksaw. I do so wish I knew what had happened to the head."

I dared not look at Vanessa. "Audrey—"

"And then he was left for us to find at the church door." She swallowed and her eyes filmed with tears. "Hanging by his tail."

Michael gave a strangled giggle. I could not blame him. Audrey was one of those unfortunate people whose tragedies are tinged with farce.

"David," she hissed. "You do realize how *diabolical* this is? Every detail so carefully thought out."

I nodded.

"It's a sort of blasphemy," Rosemary muttered.

"Yes, dear. Exactly." Audrey smiled at her. "And the police may be content to pretend it never happened, but I'm not. Why, this is the next best thing to murder. I'm simply not prepared to hide my head in the sand. If the police won't do their job, I shall just have to do it for them."

"Like Miss Marple," Rosemary suggested. "In a manner of speaking."

"Precisely. Though I say it myself, I do have *some* knowledge of human nature."

I made another attempt to sweep Audrey into the study. She wouldn't move. She wanted an audience.

"Don't you think this sort of thing is best left to the police?" I said.

"Fat lot of good they'll be. If I leave it to them, nothing will happen."

"Sometimes it's wiser to try to put something like this behind one."

"I'm not putting Lord Peter behind me. Not until I've got to the bottom of how he died."

"We found something yesterday afternoon," Rosemary said. "I think it's a clue. It was in Carter's Meadow."

Audrey spun around, still blocking the doorway. "What?"

Rosemary had the Golden Virginia tobacco tin, which had spent the night on the hall table, in her hand. She opened it and showed Audrey what it contained.

"What is it?"

"We think it may be a piece of Lord Peter's fur. And that browny stuff—see?—I think that may be blood."

Audrey seized the tin. While she examined its contents, her mouth worked uncontrollably.

"Toby—that's Toby Clifford, I mean—he was with me when we collected it. It's his tin, actually. Toby thought perhaps you could compare the hairs with Lord Peter's. Perhaps the vet—"

"If it can be done, then Mr. Giles will do it. I'll make sure of that." Audrey raised a pink, shiny face. "Thank you, my dear. This is a start. Now, tell me exactly where you found it."

Prodded by Audrey's questions, Rosemary described what had happened the afternoon before. When it transpired that I had seen the fur in its original position, Audrey was delighted.

"You'll make an ideal witness, David. People trust what a clergyman says."

That had not always been my experience.

"There was also an empty bottle of cider nearby," Rosemary was saying. "Toby says glass is very good for fingerprints, so we brought that away."

"What sort of cider, dear?"

"Autumn Gold."

"I knew it." Audrey vibrated with excitement. "I've seen them drinking it in the bus shelter. They leave the empty bottles there—"

"It's in Daddy's study if you need it. Toby says that it could be important if the fur turns out to be Lord Peter's."

"How very thoughtful of him," Audrey said. "He sounds a very nice young man."

"Yes," said Rosemary; and paragraphs were compressed into that monosyllable.

Vanessa cast a longing glance at the coffee pot. "Well, now that's settled, should we—?"

"The evidence is beginning to build up," Audrey announced. "I've been approaching the case from another angle. And I've managed to uncover another piece of evidence." She paused for an instant, as if expecting a round of applause. "I happened to be in Malik's Minimarket this morning, and Doris Potter was there. A very good sort of woman . . . She was asking me about Lord Peter. People are so kind. Even Mr. Malik expressed his sympathy, and being Muslim—or is it Hindu?—he can't really be expected to appreciate how terrible it all is. But at least he tried. Where was I? Doris. Yes, she actually popped into church on Thursday afternoon. Heaven knows why—it's not her week for the flowers and she's not on the cleaning rota at all." The possibility that Doris might have some other purpose in going to church had eluded Audrey. "She was on her way to Lady Youlgreave's. So she thinks it must have been about four. The point is, she's absolutely sure that Lord Peter wasn't in the porch then. She remembers looking at one of the notices, the one about South Africa, when she came out. So—that's useful, isn't it? Slowly we're building up a picture. I know we still have an awful lot to learn. But at least we know that Lord Peter was brought to church sometime between four o'clock and seven o'clock on Thursday evening." She beamed at Rosemary, revealing teeth to which clung small yellow specks, perhaps corn flakes. "And if we put that information together with what you've found out, dear, it's possible that whoever did it came into the churchyard by the gate into Roth Park rather than from the road." Once again she hesitated. Then she added, with a devastating lack of subtlety, "What time exactly did the Cliffords arrive here in the evening?"

The rest of the weekend was quiet. On Saturday afternoon I drafted a sermon which after tea I redrafted because on reading it seemed abstruse and pompous. I had planned to spend some of the evening tracking down the origin of the phrase which presumably had given Francis Youlgreave the title of his poem: *Cursed is he that perverteth the judgement of the stranger, the fatherless, and widow.* In the event, however, I spent most of the evening at the bedside of a man who eventually died shortly after midnight. Neither he nor his wife was a churchgoer, which led later to a heated argument with Rosemary, who could not understand why these people were as much my responsibility as Audrey Oliphant or Doris Potter.

On Sunday, I celebrated Communion twice in the morning, dozed after lunch and conducted Evensong. I went to bed early.

Externally the pattern was familiar and comforting. But my mind was less placid than I would have liked. I thought a great deal about the Cliffords. Where had their money come from? Who had their parents been? Was their father alive? I found that I could visualize the faces of both Toby and Joanna with unusual clarity—Toby's with its bony features, its frizzy curls, and the nostrils permanently flared, which gave him an apparently misleading effect of perpetual disdain. And Joanna—what I remembered most clearly about her was the down on the curve of her cheek and the green eyes with a dark edge to the iris, and the green dappled like a pond under trees on a sunny day. Most of all, I wondered about the relationship between them, whether Toby was all he seemed, and whether Joanna's apparent fear of him was due to calculation, paranoia, or a simple and entirely rational response to a genuine threat. There was Rosemary to consider, too: she seemed to be attracted to Toby.

I tried to talk about some of this with Vanessa on Sunday evening as we were going to bed.

"Puppy love," she said briskly. "Rosemary's too young for him. Nothing to worry about—he seems a perfectly sensible young man so it will probably die a natural death. As for Joanna, from what Toby said, she's had some sort of nervous breakdown. But she'll get over it, I'm sure, with Toby's help. I wish I could warm to her more, though. She's rather off-putting, don't you think?"

I wasn't sure what I thought about Joanna Clifford. What I needed very badly was to talk to my spiritual director about the Cliffords in general and Joanna in particular. But Peter Hudson was out of the country and I had not yet met his successor. To make matters worse, I wasn't sure whether I thought of Peter's absence as a problem or as a stroke of good fortune. I did not really want to talk about the Cliffords with anyone—not with Peter and certainly not with a priest I did not know well. By arranging for Peter's absence at this juncture, it was as if Providence had allowed me to stray briefly into limbo.

"No, Rosemary will be all right," Vanessa went on. "But I'm not so sure about Audrey."

"The Miss Marple business?"

"It's absurd, isn't it?"

"She's so obstinate it's almost magnificent."

Vanessa clicked her tongue against the roof of her mouth. "She's a grown woman, David. There's nothing magnificent in having absolute faith in the forensic wisdom in the novels of Agatha Christie." She glanced at me and her eyelids fluttered. "If you ask me, it's unwise to have absolute faith in *anything*."

I smiled at her. "Are you sure?"

She laughed. "Now you're trying to make a fool of me." That was how matters stood on the morning of Monday, the 17th August. Vanessa and I were in the kitchen preparing breakfast and listening to the eight o'clock news on the radio. Michael was doing his teeth in the bathroom, clearly audible in the kitchen below. Rosemary was still in bed; recently she had taken to sleeping late. The telephone rang.

"I don't think I can stand much more of this," Vanessa hissed at me. Her face had reddened. "They never leave you alone. Can't you let it ring? Just this once."

I already had my hand on the door. "No—I'm afraid I can't."

"But this is an utterly ridiculous time," she snapped, her voice rising. "Tell them you'll ring back."

She glared at me and, God help me, I glared back. I went into the hall, closing the door rather more loudly than I should have done. In a cloud of childish indignation I stormed into the study and picked up the telephone receiver. Outside in the main road, the dustcart had drawn up outside the Vicarage. A dustman dropped the lid of our bin on the ground with a clatter and hoisted the bin itself on to his back.

"The Vicarage."

There was a strangled sound on the other end of the line, which after a moment I identified as sobbing.

I tried to make my voice gentler. "Who is this, please?"

The dustcart drove away. Someone was whistling. On the other end of the line, the sob mutated into a snuffle.

"It's me. Doris."

"What's wrong?"

"She's dead. The old lady's dead." There was a fresh burst of sobbing.

"Doris, I'm so sorry."

The sobbing continued. I had not realized that Doris was quite so attached to her employer; nor would I have said that she was an hysterical woman—quite the reverse. But death is a great revealer.

"You've just found her, I imagine?" There was no reply, except sobbing, but I persevered. "My dear, she was an old lady. It had to happen. Probably sooner rather than later." The familiar platitudes slipped out of my mouth automatically. "She was in a great deal of pain, and there was nothing to look forward to, either." Platitudes have the outstanding advantage of being true. "And think how she would have hated having to go into a home or a hospital. At least she died in her own bed."

"But she didn't," Doris wailed.

"She'd managed to get up in the night, had she?" Perhaps she had wanted her commode. "After the nurse had—"

"I could kill her."

"Who?"

"That nurse. The bloody woman didn't turn up. The old lady's been lying there for days." The voice rose into a wail again, but the words, though distorted, were clear enough. "And the dogs have been eating her."

*Chapter Twenty-Two*

R ONALD TRASK loved committees the way other men love football or train-spotting. He was in his element, especially when he was in the chair. He had the knack of driving his way through the agenda, achieving his own aims while preserving the appearance of democracy. He had become archdeacon two years before; and since then he had invited me to more meetings than his predecessor had done in the previous eight years.

One of Ronald's little gatherings was scheduled for half past ten on the morning of Monday the 17th August. The weather was cool and cloudy. Six of us sat at the round table in the Trasks' dining room. We could see our faces in the polished surface. There were flowers, a carafe of water, glasses, pristine ashtrays and in front of each of us a neatly typed agenda, the work of Cynthia. The details stuck in my mind like pins in a pin cushion—hard, sharp particles of reality embedded in a sponge of uncertainty; I concentrated on them because they left less room for what I had seen an hour earlier at the Old Manor House.

"We are not so much a committee," Ronald informed us, "as a working party."

He and the others murmured soothingly in the background. Our purpose was to examine ways of halting the decline of Sunday School attendance. On two occasions

Ronald tried to draw me into the discussion but without marked success. Afterward, as the others were leaving, he asked me to stay behind for a word. He took me into his study.

"Are you all right, David? I thought you looked a little out of sorts in the meeting."

"I'm sorry—I do have a headache." I couldn't face telling him the details about Lady Youlgreave so I merely added, "Two of my parishioners died over the weekend."

"It's always a bit of a shock, isn't it? Even when the death's expected. Do sit down." Ronald waved me to a chair in front of his desk and hurried on. "Tell me, have you seen any more of the Cliffords?"

"In a manner of speaking, we're neighbors. They're very kindly lending us their paddock for our fete on Saturday week."

"Ah."

"What is it?"

"Don't worry, there's nothing wrong," he said, eyeing me curiously. He settled himself behind the desk, and his fingertips stroked the leather cover of his diary—tenderly, as though it were a woman's skin. "Just grounds for caution."

"What on earth do you mean?"

"We had lunch with the Thurstons yesterday. Victor had been at some Masonic do the night before, and he'd been talking to one of his policeman friends. I thought I'd pass on what he'd told me. Word to the wise, eh?"

"What's wrong with the Cliffords?"

"Nothing's wrong with the children—not as far as I know, nothing for certain, though the boy seems to have some unsavory friends. No, the problem is the parents. Ever heard of Derek Clifford?"

I shook my head.

"Nor had I until yesterday," Ronald went on. "Not the name he was born with, by the way—his parents came from Poland. Apparently, he owned a chain of clubs in London. Little nightclubs, I gather. Most of them had a short life. Nothing was ever proved, but the police were absolutely certain that Clifford was running them as a front for all sorts of other activities— gambling, prostitution, even receiving stolen goods."

"But nothing was proved?"

"Not in a way that would stand up in a court of law. But I understand that there was no real doubt about it."

"Is the father alive?"

"He died last year. The mother died in the spring. There was an inquest." Ronald interlaced his fingers and stared at the ceiling, as if praying, as perhaps he was. "The poor woman was an alcoholic, and on the night in question she'd taken some sleeping pills. She choked on her own vomit. There was some question about the death—whether it was suicide or accident."

I thought of Joanna finding her mother's body.

"And then there's the question of money," Ronald was saying. "I don't know what those young people paid for Roth Park, but presumably the money ultimately came from their father. The odds are, it wasn't honestly come by."

"You can't blame them for that."

"It depends, doesn't it?"

"What do you mean?"

Ronald leaned forward, his elbows resting on the desk, and smiled at me. "It depends on whether the children were involved with their father's activities. Thurston's asked his policeman friend to have a word with a few colleagues in London. Just in case there's something there."

"I don't like it." I stood up. "I'm sorry, Ronald, but it seems as though the Cliffords are being condemned because of hearsay evidence about what their father might or might not have done."

"Condemned?" Ronald stood up as well. "Of course not. My fault—I can't have made myself clear. All I'm saying is that it's wise to take elementary precautions. Especially in our position. Don't you agree?"

"If you say so." I didn't bother to keep the anger from my voice. "Is there anything else?"

"No, not at present." He followed me into the hall. "I'll keep you informed."

We said goodbye. I wondered whether Ronald was doing his job, or using the Cliffords as a way to make my life a little uncomfortable. Or perhaps both—motives are often muddled. As I drove back to Roth, I thought about my reasons for taking an interest in the young Cliffords. I had no right to condemn Ronald or anyone else for mixed motives.

Vanessa was at work so there were three of us for lunch in the Vicarage kitchen. No one was hungry. We nibbled at cold ham and elderly salad.

Afterward, while we were washing up, Rosemary said, "You know this thing about perverting the judgement of strangers—did you have time to look it up?"

"Not yet. It's Old Testament. I'm almost certain it's from Deuteronomy."

"Does it mean muddling strangers?" Michael asked suddenly. "Making visitors confused?"

"No." I smiled at him. "It was about legal disputes in Israel. Widows and orphans and strangers were the vulnerable people in a community."

This seemed to satisfy the curiosity of Rosemary and Michael, but it stimulated mine—and reminded me that I had promised Vanessa to look into the origins of the phrase. After washing up, I took my coffee into the study.

I found the relevant verse in Deuteronomy, Chapter 27, Verse 19. Both the Authorized Version and the Revised Version had an almost identical translation to that in the Prayer Book. I looked out my copy of the Vulgate to check the Latin translation: *Maledictus qui pervertit iudicium advenae pupilli et viduae.* The most recent translation I had on my shelves was the Jerusalem Bible. "A curse on him who tampers with the rights of the stranger, the orphan, and the widow." The notes in the commentary referred me to parallel texts in an earlier chapter of Deuteronomy and to a much earlier one in Exodus, Chapter 23:

> *Thou shalt neither vex a stranger, nor oppress him: for ye were strangers in the land of Egypt. Ye shall not afflict any widow, or fatherless child. If thou afflict them in any wise, and they cry at all unto me, I will surely hear their cry; and my wrath shall wax hot, and I will kill you with the sword; and your wives shall be widows, and your children fatherless.*

I opened a drawer and took out a pad of paper, thinking that I should write a few notes for Vanessa. I knew, of course, that I was trying to distract myself from the thought of Lady

Youlgreave and the implications of her death. This sort of
work was a luxury for me; scholarship could be a snare just as
surely as the more traditional temptations. It occurred to me
as I was uncapping my fountain pen that I was not the only
one looking for distractions. Why else had Rosemary raised
the subject of "The Judgement of Strangers" at lunch? Why
had none of us mentioned the subject of Lady Youlgreave?

I pushed aside the questions and made notes. The Deu-
teronomic legislation of the seventh century BC had been
comparable to the Reformation and Counter-Reformation in
Europe over two thousand years later: a determined attempt
to reform the national religion. The compilers of the book
were intolerant of dissent, but their moral teaching was remarkably humane. The fact that the phrase "perverting justice" was so well established in the Old Testament suggested
that such abuse was a long-running problem.

I turned to the original Hebrew and to the Septuagint, the
most influential of the Greek translations of the Old Testament. The word I wanted to check, the crucial word in the
passage, was *stranger*. In Hebrew the word was *gêr*, which
meant "protected stranger"—in other words, a stranger who
lived under the protection of a family or tribe to which he did
not belong. (The Arabs had a similar word for the protected
stranger, the *jâr*.) The life of a *gêr* could be hard—I made a note
about Jacob's complaint concerning his treatment by Laban
in Genesis 31. A whole clan or family might be *gerim*. The
same distinction was preserved in the Greek of the Septuagint. "Stranger" was not translated by the obvious word, *xe-
nos*, but by *proselutos*, which meant a licensed foreign resident.
Was the implication, I wondered, that complete strangers

were unprotected, that they were the legitimate prey of those whose territory they strayed into?

As I was making a note of these points for Vanessa, I heard a car pulling off the main road into the Vicarage drive. I glanced out of the window and saw an Austin Maxi drawing up. The passenger door opened and Sergeant Clough climbed out, pipe in mouth. Franklyn wriggled out of the driver's side. My tranquillity evaporated. I reached the front door before they did.

"Good afternoon, sir." Clough rubbed his bald head and stared past me into the hall. "Mind if we come in? Just for a quick word."

I took them into the study, and settled them in hard chairs in front of my desk.

"Mrs. Byfield not in? She works, doesn't she?" Clough made the idea sound slightly indecent.

"How can I help you?"

"It's Lady Youlgreave, this time, not the cat." He raised his eyebrows, perhaps signaling that he was making a mild joke; the rest of his face remained serious. "Sad business."

"Indeed."

Franklyn took out his notebook and a pencil.

"Don't mind Frankie taking notes, sir. Just for the record."

"I'm not sure I see how I can help you. I didn't actually find the body—Doris Potter did that. And Dr. Vintner can tell you more about Lady Youlgreave's injuries—he must have arrived about fifteen minutes after I did."

"Oh, we have to look down every avenue, sir. It may be a cul-de-sac, so to speak, but we have to check. You wouldn't believe how much of Frankie's time is spent taking notes that turn out to be absolutely useless. But you never know, do you? You can't take anything for granted."

Clough in his role as homespun philosopher was irritating me. "What exactly do you want to know?"

"I wish I knew, sir—in a manner of speaking, that is. Something and nothing. In cases like this—sad death of old lady, who is already very ill—bound to have happened sooner or later, probably sooner—well, usually there's no problem. Not as far as we're concerned. And there may not be a problem in this case, either. But Dr. Vintner thought that he should have a word with the coroner's officer, and he thought we should have a word with you. In view of the circumstances, you see."

"Which circumstances?"

"Well, first of all: the last person to see the old lady was apparently her cleaning woman, Mrs. Potter. And that was at about seven o'clock on Friday evening. But the body wasn't found till Monday morning. Now that's—"

"One minute," I interrupted. "Why didn't the nurse from the Fishguard Agency go in over the weekend? Mrs. Potter goes in—went in—during the week, Mondays to Fridays. But the agency nurse came in on Saturday and Sunday. Twice a day—morning and early evening."

"But not this weekend, Mr. Byfield." Clough was watching me closely. "Curious, eh? Apparently, Lady Youlgreave phoned the agency on Friday evening—must have been about seven-thirty, they reckon—and said some relations had come to stay for the weekend, and they'd look after her."

"I wasn't aware that Lady Youlgreave had any close relations. But I do know that she didn't like using the telephone."

Clough struck a match and held it over his pipe. The pipe made a gurgling sound. "Why did you go and see the old lady on Friday, sir?"

I did not want to involve myself in explanations concerning the bird table. I could imagine Clough's reaction. Lord Peter had already made me ridiculous enough in the eyes of the police. I took the morally dubious course of avoiding the question while seeming to answer it. "I regularly visited her, Sergeant. It's part of my job to visit the old and infirm."

He nodded, and I had an uneasy sense that I might not have misled him. "How did she seem? In good spirits?"

"As well as could be expected. Dr. Vintner can fill you in on her state of health, if he hasn't already. But she was declining rapidly. She was also in a great deal of pain. But yes, we had a chat, and I left at about half past five."

"How mobile was she? In general, I mean."

"It rather depended how she felt." I could not see where these questions were tending. "She spent most of her time in her bed or in her chair. But she could move about with the help of a walker."

"Could you describe to us exactly what happened this morning? What you saw at the Old Manor House?"

"Everything? I don't understand."

"It was unfortunate, sir. After you and the doctor had been, Mrs. Potter was by herself in the house for upward of an hour. No doubt the poor lady was in a state of shock. Anyway, she started tidying up. Moved the old lady into her chair. Covered her up. Hoovered. When she opened the door to us, she had a duster in her hand."

"Perhaps she didn't realize that she shouldn't move anything."

"The doctor said he'd told her."

"Then," I said, "as you say, it must have been the shock. But why is this so important? Does the coroner think that Lady Youlgreave's death was suspicious?"

"We have to tie up the loose ends." He veered away on a tangent. "Talking of which, how did people get in if they called at the house when Mrs. Potter wasn't there?"

"There's a key hidden at the back of the house. It's been there for years."

"Who knew about it?"

"Anyone who needed to, I imagine. I think Mrs. Potter has her own key, but there are a number of other people who went in regularly, and they would use the key in the kitchen yard if Mrs. Potter wasn't there to let them in. It's under the flowerpot by the door." I paused, assembling the possibilities. "I knew about it, and so did Dr. Vintner and the Fishguard Agency. There's a weekly delivery from Harrods, and I know the man sometimes let himself in when Mrs. Potter wasn't there. And there may well have been others. Do you think that Lady Youlgreave had another visitor after Doris Potter left on Friday evening?"

"I don't know what to think yet, sir. I'm just working out the possibilities. Would Mrs. Byfield know about the key?"

"Yes, she did."

Clough looked at me, waiting for more.

"My wife has been working on Lady Youlgreave's family papers during the last few weeks. She used to sit with Lady Youlgreave in the dining room, and work on them there."

"What about the dogs? How do they react to visitors?"

"They bark if they have the energy." I swallowed. "Too old to do anything else except eat and sleep."

"So if a stranger turned up, they wouldn't have seen him off the premises?"

"I doubt it. They might have barked, but no one outside the house would have heard."

Clough nodded. "And now, could you tell us what happened this morning?"

I leaned back in my chair. "We were having breakfast in the kitchen when Mrs. Potter phoned. It was a little after eight o'clock. She was very upset. But I understood from her that Lady Youlgreave was dead. She said something about the dogs, too, but . . ." I swallowed. "But I thought the shock had made her confused—even hysterical. I phoned Dr. Vintner and then went round to the Old Manor House at once. The dogs were in the back garden. There's an iron gate at the side of the house and they were poking their noses through the bars and barking at the dustmen."

"Did the dustmen know what was happening?"

"Not as far as I know. Their lorry was parked on the road. One of them had just collected the bin by the gate." He had been a grimy little man who had not wanted to meet my eyes. I had said, "Good morning," automatically, but he walked past me as though I were somewhere else; and all the time he whistled "Waltzing Matilda" at a tempo suitable for a funeral.

"And where was Mrs. Potter?"

"She opened the front door before I rang the bell." *Pink-rimmed eyes but no tears. Cheeks pale and lined like crumpled handkerchiefs.* "She took me along to the dining room straight-away and showed me Lady Youlgreave."

Clough was turning his pipe around and around in his hands. "Take your time, sir. Take your time. Tell us exactly what you saw, what the room was like, where the old lady was."

I swallowed again. "She was lying face down on the carpet near the window. Roughly midway between her chair and the fireplace. Her head was by the corner of the fender. The walker was on the hearthrug, lying on its side."

I paused and reached for a cigarette. The room had smelled of feces and urine, human and canine. I saw the telephone on the table and the tin trunk on the floor. Lady Youlgreave's father-in-law glowered down on us from his vantage point above the fireplace.

"She was in her night clothes." *A nightdress, bed socks up to the knee, a dressing gown. Her head lying on its side on the hearthrug, eyes open wide as if in astonishment, and mouth open wide, too, as though snapping at a fly. Bare pink gums. I had never seen Lady Youlgreave without her teeth.* "The nightdress had ridden up, or perhaps the dogs had pushed it up. Up to the waist." *Pale, wrinkled legs; not much strength in them and not much nourishment either. Brown stains, and in those parts which were relatively fleshy, the sight of raw meat.* "The dogs had obviously been starving," I went on slowly. "I suppose that's why James Vintner had to get in touch with the coroner's officer . . . You know what dogs are like when they get old, Sergeant? Often their training begins to slip away from them. Their taboos no longer have the same force. Like humans, really. They had tried to eat her—"

I broke off. Clough stared blandly across the desk at me. Franklyn wrote in his notebook.

"Damn it," I burst out, surprising myself as much as the two policemen. "What have you done with the dogs?"

"Don't you worry about that, sir," Clough said. "We'll look after them for the time being. Now, to go back to this morning: tell me about the rest of the room."

"It was much as usual." Apart from a pile of dogs' excrement beside Lady Youlgreave's armchair.

"Were the curtains drawn across the window?"

"No."

"The table by the chair: was there anything on that?"

"I think there was a book." A slim volume in a green leather binding: *The Voice of Angels*. "I suppose she must have got up after Mrs. Potter left her in bed. Her bedroom's next to the dining room. She probably went in there and read for a bit. And then she stood up and tripped, I imagine."

"Suppose you're right," Clough said. "She stands up. Why should she move toward the fireplace?"

"Her medicine was there."

"Ah. The medicine." Clough scratched the sparse tuft of hair above his right ear. "Now that's interesting. It's in a bottle, right? You know what it looks like?"

I nodded.

"And did you notice it this morning?"

"No. I had other things on my mind." I remembered Lady Youlgreave's hunger for her medicine. "I suppose she was going to give herself a dose, and as she walked toward it, she stumbled on something. The edge of the hearthrug, perhaps."

There was a silence. Something was wrong, and I couldn't put my finger on it. Franklyn yawned. Clough stared over my shoulder and out of the window, his face sad.

"Wait a moment," I said slowly. "When I was there on Friday, Doris said something about leaving her medicine out in the bedroom."

"She did. In three separate glasses to cover the period until the nurse turned up on Saturday morning. But they'd been knocked over."

"So that would explain her going into the dining room?"

Clough did not answer. "Tell me, Mr. Byfield, have you known Mrs. Potter long?"

"A good ten years."

"Reliable, is she?"

"Extremely reliable. She's a regular churchgoer so I know her well. And she's done a great deal for Lady Youlgreave."

"Surely she was paid for that?"

"I don't think the money was particularly important. Lady Youlgreave and Mrs. Potter had known each other for years."

I pulled myself up short, knowing that I was on the verge of becoming angry. In their own way, the two women had been friends; and Doris had given far more than she had ever received. Clough's questions were like a cynical chisel, chipping away at Doris's kindness.

"So Mrs. Potter and the old lady got on well?"

"Very well."

Clough sighed. "We have to ask these questions, sir. I know it must seem tiresome, but there it is."

"Will there be an inquest?"

"Not for me to say, sir. It depends on what the coroner thinks."

I allowed my eyes to stray back to the notes I'd been making for Vanessa. "Is there anything else?"

"No, not at present." Clough stood up and extended his hand to me. "Thank you for your time."

We shook hands and I came around the desk to show them out. As I stood up, I caught movement in the corner of my eye—movement on the other side of the window. I looked out and was just in time to see Michael running to the side of the house. Had he been eavesdropping? The window was open. Clough and Franklyn seemed to have noticed nothing.

I followed them into the hall. "Sergeant?"

Clough turned back. "Yes, sir?"

"Just a couple of points about Miss Oliphant's cat."

"Ah. This won't take long, will it?"

"No. But I thought I should let you know that there was something on Lady Youlgreave's bird table the other day. She told my wife and me that she thought it was a head."

"A *head*?"

"A small one, badly pecked by birds. We wondered if it might have been the cat's."

"Did you have a look?"

"Yes, but by the time I did, there was no trace of it." I paused, then added: "She said someone brought it there in a paper bag."

There was a snuffling sound from Franklyn: barely concealed laughter.

"So who did she say put it there?" Clough said.

"She couldn't or wouldn't say."

"I see." He put his hand on the door handle. "And did you say there was something else?"

"You remember I phoned you about the place where the cat might have been cut up?"

Clough nodded.

"It's called Carter's Meadow. Our local poet, Francis Youlgreave, is said to have cut up a cat in the same place."

After another pause, Clough said, "Thank you, sir. All a bit speculative, if you don't mind me saying so, a bit vague. But I'll bear it in mind." He opened the front door. On the threshold, however, he stopped and turned back to me. "Oh—by the way. You know those young people up at Roth Park? The Cliffords?"

I felt myself tense. "Yes."

"Do you know if they ever met Lady Youlgreave?"

"Not to my knowledge. They've not been living here that long."

"Thank you, sir."

Clough put his hands in his pockets and sauntered toward the car, where Franklyn was unlocking the driver's door. Franklyn was still snuffling happily.

"Why?" I called after him. *First Trask, now Clough.*

"Just wondered," he said over his shoulder. "After all, they were neighbors."

# Chapter Twenty-Three

S HORTLY AFTER THE POLICE LEFT, I went to visit the widow of the man who had died over the weekend. She lived in one of the council houses on Manor Farm Lane, not far from the Potters'. The house was full of relations, and the television was on all the time I was there. I did what I could and left as soon as was decently possible; now that the man was dead and the funeral was arranged, I was no longer wanted.

I walked back along the north side of the green. As I was passing the bus shelter, I heard a voice call my name. Audrey was leaning from the window of her first-floor sitting room.

"Can you spare a moment?" Her face was bright and alert. "One or two points about our fete."

She came down to meet me in the hall. The tea room had just closed, and Charlene Potter was clearing the tables. She gave me a smile as I passed. I followed Audrey upstairs. She settled me in the wing armchair that had been her father's. ("It's a chair meant for a man, don't you think? I never sit in it myself.") She opened the door of her sideboard and took out glasses and a bottle.

"You'll join me in a glass of sherry, won't you?"

"Thank you."

She was already pouring sherry into the glasses. "Such terribly sad news about Lady Youlgreave. Of course, she was very old and I suppose it could have happened at any time—living by herself in that wreck of a house with only those dogs for company." She handed me a brimming glass. "I wonder who will inherit. I believe there are Youlgreave cousins in Herefordshire somewhere, but I don't think they were in touch. And some of them emigrated. New Zealand, was it?" She settled herself in the chair by the window, sighed with satisfaction, and raised her glass. "Chin-chin. She should have gone into a home years ago. She would have had to if Doris hadn't been there. I told Charlene, 'Your mother may think she's doing Lady Youlgreave a kindness,' I said, 'but the poor dear would be much better off in a proper nursing home.' Still, some people just won't be told."

I sipped my sherry.

"Do smoke. It's Liberty Hall here!" Audrey jumped up to fetch me an ashtray. "Charlene tells me you were actually *there*."

"Doris phoned me when she found the body."

"It must have been frightful," Audrey said with relish. "Of course, the police have got it wrong as usual. Typical. I'm not surprised after the way they handled Lord Peter's death."

"What have they got wrong?"

"Apparently they think that Lady Youlgreave was trying to reach her medicine on the mantelpiece, and she tripped. But it can't have happened like that. Charlene was quite upset about it. She thinks the police are trying to blame her mother—for leaving the medicine out on the mantelpiece. But that's nonsense. The whole point of leaving it on the mantelpiece was because Lady Youlgreave couldn't reach it there."

Startled, I said, "But the mantelpiece isn't that high."

"You obviously hadn't seen Lady Youlgreave walk lately."

Audrey wagged a finger at me in playful reproof. "She was bent almost double, apparently—because of the crumbling of the spine or something. And she couldn't raise her arms above her shoulders. That's why they chose the mantelpiece: for the simple reason she couldn't reach it. You know how confused these poor old dears can get about whether or not they've had their medicine."

I had found a cigarette and was patting my pockets, searching for matches. Audrey leaped up again to bring me a light. While she was on her feet, she topped up our sherry glasses.

"And then there's the fact that she canceled the nurse from the Fishguard Agency: *very* puzzling." Audrey sank down again in her chair, sitting more heavily than before, and sipped her sherry. "She didn't like having a nurse, of course. She was only really happy with Doris. But Dr. Vintner made her, for Doris's sake."

"You mentioned something about the fete—"

Audrey was still speaking. "There's also the point that she didn't like using the telephone . . ."

She half closed her eyes and stared out of the window. It was an unnatural pose, as rigid as a waxwork's—and, also like a waxwork, a pose designed with the viewer in mind. I realized suddenly that what I was seeing was the great detective at work: Roth's answer to Miss Marple.

"To my mind, there are two alternatives," Audrey went on. "Either Lady Youlgreave canceled the nurse, intentionally intending to commit suicide over the weekend. Or she canceled the nurse simply because she didn't like her. We have to remember that she was very confused. What with the pain and the morphine she was hardly human any more, was she?"

"We shall all grow old," I said. "Or most of us will. Does that make us any less human?"

Already pink, Audrey's face darkened to red. "Just a figure of speech. I'm as sad as anyone that Lady Youlgreave has passed on. It's the end of an era. The last Youlgreave in Roth. She was so striking as a young woman, too. So dashing. She used to have wonderful parties before the war . . . I was telling Rosemary how she seemed to us children only the other day—Rosemary could hardly believe me."

I stubbed out my cigarette carefully in the ashtray. "It's good of you to let Rosemary spend so much time with you."

"It's a pleasure," Audrey cooed, allowing herself to be diverted from Lady Youlgreave. "Between you and me, I think she's rather lonely. If Vanessa were at home in the week, it would be a different story—but Vanessa is a working woman." She giggled. "So am I: I have always been a career woman and proud of it. But you see, I work at home, and I can choose my own hours. It's been a real pleasure to see more of her this holiday. Such a lovely girl. More sherry?"

"No, thank you." I glanced at my watch. "I really should be—"

"I think I might have a teensy little one." Audrey reached out for the bottle. "Dr. Vintner says that a glass or two of sherry is just the thing to help one unwind after the day's work." The neck of the bottle trembled against the rim of Audrey's glass and a drop of sherry snaked down the curves of glass and stem, slid across the base and formed a miniature puddle on the gleaming surface of the wine table. "She's been terribly useful in my investigation."

"Rosemary has? What's she been doing exactly?"

Audrey dabbed at the puddle of sherry with a lace-trimmed handkerchief. "Nothing to worry about, I promise you. No, she's made one or two useful suggestions about lines of approach. It was her idea that I ask Mr. Malik about who buys his cider. You remember you found a bottle of Autumn Gold with the fur and the blood?"

"I expect dozens of people buy that particular brand of cider."

"Perhaps. But I felt one name was especially significant." She lowered her voice to a hiss: "Kevin Jones—he's Charlene's boyfriend."

"I really think you must be very careful."

"Oh, but I am. I lock up very carefully and I take the poker upstairs with me."

"That's not what I mean. We don't know that the cider bottle had anything to do with what happened to Lord Peter. There's no proof whatsoever. And even if there were, there's no proof that Charlene's young man bought the bottle. And even if he did, it wouldn't follow that he played a part in what happened to Lord Peter."

Audrey waved her glass and the little liquid it contained slopped dangerously near the brim. "I've seen him in the bus shelter. He's one of that gang of louts. He wasn't there when I called the police. But he might have been. And the others were his friends. I hate to say it, but I have to consider the possibility that"—once again she lowered her voice to a conspirator's whisper—"there's a traitor in the camp. Lord Peter trusted Charlene completely. He would have gone anywhere with her."

"Audrey," I snapped. "You must stop this."

She flung herself against the back of her chair, flinching as though I had hit her. "But—"

"I'm serious. For your own sake. Saying this sort of thing without evidence constitutes slander. If you repeat it in public, you might end up in court." I watched her lips tremble and tried to soften my tone. "I don't know Kevin, but Charlene seems the last person to become involved with a business like this."

"Slander? I suppose you're right." She had her face under control once more. "I should have thought of that. It's so infuriating, the difference between knowledge and proof. But those louts must have been involved. Lord Peter's collar was in the bus shelter. You can't get away from that."

I looked at my watch, more openly this time. "Dear me." I pantomimed mild shock. "Time's getting on. Now, what did you want to discuss about the fete?"

Audrey swallowed and for a moment I thought she would take the change of subject as a reproof. Instead she smiled. "Dear Rosemary. A wise head on young shoulders. I would never have thought of it. It's the car parking."

"I thought we'd sorted that out."

"Rosemary reminded me that last year we had a number of people who parked on the double yellow lines round the green. Do you remember? The police were rather annoyed. Nowadays, every Tom, Dick and Harry has his own car. None of them walks anywhere at all, as far as I can see. Rosemary wondered whether the Cliffords would let us use the verge of their drive as an overflow car park once the paddock's filled up. I know we asked the Bramleys one year, and they said no, because they felt it would upset their residents. (They always said that when they didn't want to do something.) But the Cliffords are quite a different kettle of fish. Rosemary said she was quite friendly with them so she would ask them. I said, how splendid, naturally—I didn't want to hurt her pride. But I did wonder if the request might come better from you."

I put down my empty glass very carefully on the table. "I'll see if I can have a word with them."

"That would be marvelous. And do you think you could also manage to see how many cars might fit? I know it can only be an estimate, but it would be a help. I've already added 'Car Parking' to next week's advertisement in the paper."

I promised I would see what I could do. Audrey had always been inclined to fuss about the details of the fete, but this year she was fussing even more than usual.

I stood up, determined to leave. She took me downstairs, chattering brightly about James Vintner's barbecue ("I hope it won't encourage the wrong sort of people") and the enormous quantity of home-made cakes which had been promised for the cake stall. As we reached the hall, the kitchen door opened and Charlene came out with a handbag draped over her arm. She had taken off her overall.

"Are you off home?" Audrey asked. "Already?"

"It's after half past six," said Charlene. "Everything's cleared. The tea towels are soaking in the sink."

"I see," Audrey said darkly, and paused as if searching for some flaw or omission in this. "Good. Well, see you tomorrow. Are you and your young man going out tonight?"

Charlene shot her a wary glance. "Maybe."

"Well, be careful," Audrey said enigmatically. "That's all I ask."

I stood aside to let Charlene go first.

Audrey brought her head close to my ear. I could smell sweat on her body and sherry on her breath. "Such a coarse girl," she hissed. "And quite untrainable. My poor mother would be turning in her grave."

"Thank you so much for the sherry," I said. "I'll let you know about the car parking as soon as I can."

We said goodbye. Audrey waved from the doorway as I walked through the little front garden and up the steps to the wrought-iron gate. Only when I was on the pavement did the door close at last.

Charlene was standing outside Malik's Minimarket, apparently studying the window display. As the door closed, she looked at me.

"Mr. Byfield? Could you spare a minute?"

I smiled at her. "Of course." I wondered if I would ever get home that evening. "What is it?"

"Would you—would you mind coming over here?" She beckoned me toward where she was standing. When we were both in front of the shop window, she went on, "It's only that Miss Oliphant will see us standing outside her gate, and she'll wonder what we're talking about."   .

"Would that be awkward?"

"She'd badger me tomorrow until I'd told her what it was about."

We stood side by side, staring at an array of cereal packets. Neither of us said anything, but it was not an uncomfortable silence. She snapped open her bag, took out a packet of cigarettes. "Do you mind?"

"No." I shook my head when she offered me the packet.

"She doesn't let me smoke on the premises." Charlene grinned up at me, suddenly wicked. "It's not ladylike. Nor's smoking in public."

I nodded, and waited.

"Don't get me wrong," Charlene told the cereal packets. "She's been good to me, really. Her bark's worse than her bite."

*Like Beauty and Beast?*

"The thing is, I'm worried about her. I told Mum about it last night, and she said the best thing to do was have a word with you." Charlene shot off on a tangent. "Poor Mum. She's really knocked sideways."

Doris was someone else I should see. In a sense she was the one most affected by Lady Youlgreave's death: the principal mourner. Those who care for dependent persons become themselves dependent. And Doris and Lady Youlgreave had been friends, though perhaps neither would have used the word in relation to the other.

"Miss Oliphant's always had her little ways. You know, going on about how things have changed since she was a little girl. And—and things like that." Charlene glanced up at me to see how I was taking this. "But these last few months she's been different. Now she's always up and down. Right up and right down. And since her cat went, it's got even worse. She talks to herself, you know—she never used to do that. And once or twice she's shouted at me, really screamed. I don't think she's eating much, either. And she gets these ideas in her head—like she thinks the kids are after her."

"And are they?"

Charlene looked startled. "They've got better things to do.

Mind you, she's not their favorite person. But that's neither here nor there. What worries me is, she really seems to think she's some sort of detective. Like in them books she reads." Charlene's voice slid into high-pitched, genteel mimicry. "It was the butler did it in the library. With the lead piping. And—Mr. Byfield—don't think I'm talking out of turn, but I don't think Rosemary's helping. She's sort of encouraging her."

"What do you mean?" I knew I must have spoken sharply by the expression on Charlene's face. "How?"

"You know," she mumbled. "Looking for clues. Stuff like that."

"Clues about what happened to Lord Peter?"

Charlene nodded.

"Yes, I know something about that," I said. "Don't worry. I'll have a word with Rosemary, and we'll all keep an eye on Miss Oliphant."

A moment later, I said goodbye and walked home. I was aware that I had not handled the interview well. I liked Charlene, but I thought it likely she was exaggerating. In every parish there tends to be at least one unmarried, churchgoing middle-aged lady who occasionally acts oddly; there are men, too, for that matter; and the older they get, the more oddly they tend to behave. But in ninety-nine cases out of a hundred, it was nothing more than harmless eccentricity. Why should Audrey be any different?

Vanessa's car was in the Vicarage drive. I let myself into the house. Michael was watching television in the sitting room.

"Hello. Where is everyone?"

"Rosemary's out still," he said. "Aunt Vanessa's upstairs."

I was about to leave when a thought delayed me. "Michael?"

He dragged his eyes away from the gray figures flickering on the screen. I had intended to ask him if he had been listening to my conversation with Clough and Franklyn earlier this afternoon. Suddenly I no longer wanted to. It would be tantamount to making an accusation. The boy had probably just been playing a game. Nor was it likely that he would have heard much, even if he had been eavesdropping. Clough and I were both relatively soft-spoken.

The phone rang, giving me the excuse I needed.

"Nothing." I smiled at him and went into the study. It was James Vintner, sounding harassed.

"Have you heard?" he said.

"Heard what?"

"There's going to be an inquest."

"When?"

"Wednesday, probably. Waste of an entire afternoon."

"Do you know if I'm likely to be called as a witness?"

"I doubt it. If they wanted you, I think they would have been in touch by now. But I thought I'd better warn you."

"You don't think—?"

"I don't think anything. In normal circumstances I'd have certified the death without another thought. Old lady, I'd seen her in the morning of the day she died. Terminally ill. Has a fall, and off she goes: all very sad, but just like dozens of other old ladies. Nothing suspicious about it."

"So why aren't these normal circumstances?"

"Ask your Mrs. Potter. It's all her fault. Her and those

damned dogs." He hesitated. "Sorry to sound off like this. It's been a long day. And I don't like it when my patients die." He cleared his throat, perhaps aware that for once he had openly admitted that he cared about his job. He added hurriedly, "Especially the private ones. Like gold dust, these days."

A moment later we said goodbye. I went upstairs. Vanessa was in our room, sitting on the bed and staring grimly into space.

"That was James," I said. "There's going to be an inquest on Lady Youlgreave."

She nodded but did not reply.

"What is it?"

She turned her head to look at me. "Nothing, really. I suppose it's her dying. It seems strange that I won't be able to go and sit in her dining room any more."

"I suppose it may cause problems with the book."

"It's not just that."

"Then what is it?"

Vanessa glared at me. She said, "Oh God," and began to cry quietly. I sat down beside her on the bed and put my arms around her. She leaned against me. I hugged her, feeling her warmth. Desire stirred inside me and began to uncoil. Gradually she relaxed, and the tears stopped.

I stroked her back, running my fingertips down the knobs of her spine. How many weeks was it since we last made love?

"Vanessa?"

She pulled herself gently away from me. "I need to blow my nose," she said. "And then I really must do something about supper."

*Chapter Twenty-Four*

ON TUESDAY MORNING, I waited until I had the house to myself.

Vanessa went to work. Half an hour later, Rosemary left to catch a bus—she was going into London to spend the day with a schoolfriend. Michael had already gone to spend the day with the Vintners. He and Brian had an ambitious project to build a tree house in the back garden. I had two hours before my first engagement of the day, a routine meeting with the diocesan surveyor.

When I was alone, I went into the study, shut the door and telephoned Roth Park. I wondered if I had a temperature. I felt unlike myself—excited, and almost furtive. I let the phone ring on. I was on the verge of hanging up when Joanna answered.

I apologized for disturbing her and asked if we could use the drive as an overflow car park at the fete.

"Of course you can. You can park anywhere you like." It was almost ten o'clock yet she sounded half asleep. "It's not exactly going to harm the lawn or damage the flowers."

"Should I check with Toby that it's all right for us to park in the drive?"

"Toby's not here. Anyway, it's nothing to do with him."

"I beg your pardon?"

"It's my house," Joanna said, her voice suddenly distorted

as though she were yawning. "My land. Nothing to do with Toby."

"I see. I wonder—would it be convenient for me to walk up the drive and estimate how many cars there'd be room for? Audrey Oliphant feels it's important to have a good idea."

"Now?"

"If it's not inconvenient."

"You know the oak trees near the paddock?" she asked. "I'll be there in about ten minutes."

I hesitated too long. "There's no need for you to come."

"I'd like some air. Besides, I—I need to see where the parking will be. Just in case there's a problem."

We said goodbye and I put down the phone. I observed my own symptoms with a proper scholarly detachment: with perfect propriety, I was making arrangements for the church fete; yet I felt guilty: almost as though I had arranged a furtive assignation.

It was a sunny morning, a relatively rare occurrence in that dreary August. I strolled through the churchyard and into Roth Park. A moment later I reached the oaks. I leaned against a tree trunk and smoked a cigarette. From where I was standing I could see the rutted drive; I followed it with my eye as it curved around the hillock that concealed the house. It was very peaceful. Such moments of leisure were a rarity in my life. The only things moving were the smoke from my cigarette and a few wispy, almost transparent shreds of cloud high in the blue sky. In the real country, there would have been birds, and there would not have been the omnipresent rumble of traffic. But for the time being this would do very well.

Then I saw Joanna on the drive. She raised her hand in greeting and I waved back. I threw away my cigarette and watched her approaching. She wore a thin cotton dress that came down almost to her ankles. Her hair was loose. As she drew closer, I saw that her feet were bare. Closer still, I saw that she wore no make-up and her eyes were smudged with tiredness. She looked up at me with those green eyes with their dark rims and their fragmented depths, shifting like a kaleidoscope. For a moment I did not know what to say. All I knew was that I should not have come. I was in danger. Joanna was in danger, too.

"Can I scrounge a fag?"

I gave her a cigarette and lit it for her. She touched my hand, quite unselfconsciously, to steady the flame. That was good, I told myself: if she had been aware of what I was feeling, she would have avoided touching me.

"I must get some more from Malik's," she said. "Typical Toby. Drove off this morning with the last packet of cigarettes in the house."

"Where's he gone?"

She shrugged, then yawned. "Sorry. Can't stop yawning this morning."

"Didn't you sleep well?"

She smiled, slyly. "I tried not to sleep at all."

"Why?"

"I wanted to find out if the ghost would come back. You remember? The footsteps? So I took something to help me stay awake and I waited. But nothing happened. Except I grew more and more scared." She turned aside to stub out the half-smoked cigarette on the bark of a tree. "I didn't see anything, or hear anything. But I felt something." She swung back to face me. "Something waiting. Silly, isn't it?"

"Fear isn't silly. It's frightening."

She nodded.

"What about Toby?"

"What about him? As far as I know he slept all night. I heard the car start up a little after nine. Off he went. No note, no cigarettes."

"Did he know you were staying awake?"

"He'd have laughed at me. Especially after the fuss I made the other night."

I wasn't sure whether she liked or disliked her brother. "Perhaps the other night was a bad dream. Sometimes one can have these dreams between sleeping and waking."

She shook her head vigorously. "David—could you do something about it? Say some special prayers. What do you call it? Exorcism?"

"I could come and say some prayers, if you wanted."

"Would you? It can't do any harm."

I felt my hackles rising. "It can only do good."

"Oh God—I'm sorry. And I didn't mean to say that, either." She looked so contrite standing there in the dappled shade of the trees. "Double sorry."

"It's all right. Do you want to do it now?"

"Don't you need equipment?"

"The candle, book and bell?" I smiled at her. "We save those for special occasions. To be honest, I don't know much about exorcisms. I think the diocese might have an official exorcist, who goes where the bishop tells him. But full-dress exorcisms are very rare these days. Something less formal will often do the trick just as well."

She giggled. "You make it sound so normal."

"In a sense it is."

We walked up the drive to the house. Joanna speculated about the number of cars they could fit in. "At least another fifty if we use the bit outside the front door." While she was talking, I told myself that I was only doing my duty: my duty as a priest. We reached the dry fountain commemorating the visit of Queen Adelaide. Joanna stopped and leaned against the worn stone of the basin. She stared up at the facade of the house.

"Ugly place, isn't it?"

"Why did you buy it, then?"

"Toby wanted to." She glanced up at me through long lashes, as if assessing the effect of her words. "He can be very persuasive. He said it would be a good investment. He said I needed to get away from London." Suddenly her voice rose, and she turned to face me. "He's told you, hasn't he?"

"He told me that your mother committed suicide," I said. "And that you found the body."

For a long moment we stared at each other. Then she dropped her eyes.

"Did he tell you that after that I was ill?"

"Yes."

"It's not true. I wasn't ill. He likes to tell people I've had a nervous breakdown. He likes to hint I'm mad. I bet he's done it with you." She paused, but I said nothing. She went on, speaking slowly and carefully: "He gives the impression that he's looking after me out of the kindness of his heart. That without him I'd just fall apart. That I'm something fragile that he has to treat very carefully."

"And you're not?"

"Do I look fragile?" she demanded.

I shook my head. *Yet you hear ghosts.* "Then why does he do it?"

"I told you. He likes to. It makes him feel good." She shivered. "Let's go inside and get this over with."

We walked toward the front door, our footsteps loud on the gravel. The door closed behind us with a dull boom like distant thunder. The house was cool and silent.

Joanna said, "Should I offer you coffee or something?"

"No. This isn't a social call."

She looked at me again—why did she keep on looking at me?—and I hoped that she could not see too far. There's no fool like a middle-aged fool: old enough to know better, and young enough to do something about it.

I followed her upstairs, watching her dress frothing and whispering above her ankles. At the mezzanine level there was a window, and as Joanna walked past it, with the light beyond her, her body was outlined through the dress, just as Vanessa's had been all those months ago at the Trasks' party. History has a habit of almost repeating itself, like the pattern in a hand-woven carpet.

"It's quite a long walk," Joanna said over her shoulder. "I'm glad I wasn't a maid in those days. It must have been sheer hell."

"I've never been upstairs before." I wanted to bite the words back. They seemed loaded with hidden meanings.

We reached the main landing. A long corridor stretched

into the heart of the house, its boards uncarpeted, the plaster bulging and cracking on walls like a relief map of the desert.

"It's less posh than downstairs," Joanna said. "I reckon the Youlgreaves ran out of money." We walked together down the corridor, our footsteps setting up a drumming in the silence. "I don't know why they needed a house this big. It's stupid. I'd much rather live somewhere smaller."

"Why don't you?"

She shrugged.

I wanted to ask: *Has Toby some way of keeping you here? Why did you buy this house for him?* But of course I did not.

"Mind the hole," Joanna said, steering me around it. "Toby put his foot through there the other morning. Woodworm."

"Are you going to start renovating soon?"

"We need more money. Toby wants to find an investor." She glanced at me. "When Dad died, the money was left in trust to Toby and me. Mum had the use of it while she was alive. But Toby borrowed against it; he had this company which was importing stuff from India. But it didn't work out. When Mum died, he had to use his share to pay off his debts."

I felt rather embarrassed. Englishmen do not like talking about money. Joanna stopped at a door near the end of the corridor. "We're in the tower bit now." She opened the door and we went into a large square room with windows on three sides. "I always wanted to live in a tower." She led the way to another door in the corner. Beyond it was a spiral staircase with uncarpeted wooden treads. The stairs were lit by narrow windows like anachronistic arrow slits designed with dwarfs in mind. "I'm on the floor above. And the floor above that is the top room. Francis Youlgreave's room."

"Who told you that?"

"Toby." She was already climbing the stairs and her voice floated down to me. "He mentioned it again last night."

*To scare her?*

We came to an open door. My first impression was that emptiness and light lay beyond it. The room was square, with a round-headed sash window in each wall. The wallpaper—stylized golden tulips on a faded blue background, perhaps as old as the house—was beginning to part company from the walls. In the opposite corner from the door was a plain, cast-iron fireplace, the grate littered with cigarette ends and ash. A carpet designed for a suburban sitting room filled about a third of the floor; the rest was bare boards. On the carpet, as if on a castaway's raft, were Joanna's belongings—a mattress, the radio I had seen her with on the terrace, a green trunk, a pair of suitcases, an archipelago of discarded clothes, an ornate walnut-veneered dressing table with a tall mirror attached to it. The top of the dressing table was littered with cosmetics, paperbacks and an overflowing ashtray. The room smelled of a powerful, crude perfume, which overlaid another smell, sweet and spicy, reminding me of Indian food.

"It's a bit of a tip, I'm afraid." Joanna gave me a crooked smile—one corner of her mouth turned up and the other turned down. "If I'd known you were coming, I'd have done something about it."

"It doesn't matter."

The bedroom was like a glimpse behind a drawn curtain. Rosemary and Vanessa were both tidy people. Their bedrooms showed only that they disliked clutter and knew how to control it. Joanna's made a present of her personality to a visitor, and I was touched. For a moment I felt young and full of daring. For a moment it amused me to imagine what Audrey Oliphant or Cynthia Trask would make of my situation.

I walked to the window and looked down on the drive, on the roof of the canopy over the front door with its slipped slates and its outcrops of moss like green pimples. The knowledge of my indiscretion sank in: a middle-aged clergyman alone with an attractive young woman in her bedroom. I turned back, eager to finish what had been started. Joanna was still standing just inside the doorway, watching me.

"What will you do?" she asked.

"Just say a prayer."

"OK."

I fancied that she looked disappointed, as if she had been hoping for something more dramatic. She bowed her head and I prayed for the room to be filled with God's peace. Then I invited Joanna to join me in the Lord's Prayer. Her voice stumbled softly after mine, like a distant echo.

When it was over, she said, "Is that all?"

"Yes. Shall we go upstairs?"

She nodded, and without a word slipped out of the room. I followed her up the spiral staircase. Our footsteps thudded on the bare wood. I kept my eyes on Joanna's ankles, pale and flickering before me. At the top was a tiny landing, barely large enough for one person, and a closed door. It seemed colder to me here than it had been on the floor below.

Joanna twisted the handle and pushed open the door. The room was a copy of hers—the same dimensions, the same round-headed sash windows, the same cast-iron fireplace. One of the windows was slightly open—the one overlooking the canopy and the fountain; and I had the foolish thought that this must have been the one from which Francis Youlgreave jumped into the arms of his angel. The wallpaper was modern—flowers once more, but psychedelic daisies in turquoise and orange.

I moved slowly into the center of the room. It was empty— no furniture, no carpet, no dust on the bare boards. Francis Youlgreave had left behind him a vacuum, waiting to be filled.

"Well?" Joanna was standing by the fireplace, the fingers of her right hand kneading the flesh of her left forearm. "What do you think? Can you feel anything?"

"No." The room was merely a room, somehow incomplete like all unused rooms, but nothing more than that. "Can you?"

"I don't know what I feel any more."

Suddenly I wanted to be gone—away from this house and away from Joanna. In a brisk voice, I repeated the prayer asking for God's peace. Once again I said the Lord's Prayer, galloping through the familiar words with Joanna's voice stumbling after mine. I wondered whether to say another prayer, one specifically for Francis Youlgreave. I glanced at Joanna. She was still clutching her arm, but the fingers were still. Her eyes met mine. She stared at me as if I were a stranger— or, for that matter, a ghost.

"Did you hear that?" she asked.

"What?"

She took a step toward me, stopped and looked over her shoulder. "I thought I heard someone crying. A child." She held up a hand, and for thirty seconds we listened to the silence. Then she shook her head. "It's stopped." She took a step toward me, and then another, and another; her feet faltered; as if each footstep required a separate decision, and as if sometimes the decisions were unwelcome. She stopped a few feet away from me and raised her face to mine. "Do you think I imagined it?"

"I don't know." I wished she would look away from me. "Perhaps."

"Do you think I'm mad?"

"Of course you're not." I took a step backward. "Now—"

"David," she interrupted.

I looked at her. Once, years ago, driving late on a winter night across the Fens to Rosington, I almost ran over a young badger who was playing in the middle of the road. The car went into a skid but stopped in time. For a long moment the badger did not move: he stared into the beam of my headlights.

"It's so strange . . ." Joanna whispered.

Another silence grew between us, and I did not know how long it went on for. What was so strange? This house? The crying child? Francis Youlgreave? Or even the two of us alone in this room?

We did not move. There was a hair on Joanna's cheek, and I wanted desperately to brush it away. Then I heard, or thought I heard, the beating of distant wings on the edge of my hearing. In my mind I saw the badger abruptly recollecting himself and stumbling into the darkness of the verge.

"I must go. Goodbye."

Without another word, I scuttled out of the room and almost ran down the stairs.

## Chapter Twenty-Five

THE INQUEST was at 2:3o p.m. on Wednesday the 19th August. I myself was not called as a witness, but I drove Doris Potter there.

The proceedings did not take long. The coroner was an elderly doctor named Chilbert, a sharp man who kept glancing at his watch as if impatient to be gone. There was a jury of seven men and three women—two in their twenties, two in their sixties, and the remainder scattered between; the only thing they had in common was an expression of wary self-consciousness, but even that wore off as the proceedings continued.

Dr. Vintner was the first witness to be called. He gave evidence of Lady Youlgreave's identity. Then Chilbert took him through her recent medical history. James had seen a good deal of her because she had a terminal malignancy—breast cancer. It was clear that he thought she could have died at any time in the last few months. He described how he had tried and failed to persuade her to move into a nursing home. Her mind had been increasingly confused, he said, because of the morphine. It was true that osteoarthritis of the shoulders had made it impossible for her to raise her arms. But she had been quite capable of forgetting that she could not reach the bottle on the mantelpiece.

Beside me, Doris sucked in her breath.

The pathologist's report confirmed what James had said.

He said that Lady Youlgreave had fractured her skull when she fell, probably on the corner of the hearth. There was a laceration with swelling and bruising around it. Her injuries were entirely consistent with her having tripped on the hearth-rug. Finally, he briefly described the postmortem damage inflicted by Beauty and Beast—but in technically obscure vocabulary designed, I suspected, to confuse the two journalists in the public gallery.

The coroner nodded with monotonous regularity while James and the pathologist were speaking. But he stopped nodding when he questioned Doris, the next witness to be called. She was trembling and her voice shook. But she insisted that Lady Youlgreave, however confused about other matters, knew that she could not reach her medicine. She also mentioned her employer's dislike of using the phone.

Chilbert screwed up his lips and then said, "In general, no doubt you're right, Mrs. Potter. But we have just heard from Dr. Vintner how muddled Lady Youlgreave had become." He glanced at James as if drawing support from a colleague. "It's a sad truth, but people in her condition do deteriorate. So I find it hard to believe that her behavior was still predictable by normal standards. In fact—"

"But, sir, I—"

"This is a medical question, Mrs. Potter, and we should leave it to those competent to answer it." Chilbert raised a heavy eyebrow. "You're not a doctor of medicine, I take it?"

"But why would she want to say her cousins were coming?"

"Who knows? She may have dreamed that they were. But we're not here to speculate. Now, perhaps you would like to tell us why you moved Lady Youlgreave's body and tidied the room before the police arrived?"

She shrugged. "I just did it. It seemed right. She would have liked to be decent."

"You should have left everything as it was."

"Left the dogs in there with her, do you mean? Left her all uncovered for all those men to see? She wouldn't have wanted them to see her like that."

Chilbert looked at Doris's flushed face and—showing more wisdom than I had credited him with—told her she could stand down. Next he talked to the teenager who had taken Lady Youlgreave's call canceling the nurse. The teenager's mother ran the Fishguard Agency, but she had been away. The boy, younger than Rosemary, was quite definite about the time of the call.

"What did the caller sound like?" Chilbert asked.

"I don't know. An old lady, I suppose. She said she was Lady Youlgreave."

"What exactly did she say to you?"

"Her cousins had come down for the weekend. Out of the blue, like. And they were going to look after her so she didn't need the nurse to call until the weekend afterward."

"So what did you do?"

"I phoned the nurse and canceled her." Stolid as a suet pudding, the boy stared up at Chilbert. "I knew what to do. I often look after the phone when Mum's out, and there's always people ringing up to change things."

Sergeant Clough confirmed that there had been a call from the Old Manor House to the agency number at that time on Friday evening. His bald scalp gleaming in the striplight above his head, he emphasized that there had been no sign of a break-in.

The coroner reminded the jury that the probable time of death was Friday evening: the agency nurse had been due at 7:45 a.m. on Saturday morning so, even if she had come, she could not have prevented Lady Youlgreave's death. The jury, suitably instructed, returned a verdict of accidental death.

Afterward, Doris and I walked back to the car.

"I don't believe it," she said. "She wouldn't have phoned the agency."

"But she must have done. They traced the call."

"Anyone could have got in. Everyone knew where the key was."

"I know it's hard to accept," I said, "but I have to say that I think the verdict is probably right. People do odd things. Especially when they're old and confused. And there was nothing to suggest otherwise, was there?"

She screwed up her mouth like an obstinate child, but said nothing.

"I know it was ghastly," I went on, unlocking the door of the car, "and the fact you found her like that was even worse." I held open the door for her. "Wretched animals."

Doris scrambled inelegantly into the passenger seat. "What's going to happen to them?"

"The dogs? I imagine they'll be put down."

"No." Doris's head snapped up, and she looked at me, her face outraged as though I had hit her. "They mustn't be put down. Can't I have them?"

"But, Doris—look, they should have been put down years ago."

"I'd like them. They'd be all right with me."

"I'm sure they would. But have you considered—?"

"They know me. I remember Beaut when she was a puppy."

"They need a great deal of care. Then there's vets' bills as well. And really, wouldn't it be kinder to them if they were put down?"

"How do you know? Most people don't want to die, even when they're old and ill. Why should animals be any different?"

I looked down at her and remembered the high moral tone I had taken when Audrey was a little less than charitable about old people. "You must do what you think best. And let me know if there's anything I can do to help."

"How do I set about getting them?"

"Lady Youlgreave's solicitor is the person to ask about that."

"Mr. Deakin."

"He'll know. In theory I suppose the dogs now belong to Lady Youlgreave's heirs. But I can't believe they'd object to your having them."

Doris nodded. "Thank you."

We drove back to Roth. I turned into Manor Farm Lane and drew up outside the little house she shared with her husband, and with Charlene and Charlene's two younger brothers. I tried and failed to imagine what effect the addition of Beauty and Beast to their ménage would have. Doris did not get out. I fumbled for my own door handle, intending to walk around and open the passenger door for her.

"Vicar?"

"Yes?"

Doris was sitting upright in the seat, her fingers gripping the strap of her handbag. "There's something I maybe should have told them."

"Told whom?"

"The police. That coroner."

I stared at her, alarm creeping over me. "What do you mean? Something to do with Lady Youlgreave?"

"On Friday—as I was going—she wanted me to put some stuff in the dustbin. I always move the dustbin just before I go, you see, put it by the gate. It's not something the nurse would want to do, and sometimes the dustmen come early on Monday, before I get there."

"So why was this any different?"

She turned to look at me. "It was some stuff from the tin box. You know, the one Mrs. Byfield's been looking at. Not all of it—just a few of them notebooks and letters and things."

"But they were family papers, Doris. They might have been important."

She shook her head. "Lady Youlgreave said this was stuff no one wanted."

"I don't think she was necessarily the best judge."

"But she wanted me to throw them away so badly. Said it was nasty." Doris's face was miserable. "She was crying, Vicar. Like a child. And when all's said and done, what did they matter? She was all upset, and they were only papers."

"You could have taken them away," I suggested, trying to speak gently. "And then perhaps discussed what to do with—"

"She made me promise I'd do it. It was the only way to stop

her crying." Doris stared defiantly at me. "I don't break promises."

There was a silence in the car. I bowed my head.

"No," I said at last. "Of course you don't."

"But should I have told the police? Or should I tell them now?"

I thought for a moment. "I don't think so." It would only complicate matters. The information would not have affected the verdict: it merely confirmed Lady Youlgreave's confused mental state. "Perhaps I should have a word with my wife. She may be able to tell if anything significant is missing. If necessary we can mention what happened to the solicitor."

"All right." Doris opened the car door. "Thanks for the lift." Before she shut the door she turned back to me and added, "She did it for the best, you know. It wouldn't have been nice for the Youlgreaves, she said, and she didn't want your wife to see. Not *suitable*. That's what she said, Vicar. Not *suitable*."

Doris slammed the door. I watched her walking with a suggestion of a waddle up the concrete path to her front door. I wondered which of Francis's shabby little scandals Lady Youlgreave had wanted to conceal.

I drove home. As I had expected, there was no one at the Vicarage. Vanessa was still at work. Michael was out with Brian Vintner. Rosemary had announced at breakfast that she was going up to London again, with the same schoolfriend. I was relieved. I was not used to sharing a house with three people, and the longer the summer went on, the more the attractions of solitude increased.

I took off my jacket and tie and dropped them on a chair in

the study. I put the kettle on and went to the lavatory. In mid-performance, the doorbell rang. I swore. Hastily buttoning myself up, I rinsed my hands and went to answer the door. It was Audrey. Some people have a talent for arriving inconveniently which amounts to genius.

Pink and quivering, she advanced toward me, forcing me to step back. A moment later, she was in the hall beside me. She was wearing a dress of some synthetic, shiny material—a loud check in turquoise and yellow. The dress clung to her like a second skin. I noticed smears of mud on her stockings. Her jowls trembled.

"I'm sorry, David. I've come to complain."

I blinked. "What about?"

"That boy. Michael. I know he's your godson. I know his parents are great friends of yours. But I just can't put up with it."

"But what's he been doing?"

"Spying on me. I was walking in the park yesterday afternoon and there he was. I kept seeing his face peering at me round trees or through bushes." She hesitated, her jaws moving as though she were chewing over the insult. "And this afternoon he's been doing the same thing."

"In Roth Park?"

She flushed. "I'd been taking a little exercise after lunch. I've not been sleeping well lately."

I wondered if the unaccustomed exercise had something to do with her detective work. "The footpaths are public rights of way, Audrey. Perhaps Michael was playing there. There's no reason why he shouldn't have been there as well as you."

"He was snooping. Him and that nasty Brian Vintner. I won't put up with it."

I felt a rush of anger. "I don't think Michael's the sort of boy who would snoop."

She glared up at me. "Are you saying I'm a liar?"

"Of course not." I stared at her, realizing how close I had come to losing my temper and realizing how inappropriate my behavior was. "I'm sorry. I shouldn't have spoken like that."

She grunted. To my dismay, I saw her eyes were glistening.

"The fact is," I hurried on, "I'm just back from Lady Youlgreave's inquest."

"The inquest?" The jowls wobbled once more. "I was thinking of going myself, actually. I had hoped you might be able to give me a lift. But nobody answered when I phoned."

"We've all been out for most of the day."

"What happened?"

"What you'd expect." I was puzzled by Audrey's change of tack. "They decided it was an accident."

Audrey sniffed. At that moment, the whistle on the kettle began to squeal, higher and louder.

"I was about to make some tea," I said reluctantly. "Would you like a cup?"

Audrey allowed herself to be mollified. She followed me into the kitchen and talked while I made the tea. I promised I would have a word with Michael, and she promised she would say no more about it. Audrey stayed for half an hour. While I tried not to think of the work I should be doing, she talked about Lady Youlgreave in a manner which suggested she had been to Roth what the Queen Mother had been to the country.

She also talked, at length, about her determination to bring to justice whoever was responsible for Lord Peter's mutilation. Finally, she talked about the fete. I am afraid I did not listen very carefully.

At last she went. I returned to the kitchen to wash up the tea things. Afterward, I was crossing the hall on my way back to the study when I heard a key in the lock of the front door.

Rosemary burst into the house. She was dressed in denim, jeans and a shirt with studded poppers which I had not seen before. Around her neck was a silk scarf, also new. The colors were dark green and bronze: they would have suited Vanessa. I registered all this automatically. What I really saw was her face: red and tear-stained, framed by disheveled blonde hair.

"Rosemary—whatever's happened?"

Her face working, she stared at me. Then, without a word, she ran up the stairs and into the bathroom. I heard the bolt on the door click home.

The Vicarage walls and floors were thin. A moment later, I heard the sound of vomiting.

# Chapter Twenty-Six

ON WEDNESDAY EVENING I went reluctantly to St. Mary Magdalene. The reluctance had been growing on me over the last year. I had always tended to anthropomorphize churches, to endow the buildings with personalities: as with humans, some personalities were more attractive than others. For most of my time at Roth I had liked St. Mary Magdalene. If I had had to find a human equivalent to it, I would have chosen Doris Potter.

In the past twelve months, however—ever since that odd experience just after Vanessa and I had met—I had no longer felt the same about the place. The feeling was almost impossible to pin down. It was like the faint blush of damp spreading almost imperceptibly on a whitewashed wall. I knew it was there. I could not see it, but I thought I could feel it. I felt as though the church were no longer entirely mine, as though something or someone were trying with gradual success to take it over. On one level, I knew very well that I was imagining things. As a man and as a priest, I was prone to see shadows where there were none.

I came out to lock the church before supper. After a gray day, it was a fine evening, though there were dark clouds over much of the sky. The churchyard was bathed in strong, metallic light: it looked like a stage set. I left Vanessa cooking supper. Michael was spending the evening at the Vintners'.

Rosemary was resting in her room; she had told me that she had an upset stomach—something she had eaten at lunch must have disagreed with her. I did not know whether or not to believe her.

Before I locked up, I went inside the church to make sure everything was all right. The ladies had been in recently, and the place smelled of flowers and polish. The somber colors of the Last Judgement painting glowed above the chancel arch. I walked slowly up to my stall in the choir, intending to pray. My footsteps sounded louder than usual, as though I were walking on the skin of a drum.

As I passed under the chancel arch, a movement caught my eye—to the left and above my head. I looked up. I was directly beneath the marble tablet commemorating Francis Youlgreave. Nothing was moving. Sometimes, I told myself, the flutter of your own eyelash can give you the impression of movement beyond yourself.

In my mind, Francis's tablet coalesced with the idea that I was walking on a drum. If this was a drum, then inside the drum, the home of its resonance, was the vault beneath the chancel where the Youlgreaves lay. Not that there were very many Youlgreaves in there. I had not been down there for years, but I remembered a small, dusty chamber laid out rather like a wine cellar with deep shelves on either side; there had been only three coffins, one of them presumably belonging to Francis Youlgreave. There was ample room for at least a dozen more.

The vault must have been built in another time for other families, but there was no sign of them now. The first of the Youlgreaves had wanted to make the place his own, and now only Youlgreaves waited there for the Second Coming. I assumed that the vault would need to be reopened for Lady Youlgreave.

Suddenly I did not want to pray. I told myself I was in the wrong frame of mind. I shivered as I walked back to the south door. I did not know why but I was frightened. I felt like a weary swimmer, alone, out of his depth and too far from land.

I left the church, locking the door behind me. As I came out of the porch the full force of the sunlight hit me. On the right, beside the path which led to the private gate from the churchyard to Roth Park, there was a wooden bench, donated by Audrey in memory of her parents. A figure was sprawling on it, arms outstretched along the back of the seat, a silhouette against the blinding light of the sun. For an instant my heart lurched. I thought it was Joanna.

"Hello, David," Toby said. "Lovely evening."

I blinked in the light. He sat up and moved along the bench, as if making room for me to sit. He looked particularly androgynous this evening in red trousers and a deeper red T-shirt whose low neck and long flared sleeves gave him a faintly medieval air. His feet were bare and he was smoking a cigarette.

"Was there something you wanted?" I asked.

"Yes and no." He laughed. "I didn't realize you were in there, actually, but now we've met, there is something."

With sudden, irrational terror, I wondered if Toby knew: that I had seen his sister without his knowledge; that she had taken me to her room, that she had talked to me about him. I realized how vulnerable I was. Toby was speaking and I had to ask him to repeat what he had said.

"How was the inquest?"

"They decided the death was an accident."

Toby laughed again, a shrill squirt of sound. "Which everyone knew already. Our legal system has a genius for stating the obvious, hasn't it?"

"I suppose they have to make sure."

Toby bent forward and carefully stubbed out his cigarette in the grass. "I wanted a word about the fete actually. I wondered if you have a fortune-teller."

"Not as far as I know. I don't think we've ever had one."

"I thought it might add to the fun. If you've no objection, of course."

"As long as it's suitably light-hearted, I don't think there'd be a problem. But I wouldn't want anyone to take it seriously."

"Oh no," said Toby.

"Who had you in mind?"

"Actually, I thought I could do it myself. I did it at school once. Just for a joke, at a sort of show we had. I wore a wig, and a long dark robe covered in stars." The fingers of his left hand fluttered as though miming the flowing folds of the robe. "Just a bit of fun."

I thought about it for a moment. The idea was attractive. I had felt for some years that under Audrey's hand the fete was becoming rather a dull affair, with the same stalls and the same sideshows coming round monotonously every year.

"There's an old tent in the stables up at the house," Toby went on. "It looks sound enough. I could use it as my booth."

"What sort of fortune-telling?"

Toby shrugged. "I'm not choosy. Palmistry, the cards, astrology, the I Ching. Whatever the customer wants."

"I'm sure people would enjoy it. And it's very kind of you, too. But I'd better have a word with Audrey first. She's doing most of the organizing."

"I shall have to think of a name." He grinned up at me. "The Princess of Prophecy: something like that."

I glanced at my watch. "I must be going. Vanessa will have supper on the table soon."

Toby stood up. "How's the research going, by the way?"

"Lady Youlgreave's death is a complication. We're a little concerned about what will happen to the papers."

"It all depends on who the heir is, I suppose. No news on that?"

I shook my head.

"The solicitor must know," Toby went on, half to himself. "There must be a solicitor."

I nodded but said nothing. I had never met Mr. Deakin, though Lady Youlgreave had mentioned him once or twice. I wondered if he'd been at the inquest, one of the anonymous men in dark suits.

Toby took a step away from me, then stopped, as if something had occurred to him. "Why doesn't Vanessa come and see Francis's room on Sunday afternoon? I know we were going to wait till the party after the fete, but it would be much better to do it in daylight. Besides, you know what parties are like. Full of distractions."

"That would be very kind, but—"

"It's no problem," he rushed on. "Tell you what, why don't you all come? And if any of you would like a swim, you can bring your costumes. The pool should be sorted out by then."

I thanked him, and said that Vanessa or I would phone later in the evening.

"Do come," he said. Then he smiled and loped away—not along the path but among the graves. The cuffs of his T-shirt and of his trousers swayed as he walked. He looked like a blood-red pixie.

Later that evening, Vanessa and I had another whispered conference in our bedroom. It was a warm evening and we sat propped up against pillows on top of the bed, I in my pajamas and she in her nightdress. The nightdress was dark-blue with cream piping around the neck and the cuffs. I dared not look at her too much because it made me want to make love.

"What on earth's wrong with Rosemary?" she hissed. "She's been very subdued all evening."

"She's got an upset stomach."

Vanessa shook her head vigorously. "I don't believe it for a moment."

"She was sick when she came home. I heard her."

"Perhaps she was. But no one with an upset stomach eats the supper she did. No, if you ask me, it's something else. Maybe something shocked her." She paused. "Who is this mysterious schoolfriend?"

"I think she's called Clarissa. Or Camilla. Something like that."

"Are you sure she exists?"

Startled, I turned and looked at Vanessa. Her hair floated

on her shoulders. Her face was very close to mine. The neck of her nightdress was open and I could see her left breast. I longed to be old—to reach an age where sexuality was no longer a distraction and a temptation.

"Why shouldn't the friend be real?" I said, clinging to the safety of words.

Vanessa picked up an emery board from the bedside table and began to buff her nails. "I may be maligning her," she said thoughtfully, "but it's a classic tactic—the old schoolfriend, going shopping, that sort of thing." She smiled at me. "We used to use it when I was young. I suspect my parents knew perfectly well what I was up to, but they chose to turn a blind eye."

"But I thought she was interested in Toby Clifford."

"She is. I wouldn't be at all surprised if he's the mysterious schoolfriend."

"But—" I stopped. But what? *But he's years older than she is. But he's a hippy, or at least he dresses like one. But I was talking to him only a few hours ago. But I don't like to think of my daughter with a man like that, perhaps with any man.*

"Just a thought," Vanessa said. "He might have tried something on. That might account for her being so upset."

"So upset it made her sick?"

"It happens."

"What does?"

She glanced at me, then away. "Sudden physical revulsion. In some ways, Rosemary's very young for her age."

"You really think he may have made advances to her? Physical advances?"

"I don't know," Vanessa said. "I'm just saying it might have happened that way: if Rosemary had her head stuffed full of romantic dreams about Toby, and he misinterpreted how she was responding to him, he might have made a pass at her, and she might have found the whole thing totally revolting. Men and women look at these things very differently."

*After all, you and I look at these things differently.* The words lay between us. There was no need to speak them aloud.

"Rosemary said she didn't want to come on Sunday," I said haltingly, as though in a language I did not fully understand. We had discussed Toby's invitation over supper.

"Exactly. Yesterday nothing would have kept her away from Roth Park. Still, maybe it's all for the best. He's very charming, but really too old for her. And I'm not altogether sure I trust him."

We sat there in silence for a moment. Traffic grumbled in the main road.

"Audrey came round this afternoon to complain about Michael," I said.

"Hush." She darted a glance at me. "They'll hear if you're not careful. What's he been doing?"

"She claimed that he and Brian Vintner had been spying on her."

"Where?"

"In Roth Park somewhere. I suspect she's been out looking for clues. I had a word with Michael but he denied it. He did say that they had seen her in the park this afternoon."

"Audrey will always find something to complain about."

"She's having a difficult time."

"So are we all," Vanessa snapped, forgetting to lower her voice. "The woman's a cow and that's all there is to it. A menopausal cow at that."

"You may be right. But she's a victim as well. What happened to Lord Peter would have been a terrible shock for anyone."

Vanessa glared at me.

"By the way," I said before she had time to reply, "there's something we need to discuss. It's about the Youlgreave papers."

"You're trying to change the subject."

"Yes, but we still need to talk about this. And I'm not sure there's much more we can usefully say about Audrey."

She held up her hand and examined her nails. "All right. What's this about the papers?"

"After the inquest, Doris told me something. I think we should treat it as confidential. She knows I'm going to mention it to you, though. It seems that on Friday evening, Lady Youlgreave asked her to throw away some of the papers. They went out with the rubbish on Monday morning."

Vanessa stared at me. The color in her cheeks receded, and suddenly there were freckles where I had noticed none before. "Oh my God—the ones in the box? Which ones?"

I passed on what Doris had told me. Vanessa rested her head on her hand.

"I could *kill* her," she said slowly. "If only Doris had had the sense to *pretend* to throw them away."

"She's not that sort of person."

"Then I wish she was. I wonder what we've lost. The old lady was very cagey about letting me see some of the stuff."

"About Francis's time in Rosington and afterward?"

"Yes." Her eyebrows wrinkled. "How did you guess?"

"That seems to have been the most controversial period in his life."

"There's no hope we could get them back, is there?"

"By now they'll be yards deep in rubbish in some land-fill."

"Is the box still at the house?"

"I don't know. Doris said that someone from the solicitors came to take away any easily portable valuables. Just in case. Would you be able to know what was missing?"

Vanessa shook her head. "Lady Youlgreave never let me catalog the entire contents of the box. She doled things out to me as she saw fit." Unexpectedly she put her hand on top of mine, which was lying palm down on the bedspread. "You are very patient with me, David. All this must seem rather unimportant."

I twisted my hand so I could grip hers. "It's important to you so it's important to me. But part of me thinks Lady Youlgreave was right. Perhaps the least said about Francis Youlgreave the better."

She drew away. "I never knew you felt like that."

"I don't want to put it too strongly. But maybe in the long run this is a blessing in disguise."

She said nothing. I turned on my side, facing her, and ran the fingers of my right hand lightly down her arm from the shoulder to the hand. I brought my head closer and kissed her on the lips.

"David," she said softly. "I'm sorry. I just don't feel like it."

I drew back. "Not to worry. It doesn't matter."

"I know you're disappointed in me," she went on, "but sometimes I wish we could just leave sex out of it. Just for the time being. I've tried and tried. But at present it just won't work. It's not that I don't love you. I just don't want to show it like *that*. Not now. Perhaps later, when I've had time to get used to the idea."

"Vanessa—"

"You were celibate for ten years. You must have got used to it. Couldn't you get used to it again? Just for a little while. What I'd like to do is live together, like brother and sister almost." She paused. "Like Toby and Joanna."

*Chapter Twenty-Seven*

T HE SECRETARY SPOKE with an upper-class drawl of the type that takes generations to perfect. She telephoned me from Lincoln's Inn on Thursday morning to arrange a meeting with Lady Youlgreave's solicitor. Mr. Deakin, she said, was going to be at the Old Manor House for most of the day and he wondered if we might be able to discuss the arrangements for the funeral. I had a busy day in front of me, but I knew that I would be free at some point in the early afternoon, so I suggested that I call at the Old Manor House between two and three.

The sunshine of yesterday evening had given way to dull, clammy weather, neither hot nor cold. It mirrored my mood. When I reached the Old Manor House, it was about a quarter past two. I had been there less than a week ago, on the day that Lady Youlgreave died, but already the shabby house looked even shabbier.

I rang the doorbell. A moment later, the door was opened by a thin-faced, ginger-haired youth with long sideburns and a tweed suit with a mustard-yellow-and-black check.

"Afternoon, Reverend," he said, extending a hand. "Good of you to pop round. I'm Nick Deakin."

We shook hands, and he took me into a little room at the back of the hall which was furnished as a study; I'd never been in there before. I had been expecting a different sort of

solicitor—a pinstriped family lawyer, a man to match the secretary, overbred and pompous.

"Afraid the whole place stinks," Deakin said. "Those dogs,
I suppose. Let's sit down and make ourselves comfortable.
Would you like a coffee or something?"

"No, thank you."

The room was very dirty, every horizontal surface covered
with a layer of gritty dust. Deakin had flung open the window,
which overlooked the tangled garden at the back of the house.
The furniture was old and heavy; like that in the dining
room, it had been designed for larger rooms in a larger house.
There were two armchairs near the window, upholstered with
brown leather, dry and cracked. Deakin waved me toward the
nearer one.

"I gave them a good dust." He grinned, revealing projecting front teeth which gave him the appearance of a friendly
red squirrel. "Poor old Mrs. Potter, eh? Must have been a hell
of a job trying to keep this house clean as well as keep the old
lady on the straight and narrow." He sat down and offered me
a cigarette. "You know Mrs. Potter?" he went on.

"Very well."

Deakin clicked an enormous gold lighter under my nose.
"She says she wants the dogs."

"She told me that, too."

"I don't think anyone else would mind. They're practically
dead on their feet, eh? Besides, after what happened, you'd
think they'd be better off in the Great Kennel in the Sky.
Still, none of my business. But she knows what she's doing,
does she? I thought I'd better check before we made any decisions."

"Oh yes," I said. "More than most people."

We went on to talk about the arrangements for the funeral. Deakin had already discussed possible times with the undertaker, and we soon agreed on Monday, at 2 p.m.

"Burial or cremation?" I asked.

Deakin opened his briefcase and took out a sheet of paper. "Cremation—she specified it in her will. There's another point: she doesn't want to go in the family vault. She's left quite detailed instructions about the headstone, et cetera, but that needn't concern you."

Relief washed over me, surprising me with its intensity. I had not wanted to go into that vault under the chancel of St. Mary Magdalene. I felt reprieved. I also wondered why Lady Youlgreave had not wanted her mortal remains to wait for the Last Judgement beside Francis Youlgreave's. Perhaps she had known too much about him to feel comfortable in his company, dead or alive.

"Will any of Lady Youlgreave's relations be there?"

Deakin shrugged. "Almost certainly not. There's no close family. But we'll put a notice in *The Times* and the *Telegraph*. Maybe the odd friend will turn up."

"Some local people may want to come as well. I'll pass the news around the parish. What about afterward?"

"Eh?"

"People often expect something. If only a cup of tea."

"Oh, I see. What do you suggest?"

"We could use the church hall. It's on the green, next to the library. One of our churchwardens has a tea room—if you like, I could ask her to provide tea and biscuits. It shouldn't be expensive."

"Sounds OK to me. Can't exactly have it here, can we?" He leaned forward and stubbed out his cigarette in a discolored brass ashtray embedded in what looked like the foot of an elephant. "Not unless we have the place fumigated first."

"What will happen to the house?"

He hesitated, then grinned at me. "No reason why you shouldn't know. Under the terms of her husband's will, Lady Youlgreave only had a life interest in most of the estate. It'll go to some of his relations—second cousins, once removed; something like that. They live in South Africa now, so I doubt if they'll be at the funeral."

"My wife was working on some Youlgreave family papers. I don't know if you've heard of Francis Youlgreave?"

Deakin shook his head.

"He was a minor poet at the turn of the century. My wife was going to write a biography of him—with Lady Youlgreave's approval. But what's the position now?"

"She'll need to discuss that with the heir. Why don't you suggest she write to them? We can forward a letter, if you'd like. There are one or two bequests from Lady Youlgreave's personal estate, but Youlgreave family papers won't come into that."

Shortly afterward, Deakin saw me out. We shook hands on the doorstep.

"She was a game old bird," he said cheerfully. "You know, in a funny way I'll miss her."

We said goodbye. It was not until I was crossing the bridge over the Rowan that the obvious question occurred to me. How had Nick Deakin known Lady Youlgreave? Deakin could not have been qualified for very long—he looked in his mid-twenties, at the most. He must have seen her recently. I wondered why.

As I was passing the entry into the drive of Roth Park, I glanced across the green and noticed Audrey coming out of Tudor Cottage. I waved to her, but she appeared not to see me. There was a sudden gap in the traffic so, on impulse, I crossed the road to the green. She too had crossed the road outside her house and was now on the green as well. She would need to know about the arrangements for Lady Youlgreave's funeral, and about the tea and biscuits afterward. Now was as good a time to tell her as any. If I intercepted her on the green, I thought, there was less chance of her delaying me.

Audrey still had not seen me. She veered toward the bus shelter. I began to walk more quickly across the grass. I heard her talking but could not see her, because the bus shelter was between us. Her voice rose higher and higher. I swore under my breath and broke into a clumsy run.

She was standing just outside the bus shelter haranguing the people inside—three hairy youths in T-shirts and jeans, and a fat girl with dyed blonde hair and a short pink dress.

"Parasites," she was saying. "You ruin the village for everyone. If I had my way, I'd bring back the birch. And which of you did those horrible things to my cat?"

"Audrey," I said, laying a hand on her shoulder, "let's go back to the cottage."

She whirled around. Her cheeks wobbled—by now she was gobbling like a turkey, making half-articulate sounds. Her breath smelled of sweet sherry. I took her arm, but she tore it away from me. She swung back to the young people in the bus shelter. Before I could stop her, she darted toward the tallest of the youths, a strapping boy with several days' growth of beard on his face.

"You're scum," she shrieked. And she spat in his face.

I seized Audrey's arm again and tried to drag her away. Simultaneously the girl in the pink dress slapped Audrey's face. Audrey screamed, a high animal sound.

"Shut up, you dried-up old bitch," the girl yelled, bringing her face very close to Audrey's. "What the fuck do you think you're doing, swanning around pretending to be Lady Muck? Don't you know everyone laughs at you?"

There were running footsteps behind me. Charlene appeared beside me in the doorway.

"You can shut that big mouth of yours, Judy." Charlene took Audrey's other arm and pulled her gently outside. "Come along, Miss Oliphant."

Judy, the girl in pink, took a step after Audrey but stopped when Charlene glared at her.

"Kevin," Charlene said to one of the boys, "aren't you meant to be at work?"

He stared at his shuffling feet and said he was just going.

Charlene and I helped Audrey across the road and into Tudor Cottage. Fortunately there were no customers in the tea room. We took Audrey upstairs and into the sitting room, where she sank into the armchair by the window. She was still trembling, but less violently than before and her face was pale where it had previously been red. I glanced out of the window. The bus shelter appeared to be empty.

"I'm going to fetch her a cup of tea," Charlene told me. "And one of those pills Dr. Vintner left. Can you stay with her? I won't be long."

Charlene left us alone.

"Do sit down," Audrey said faintly. "I always think that chair needs a man. There's a clean ashtray over there . . ."

The effort to act normally seemed to exhaust her still more. For a moment she said nothing. I noticed on the little table beside her chair an empty glass and a red exercise book, probably the one I had seen in her office the other day.

Audrey peered out of the window, down at the empty bus shelter. "I was sitting here after lunch, writing my journal, when I saw them," she said quietly, looking not at me but the bus shelter. "I knew they were up to no good. They had been in the pub. The three of them with that dreadful girl. No better than she should be . . . And they were laughing and giggling, and I knew they were laughing at me and Lord Peter. I had to say something. No one else will. It's not right that evil should go unpunished." She stared at me. "And if no one else will punish evil, then we must do it ourselves. You do agree with me, David, don't you? David?"

On Friday evening, after Evensong, Doris Potter was waiting for me on the bench by the south porch.

"Can you spare a moment, Vicar?"

I went and sat beside her on the bench. I had noticed her in church but thought nothing of it. I said Evensong on Tuesdays and Fridays, and she usually tried to come to at least one of them. I was in no particular hurry to get home. I knew we were having a cold supper. Besides, since our conversation on Wednesday evening, Vanessa and I had not had a great deal to say to each other.

"I saw that solicitor the other day," Doris said.

"Mr. Deakin?"

She nodded. "He's asked me to stay on at the house for a while—try and clean it up a bit." She stared down at her rough, red hands. "He says the old lady left me something in her will."

"I'm not surprised—after all you did for her."

She shrugged impatiently. "There's a bit of money which will come in handy, I don't mind admitting. There's something else too. She added it to her will a few months before she died. A—a—what's it called?"

"A codicil?"

"That's it. She got me to ring Mr. Deakin and he came to the house a couple of times. I knew it was about her will, but she didn't tell me what it was. But Mr. Deakin did. She's gone and left me some land. Carter's Meadow. You know—that bit of land in Roth Park—between the garden and the housing estate near the reservoir." She glanced at me, her gray eyes calm and serious. "Where you and Rosemary found the blood and Lord Peter's fur."

"But doesn't that belong to the Cliffords?"

Doris shook her head. "It wasn't sold with the rest of the land. The Bramleys didn't own it. And it's not Youlgreave land either, not family—it doesn't go with the Old Manor House. It was Lady Youlgreave's."

From what Doris told me, Carter's Meadow was an anomaly. According to Lady Youlgreave, it had once belonged to a large farm in the northern part of the parish, the part which was now underwater. For many years it had been leased to the Youlgreaves, but the owner had refused to sell it to them outright and had even tried to break the lease.

"There was bad blood between him and the family," Doris

said, watching me carefully. "Something to do with Francis, she thought."

*Because Francis killed a cat in Carter's Meadow?*

In the nineteen-thirties, Doris went on, when they built the Jubilee Reservoir, Carter's Meadow had at last come on the open market and Lady Youlgreave had bought it, intending to give it to her husband as a present. But the sale of Roth Park and then the war and her husband's death prevented this; because the land belonged directly to Lady Youlgreave, it had not been sold with the rest of the estate.

"I think she'd forgotten all about it until that man came to call," Doris said. "He wanted to buy it, you see, but she took against him."

"Which man?"

"Toby Clifford. He tried to push her into selling it, but she wouldn't budge. You know what she was like—she could be so obstinate. Then he tried to get me to do his dirty work for him." Doris frowned. "Bare-faced cheek. We were in the hall and I was showing him out, and he pulled out a wallet. Said maybe we could come to an arrangement." She snorted. "I told him he and his money weren't wanted."

"Why did he want the land?"

"Something to do with his plans for Roth Park. He thinks big, that one. Eyes bigger than his stomach." Her face creased into a smile full of mischief. "The only reason she took against him was because he looked like a girl with all that hair. The thing is, now she's gone and left *me* that land. The Clifford boy's still interested in buying it—Mr. Deakin told me. But I don't know what to do for the best. *She* wouldn't have liked me to sell Carter's Meadow to him."

"I don't think you should worry about that," I said. "You can do whatever you like with the land, unless Lady Youlgreave laid down any conditions in the will."

"So do you think I should let him have it? If he offers a fair price, that is."

I thought of Toby and Joanna, camping like a pair of waifs in that tumbledown house. And I thought of the hints I'd heard about Toby. I thought of the things that Toby had told me about Joanna, and Joanna had told me about Toby.

Toby was a determined young man, and if Carter's Meadow was essential for his plans for Roth Park, then the timing of Lady Youlgreave's death must have been convenient for him. I glimpsed melodramatic possibilities: a visit to a vulnerable old woman when the house was empty; another refusal countered by a quick push; a disguised voice on the telephone; knocking over the medicine in the bedroom to suggest a reason why Lady Youlgreave might have tripped on the hearthrug. I shook my head, trying to clear it of these fancies. But a residue of doubt remained.

"If I were you," I said to Doris, "I'd hang on to the land for a while. Wait and see."

# Chapter Twenty-Eight

A T LUNCHTIME ON SUNDAY, Rosemary said that she could not possibly spare the time to come to Roth Park: she had to work. We did not press her. Michael wanted to go because of the swimming pool. Vanessa wanted to go in order to see Francis Youlgreave's room. Even though her access to the family papers was now in doubt, and some of the papers had been destroyed, she was still determined to write the biography—far more so than she had been when Lady Youlgreave was alive. It was as if the Youlgreaves had infected her with a bacillus, and the disease would have to run its course.

"There must be other materials," she said over lunch. "Just because nobody's found them yet, it doesn't mean they're not around if one only looks in the right place. Perhaps I should go to Rosington."

"I doubt if you'll find much there."

"How do you know?"

"I'm sure there's some public record of him," I said carefully, aware that Rosemary and Michael were listening to us. "The dates of his appointments, where he lived and so on."

"Yes—but did people talk about him when you lived in Rosington?"

"Occasionally. Gossip, mainly. But that's not really what you want, is it?"

"It all helps." She looked at me across the table, and I had the feeling that she saw me properly for the first time since our conversation on Wednesday evening. "I'm going to write this book, David, I really am."

We finished the meal in silence. I wanted to go to Roth Park because I would see Joanna. I didn't want to go for the same reason. Every night since Wednesday I'd dreamed about her. Try as I might to forget her, the image of her lingered in my waking hours as well.

At half past three, Vanessa, Michael and I walked slowly up the drive of Roth Park. Michael had his bathing costume and a towel, Vanessa carried a notebook and I had a bunch of roses from the Vicarage garden. Vanessa had insisted that we take the roses.

It was a warm afternoon, still sultry, but sunnier than it had been in the past few days. The house came into view. The E-type Jaguar was parked beside the empty fountain. I felt uneasy, as if some primitive part of me sensed that we were being watched, as if we might be walking into an ambush. I glanced up at the tower at the far end of the house. My eyes found the windows belonging to Joanna's room, the one under Francis Youlgreave's.

Vanessa said, "It's quite a drop, isn't it? I wonder if he was killed instantly. I must try the local papers. They must have something in their back files about it."

"I imagine the Youlgreaves tried to hush it up."

"Yes, but there'll be something. But of course the big question is what is—or was—in the journals. There may have been a suicide note or something." She hugged her notebook. "It's so frustrating."

Michael watched us as we talked, his eyes flicking from one to the other. He spent most of that summer watching us.

"Hello." Toby was standing in the path through the shrubbery at the corner of the house. "Come through this way. I've got chairs down by the pool."

He was wearing a pair of shorts—cut-off jeans—and nothing else. Even his feet were bare. His hair flowed on either side of his central parting, twin waterfalls of ginger curls. The bones of the shoulders and the ribcage stood out clearly. His body was slighter than I had expected and almost hairless. I remembered then what he usually made it so easy to forget: how young he was.

"Rosemary not with you?"

"She felt she had to work," Vanessa replied. "She's got a holiday reading list as long as my arm."

"Shame." Toby led us into the shrubbery. "Joanna sends her apologies, by the way. She's lying down. She woke up with a foul headache, and it's been growing steadily worse."

*Lying down in the room below Francis Youlgreave's.* I was both frustrated and relieved. *Thank God she's not here.* Yet while I thought this, my nails were digging into the palms of my hands because I had wanted to see her so badly.

We reached the path beside the terrace. Someone had cut back the grass to an uneven stubble. To our left, the east facade of the house reared up to the sky. We picked our way across the ragged lawn.

"I'm beginning to think we're making a difference here at last," Toby said. "I hope we'll be playing croquet by this time next year."

I doubted it. Among the stubble were molehills and stumps

of thistles. Brambles had colonized the former flowerbed beneath the terrace and in places were spreading into the lawn. It struck me then with renewed force what an insanely difficult job Toby had taken on. Surely he was too intelligent not to realize that Roth Park needed an ocean of money poured over it? Or was his belief in his own powers so strong that he had drifted into fantasy? Or was it simply that age had not yet blunted his ambitions, that the never-ending compromises that come with maturity had not yet hit him?

"Gosh," Michael said, and whistled.

He was a few paces ahead of us and had seen the swimming pool first. Freshly painted, it glowed in its stone-lined hollow. It seemed much larger than it had in its derelict state. The water was clear and blue. The flagstones around the pool had been weeded and swept. The little changing hut with the verandah, where Rosemary and I had sheltered on the afternoon of the storm, gleamed a fresh, clean white in the sunshine. The springboard had either been replaced or re-covered.

"Not bad, eh?" Toby said. "Take care of the luxuries and the essentials will take care of themselves."

Near the changing hut was a row of four deckchairs. Beside one of them was the radio, a heavy cut-glass ashtray and a paperback novel.

Vanessa and I made appropriate noises of admiration. Toby smiled and stretched his arms above his head, reminding me suddenly and incongruously of Lord Peter when he was well fed and pleased with life.

"How would you like to do this?" Toby asked Vanessa. "Would you like to see the room first or have a swim? Or you might like a cup of tea?"

"I'd like to see the room, please."

Toby smiled at her. "I'm afraid there's not much to see. Not unless you're psychic and can decode the vibrations, or whatever psychics do." He turned to Michael and me. "Would you like to come?"

I didn't want to see the room again. I did not want to remember my last visit. Besides, if I went up to Francis's room, there was a very real risk that I would bump into Joanna. I could not say that I had seen the room before, because Toby did not know of that visit to Roth Park and my conversation with Joanna. Nor for that matter did Vanessa. I glanced at Michael: he was staring wistfully at the water and that gave me my cue.

"I'll stay here with Michael," I said. "Watch him swim."

Vanessa looked sharply at me.

"It's up to you," Toby said. "There're towels in the hut. Are you sure you'll be all right?"

Toby seemed excited, in a hurry to be gone. I even wondered if for some reason he wanted to be alone with Vanessa; but that was ridiculous. The two of them walked toward the house. Michael went into the hut to get changed. I moved one of the deckchairs, the one nearest the pool, into a patch of shade. There was a wet footprint on the slab that had been under the deckchair: a small, bare foot—too small for Toby's so it was almost certainly Joanna's. Presumably she had been out here until a few moments ago. Had she suddenly felt unable to cope with us? Or unable to cope with me?

Michael came out of the hut, suddenly shy in a pair of black swimming trunks. I smiled at him and he darted toward the water. There was a great splash. His head appeared, the hair plastered against his skull.

"What's it like?" I shouted.

"Freezing. It's wonderful."

He looked younger in the water, less guarded, less self-conscious. He turned away from me and began to swim toward the shallow end of the pool, using a primitive crawl that made a lot of noise for very little return. Watching Michael, I stepped forward to the side of the pool. I heard a noise behind me, half concealed by the splashing. I turned.

Joanna was sitting in the deckchair I had moved from the edge of the pool.

For a second I could not speak. I knew I must look a fool, standing there open-mouthed. Joanna wore a white wrap that came down to her ankles. It was made of fine cotton, or perhaps silk, and there were long splits in the material from the armpits down to the thighs. Underneath the wrap was a green bikini, still damp to judge by the marks on the wrap. She smiled up at me. It was the sort of smile that hints at shared secrets.

"Toby said you were lying down. Is your headache better?"

"I haven't got a headache." She spread her arms wide, a gesture which made the wrap fall open, revealing the bikini, revealing the high, firm breasts. "He thought I wasn't in a fit state to receive visitors."

"Well, I'm glad you're not ill."

"Come and sit down."

I glanced back at the pool. Michael had reached the far end and was swimming back to us. Joanna waved to him. There could be no harm in talking to Joanna, I told myself. Michael was our chaperone. Not that we would need one, of course. I sat down beside Joanna and tried not to stare at her. Her voice was slightly slurred and the whites of her eyes were blood-shot. I wondered if she might be on drugs. That might explain why Toby did not want her to meet us.

Her eyes slid toward me and away. "So Rosemary didn't come?"

"She had to work, I'm afraid. Oxbridge entrance coming up, and she's very tense about that."

"I think she didn't want to see Toby."

I didn't say anything. In a sense, I did not want to hear any more.

"I think they had a quarrel," Joanna went on. "They were both up here, in the house."

There was a silence. Then I moistened my lips and said, "When?"

"On Wednesday. He drove her up to London the day before. But on Wednesday they came here." The green eyes slid toward me again and this time they did not slide away.

I heard myself saying, "You don't have to tell me this."

"I do. I saw her running down the drive afterward. She was crying." She bit her lip. "I don't know. I'm just trying to do what's best. I thought you should know."

I was not sure whether to believe her. Wild accusations might be no more than a symptom of psychological distur-bance. On the other hand, what she had said fitted neatly with what had happened on Wednesday afternoon, and with Vanessa's speculations about why Rosemary had been upset.

"Don't tell Toby I told you." Joanna's voice was urgent now. "He'd take it out on me."

For a few minutes we watched Michael swimming up the pool toward us. He clambered out and ran on to the springboard. He turned to make sure we were watching him and plunged in with an even greater splash than before.

"I'm not like Rosemary."

Startled, I looked at Joanna. "I'm sorry. I don't follow."

She ran a fingernail down her bare forearm. Suddenly she stretched out her hand and touched mine. As if stung, I jerked away from her. We stared at each other.

"Do you understand what I'm saying, David?"

I looked at Michael. He was swimming underwater. I turned back to her. She made no further attempt to touch me, but she leaned a little toward me. She was smiling. I wanted to touch her face, her neck, her breasts.

"No," I muttered.

But she was no longer looking at me. She was looking past me, toward the house.

Vanessa and Toby were walking across the lawn toward us. Vanessa was laughing at something Toby had said. At a distance, they looked much of an age. As a couple she and Toby were far better matched than she and I were.

They came down the steps from the lawn. I stood up. It suddenly occurred to me that we might have been visible from one of the windows of the house. Toby or Vanessa might have seen Joanna touch my hand.

"You sure this is wise?" Toby said to Joanna as he came down the steps from the lawn. "The sunshine won't do your head much good."

"I'm feeling much better now." She sat back in her deckchair, as though resisting any attempt to pry her away from it. She asked Vanessa: "What did you think of Francis Youl-greave's room?"

"A very lonely place," Vanessa said.

"With a very long drop from the window," Toby added dryly. "What about some tea?"

We drank tea from cracked mugs and ate digestive biscuits from the packet. Michael swam on and on. He gave us all something to look at, a useful activity to fill the silences. There were many silences. The urge to look at Joanna was almost overpowering.

At last it was time for us to go—I was due to take Evensong, at which I would be lucky to have a congregation of more than three people. The Cliffords both came out to the drive to see us off.

"Oh, by the way," I said to Toby, "I had a word with Audrey Oliphant after church this morning. She'd be delighted if you could do some fortune-telling at the fete."

"Madam Mysterioso. Your fate is in her hands." He grinned. "And indeed your fete, if you'll excuse the pun."

Michael got the joke and burst out laughing.

"She'll have a word with you about the details during the week," I said. "It's very kind of you."

Joanna was standing just behind her brother and I could not help seeing her face when I said the word "kind." Her eyebrows lifted. It was as if she had whispered in my ear: *Kind? You must be joking.*

We said goodbye and walked down the drive.

"Was it worth it?" I asked Vanessa. "Have you learned anything?"

"Nothing concrete. But it's odd. Being in that room, looking out of those windows—it was as if I was suddenly much closer to him. As if I knew him slightly before and now knew him much better. I know that sounds fanciful, but that's how I feel."

"I understand." I felt rather the same about Joanna.

"What was the water like?" Vanessa asked Michael; and for the rest of the way we talked about the swimming pool.

When I opened the front door of the Vicarage, the first thing that greeted me was the smell of alcohol. We went into the sitting room. Rosemary was dozing on the sofa with the television on at a deafening volume. On the table beside her was a bottle of sweet sherry, almost empty.

The following day was Monday the 24th August. Lady Youlgreave's funeral was in the afternoon. Doris Potter was there, of course, and so were Audrey Oliphant and Nick Deakin. There were half a dozen others—all female, all elderly, some of whom I did not know. There is nothing like a funeral for flushing out unfamiliar faces. Apart from Deakin, no one came to represent the family.

No one, that is, apart from the dogs. Doris had asked me if she might bring Beauty and Beast into the church. It was a bizarre request and, had someone else made it, I would probably have refused. They sprawled on the floor at the west end of the church, at the foot of the font. Doris sat beside them. Beauty snored occasionally, but apart from that I would not have known they were there. Afterward, the only sign of their presence was a large puddle where they had lain. Doris's husband loaded them into his car and drove them away, back to their new home in the little house on Manor Farm Lane.

Doris, Deakin and I went with the coffin to the crematorium. Audrey conducted the other mourners over the road to the church hall. When we joined them later, we found them sipping tea and talking in whispers. It was one of the quietest, saddest funerals I could remember taking.

After it was over, Audrey wanted to complain to me about the behavior of the dogs in the church. I managed to escape from her. I felt I needed air, as though I were suffocating. On my way home I met Mary Vintner. She wanted to ask me about the funeral but I muttered an excuse and brushed past her.

I knew I should go back to the Vicarage. I had letters to write, phone calls to make, and Audrey had been pestering me for my monthly contribution to the parish magazine. Over the last week or so, I had allowed work to pile up. The business of running a parish seemed unbearably tedious. There was nothing new in that. What was new was my inability to ignore the tedium and get down to the job.

On impulse, I turned into the gates of Roth Park. Once I was past the church, I turned right, following the route that Rosemary had taken me on the day that she had found the fur and the blood in Carter's Meadow. I had the curious sensation that everything was out of my hands now, that it was too late for me to intervene in the course of events.

It was almost with relief that, a moment later, I saw Joanna coming toward me down the path from Carter's Meadow. She was wearing the green dress I had seen her in before, and sandals. When she saw me, she broke into a run. I held out my arms and she walked into them, as naturally as if she had been doing so for years. Her body was firm and warm. She slipped her arms around my waist.

For a while we stood there, not moving. A devil within me said, *It's all right, there's nothing sexual in this, you are comforting a friend, a parishioner.* If I allowed the situation to develop, yes, I would move toward mortal sin and I would no longer be fit to be a priest. But that would not happen. There was nothing to worry about. Joanna's feeling for me must be purely filial, the orphan's desire to replace a lost father. It would be sheer vanity on my part to suppose otherwise. My friendly devil obligingly pointed out: *How can anything so sweet be bad?*

"David, look at me."

I looked down into Joanna's eyes, green and dark-rimmed. I opened my mouth to say something but she shook her head.

"Kiss me," she said. *"Please."*

I bent my head and obeyed.

*Chapter Twenty-Nine*

THERE WAS A KIND OF MADNESS in the air that summer, spreading like a disease, infecting first one person and then another, until the final weekend in August. That does not excuse what I did. Out of all of us, I was the one who should have known better. I was the one who could have prevented it.

The first time I kissed Joanna was late in the afternoon of Monday, 24th August—the day of Lady Youlgreave's funeral; the church fete was the following Saturday. After the kiss, we stood there, neither moving nor speaking for at least a minute. Suddenly she pushed me away from her. Her nipples were erect under the thin material of her dress. And she had had an effect on my body, too.

"I'm sorry," I blurted out. "I should never—"

"It's not that," she whispered. "Someone's coming."

She was looking behind me. I turned. There were two small figures among the oak trees near the drive. Michael and Brian Vintner had their backs to us. Michael seemed to be pointing to something down by the river.

"They didn't see us," Joanna said. "I'm sure."

"I must go."

She stared at me. "I don't want you to go."

"I'm a married man, a priest." My tongue stumbled. "It's out of the question. I should never have—"

"I've wanted to touch you for ages. Almost since we met. It

wasn't the first time, when you came to the house to talk about the fete. I didn't know what to make of you then. It was the time after that—do you remember?"

I remembered.

"I was in the church," she went on. "Everything was so quiet, I thought I was going to go mad. And I had this feeling someone was watching me, someone nasty. And then you came in, and everything was all right."

"But everything isn't all right. I must go now."

"I wish you wouldn't. I've never met anyone like you."

"I must go." But I did not move away.

The boys were walking away from us, toward the river. A moment later, they were out of sight.

"I need your help," she said.

"Why?"

"Because of Toby. Because—oh *hell*. There's someone else coming."

She was looking in the opposite direction—toward the path to Carter's Meadow. The remains of a hedge ran along what had been the eastern boundary of the meadow. Someone was walking along behind it—slowly, head bowed, as if looking for something. It was Audrey.

"Please," Joanna said. "I need to talk to you."

Without warning, she darted away, aiming for the drive at a point nearer the house than the oak trees. I glanced back at Audrey. She still had not seen me—or so I hoped. I began to walk—almost to run—toward the gate from Roth Park into the churchyard.

I slipped inside the church. It still smelled of the funeral—of flowers and recently extinguished candles. I walked up to the chancel and sat down in my stall in the choir.

I lifted my eyes, trying to pray, and instead saw the memorial tablet of Francis Youlgreave. His mortal remains lay somewhere beneath my feet. But for an instant it was as if he were with me in the church, a dark shape leaning against the whitewashed wall beneath his own memorial. I thought he was laughing at me.

"Is this your fault?" I heard myself saying.

There was no answer. How could there be? I was the only person in the church. There was nothing and no one beneath the tablet, not even a shadow. *Is this your fault?* A faint, mocking echo of the words floated in the still air. The question twisted like a snake that bites its tail: and for an instant I thought someone else had spoken the words—*Is this your fault?*—and that the question was directed at me.

"Not me," I said aloud. "*Francis?*"

Francis Youlgreave was the thread, almost invisible, that bound us. I came to Roth, all those years ago, because of him. Vanessa's original interest in me was sparked by the fact that I lived in the place where Francis Youlgreave had died. Lady Youlgreave had provided fuel to feed the fire. Now Lady Youlgreave was dead, gnawed by her pets. Francis Youlgreave had mutilated animals, and Audrey's Lord Peter had been mutilated in his turn. Vanessa was increasingly determined to write his biography. And I—there was no point in trying to fool myself—was in love with a young woman who lived in Francis Youlgreave's family home and thought she heard his footsteps in the room above hers at night.

Sitting there in the empty church, I felt a coldness creeping over me. There was no pattern in this, or none that I could discern. Where were we going? Where would this end? On the edge of my range of vision, the marble tablet stared down like a blank white face.

I was not going mad, I told myself. True, I was under considerable stress. There was a great deal to worry about. But I was not going mad. What I needed now was a little peace in which to pray for guidance, to work out how best to deal with the situation. I closed my eyes and tried to focus inwardly.

There was a crack of metal on metal followed by a long creak. Someone was at the south door. Hastily I stood up. I picked up a hymnal and pretended to leaf through it.

Audrey came into the church. She had changed from the black dress she had worn for Lady Youlgreave's funeral, and was now wearing a blouse and skirt. She saw me and advanced up the nave.

"I thought I might find you here. I'm not interrupting, I hope?"

I tried to smile. I was terrified that she had seen me with Joanna.

"I felt I had to show you this right away. I was walking in the park just now and I happened to be near where Rosemary found the fur and the blood. And I saw something in the hedge."

She held out what looked like a piece of rust-stained rag. I reached out to take it but she pulled her hand back. "Better not. The police may need to send it for analysis."

"What is it?"

"It's a handkerchief," Audrey said. "And it's stained with blood. A pound to a penny it's Lord Peter's blood. The vet should be able to tell us." She looked up at me, and suddenly her eyes were wary. "But first there's something you should know. Look."

Once again she held out the handkerchief. She took one of the hems in both hands and pulled it apart so the material became flat. The rusty stains could easily be blood. There were other stains, grass, perhaps, and mud. Audrey clicked her tongue against the roof of her mouth as she ran the hem of the handkerchief through her fingers. She was looking for something. Then she found it.

She held up the handkerchief to me, closer and closer until it was a few inches from my eyes. I took a step backward to bring it into focus. A tape had been sewn to the hem. Scarlet capitals trembled, then steadied into a name: M. D. H. APPLEYARD.

"If you don't talk to Rosemary," Vanessa said, "I will. Someone's got to."

"You don't think we should let sleeping dogs lie?" I suggested. "She's already paid the price."

"If you drink more than half a bottle of sherry, of course you're going to feel awful. But only for a few hours. The thing is, we need to have a word with her so she understands very clearly that we don't approve of that sort of behavior."

"There must be a reason for it."

"I'm sure there is. Probably this wretched squabble with Toby Clifford. Or perhaps it's the A level results not being quite as brilliant as she would have liked. But that's neither here nor there. In any event, we need to say something. And you're her father, so you're the best person to do it."

"All right. You've made your point."

Then the silence grew between us again. We were in the kitchen, just the two of us, washing up after supper. Michael had gone to bed, and Rosemary was in her bedroom, technically working. She seemed none the worse for drinking herself into a stupor yesterday afternoon.

Afterward I went wearily upstairs. Michael was reading in bed and we waved to one another through the open door of his room. It had taken me more than half an hour to persuade Audrey that the bloodstained handkerchief was not incontrovertible evidence of his guilt. She was still determined to consult the vet, to see if he could identify the stain as cat's blood, compatible with Lord Peter's; I could not change her mind about that.

Everything was irritating me this evening. Vanessa had spent most of supper talking about her intention of writing to Lady Youlgreave's heir to see if she could continue her researches into the family papers. I wished that Doris Potter had thrown the lot away.

All I wanted to do was lie down and close my eyes. Not to find refuge in sleep: I knew I would see Joanna's face, and I knew that I would relive what had happened this afternoon in Roth Park. I had to remember what had happened, I told myself, if only to decide what to do about it. I was lying to myself—I wanted to remember because to do so brought me a blend of pain and pleasure that I could not do without.

I tapped on the door of Rosemary's room. There was no answer.

"Rosemary?" I murmured, keeping my voice low because of Michael. "May I come in?"

There were footsteps on the other side of the door, destroying my hope that she might be asleep. The key turned in the lock and the door opened. Her hair was pulled back from her scrubbed face and she wore a long dressing gown.

"What is it?"

"May I come in?" I said again. "I'd like a word. We can't talk on the landing."

Rosemary hesitated for a second and then opened the door more widely. The room was very neat and, apart from the books, impersonal, as though in a hotel. She sat down on the bed, her back straight, her knees close together. I took the chair in front of the table by the window.

The window was open and there was enough light to see across the garden to the trees of Roth Park. It was much quieter than at the front of the house where Vanessa and I slept. I looked at the trees and thought: *Beyond the oaks is the little hill, and beyond the little hill is the house, and at the far end of the house is the tower, and in the tower is Joanna. I love you.* I wanted to fire the thought like an arrow through her window.

I turned back to look at Rosemary. Her face was as blank as Francis Youlgreave's marble tablet. She wasn't looking at me but at the cover of a book that lay beside her on the bed. It looked familiar; and a second later I recognized it: Vanessa's copy of *The Four Last Things*, the collection of poems which included "The Judgement of Strangers." I wondered if Vanessa knew that Rosemary had borrowed it.

"It's about yesterday," I said.

Rosemary gave no sign that she had heard.

"When we came back from the Cliffords', you were flat-out

on the sofa with a bottle of sherry beside you. Or what was left of it."

Still she said nothing.

"I presume you'd drunk quite a lot of it, and that's why you fell asleep." I waited, but she neither confirmed nor denied what I had said. "It's not that we mind you having the occasional drink but—"

"*We.* I wish you wouldn't keep saying *we*."

"Vanessa's your stepmother. She cares about you very much, as do I. I don't know if you drank all that sherry because you were unhappy, but take it from me that alcohol doesn't dissolve unhappiness."

That at least earned a reaction. Rosemary raised her head and stared directly at me, her eyes brilliant. "Audrey thinks it does," she said. "When I saw her the other evening"—Rosemary paused for effect—"she was as pissed as a newt."

I stared at her. "I don't like you speaking like that about anyone, let alone a friend such as Audrey."

"She's not a friend of yours. You hate her. You take everything she gives you, all the help with the church, but really you think she's an embarrassment."

"Don't be silly." But there was enough truth in what Rosemary said to make me feel even more uncomfortable than I already was. I wondered too if she really had seen Audrey drunk. Audrey had always liked her glass of sherry, but recently she had been drinking rather more than usual.

"You laugh at her," Rosemary said softly. "As if she's just a bad joke."

"That's absurd. In any case, I've not come here to talk about Audrey. I've come here to talk about you."

"But I don't want to talk about me. There's nothing to say."

"Darling, I know life seems hard sometimes. But it will get better. I know your results weren't quite as good as you wanted, but it doesn't really matter."

She turned her head away from me.

"Your results are more than adequate. Anyway, as far as Oxford is concerned, it's the entrance exam that counts. That and the interview."

Her head was lowered. With a fingertip she traced an invisible spiral on the cover of *The Four Last Things*.

I wondered whether to mention Toby. Better not—Rosemary wouldn't thank me for breaching her privacy. I persevered for a few more minutes, trying to encourage her to respond to me, but got nowhere. She needed help, I knew, but I could not find a way to give it to her. Another failure; and the fact that this failure concerned my own daughter made it worse. When I left I kissed the top of her head. She opened the book and began to read.

I closed the door softly and went across the landing to Michael's room. Rosemary and I had kept our voices low automatically—as one had to in this house—but I wondered if he'd heard anything. He was still sitting up in bed.

"Good book?"

"Yes." He marked his place with a finger. "Agatha Christie. *Five Little Pigs*. But I think I know who did it, and I'm only a third of the way through."

I perched on the end of the bed and for a few minutes we talked about Agatha Christie. "By the way," I said as I was leaving, "Miss Oliphant found one of your handkerchiefs this afternoon."

"Where?"

"In the park."

"I expect it was down by the river. We usually go there."

"No—it was on the other side. Between the Cliffords' garden and the council estate."

Michael looked sharply at me. "In Carter's Meadow? Where Rosemary found the fur and blood?"

I nodded.

"Well, I don't know what it was doing there," he said carefully.

"Not to worry. Anyway, I expect Miss Oliphant will give it back to you soon." I cast around for a reason for the delay. "I wouldn't be surprised if she wants to wash it first."

Michael smiled politely at me. He looked vulnerable in his pajamas, and younger than he was. I would have liked to give him a hug, as I used to do when he was much younger, but I was afraid of embarrassing him.

I said good night and went downstairs to report my failure with Rosemary to Vanessa. On the way down, I thought that a bloodstained handkerchief was just the sort of clue you would expect to find in an Agatha Christie novel. But if Agatha Christie presented you with a handkerchief marked with the name of the suspect, you knew it was probably a false clue. And you also knew that when you had found the person who had planted the false clue, you had almost certainly found the criminal.

## Chapter Thirty

AFTER BREAKFAST ON TUESDAY, I went across the road to buy cigarettes at Malik's Minimarket. Audrey and two other women were talking to Mr. Malik, their heads nodding together over the counter. When I came in there was a lull in the conversation.

"David!" Audrey cried. "And how are you this morning? Bright and breezy?"

"Fine, thank you." I noticed that the other women had turned aside to study a poster advertising a new brand of instant coffee. "And how are you?"

Audrey smiled bravely. "As well as can be expected. Now—you go first." She opened her handbag and peered inside. "I'm looking for my shopping list."

I asked for a packet of Players No 6.

"So Mrs. Potter is now a landowner." Mr. Malik grinned at me as he gave me my change. "To be sure, I shall be treating her very respectfully in future."

"Carter's Meadow," Audrey said at my elbow. "At least two acres. It does seem a little odd. After all, when all's said and done, Doris was only the charwoman. Still, Lady Youlgreave wasn't really herself in the last few years, was she? When I think what she was like before the war . . . Of course, I'm sure we're all delighted for Doris, but I wouldn't be surprised if she finds it a bit of a white elephant."

I smiled and said goodbye. To my dismay, Audrey followed me out of the shop.

"You'd think she'd have had the decency to leave something to the church, wouldn't you? After all, she was the patron of the living."

"We'll survive without it."

"And singling out Doris in that way—really most peculiar. And have you heard that she's taken in those dreadful dogs? After what they did to Lady Youlgreave! I was never so shocked in my life. Not a very *sensitive* thing to do."

I looked at my watch. "You must excuse me."

Audrey laid a hand on my sleeve. "Just one more thing. No, I tell a lie—two. I phoned the vet, but unfortunately he's on holiday. So we'll have to wait until next week until he can run the tests."

"Do you really think it's necessary? I had a word with Michael last night, and I'm sure he had nothing to do with Lord Peter."

Audrey looked at me, and her look said, *You would think that, wouldn't you?* She rushed on, "The other thing, of course, is the fete. Toby Clifford rang up this morning. So nice and friendly. We're going to add fortune-telling to our advertisement in the paper. And if you agree, we thought we'd put his tent beyond the books and the home-made cakes and jam. Right in the corner of the garden. I think there'll be enough room if we move the white elephants along a little. Rather a squeeze, perhaps, but I'm sure we all agree that Toby's well worth a little inconvenience."

"I'm sure he'll be wonderful—"

"I must fly. Such a lot to do. If I'm not there to chivvy her, Charlene works at a snail's pace."

With a wave of her hand, and a whiff of cologne and body odor, Audrey was gone. I turned to cross the road. I was just in time to see Joanna emerging from the drive of Roth Park.

At that moment, a heavily laden gravel truck rumbled slowly down the main road, shielding Joanna from me. I waited outside Malik's Minimarket. Thoughts chased across my mind at breakneck speed during the tiny patch of time while the truck blocked my view of her. Perhaps she would not be there when the truck had passed. Perhaps I wanted to see her so badly that I had imagined her. Or I had projected her appearance on to some other young woman. Or Joanna had been real; but she would have glimpsed me and, embarrassed and mortified by the memory of what had happened yesterday, she would have ducked back into the drive to avoid meeting me or even seeing me. And, of course, it was quite out of the question that I should talk to her or have anything to do with her at all. A lover's logic is as elaborately fantastic as a schizophrenic's.

The truck rolled over the bridge. Joanna was still standing in the mouth of the drive. She waved to me. No, she *beckoned* me.

At that moment there was a gap in the traffic and she darted over the road to the green. I crossed to the green myself and we walked slowly toward each other over the scrubby, litter-strewn grass. Her hair bounced on her shoulders as if endowed with separate life. I wanted to break into a run and put my arms around her. When only two or three yards were between us, we both stopped.

"I hoped you'd be here," she said. "I hoped you'd be early. I couldn't stop thinking of you."

"We mustn't—someone might see."

"What is there to see?" She smiled at me. "We're neighbors." The smile twisted and slipped away. "We *mingle* with each other socially."

"The family at the Vicarage and the family at the big house," I said wildly. "Just like a Jane Austen novel."

"I want to kiss you again."

"Joanna—"

"And we need to talk."

I felt as though she were older than I. Not that it really mattered, in one sense. When you are in love, your respective ages shrivel into irrelevance.

"I'm worried," she murmured. "Not just about us. It's Toby."

"What's he been doing?"

"Cooee!"

I turned around. Audrey was standing at the gate of Tudor Cottage. She waved vigorously at us.

"Cooee! Miss Clifford! Can you spare a moment? It's about the parking for the fete."

"Coming," Joanna called. In a lower voice, she said to me, "I'll come out for a walk at about eight this evening. No, let's make it nine—it'll be beginning to get dark. I'll be on the drive, or near it, or perhaps in the churchyard. Please come if you can." She lifted her face, full of pleading, toward mine. *"David."*

She waved casually at me and set off across the green toward Audrey. I remembered to wave to Audrey. My hand was trembling.

I walked back to the Vicarage, narrowly escaping a collision with a speeding Ford Capri, and went into my study. I sat down and put my head in my hands.

There was a dreadful irony about all this. I had married Vanessa for the comforts of friendship and sex. Especially sex. But sex with Vanessa had become like the jam in *Through the Looking-Glass*, perpetually retreating into the past and the future. Now something far worse had happened: I wanted to make love with a woman who was young enough to be my daughter. I could cope, after a fashion, with that—after all, I had had plenty of practice at suppressing that particular urge in the last decade.

Sex was not the real problem. When I married Vanessa, I had thought in my arrogance that love in the adolescent sense—as a romantic prelude to the biological necessities of mating and procreation—belonged to a stage of my life which I had left behind in Rosington. So Providence had sent Joanna Clifford into my life.

Providence had decided I should fall in love with her. And what did Providence intend me to do about it?

"Wonderful news." Vanessa had just returned from work, and was leaning against the jamb of the study doorway. "I went to see Nick Deakin today, and really he couldn't have been nicer."

"You talked about the papers?"

She came into the room and dropped her briefcase on a chair.

"Apparently old Mr. Youlgreave phoned from Cape Town, about something completely different. But Nick mentioned that I was working on the family papers, and asked if he would mind me continuing. And Mr. Youlgreave—his name's

Frank, by the way; I wonder if Francis is a family name?—said I was welcome to carry on if Mr. Deakin could vouch for me, which of course he did, bless him. He—Frank Youlgreave, I mean—wants me to send him a sort of *catalog raisonné* of what's there, and then we'll talk about what we do next."

Vanessa's face was pink, the flush spreading to the roots of her hair; and the excitement bubbled almost visibly out of her. I thought, without particular sadness, if only I could have made her do that; not that it mattered now.

"And I've actually got them here. I've got the tin box in the boot of the car. I can't believe it. Nick said it was a bit irregular, but seeing as the new owner had given me permission, and seeing that I was a vicar's wife, he thought it would be all right. Such a sweetie."

"Do you know what's missing yet?"

She shook her head. "I've not had time to have a proper look. Would you mind if we ate early this evening? I'd like to make a start after supper."

Of course I didn't mind. That is another thing that love can do: it turns its victims into conspirators.

"On my way home I went to the Central Library. Did you know they've got a back file of the *Courier*? All the way back to eighteen-eighty-six." She stared at her hands. "My fingers are filthy."

"The report on the inquest?"

She nodded. "Took me ages to find it. Officially it was an accident. During the night Francis fell from the window of his room. He landed near the fountain."

"So it must have been the east window?"

"I suppose so. It was a very hot night, and he hadn't been

well. A maid found the body in the morning. The coroner sent his condolences to the family and warned about the danger of leaning too far out of the window. Not a hint of suicide."

*No hint of angels, either?*

" 'The distinguished poet,' the *Courier* called him. 'Formerly a Canon of Rosington until ill health forced him to retire.' " Vanessa picked up her briefcase. "Supper in about half an hour?"

She left me alone with the ghost of Joanna. I smoked and looked out of the window. Ronald Trask phoned to ask if I had finished compiling my parish statistics, which were several weeks overdue. I told him I was working on them. He wanted to discuss how I intended to implement his latest brainchild, the Diocesan Ecumenical Initiative, but I put him off by leading him to believe that I had a visitor with me. Indeed I had: the ghost of Joanna.

Eventually Michael came to tell me that supper was ready. The four of us had a hurried meal of baked beans, toast and cheese. I seemed to have mislaid my appetite. Michael and I washed up while Rosemary made coffee.

Everyone made it easy for me. Vanessa wanted to examine the Youlgreave papers. Rosemary went upstairs to work in her bedroom. Michael asked if he might listen to a program on Radio Luxembourg while he wrote to his parents.

At ten to eight I went into the sitting room. Vanessa was at her desk with the black box on a little table by her chair. She was working her way through a bundle of letters and making notes on a sheet of foolscap.

"I'll lock the church," I said, trying to make my voice sound casual. "Then I might make one or two parish calls."

The pen continued to travel over the paper. "OK."

"I'm not quite sure how long I'll be."

Vanessa unfolded another sheet of paper. "I'll expect you when I see you." Suddenly she looked up. "You don't mind me doing this, do you?"

"Of course not." I forced a smile. "Have fun."

"I've already found a holograph poem that's not in any of the collections. It's called 'The Office of the Dead'—undated but middle-to-late period, I think; probably Rosington."

"You're really enjoying this, aren't you? I'm so glad."

She reached out and touched my hand. "You are good to me. I know we don't get much time together. I feel guilty."

"But you mustn't feel guilty. Please don't."

Guilt was my prerogative, not hers. Besides, I wanted Vanessa to be happy. And I also wanted Joanna. I said goodbye and left the house. Feeling like a truant sneaking out of school, I walked through the garden and through the gate to the churchyard. I followed the path that skirted the east end of the church. Absurdly superstitious, I averted my eyes from the steps leading down to the Youlgreave vault.

*What if Francis is down there, watching me?*

I let myself into the church by the south door. I made a circuit of the inside of the building rather more quickly than usual. I found that I did not want to let my eyes linger on certain objects—on the cross on the high altar, for example, on the smoky colors and swirling shapes of the Last Judgement panel painting, and on the moonface of Francis Youlgreave's memorial tablet.

As I returned to the south door, I thought, quite dispassionately, that my behavior was abnormal; I might well be on the verge of a nervous breakdown. I should go and see somebody about it, preferably Peter Hudson when he returned from Crete. Not yet, though; I was not ready to share my possible nervous breakdown with anyone except Joanna. But should Joanna be considered as its cause or its effect?

I locked the door behind me and walked slowly through the churchyard. I looked at my watch. It was ten past eight. I was fifty minutes early. I did not mind. There was pleasure even in being alone and being able to think of her.

I passed through the gate from the churchyard into the grounds of Roth Park. It was cool under the oaks and noticeably darker than in the churchyard. The sky was cloudy. I stopped for a moment and waited, looking around. This was, after all, a public place. People walked their dogs along the footpaths. Children played here. Adolescents found other pleasures. For all I knew, Audrey had chosen this evening to mount another detective expedition into the grounds of Roth Park. The need to be furtive heightened my pleasure.

I looked at my watch again. Another forty-five minutes, assuming Joanna was on time. I knew nothing about her, I realized—not even whether she was the sort of woman who was usually early or late. I patted the pockets of my jacket, looking for cigarettes.

At that moment, Joanna slipped from behind the trunk of an oak tree fifty yards away from me. She wore a long, pale-colored dress that swayed as she walked and glowed against the greens of the leaves and the grass and the brown of the trees. She saw me and began to walk toward me. Faster and faster she came. I held out my hands to her and, at long last, I felt the touch of her fingers on mine.

*Chapter Thirty-One*

LOVE IS A FORM OF HAUNTING, and Joanna was my ghost.

I knew the terrible danger I was in—both socially and, far more importantly, spiritually. I ran the risk of hurting all those I loved. I was wantonly endangering the happiness of Vanessa and Rosemary. The feelings that Joanna and I shared had no future. We had very little in common.

I also knew that, even if I had the power to rewrite the immediate past and to prevent what was happening now, I would not choose to exercise it.

Joanna and I packed a great deal into that week, into a handful of meetings.

"You're early," she said on Tuesday evening, still holding my hands in hers.

I was so happy I could not stop smiling. "So are you."

"Toby's out."

"When will he be back?"

She glanced to her right, toward the drive. "I don't know. He didn't say." Her fingers tightened on mine. "I think someone's coming."

We snatched our hands apart. For a moment we listened. I heard traffic on the road and a distant burst of laughter, perhaps from one of the televisions in Vicarage Drive.

"It's no one," I said.

"Come into the garden."

"But if Toby—"

"We'll hear the car on the drive." She smiled at me. "Trust me."

She led me through the oaks and up the drive toward the house. We cut through the shrubbery on to the lawn. As we came on to the grass, she took my hand.

"We can go into the house if you like."

I felt a shiver running through me. Fear and desire, inextricably mingled. "We'd better not."

"Then let's go down to the pool."

Hand in hand, we walked quickly across the lawn. The pool was a good choice. It was masked by trees and set lower than the surrounding garden. We could hear and not be seen. If need be, if someone came from the house, I could slip away through the fence into Carter's Meadow. Conspirators plan ahead.

We sat on one of the benches recessed into the stone wall around the pool. The stone was warm to the touch. The evening sun slanted across the swaying waters of the pool, creating shifting black stains of shadow against the clear blue of the water. A passenger jet flew overhead and Joanna covered her ears with her hands and pushed her face against my shoulder. Slowly the sound diminished and silence flooded back. She reached up, cupped the back of my head with her hand, and pulled my face toward hers. With my free hand I stroked her arm. Without moving her mouth, she took my hand and placed it over her breast.

I pulled away from her. I was trembling like a man with a fever. "I can't do this."

Her face was flushed and smiling. Suddenly she kissed me again. This time her tongue darted into my mouth and flicked to and fro like the tail of a landed fish. Despite myself I responded.

Afterward she said, "I've wanted to do that since I met you in church."

"You were in there when I came to lock up. You said you couldn't get used to the quiet here."

At that moment another airplane went over our heads. We looked at each other and started to laugh.

"Do you remember when we found that cat?" she asked. "You put your arms around me."

"I remember."

Joanna's hands were under my jacket now, exploring and stroking my body like two small animals. Suddenly the hands stopped moving. She pulled her face away and looked up at me.

"We mustn't let Toby find out."

"We mustn't let anyone find out."

"No, you don't understand. If Toby finds out, he'll use the knowledge."

"How?" I tried to smile. "Blackmail?"

I had intended the suggestion as a joke. But Joanna nodded.

"He'll be out of luck," I said. "I haven't any money."

"He'd find something else you could give him. Or do for him."

"You make him sound like a monster."

Joanna said nothing. She looked away from me and stared into the dappled surface of the pool.

"Joanna," I whispered; even saying her name was a pleasure, intensified because the pleasure was touched with pain.

"He's my brother." She spoke to my chest; she would not look at me. "I've known him all my life. But I don't know *why* he's like he is. All I know is *what* he is." She swallowed. "How do you think he got that car? His precious bloody Jaguar?"

*A rich boy's toy.* "Tell me."

"He was dealing. Not dope, or acid, or even speed. I could have handled that. He was dealing heroin. He was going out with a girl called Annabel. Poor little rich girl. Her dad gave her everything, including the E-type. Toby got her into heroin, I'm sure of that. Then he started using her as his front for the dealing. She had a flat at the back of Harrods. He was very clever. When the police began prowling around, everything led to her not him. They busted her. They could have done her for dealing, but the father could afford a good barrister. Toby's name just didn't come into it. In the end they did her for possession, instead, and now she's in a nursing home in Switzerland. She worshipped Toby, you know. Still does, I expect. She told him he could use the car while she was gone."

"And you?"

She stirred in my arms and looked up at me. "What?"

"Do you use drugs?"

"Nothing you need worry about."

"What about you and Toby? Why are you together? Why did you buy this house with him?" I hesitated and added a further question, one that bubbled up unexpectedly, surprising me perhaps more than her. "And why are you so scared of him?"

Joanna did not reply. My lips brushed her hair. She was breathing rapidly and shallowly. A small black ant scurried along the stone bench and climbed rapidly up to the top of my left thigh. It ran down to my left knee. It stared over the swimming pool like stout Cortez over the Pacific. Suddenly it turned through 360 degrees as if searching for his fellows. Finally it plunged over my kneecap and ran down the shin to the unknown territory of my foot and the paving slabs beyond. Like myself, the ant had gone too far to turn back.

"Joanna? Why?"

I wanted to say that I loved her so much that I had a right to know, but I felt that that would be putting unfair pressure on her. She raised her head and stared at me with those green-brown eyes, wide and innocent. Her lips parted but, instead of speaking, she pulled my mouth down on hers.

While we were kissing, we heard the dark throb of the Jaguar's engine on the drive.


For the rest of the week, time behaved capriciously, sprinting and crawling by turns. Joanna and I managed to meet every day, usually in the evening. On Wednesday, we went to the cinema in Richmond. I cannot remember what the film was. We bought tickets separately and met in the darkness. We sat side by side, unable to speak, our fingers exploring each other. Afterward we left separately, just before the lights came on. I had parked in a side road near the green and Joanna joined me in the car. While we were kissing, I thought how easy it would be for a policeman to pass by and shine a torch into the car; how easy for a colleague or parishioner to recognize the car and come over to talk to me.

Joanna pulled slightly away from me. "I want all of you. I want you inside me."

"No. That's impossible."

"I'm not a virgin, you know. Not since I was sixteen."

I wanted to ask about those nameless lovers she had known before.

"I wish you were my first," she went on. "I've never felt like that before."

I kissed her again.

A few minutes later she returned to the subject: "So why don't we make love properly?"

*Why not indeed?* "Not yet," I managed to say.

"But why? You want me." Her hand was working between my legs and I could hardly deny what my body made so clear. "I don't care where. We can do it here if you like. Now."

"No."

"Why not?"

"Because . . ." For me, I knew, penetration would be the final step, the point of no return. I had surrendered so much else but I was not—illogically but powerfully—prepared to surrender that. "I'm not ready. Just give me a little time."

"That's the one thing we don't have."

"One of several things we don't have, actually."

Joanna giggled. "I love you." Her hand began more vigorous operations. "Still—"

"Yes," I said faintly. "There are other possibilities."

She lowered her head over me. I stroked her hair.

All this should have been squalid, even ridiculous. Many

people would have used worse words, and perhaps they would have been right. There are few defenses left for a married, middle-aged clergyman who furtively exchanges sexual favors with a vulnerable young woman in a variety of undignified and uncomfortable situations.

I thirsted for Joanna as, at other times, I had thirsted for God. Discomfort, guilt, fear of discovery, lack of time—everything fed whatever emotion bound us together. It was not merely lust, because lust is straightforward and this was not; and lust can be satisfied, at least briefly, and this never was. Obsession? No, because that is entirely selfish and neither of us wished solely to take from the other—we also wished to give. What else was left? Only love, that vague and much-maligned word: a love that embraced lust and obsession.

During that month, I skimped and neglected the religious framework of my life, the framework that had sustained me for so long. I was afraid of God. I felt as though I were in the Garden of Eden but had no right to be there, and at any moment the order for my expulsion would come. Nor did I have time for Him. There was no longer enough room in my life.

There was little room for anything except Joanna. My in-tray filled up with unanswered letters and unpaid bills. The pad by the telephone filled with messages asking me to phone people I did not want to phone.

On Thursday I invented an attack of flu to avoid a diocesan meeting, a lie which gave us five whole hours in the afternoon and early evening. Joanna and I drove down to Hampshire, parked the car in a lay-by and followed a footpath into a wood. We left the footpath and followed tracks made by small animals until we came to a little clearing in a hollow. I laid out the rug from the car. Then, for the first time, I saw Joanna naked.

Despite everything that happened later, that afternoon glows in my mind. Sunlight trickled down through the leaves, casting shifting patterns on our bodies. I had never known such pleasure, such excitement, such happiness. Morally, I knew, avoiding penetration was a mere quibble—my guilt was already absolute. But I clung to the quibble as if it meant something, like a man holding a life belt in the face of a tidal wave.

What happened did not feel squalid: it felt inevitable, sad, guilt-ridden and wonderful. We knew that there would be a price to pay; and there was. But neither of us could have known how high that price would be.

*Chapter Thirty-Two*

EVEN VANESSA, at work during the day and immersed in the Youlgreave papers during the evening, noticed that something had changed.

"Did you have a good meeting?" she asked, as I got into bed on Thursday evening.

"The usual sort of thing."

She smiled at me. "Except that it went on for even longer than usual. Still, you seem quite cheerful about it."

"I've known worse." I was appalled by my automatic hypocrisy, by my careful choice of words designed to avoid an actual lie.

"I forgot to tell you: Mary Vintner phoned. James wants to do the barbecue on the paved bit outside our kitchen window. Is that all right?"

"Do you mind?"

"Not if I don't have to do it. She said they'll bring everything, including food to cook, and she'll make sure he clears up afterward." She sniffed. "You smell nice."

"I rather overdid the talcum powder, I'm afraid." It had worried me that Vanessa might smell Joanna on me so I had taken precautions.

"I like it. You've been very busy this week. We've hardly seen each other."

"Sometimes it's like that. Parish life tends to be unpredictable. You've been fairly busy yourself. How's it going?"

"With Francis?" Vanessa sat down at the dressing table and began to brush her hair; once I had loved watching her at this nightly ritual. "Rather well, actually. I've nearly finished cataloguing what's there."

"Have you read everything?"

"Not really. Just enough to get an idea of the contents. His handwriting was appalling, and as he grew older it got worse. You remember that poem I found?"

" 'The Office of the Dead?' "

"Yes—I've still not been able to decipher it all. And there's another complication—the spirit regularly moved him to write when he wasn't exactly sober. Laudanum, brandy and sodas, opium—you name it, he liked it. Plus, there's a lot of semi-coded references whose meaning I haven't worked out."

"What about the papers that Doris threw away?"

Vanessa frowned at the mirror. "Honestly, I know she's a nice woman, but sometimes I could strangle her. I think two volumes of the journal went, and quite a lot of letters and things. As far as I can see, Lady Youlgreave wanted to weed out anything that dealt with that Rosington episode. So frustrating."

I shivered.

"Are you cold?" her reflection asked me.

"It is beginning to get cooler at night, don't you think? A hint of autumn."

"How depressing. It's been such a rotten summer." She put down the brush and got into bed. "Are you—are you very disappointed?"

"About what?"

"About me?"

"Of course not."

"You are good to me. I don't think many husbands would be so—so *gracious* about having to share me with Francis."

"I can understand the fascination," I said. "Anyway, it's important."

"Francis?"

"Discovering the truth. Separating fact from speculation. You should have been an academic."

She stroked my arm, then let her hand rest on mine. "And you?"

"I told you—at one time I thought I wanted to be an academic, but then being a priest seemed more important."

"So we're two of a kind. I wanted to do research, but I married Charles instead and turned into a publisher." She shifted beside me in the bed, moving a little closer. "Why couldn't you combine being a priest with being an academic?"

"I tried. But it didn't work out." I turned my head and smiled at her. "But it's all right. Everything's worked out for the best."

*If I hadn't become Vicar of Roth, how could I have met Joanna?*

"I want you to be happy," Vanessa said. "I feel I'm failing you."

"You're not failing me." I patted Vanessa's hand and thought of Joanna. "And I'm very happy."

On Friday, Audrey temporarily delegated control of Ye Olde Tudor Tea Room to Charlene, moved her headquarters into the Vicarage and presided over the preparations for the fete. This year she seemed to take it even more seriously than usual. She camped in the dining room, the room we used least. Rosemary acted as her aide-de-camp.

The dining room filled up with smaller items of jumble, and the garage served as a dump for the larger pieces and for a heterogeneous collection of wallpaper-pasting tables, chairs and home-made signs. Toby phoned me and asked if it would be all right if he and Joanna brought the tent in the afternoon and put it up in the garden.

"You've come to see what we've been up to," Audrey informed me when I took some coffee to her and Rosemary in the middle of the morning.

"You're doing wonders." I edged toward the doorway. "Let me know if there's anything I can do."

"Let us pray for fine weather," Audrey said, eyeing me in a way that suggested she had earmarked this responsibility for me. "People always enjoy themselves more when the sun's out, and then they spend more."

Vanessa was at work, but Michael was recruited to help with the preparations as well as Rosemary. He helped willingly, excited by the break in routine.

During the day a steady trickle of people arrived at the Vicarage. Some came to help, some brought items for selling, some came simply to gossip. There would be more in the morning. I sometimes thought that the real importance of the fete was not the money it made, never very much in comparison with the effort that went into it, but the way it brought people together.

All day I found it hard to concentrate. I did not know when

Joanna would come. Or even whether she would come. We had not been able to arrange another meeting for today—I was fully occupied until the evening, and we might not be able to see each other alone later on. My love for her was like an itch: the more I scratched it, the worse it became.

As the day went on, frustration and uncertainty made me increasingly irritable. I snapped at Michael when he dropped a fork while laying the table for lunch. During lunch itself Rosemary said nothing: she sat with her head bowed so that her hair fell to either side of her face, effectively curtaining it. When I tried to make conversation, she answered in monosyllables.

"For heaven's sake," I burst out at last. "Must you be quite so gloomy?"

Rosemary made a sound that might have been a sob, scraped back her chair and left the room. Michael stared at his plate, flushing with embarrassment. I went up to Rosemary's room afterward, intending to apologize. I'd hardly begun when she interrupted me.

"You don't care about me. You never have."

"Of course I do. You're my daughter."

She lowered her head once more, retiring behind her golden curtain. "I wish I lived anywhere but here. Anywhere in the world."

"My dear—"

"It's all changed since you married Vanessa. You never have any time for me. You talk to *Michael* more than me."

I sat down on the bed beside her and tried to take her hand, but she stood up at once and moved to the window. "That's simply not true. I love you very much and I always will."

"I don't believe you." She looked out into the garden, toward the trees of Roth Park. "I don't want to talk about it. There's no point."

"Rosie, you really—"

"*Don't* call me that."

The doorbell rang. My first thought was that it might be Joanna and Toby.

"Go on, answer it," Rosemary told me. "It might be someone important."

"We'll talk later," I said, trying to retrieve something from my failure.

She shrugged. I went downstairs and opened the door.

"It's only little me," said Audrey. Something in my face must have alerted her, for she added almost at once, "Is there anything wrong?"

"Nothing at all, thank you." I stood back to let her into the house. She surged past me, trailing clouds of perfume and perspiration.

"I've a feeling," she said gaily, "this is going to be our best fete yet."

"I hope you're right. Now, if you'll excuse me—"

She was between me and the study door, cutting off my obvious line of escape. "All the stalls are very well stocked, and we've got a really good band of helpers this year. And I think that Toby Clifford's fortune-telling tent is going to make all the difference. Even the Vintners' barbecue."

"Good."

"I wanted to ask you—what time do you think we should announce the result of the Guess-the-Weight Competition? Last time we left it until the end, and I'm not sure that was a good idea—a lot of people had already left, including the winner, in fact. Do you remember? It was Mrs. Smiley, that woman with the poodle who lives in Rowan Road."

"You must do whatever you think best." I edged toward the study door, but Audrey held her ground.

"I thought perhaps we should announce the winner just before tea—at about ten to four. I mean, let's face it, if anyone's going to guess the weight, they're going to do it in the first two hours, aren't they? Doris told me that they took most of the guesses in the first hour."

"I'm sure that'll be fine, then."

"There was one other thing—the cups and saucers. Last year several of them got broken. The Church Hall Committee were rather upset. If you're happy with it, I'll say at the outset that we'll replace any breakages from our profits so there's no doubt about the matter."

"Audrey," I said desperately, "I'm sure you'll make all the arrangements marvelously. You've already made the decisions. You do not need me to rubber-stamp them for you."

It wasn't so much what I said as the way that I said it. I watched the color flooding into her face. I saw her mouth trembling and her eyes screwing up. It was as if her features were disintegrating. And it was my fault.

"I'm so sorry." In my agitation, I laid a hand on her arm. "I didn't mean to snap. You're doing a wonderful—"

To my horror she came even closer to me until her body was nudging against mine.

"Oh, David," she said between sobs. "I hate it when you're like that."

I tried to back away from her but succeeded only in backing

into the wall. "Now there's nothing to worry about. Why don't I make us some tea?"

"Everything's changed," she wailed. "You never used to be like this."

"There, there." I patted the doughy flesh of her bare fore-arm. "Everything's all right. Now, there's a great deal to do before tomorrow."

By now I was sandwiched between Audrey and the wall. It was a ridiculous situation. I could have stamped my feet with rage, irritation and embarrassment. Each of us has a child inside him, and mine was very near the surface and on the verge of having a tantrum.

"It's Vanessa," Audrey whimpered, her voice rising higher and louder. "It's all her fault."

At that moment the doorbell rang once again. Relieved at the interruption, I turned toward the door. As I did so, I realized that Audrey and I were not alone and might not have been for some time.

Rosemary was standing at the head of the stairs, with the light from the window behind her outlining her body and streaming through her blonde hair. In that instant, she looked as beautiful, and as implacable, as an angel.

The tent was contained in a great canvas bundle, the foot of which rested on the floor in front of the front passenger seat of the Jaguar. The top of the bundle poked through the sun roof. When I followed Toby into the drive, leaving Audrey to compose herself in the dining room, Joanna was disentan-gling her body from the tiny back seats. The despair and frustration I had felt a moment earlier dropped away from me. In her absence, I imagined Joanna so intensely that the reality was almost more than I could cope with: she was, literally, a dream come true.

She clambered out of the car by the driver's door, said hello to me in an offhand manner, and walked round the long bonnet to the passenger door.

"Joanna was once in the Girl Guides," Toby told me. "So she'll be able to tell us how to put up the tent."

"You're a liar," she said over the roof of the car. "I was never in the Guides any more than you were."

"It makes a good story, though. And you'd have looked very fetching in the uniform."

Joanna ignored him. She opened the passenger door and tried to lift the base of the bundle on to the seat. Toby and I went to help her. The nearer I came to her the more unsettled I felt.

"How's the family?" Toby asked me.

"Fine, thank you."

"And Vanessa's research?"

"Quite well, I think." I was aware, as lovers are aware, that Joanna was listening. "It takes up most of her spare time, though."

"Odd to think of a dead poet coming between man and wife," Toby said with a smile. "And Rosemary's still working hard?"

I nodded. "You'll probably see her. She's here. She's acting as Audrey's right-hand woman."

Toby edged Joanna out of the way. He bent down and hoisted the bundle on to the seat. "If I push it upward, could you sort of guide it out of the sun roof? It's not as heavy as it looks."

We extracted the tent from the car and carried it around to the garden, with Joanna following. I glanced up at Rosemary's window, but I could not see if she was watching us. I explained where Audrey wanted the tent to go—in the corner of the garden where the churchyard wall joined the boundary wall of Roth Park. I offered to help but Toby said he was better off by himself, at least at first.

"I'll let you know, though, when I need a second pair of hands."

"I'll go and put the kettle on."

"Is there anything I can do?" Joanna said, looking at me. "For the fete, I mean."

"I'm not sure." I hesitated. "We could ask Audrey. She's in the dining room."

The dining room overlooked the back of the house, and I guessed that Audrey was monitoring developments in the garden. Joanna and I walked sedately across the lawn to the back door, keeping a safe distance apart from each other. We went into the house. The door from the kitchen to the hall was closed. Keeping well back from the window and to one side of it, I turned to Joanna. She put her hands on my shoulders, stared at me for a moment and then kissed me slowly and gently.

"I feel like a bee," she said, "sucking honey from a flower. Does that sound stupid?"

"No." If she had said that the moon was made of solid silver, that would not have sounded stupid either. She smelled of mown grass and cigarettes. We kissed again, keeping our bodies apart.

At last she drew away from me. "You'd better put the kettle on. And I suppose I'd better go and find Miss Oliphant."

"Don't go."

"No, not yet." She watched me filling the kettle and putting it on the ring. "David?"

"Mm?"

"I can't bear this. Not being with you all the time. Not even making love properly."

"I know." I thought of what the future might contain: leaving the priesthood, divorcing Vanessa, finding some other job—and in that instant all that seemed as irrelevant as an old skin seems to a snake. What did it matter, as long as Joanna and I could be together?

"I'm scared," she said.

I reached for her hand.

"I want everything from you," she said slowly. "I want your children. That's why we have to make love before it's too late."

"Too late?"

"You know what I mean. Just in case . . ."

I played with her fingers. *Make love now, just in case we have no future?* But we would have a future. Of course we would. *But just in case?*

"All right." My voice was hoarse.

"You mean you will? Properly?"

I cleared my throat. "Yes."

"This evening?"

"We've got the Vintners coming round."

"Tomorrow, then?"

"There's the fete. I'll have to be on parade for that. And

afterward there'll be your party. Won't you be very busy with that?"

She shook her head. "Toby's ordered stacks of booze and crisps and things. He's hiring glasses. It's not as if there's any point in our cleaning the house. So there's nothing to do. We'll just let people get on with it."

"It'll be getting dark by then."

Her eyes gleamed; they looked greener and deeper than ever. "And if it's fine we'll be in the garden as well as the house. I'm sure we can slip away. And if we don't manage then, we'll manage afterward."

I nodded. I wanted her now.

"We'll have to be careful about Toby, though," she said. "He's so sharp, especially where something like this is concerned."

I felt a spurt of anger: something like what? Did his sister often have clandestine affairs with married men?

"He can be very malicious," Joanna went on.

"Then why do you stay with him?"

My voice was suddenly harsh. I was not angry with her. I was jealous of past lovers, furious with Toby for making his sister afraid, and desperate to have more of Joanna than at present I could.

She moved away from me. "There are reasons." It was as if a light had gone out behind her face. "I will tell you. But not now."

"Why not?"

"This isn't the right time."

"But you would leave him, wouldn't you? You would leave him to come with me?"

She smiled at me and ran her fingers through her hair. "Yes. If you still wanted me."

"Is it that bad?"

She did not speak.

"Joanna. Please tell me."

She looked up at me and I saw the tears in her eyes.

"I love you," I said.

"David—"

The door opened and Audrey came into the kitchen. Apart from a reluctance to meet my eyes, she betrayed no sign of the last conversation that we had had.

"Hello, Joanna. Come to help? Are you any good at lettering notices? Oh jolly good! You've put the kettle on. I'm dying for a cup of tea."

# Chapter Thirty-Three

WHEN I WOKE on Saturday morning, rain was rattling on the windowpane. I drew back the curtains. Black clouds hung low over the green and spread out to the eastern horizon, threatening London. Traffic threw up a fine spray as it passed up and down the main road, and puddles dotted the gravel of the Vicarage drive.

At breakfast, Vanessa said cheerfully, "So it looks like the church hall, doesn't it?"

I stared out of the window at the back garden. Toby's tent stood forlornly in the far corner, its canvas stained with damp. The church hall was Audrey's contingency plan for wet weather. Some of our attractions, such as the barbecue, would have to be abandoned. There would not be room for many members of the public, either, even if they felt like trekking through the rain across the green from the paddock of Roth Park to the church hall.

The telephone rang. It was Audrey.

"We shall just have to pray for a miracle," she said, her voice shrill. "I simply can't *believe* this wretched weather."

Whether Audrey prayed or not, the miracle duly appeared: by half past nine, it had stopped raining; and by ten o'clock, the dark clouds were receding over London, while blue sky was coming in from the west. By half past ten, the Vicarage felt as crowded as a railway terminal in the rush hour.

The sun had broken through the clouds and the grass was steaming. Stalls were going up all over the lawn, according to Audrey's directions. After a while, I realized that I was redundant—in fact, that my presence was actually impeding people because they felt they had to consult me or merely make conversation. I retired to the study, where I angled my chair so I could see out of the window. Joanna and Toby were not due to arrive until after lunch, but there was always the possibility that they might change their plans.

The room felt alien to me. Joanna had that effect. She had cut me adrift in my old life, made me a foreigner in a country which had once been my home. I looked at the shabby cloak hanging on the back of the door, at the books—rows and rows of theology, at the stack of parish magazines on the window-sill and finally at the crucifix on the wall. All these things belonged to another person in another life; they were no longer familiar.

Toward lunchtime, Vanessa stormed into the study. I felt a stab of guilt that she had caught me doing nothing. Not that she noticed. She was carrying the tin box in her arms and her face was flushed.

"I'm going upstairs to our bedroom," she told me. "And I do not want to be disturbed for anything short of an earthquake."

"What's up?"

"I've been trying to work in the sitting room, but people keep coming in and asking me for things. If it isn't Audrey, it's James; and if it isn't him, it's Ted Potter. I may be your wife, but I'm not a parish amenity." She grinned at me. "I feel better for getting that off my chest. You know where I am if you want me."

I heard her footsteps on the stairs. I knew that people like Audrey thought that Vanessa was an unsuitable wife for a parish priest. What would they think of Joanna? My mind filled with the memory of her on Thursday afternoon—naked in the wood, sprawling on the blanket, smiling wantonly up at me. My body began to respond to the memory. This would never do. I got up and went to the kitchen to make myself some coffee.

James Vintner poked his head through the open window. "Got any paraffin?"

"I'm afraid not."

"I can't get this damn charcoal to light. Want to have a look?"

I went outside. "I've never used a barbecue."

"Needs to burn well for an hour or so before you can cook on it." James sniffed appreciatively, his mind leaping ahead. "Nothing like meat barbecued in the open. Irresistible."

"Perhaps Audrey has some paraffin."

He clapped his hands. "I don't see why petrol shouldn't work. I've got a can in the car."

He fetched the can and poured some of the petrol over the charcoal. There was a whoosh of flame when he lit the match. For an instant, tongues of fire danced over his hair.

"Bloody hell!" He slapped his head vigorously and glared at me. "No harm done."

At least the charcoal seemed well alight. James asked Rosemary to put the can in the garage in case he needed it again. Audrey pounced on me and towed me away to look at the book stall—at the center of which was a carefully arranged pyramid of *The History of Roth*, donated by its author.

"I've put out thirty-six copies," Audrey said. "Do you think that will be enough? I've got some more under the table."

"I'm sure that will be enough. It's very generous of you."

Audrey simpered. "Every little bit helps. And it's all in a good cause." Her eyes slipped past me toward the tent in the corner of the garden. "No sign of Toby?"

"He's not due till after lunch. Do you need him for something?"

"I'd just like to have more of an idea of what he's going to do. After all, this is a *church* fete. One wouldn't want anything *inappropriate*."

As she was speaking, she walked toward the tent. She opened the flap and we looked into its cool green interior. Despite the rain in the night, it was perfectly dry. In the middle of the tent was a card table covered with a blue chenille cloth. Two kitchen chairs faced each other across the table.

"It might be wise if you were his first customer," Audrey suggested. "If you wouldn't mind, that is."

"Why?"

"Well, you could make sure that what he's doing is all right. And also, if you go and see him, it'll encourage everyone else." She giggled. "In fact, I almost think I might try him myself. I've never had my fortune told." She looked up at me. "Of course, I know it's complete nonsense—just a bit of fun." She giggled once more. "Still, I suppose one never knows."


At first, the only problem was that there was no sign of Toby Clifford—or of Joanna.

The fete began at two o'clock. The sun shone down from a

cloudless sky. Ted Potter directed the cars in the paddock and along the drive of Roth Park. Rosemary sat at a table just inside the Vicarage gates taking the entrance money and bestowing smiles in return. Audrey even persuaded Vanessa to accept a roving commission to sell raffle tickets.

"Many hands make light work," Audrey told her.

Vanessa glanced at me, her eyebrows lifting and her mouth twitching. "I thought that too many cooks spoiled the broth."

I managed not to laugh. "Audrey—are those books quite safe? Couldn't someone knock the pile over?"

In the first five minutes, two visitors bought copies of *The History of Roth*. The barbecue settled down to a steady glow. James, whose face was glowing too, added more and more charcoal.

"We could roast a pig on this," he told me. "Maybe I should have been a chef."

At twenty past two, Mary Vintner and I were trying to guess the weight of the cake, an activity which took place at the side of the house, in full view of the drive. A group of young people had just paid their entrance fee. Among them was Charlene's friend Kevin Jones. They had spent lunchtime in the Queen's Head, and they were in a cheerful mood. Behind them I glimpsed a woman—dark flowing hair, a long dark dress and some sort of brightly colored headscarf.

I heard Rosemary say, "Excuse me. You haven't paid."

For the first time I saw the woman's face, dominated by sunglasses with mirrored lenses and a bright-red slash of lipstick across the mouth.

"Oh no," the woman squealed. "Madam Mysterioso never pays. Cross my palm with silver, dearie, and we'll see if we can find you a handsome young man lurking in your future."

Rosemary had recognized Toby and even before he began to speak her embarrassment was obvious, at least to me. She stood back, waving him in.

"Vanessa," Toby called, declining to be waved in, "come and vouch for me. We madams must stick together."

Several people laughed, including Mary. He had a gift for making people laugh when he wanted to, even when what he said was not intrinsically funny. Vanessa came into view with her roll of raffle tickets. Smiling, their heads close together, she and Toby followed the path down the side of the house toward Mary and me. Rosemary looked after them, her face pink and tight.

"Sorry I'm a bit late," Toby said to me. "I started to drive down, but some idiot had blocked the drive, so I had to reverse back up to the house and then walk. And walking in a skirt is an art I haven't entirely mastered."

"It's a splendid costume." What I wanted to say was, *Leave my daughter alone*, and, *Where's Joanna?*

"I'll get started, shall I? Is there a queue?"

As it happened, there was. When we reached the tent, Kevin and his friends were clamoring for Madam Mysterioso.

"Ah," cried Toby in his falsetto. "The price of fame. My public needs me. Hello, children! Just give me a moment to powder my nose."

He winked at Vanessa and went alone into the tent.

Audrey sidled up to me. "Shouldn't you go first?" she hissed.

At this moment there was a diversion.

"Fire!" shouted Brian.

Almost everyone in the garden turned toward the barbecue. His face purple, James was jumping up and down on a flaming tea towel. His wife took in the situation at a glance. She darted into the kitchen, lifted the washing-up bowl from the sink, returned outside and deposited several pints of dirty sudsy water over the tea towel and over her husband's trousers and shoes. James swore. Then he looked up and realized that he was at the center of attention.

"Almost ready to take your orders, ladies and gentlemen," he called, taking advantage of his audience. "Beefburgers, sausages, fried onions, rolls, mustard, tomato ketchup—we have everything you could possibly want to eat." He added, in a slightly lower voice, "Damn it, Mary, you'll have to send Brian home for my shorts and sandals. I wish you wouldn't panic like that."

By the time I returned to Madam Mysterioso, Kevin was already inside the tent, laughing hysterically.

I spent the rest of the afternoon in a daze. I wandered around the fete and talked to people. After all, as Vanessa pointed out to me during a lull in the proceedings, it was my party and I was expected to circulate. The weather was wonderful, attendance was as good as we had ever had, if not better, and both the barbecue and Madam Mysterioso were doing excellent trade.

But all I could think of was Joanna. Why wasn't she here? Had she changed her mind about me? Had Toby found out and somehow prevented her from coming? In the end, I could stand it no longer. I slipped into the house and went into the study. I dialed the number of Roth Park and waited.

The phone rang on and on. While it rang, I looked out of the window at Rosemary sitting at her table by the gate, staring out at the main road and the green beyond. I wondered if Joanna had had an accident, if she were lying in a coma at the foot of the stairs. Or she might have slipped, cracked her head and fallen into the swimming pool. I was about to give up when there was a click at the other end of the line and Joanna's sleepy voice said hello.

"It's me."

"David. Dear David. What time is it?"

"About a quarter to four. Are you coming down to the fete? I thought—"

The study door opened. Vanessa came in with a cup of tea in each hand.

"No," I said swiftly. "I'm afraid you've got a wrong number. Goodbye." I put down the phone.

"I thought we could have tea in peace and quiet," Vanessa said. "It's like a Roman circus out there. With Audrey as the principal lion." She sat down opposite me and took a cigarette from the packet on the desk. "A wrong number? I didn't hear the phone ring."

"It had hardly started when I picked the phone up," I said. "Thanks for the tea. It's thirsty work."

"I visited Madam Mysterioso," Vanessa said. "She foresaw an outstanding literary success in my life. You should give Toby a try—he's really rather good."

I was scared that Joanna might phone me back. I gulped my tea and went outside with Vanessa. The fete was beginning to wind down. James beamed at us as he dropped the last sausages on to the grill.

"Have a hot dog. Vanessa? David?"

The smell of burning meat reached my nostrils.

"*With flames to the flesh,*" Vanessa quoted, "*with brands to the burning.* Yes, please."

"Not for me, thanks," I said.

The smell made me queasy. Trust Francis Youlgreave to be both ambiguous and disgusting. *As incense to heav'n the soul is returning* . . . It had never occurred to me before that a burning heretic must have smelled of roasting meat, and that the smell must have titillated the taste buds of the spectators, especially those with empty bellies. A missionary who had talked to me when I was an ordinand had told me that roasted human flesh smelled and tasted like pork.

"Pork sausages," James said. "Can't beat them. Much nicer flavor than beef."

Four more copies of *The History of Roth* had been sold and there was no longer a queue outside Madam Mysterioso's tent. The flap was open. Toby beckoned me in. He held out his right hand, palm upward.

"Cross me palm with silver," he squeaked, his voice sounding hoarser than it had at the beginning of the afternoon.

I laid a ten-shilling note in his hand.

"That's right, my dear. Generosity shall have its reward. Shut the flap and we can be nice and private."

When the flap was closed, the tent became another place—cool, green and shadowed. A joss stick smoldered in a brass holder, filling the air with a heavy scent. Toby, hunched over the table, in his black wig, his long black dress and his shawl, seemed in no hurry to begin. He had added a silk scarf, worn as a headband, and a large necklace of imitation diamonds to his attire. On the table between us were some of the tools of his trade: a pack of tarot cards, a crystal ball, and the *Prophecies* of Paracelsus.

"Isn't this cozy?" he said. "Now, what can I do for you? A little palmistry, perhaps?"

Examining my hand with a large magnifying glass, Toby launched into an entertaining survey of my hypothetical future. Soon I would be a bishop. In a year or two I would have my own television show. Meanwhile (he threw in for good measure), my wife would become a world-famous author.

"I usually end by consulting my crystal ball," he informed me in a voice that was now reduced to an imperious wheeze. "In it I see a vision of the future, a picture that encapsulates what is to come. Frequently its meaning is symbolic. I like my clients to take away this picture and meditate upon it, if possible for years to come."

He grinned at me across the table. "Stare into the crystal," he commanded.

The two of us placed our elbows on the table and peered into its glassy depths. All I could see was a distorted image of myself and the walls of the tent. Seconds passed.

"I can see a little girl," Toby said in his normal voice. He looked up at me, his eyes wide and surprised. "She's sitting on a bed, and she's got dark hair." He frowned. "And she's *crying*."

*Chapter Thirty-Four*

A SIGN CONSISTING OF a ragged sheet of cardboard attached to a wooden baton had been pushed into the soft verge beside the drive: PARTY, it said in red letters, and underneath was an arrow pointing to the path through the shrubbery. Pop music pulsed steadily through the warm evening air.

Audrey made a face. "Oh dear. That jingly-jangly music. If music's the word I want."

She had walked with us up the drive, joining us as we came through the gate from the churchyard—her timing was so perfect that I suspected that she had been watching out for us.

It was a little before seven o'clock. The evening sun was directly in our eyes. It slanted across the facade of the house, creating black bars of shadow. The Vintners' Rover was among the cars in front of the house in the shadow of the tower. Brian ran across the gravel and annexed Michael. The two boys darted into the shrubbery.

"Hello, Vicar," said Ted Potter, coming up behind us with Doris. He beamed at Vanessa and Rosemary and sidled closer to me. His breath smelled of beer. "Never thought we'd be coming up *here* for a party. Times change, eh?"

Toby had been generous with his invitations. A stream of people, some on foot and some in cars, were making their way up the drive toward the house. Kevin and Charlene walked self-consciously arm in arm, followed by Judy, the fat girl in the bus shelter who had sworn at Audrey.

We followed the boys through the shrubbery to the ragged lawn on the other side of the bushes. The French windows were open. People were chatting and drinking on the terrace, on the lawn and down by the swimming pool. There were many faces I did not recognize.

"I wonder where our host and hostess are," Audrey said, her nose wrinkling.

There was a loud splash from the direction of the pool. For a moment we hesitated, feeling the awkwardness of those who have arrived at a gathering but have not yet been assimilated by it.

There was no sign of Joanna.

Kevin and Charlene emerged giggling from the shrubbery, with Judy trailing behind.

"David! Vanessa!"

James Vintner waved from the terrace. Somewhere in the room behind him came the familiar bray of Mary's laughter. The music stopped abruptly.

"Thank heavens for that," muttered Audrey.

"Come and get yourself a drink," James called. "Toby's made me deputy barman for the evening."

We trooped up to the terrace and into the long sitting room. A group of teenagers clustered around the record player. A trestle table had been set up as a makeshift bar at one end.

"Gin, whiskey, vodka?" James waved his arm to and fro, pointing out what was on offer. "Beer, cider, red wine, white wine, Coca-Cola, orange squash, sherry—and of course punch.

Come on, David, why not push the boat out? I see you've come in mufti so you can let your hair down. What about a large gin?"

We all asked for gin, even Rosemary, because it was the easiest thing to do.

"Where are the Cliffords?" Vanessa asked as James was rummaging in the ice bucket.

"Toby took a jug of punch down to the pool. I wouldn't advise trying it—absolutely lethal. At least a bottle of brandy went into it, and heaven knows what else . . . Jo's around somewhere—I saw her a moment ago."

Jealousy kicked me. I didn't like James calling her "Jo."

"There you are. You know where to come for refills." James leered at Charlene and Doris. "And what can I get you, my dears?"

We drifted by stages on to the terrace and down to the lawn. Rosemary was soon in conversation with two young men I did not know and to whom she did not introduce me. The three of them followed us across the lawn. Michael and Brian zigzagged like swallows around the garden. Audrey was hailed by our librarian, Mrs. Finch, who was with her husband.

"I don't think I've ever seen ground elder quite so well established as this," the husband said in a voice like a satisfied whinny. "I mean, they'll be having it growing inside the house if they're not careful."

Vanessa and I moved away.

"I'll be glad when this is over," she murmured. "Can we leave early?"

"It's been a long day," I said, not wanting to commit myself.

"It's always a relief when the fete is out of the way for another year."

"I'm dead on my feet."

"I may have to stay for a while. I feel I'm partly on duty." I added, as casually as I could manage, "But there's no reason why you shouldn't slip off whenever you want."

"I might do that. I'd like to do a little reading tonight." She paused to sip her drink, and made a face. "James's made this awfully strong."

We went down the steps into the paved area around the swimming pool. Several teenagers were swimming or splashing each other. Toby was at the center of a knot of people in front of the white changing hut where Rosemary and I had sheltered with him from the rain. He saw us and waved. We walked around the pool to join him. He stood out from everyone else because he was in white—a collarless shirt and tight, flared trousers.

"You're looking very festive," he said to Vanessa, who was in fact wearing the dress that she had worn at the Trasks' dinner party almost a year ago, on the occasion of our first meeting.

Vanessa laughed and said, "Go on with you, Toby."

He leaned forward unexpectedly and kissed her on the cheek. "Welcome to the party, anyway. If David doesn't mind, you can be our official Belle of the Ball. By the way, I've got something to show you."

"Really? What?"

"It's a surprise." She looked at him in a way that was almost flirtatious. Which *was* flirtatious. It suddenly struck me that Vanessa was not averse to flirtation when it was divorced from any possibility of leading to sexual activity.

Toby looked past us. "And Rosemary—how are you?"

My daughter was standing with the two youths only a few yards away. She ignored him.

"Why are you being so mysterious?" asked Vanessa.

"I like surprises," Toby said. "Don't you? I'll give you a clue: it's something to do with Francis Youlgreave."

"I see." Vanessa's voice did not change, but her features sharpened as if the skin of her face had tightened over the bones beneath: suddenly she looked hungry. "And when is the secret going to be revealed?"

"Soon. Give me a moment." He smiled impartially at both of us. "I need to collect my thoughts and discharge my hostly duties." He turned and in one swift movement picked up a dish that had been resting on the step of the little wooden verandah behind him. "Have some cheese."

He held out a large, chipped serving plate designed for a joint of meat. At present it held a mound of cheese diced roughly into cubes. On one side of the plate was the kitchen knife he had been using to cut up the cheese, and on the other was the remains of a hunk of Cheddar.

"We should have got some of those little cocktail sticks. But I hope you won't mind using your fingers." Toby looked up at the house. "Clouds coming up from the west. I think we're going to get rain, so we might as well enjoy the garden and the pool while we can."

Nibbling the cheese, I stared at the sky. I caught sight of Rosemary, still only a few yards away, flanked by escorts. But she wasn't listening to them. She was looking at us. I smiled at her but she appeared not to see me.

Toby popped two cubes of cheese into his mouth. "Let's go

up to the house and I'll put you out of your misery," he said indistinctly. "Have you seen Joanna yet?"

"No." Vanessa glanced at me. "Was she at the fete? I didn't see her."

"She decided she'd do a few things for the party," Toby said. "At least, that was her story. My theory is, she didn't want to run the risk of being pointed out as the sister of Madam Mysterioso."

"Audrey tells me that you and the barbecue were our top-earning attractions," I said.

"That's a comfort." Toby waved at the redbrick bulk of the house. "So if my career as a hotelier falls through, at least I can make a new life as a professional prophet."

Toby picked up the jug of punch and the three of us walked slowly back to the house, pausing every now and then to allow Toby to fulfill his hostly duties. I wondered whether the glance Vanessa had given me was significant, whether she suspected that there might be something between Joanna and me. Hindsight always colors memory; but even at that moment I felt there were strange emotions abroad, an uneasiness which affected the way that people mixed with each other.

A burst of rock music came to meet us from the sitting room. A few couples were dancing on the terrace. In the room beyond, James was explaining how to make champagne cocktails to a ravishingly beautiful Asian girl. Mary was dancing with a large young man in a leather jacket. The drinks table was surrounded by a crowd of people who had evidently decided that it was simpler to serve themselves rather than wait to be served by the deputy barman.

Mary and her partner lurched a few paces to the right. Suddenly I saw Joanna. She was standing by the fireplace talking to Audrey.

Audrey had seen us, too. "I was just asking Joanna if we could turn the music down a little," she shouted, crossing the room toward us. "It's absolutely deafening. In fact, it's so loud I'm not sure she can hear what I was saying."

"Oh, you have to have loud music at parties," Vanessa said. "Otherwise it wouldn't be a proper party."

Audrey stared at her. It was an undiplomatic remark, and Vanessa was not usually undiplomatic. Either she wanted to offend Audrey, I thought, or her mind was on other things—on Toby's surprise connected with Francis Youlgreave.

"Of course we can turn it down," Toby said, smiling at Audrey.

He walked over to the record player, but it was too late. Audrey had wheeled around on Vanessa. At that moment Toby turned the volume down. He must have turned the knob too far because suddenly there was no music at all.

"I've had enough of you," Audrey shrieked in the sudden silence. "You're quite intolerable. Why do you have to interfere? You don't belong here."

She flung a startled glance around the room, at the blank faces staring at hers. She gave a high, wordless cry and stumbled through the nearest French window on to the terrace. Simultaneously, Toby turned up the music. Audrey ran across the flags, down the steps and on to the lawn. A moment later she vanished among the bushes of the shrubbery between the lawn and the drive.

I had begun to follow her. I reached the French window.

Vanessa came up behind me and laid a restraining hand on my arm.

"Better leave her," she said. "It'll be kinder in the long run."

"Are you OK?"

"Of course." She smiled, cool and faintly amused.

James abandoned his Asian beauty and came over to the two of us. He looked from one to the other of us.

"Flew off the handle, eh?"

"You heard what happened," Vanessa said, though James could not possibly have heard what she had said to spark off Audrey's outburst.

He shrugged. "Time of life. Takes some people harder than others. How are your glasses? You can't go round with half-empty glasses. This is a party."

The buzz of conversation resumed.

"I feel responsible," Toby said, every inch the concerned host.

"There's nothing you could have done," James pointed out. "Best forget about it. Kindest thing all round. Don't let it spoil the party."

Toby turned to Vanessa. "Are you ready for the secret?"

"Where is it?"

"It *was* in the old stables. I found it when I was digging out that tent, but I didn't have a proper look till this evening."

In her eagerness, Vanessa laid a hand on his arm. "Yes, but what *is* it? It had better be good after all this build-up."

He stared at her, obviously wondering whether to prolong the tease. "All right. It's a box—a dusty old pine box full of dusty old books. Three or four dozen of them. I've not been through them, but most of them look like theology. And the ones I did look at had 'F. St. J. Youlgreave' on the flyleaf. I've moved them into the office."

As he was talking, he and Vanessa were edging toward the door to the hall. They did not ask me to accompany them and I did not want to go. As soon as they had left the room, I strolled over to the fireplace. Joanna looked up at me. The music cocooned us in a bubble of privacy.

"Look," she said; I half heard her and half saw her lips move. Her eyes showed me where to look—behind me, toward the terrace.

I was just in time to see Rosemary turning away. As I watched, she stepped down to the lawn and rejoined the youths she had been with at the pool.

"She's in a state," Joanna said. Then only her lips moved without any accompanying sound: "*I love you.*"

"Come outside?" I mouthed back.

She nodded, picked up her glass from the mantelpiece and led the way on to the terrace. It was noticeably darker and cooler than it had been even a few minutes before. We walked down the steps, away from the dancers and the drinkers. There was no sign of Rosemary or her escorts.

"I missed you. Why weren't you at the fete?"

"Because I wouldn't have had a chance to be with you. What happened when you tried to phone?"

"Vanessa came into the study."

"I want to be alone with you. I *have* to be."

We met Doris and Ted Potter at that moment. I heard myself congratulating them on their contribution to the fete and telling them how much money we had made this year—a record. I even asked about Beauty and Beast. And then, as if in a dream, they were no longer there; and Joanna and I were alone on the edge of the lawn.

"There're too many people," she whispered, turning so she could see if anyone was coming toward us. "They're all over the place. Some of the younger ones aren't going to go for hours and hours. Not until the booze runs out. And Toby's really gone to town on that." She looked at me over the rim of her glass. "He's trying to make everyone like him. Have you noticed?"

I shrugged. At that moment I was not particularly interested in Toby.

"He wants to get the locals on his side for the hotel scheme, you see." She reverted abruptly to what we'd been talking about before. "It's too dangerous outside. I thought it would be easy, once it began to get dark, but people are everywhere."

"Then what can we do?"

"Go inside the house. Up to my room."

"But—but what if someone comes?"

"We can lock the door." She waved her free hand around the garden. "We can't lock the door here. It's such a big place that no one will think it odd if they can't find us."

I ached to touch her. We had so few choices. It took me only a moment to convince myself that if we wanted to be alone, then her room was the safest place.

She knew me well enough to take my agreement for granted. "We'd better go there separately. You remember the way?"

I nodded.

"I'll go first," she said. "You can follow in a couple of minutes. Use the main stairs. Toby's put a sign to the lavatory on the landing. Everyone will assume you're going up there."

She smiled up at me and mouthed the words *I love you*. Then she slipped away across the grass. She was wearing a short dress that buttoned up the front; it was made of a soft material the color of claret. On the terrace, she paused for a moment to say something to the man in the leather jacket who had been dancing with Mary Vintner. I heard her laugh. Then she disappeared into the house. I felt sick with desire, sick with shame.

Drink in hand, I walked slowly down to the swimming pool.

"Uncle David?"

Startled, I looked up. Two small white faces loomed against the dark red foliage of the copper beech. Michael and Brian were ten feet above my head.

"It's a great climbing tree once you get up to the first main branch."

"I'm sure it is." I wanted to add, *Do be careful*, but managed to restrain myself.

He grinned down at me. "We can see everyone. But they can't see us."

"Let's hope they all behave themselves, then. See you later."

I walked around the swimming pool, arriving in time to see another fully clothed youth falling into the water accidentally on purpose. I looked down at my glass and saw to my surprise that it was empty. Surely I need not wait any longer? I sauntered back to the house.

"Have a refill," James called as I went inside.

I allowed him to give me one, because it was the simplest thing to do. I drifted across the room, smiling at faces I knew, and slipped out into the hallway. To my relief, there was no sign of Rosemary, Audrey or—most importantly of all—Vanessa. I walked down the corridor to the main hall at the front of the house.

No one had turned on the lights. The office door was closed, but there was a line of light between the bottom of the door and the threshold. I assumed that Vanessa and Toby were still inside, still examining the books which might have belonged to Francis Youlgreave. Suspicion stirred—was I not a conspirator myself? Surely they had been in there a very long time? I glanced at my watch. It seemed hours since Toby and Vanessa had left, but in fact it was no more than ten or fifteen minutes. I pushed the pair of them out of my mind.

As I went up the stairs, I glanced upward through the gloom toward the great lantern skylight on the roof. This was a monochrome world, a place of shadows.

I reached the landing. A few yards away from me, a lavatory flushed. Simultaneously I noticed the light under a door on my left.

Abandoning dignity, I scuttled along the landing. A large cupboard, stretching from floor to ceiling, stood against the wall of the corridor. I ducked beside it and pressed my back against the wall so the bulk of the cupboard was between me and the lavatory door and the head of the stairs.

A bolt shot back. There were footsteps on the bare boards, footsteps clattering down the stairs. I waited until all was silent and then continued along the corridor.

The door to the room beneath Joanna's was ajar. Despite the gathering dusk, it was lighter here than on the landing. One of the windows faced west and part of the sky was dark with rain clouds. For a moment, I hesitated. I thought I heard a faint rhythmic rustle, like the beating of distant wings.

*Francis Youlgreave's angel?*

There was a pattering sound in the fireplace. I went over to it and peered down at the flecks of soot which had fallen into the grate. Nothing to worry about. Just the wind in the chimney.

I crossed the room to the spiral staircase, whose door was also ajar. I went up the uncarpeted stairs as quietly as I could manage. It was suddenly much darker again, because the only light in this enclosed space came from the tiny arrow slits set low in the walls. Joanna's door was shut. Beyond it, the stairs carried on upward through the darkness to Francis Youlgreave's room. I tapped on her door.

*What if she isn't here?*

I barely had time to formulate the thought before the handle turned. Joanna smiled up at me. She held the door open and I slipped inside. I turned to see her closing the door and turning the key in the lock. She faced me and leaned back against the door. I saw that she was shivering.

"What is it?"

"I thought you wouldn't come."

I put my arms around her. It was very quiet. One of the windows was open and I could hear the faint sound of music, of chinking glasses and laughter; but the sounds were so far away that they emphasized the silence rather than broke it. The big room was much as I had seen it before—the mattress on the carpet, an island on a sea of bare boards—except that it was tidier.

Gradually Joanna stopped trembling. Her fingers ran down my spine, up and down, up and down, as though she were playing a musical instrument. Then she stirred, pulled herself a little away from me and smiled. Slowly she undid the buttons of her dress and let it drop to the floor. She stepped out of it and took my hand.

"Toby—" I began.

She put her finger to my lips. "Not now. Just you. Just me."

I drew her toward me. We kissed. I ran my fingertips over her breasts. She pulled at the knot of my tie. When we were both naked, I led her to the mattress.

Gradually the light ebbed from the room. Detail seeped away. The four windows became round-headed oblongs in varying shades of gray. At times, it seemed to me that the tower was rocking gently. I heard the wind moaning, almost obscuring the faint sound of beating wings. Into my mind slipped an incongruous image of Francis Youlgreave's angel carrying him up to heaven.

Afterward we lay in a warm huddle of naked limbs under a single sheet. *Now I have done the unforgivable*, I thought; and joy welled like a fountain inside me. Joanna nestled against me, her hand slowly stroking my chest. I could hardly breathe for happiness.

"I want it all over again," she whispered, so quietly I could barely hear; her breath teased the hairs of my chest.

"And again," I said.

"And again."

It wasn't funny but we laughed. Vanessa and I had never

laughed after making love. Joanna reached over me for cigarettes and lighter. Still entwined, we struggled into a sitting position, leaning against the wall. She pushed a cigarette in my mouth and lit it.

"Do you think they're missing us?" she asked.

"Probably. It doesn't matter."

She twitched. "It might if Toby notices."

"Forget Toby."

Joanna drew on her cigarette and her features acquired an infernal glow. "We should go downstairs." But she did not move.

I touched her cheek. "Why do you stay with him? Why are you afraid of him?"

She said nothing. Her face was a pale oval in the gloom. I heard her breathing, rapid and irregular.

"Is it true that this house is yours?" I persisted, my voice becoming harsh because I was anxious. "Did you tell me the truth?"

Joanna sucked in her breath. "I've never lied to you. Not really . . . I never will. We must go." She made a half-hearted attempt to scramble off the mattress, but our bodies were too entangled for her to be able to move without my cooperation. "I'm sorry. I'm not worth it, you know."

"You're worth everything. I love you."

"Really?" She stubbed out her cigarette, her head bowed over the ashtray. "It's not just sex?"

"No. Though I'm not pretending that's not important. But I love you—I want to marry you. Will you?" There was a silence. My stomach felt as though I were falling. *Falling from a high window into the arms of an angel.*

"You can't." She made a sound that was half a giggle and half a sob. "You're already married."

"There's such a thing as divorce."

"But you wouldn't be able to. You're a clergyman."

"There are other ways of making a living."

She kissed me. Then she rested her head against my shoulder. "Anyway, there's Toby."

"What's he got to do with it? I don't want to marry *him*." A monstrous suspicion sprouted in my mind. "You and Toby—surely you're not—?"

Joanna laughed, a sharp, nervy sound like a shower of stones against a windowpane. "Toby and I aren't lovers, if that's what you're worried about."

"Then what is it?"

"I told you about the heroin. I didn't lie to you. But I didn't tell you everything."

I waited. The evening air cooled my bare skin. Ash fell from my cigarette to the sheet. I brushed it off and dropped the cigarette end in the ashtray.

"You remember Annabel? Toby's friend?" She pulled herself away from me and sat up on the mattress, her arms around her knees. "Well, he used the same technique on me as he did on her."

"Heroin." My hand slipped on to Joanna's thigh, as if I needed to reassure myself that she was still there, to feel the flesh and blood of her. "Are you—you're addicted to heroin?"

"Yes."

"But you're not—"

"I'm not a half-starved junkie living in a basement room

in Notting Hill? I'm not selling my body to pay for my habit? I'm not covered in sores. I'm not subhuman."

I put my arms around her and hugged her.

"It doesn't have to be like that, you know. If you've got a regular supply of it, you can lead a perfectly normal life."

"But there was no sign of it."

"I don't use a syringe. I smoke it. That's how Toby got me started." Her voice was low and the flow stumbled. "We used to smoke dope together. Cannabis, pot—whatever you want to call it. Everyone did. All our friends. And why not? As far as I can see, it's perfectly harmless. But Toby began rolling me joints with a little something added. My special joints, he called them." Her shoulders twitched. "And after a while, I couldn't do without them. So what could I do? I didn't know anyone else who could get me heroin. Only Toby. *Keep it in the family*: that's what he said. And as long as I do what Toby wants, there's no problem there."

"There are doctors. A GP could refer you to a—?"

"But I *like* it. Besides, I'm scared."

"Why are you scared?"

"Because if I try to stop using heroin, Toby won't be able to rely on me to do what he wants."

"But that's the whole point of it, surely?"

"He'll do something. He'll try and get me back on it. And if he can't manage that, he might do *anything*. It's very easy to overdose, you see. Especially with Chinese heroin. And his stuff's all Chinese. It comes in from Hong Kong, and you never really know how strong it is or what they've cut it with. It's not pure, like the stuff you get on the NHS. Not that there's much of that around these days. But if a dealer gets annoyed with a customer, he'll sometimes give him a shot of unusually pure heroin. There's a word for it in the trade. It's called a hotshot. And it kills you."

"But what good would that do him? You said he hasn't any money of his own. Wouldn't he be killing the golden goose?"

"If I made a will, you mean? Left what I've got to someone else. I'm not sure it would work. When we bought this house, he made me sign something. A sort of option clause. It gives him the right to buy it at a nominal sum unless he agrees to the sale." By now it was almost entirely dark and Joanna's voice had sunk to a whisper. "He'd probably kill me anyway. There'd be no danger for him, because everyone would say I was just another addict who had taken an overdose. He likes to feel in control, you see. That's important in itself."

"But *killing* you?"

She twisted in my arms. "Believe me. You must believe me. He's my brother, I know him."

She reached for the cigarettes again. For a moment we smoked in silence.

"Have I made you hate me? Despise me?"

"Of course you haven't. We'll go away together. Then I can look after you, help you with the treatment. We'll find you a lawyer, too. Toby won't be able to find you. That's the important thing."

"I can't do that. I can't ruin your life."

"You don't want to come with me?"

"You know I do. But if we go away together, I'll ruin you—one way or another. And I love you—so how can I do that to you?"

"You must let me decide that. I know what I'm letting myself in for."

"You don't, not really. You don't know what living with an addict is like. You don't even know me very well." She stroked my neck, tracing the outline of the Adam's apple. "We must go. They'll be wondering where we are."

"They don't matter."

"They do. You know they do."

It was then, as if on cue, that we heard footsteps slowly crossing the bare boards of the room below. There was a faint creak.

"That's the door to the stairs," Joanna whispered. "He's coming up."

"The door's locked."

"Yes, but the key's in the lock. If they bend down and look . . ."

We clung together like babes in the wood. The footsteps were slow but not heavy. They could have belonged to a man or a woman. They slowed as they approached our door, and then stopped. Joanna squeezed my hand.

There was a faint tapping. I held my breath. Someone wanting to be quiet—why? Not wanting to disturb Joanna if she were asleep? Or afraid of a third party hearing the knock? At length—I had lost track of time—the footsteps began again.

"They're going *up*," Joanna murmured.

Enclosed in darkness, we listened to the sounds and tried to decode them. The higher the footsteps climbed, the more muffled they became. Suddenly they were louder and more crisply defined.

Joanna stirred against me. "He's in the room above." Her breath tickled my ear. "You don't think . . . ?"

"No. It's not Francis Youlgreave. You can be quite sure of that." As I spoke I wondered if I were right.

The footsteps crossed the ceiling above our heads. I thought they led to the window overlooking the drive, the one from which Francis Youlgreave had jumped to the gravel below.

Silence settled around us again. When at last the footsteps began again, I felt Joanna letting out her breath. A sigh of relief? *He hasn't jumped, this time.*

The steps stopped. What was he—or she—doing now? Staring out of another window? Then the movement began again—more rapid now, almost a run, and much louder. The steps tapped across the floor and clattered down the stairs, not pausing at Joanna's door. Somewhere below us another door slammed.

Joanna slithered away from me, rolled off the mattress and scrambled to her feet. Her naked body was a dark blur, as beautiful in the semi-darkness as it was in the light. I struggled up myself—far more slowly, for my limbs were less supple, and I was not used to scrambling up from mattresses. She tiptoed across the room to the north-facing window. Her body darkened into a silhouette in front of the paler gray of the glass.

"David—look."

I padded across the floor. The room was full of drafts, slipping through the windows, under the door, through the cracks in the floorboards. The warmth from our lovemaking had gone and I felt cold. When I reached the window, Joanna leaned against me and drew my arm over her shoulder and down between her breasts.

"See." She pointed with her free hand. "Over there—beyond the pool, beyond the trees."

On the far side of the trees, just beyond the garden boundary, flames flickered red and orange in Carter's Meadow. They had climbed high and were still climbing higher. Because of the screen of leaves and branches between us and the fire, the flames were an impressionistic jumble of sparks. The window was open a little at the top, and for an instant I thought I could even hear the crackle of the fire and perhaps a cry of pain and terror.

> *With flames to the flesh, with brands to the burning,*
> *As incense to heav'n the soul is returning . . .*

# Chapter Thirty-Five

S OMEONE'S HAVING A BONFIRE." The calmness of my voice amazed me. "Teenagers, perhaps. After all, it's Saturday night."

Joanna did not reply. She began to search for her clothes in the semi-darkness. I did the same. I felt ungainly, unclean and furtive. Joanna finished dressing before me. While I was still knotting my shoelaces, she was unlocking the door.

"It's a good time to go," she said. "They'll have seen the fire. It'll be a diversion."

I straightened up. "I wish we could stay."

"So do I."

"There's so much we need to talk about. The future."

"I don't belong in your future."

"You do."

She reached up and kissed me. "I so much want to believe you." Her arms tightened round my neck. "If I could sort out Toby somehow, could we really be together?"

"Of course we could. We can in any case."

"I've got an idea."

"What?"

"I don't want to tell you yet. I don't know if I'm brave enough to do it. I don't know if it would work."

I started to ask a question, but she covered my mouth, first with her fingers and then with her lips. A moment later, she turned the key and opened the door . . .

"Give me your hand," she murmured. "We'd better not use the light, and I know the way."

"You sound as if you're talking in parables."

She stopped so suddenly that I bumped into her, and again she reached up and kissed me. Without another word she led me down the stairs, across the room below and along the landing which ran the length of the house.

The music had stopped. The light was on at the head of the stairs. People were talking somewhere in the distance. Their voices echoed up from the hall, sounds chasing each other through the house to the lantern in the roof. Among the voices I thought I recognized James's and perhaps Vanessa's.

Joanna tugged me into a passage on the left, leading toward the back of the house. There was still enough light for me to be able to make out broad outlines and variations of light and shade; but all detail had gone. We went up and down short flights of stairs and across bare rooms smelling of dust. In one room we heard the scuttling of a startled animal, probably a rat. Joanna shied away from the sound and for an instant nestled against me.

She opened a door. "The backstairs," she whispered. "I'll go first and check there's no one in the kitchen."

A moment later, I joined her in the kitchen, a large, untidy room which smelled of damp and stale milk, and which looked in the gloom as though little had changed there since the Youlgreaves left in the 1930s.

"We'd better separate," Joanna said. "If you go through that door and carry straight on, you'll reach the hall. You could say you were looking for a lavatory. I'll go round the back."

"Where?"

"There's a kitchen yard outside, and then the stables. I can get round into the garden, near the swimming pool."

She gave me a gentle push toward the door to the hall. She herself moved away in the opposite direction. When I reached the door I stopped and looked back at her.

She, too, was looking at me. "I love you," she said softly but very distinctly. "Whatever happens, remember that."

She opened the door and was gone. Sadness swept over me like a fog. I stumbled blindly through the house.

There were lights in the hall. I forced myself toward the glare. I saw no one. The door to the office was still shut. I heard voices on my left, presumably coming from the sitting room with the bar. I could not make out the words, but the voices were no longer making party sounds: they sounded urgent and confused.

I pushed my fingers through my hair and straightened my tie. If only I could find a mirror—I was suddenly afraid that my appearance must in some way proclaim not only that I loved Joanna but that we had spent much of the evening making love. I looked at my watch. It was after nine o'clock. It felt much later.

I peered down the corridor. The door to the sitting room was open. Someone had left a half-filled glass on the hall floor. On impulse I picked it up. A partygoer has a drink in his hand; the possession of a drink helped to create an illusion of my innocence.

The sitting room was full of people. Many of them were clustered around the makeshift bar. I could not see Vanessa or Toby.

James's voice rose above the others: "Softly, softly, eh? No point in letting it spoil the party." He spotted me and waved me toward him. "Have you seen Toby?"

"He might be outside."

"He went off somewhere. Thought he might have been looking for you."

I shook my head.

"Someone's lit a bonfire in that field by the council estate."

"So I gather."

"Just a bit of fun, probably."

There were footsteps outside and suddenly Vanessa was in the room. Her face was flushed and she looked very happy—almost as though she had come from meeting a lover. She came toward me.

"I was wondering where you were," she said. "What's happening?"

"There's a bonfire on Carter's Meadow."

"That fire's on our land," interrupted Ted Potter, waving a beer bottle belligerently. The bottle was not empty and some of the contents trickled on to his face and shoulders. "Bloody trespassers, Vicar, if you don't mind me saying so. We're going to turf them out."

"It's not your land, Ted," Doris said, grabbing his arm. "It's mine. And now you've got beer all over your jacket."

"Oh Doris," he crooned. He held the bottle up to the light and saw that it was now empty. He lunged toward the bar table and beamed at James. "It's my round, Doc. What's everyone having?"

Doris looked at me. "I'm sorry. It's only once or twice a year he gets like that. Doesn't touch the stuff the rest of the time. I just wish he wouldn't do it in public."

I smiled at her. "At least he's enjoying himself. And he's worked very hard today."

"So have we all. That's no excuse."

"What have you got there, Vicar?" Ted called. "Gin, is it?"

I covered the stolen glass with my hand and shook my head. Suddenly the memory of Joanna pushed its way to the forefront of my mind and I wanted to laugh with happiness.

"Wonderful, isn't it?" Vanessa was saying. "Such a piece of luck."

I spilled a few drops of my drink. "I'm sorry—what is?"

"The books. Toby says I can take them home."

"So they did belong to Francis?"

"Yes. There must be about thirty of them. Mainly theology, but there are some oddities as well. There's a copy of *The Tongues of Angels* with the pages uncut. And a mid-Victorian housewives' manual on meat."

"On *what*?"

Vanessa stared up at me with a half smile on her face. Implacable as fate, she knew exactly what she was telling me. "Meat. Everything the housewife needed to know. How to buy it, prepare it, cook it, serve it, dress it, carve it, use up the leftovers." She paused. "How to cut it up. There was a little textbook of human anatomy, too. Some of the passages had been marked."

I sipped my drink, discovering that it was neat gin.

"I'm not going to sanitize Francis Youlgreave. I want to know the *truth*."

Ted Potter stumbled between us and sat down heavily in

one of the armchairs. "To be perfectly honest, it's past my bedtime," he confided to the glass in his hand. He nodded, as though at something the glass had replied. "Yes, tomorrow is another day."

His eyelids closed. The glass wavered. Doris removed it and stared down at her husband. Charlene came to join her. A moment later, Ted began to snore gently.

"Kevin'll have to give us a hand with him," Doris said.

Charlene shook her head. "Kevin's flat on his back. Miss Oliphant tripped over him and he didn't even notice."

"Just leave them where they are," Vanessa suggested. "Why should getting them home be your responsibility?"

"Toby!" James roared at my shoulder. "How's the Great Fire of Carter's Meadow?"

Toby was at the nearer French window. "Seems to be dying down. I don't think anyone's out there. I'm going to have a look at it now. Anyone want to come?" He turned to me. "David?"

"David'll soon sort them out," James said, and laughed loudly. "The church militant."

Vanessa followed me on to the terrace. From this angle, you could not see the fire. Audrey was standing by the steps leading down to the lawn.

"Is Rosemary all right?" Vanessa asked.

"I expect so. I haven't seen her recently."

"David?" Audrey called from the shadows at the edge of the lawn. "I'd like a word."

I could tell by her voice that she was upset. "Could it wait a moment? I gather there's a little problem in Carter's Meadow."

"The fire? I bet you anything it's those wretched boys."

"The ones from the bus shelter?"

"No—Michael and Brian Vintner." She walked slowly toward us. "They've been behaving like barbarians all evening. I'm sorry to have to tell you this, but Michael barged into me by the pool and then rushed off without apologizing. And he and Brian were playing in the trees near the fence and making a terrible racket. I think they deserve a severe punishment."

"Audrey," Vanessa interrupted. "Thank you for telling us, but I really think you should leave Michael to us."

"I'm sorry, Mrs. Byfield." Audrey spat out Vanessa's married name as if it were a curse. "It's just not good enough."

"May we talk about this later?" I said.

"Leave it to me," Vanessa said, her voice grim. "I'll talk to Audrey. You and Toby go and sort out the fire."

Coward that I was, I was glad to take the easy way out. I had no wish to become involved in yet another of Audrey's outbursts. Not that I was particularly keen to go with Toby, either. The irony was that while Audrey was merely an irritation, Toby—if what Joanna had told me was true—was capable of real evil. Yet Toby was intelligent and had good manners, and he didn't make scenes; so in one way he was the more attractive choice of companion. It is always simpler to judge by externals, even when there is no excuse for doing so.

Toby and I walked across the lawn, the beam of his torch snaking before us. Few people were out here now. A young couple were embracing on one of the benches beside the swimming pool. When they saw us they hastily sat up and straightened their clothes. It was too dark to recognize their faces. Toby and I walked around the pool and I heard the couple scurrying into the night like the startled rat Joanna and I had disturbed upstairs.

"You can't see the fire from here," I said.

"I only noticed it because I went up the tower to see if Jo was there. Have you seen her lately, by the way?"

"Not recently. I've not seen Michael or Rosemary, either."

"Michael and Brian have been having the time of their lives. But I'm afraid Audrey hasn't."

"Perhaps we should have taken the boys home."

"Why? It's their party, too. I like parties where you have all sorts, all ages."

He led me toward the path through the bushes, the one Rosemary and I had taken in the opposite direction on the afternoon when Rosemary found the blood and the fur in Carter's Meadow. There was a pattering on the leaves above our heads.

"It's starting to rain," Toby said. "It's been trying to all evening."

"At least it'll help put out the fire."

The path had swung around to the left, and we could see the fire quite clearly on the far side of the fence. A few minutes later, we scrambled through into Carter's Meadow. We set off across the rough grass toward the little spinney of self-seeded trees.

"It's at the same place we found the fur," Toby said. "Exactly the same. How odd."

I glanced at him, but the darkness hid his face. "It may be a coincidence."

We walked on toward the clump of trees. The dead elder

stood on one side, apart from the others. Its wood must have dried out still further over the summer. It was a tree of fire, burning with one last glow of artificial life. By now the flames were dying down, but many of the branches and twigs still gleamed red. Two of the neighboring trees had blackened leaves, but fortunately the flames had not spread.

Toby panned the torch beam to and fro. No one was there. Nothing moved apart from the dying flames and the rain, which was growing steadily heavier. Trapped in the beam, the raindrops looked like needles showering from the sky.

"Phew," he said. "You can feel the heat from here."

"Lucky the wind wasn't in the other direction. The other trees would have gone, too."

The beam of the torch raced across the grass to the base of the tree. "What's that?"

Picked out in the torchlight was a black oblong with a red glow along the top. Something else lay half concealed on the ground immediately behind it—something red, I thought, though it was hard to be sure because the color might simply be a reflection of the flames.

Toby stopped a few yards away from the tree; the heat made it uncomfortable to go nearer. He played the beam on the ground.

"It's a sort of box. And that might be a petrol can behind it."

"So the fire was started deliberately?"

"Probably CHBs."

"What?"

Toby turned his head toward me and the reflections of the flames danced like snakes among his ginger curls. "Council house brats." He threw back his head and laughed.

The words shocked me—not merely because of their grotesque snobbery, but because Toby had assumed I would share his amusement. Was that how I appeared to him?

He turned back to the fire. "It'll burn itself out in an hour or so, and I don't think it's going to do any damage to anything else. But it's a bit close to the garden for comfort."

"We'd better report it to the police."

"If this were my land, the first thing I'd do is rebuild the fences."

I was only half listening to him. I edged across the grass toward the tree. The heat was unpleasant but not unbearable. Beside the box, the petrol can lay on its side, its cap off.

"Do you think Mrs. Potter might sell the field to me eventually? It would round off the garden rather nicely."

I picked up a long twig, one end charred from the fire. I used it to touch the blackened side of the box. The two came together with a faint *clunk*, which suggested that the box was made of metal.

*Dear God—not CHBs. Much closer to home.*

"David—what are you doing? Mind out—that branch is going to come down."

I ignored him. Shielding my face with my free arm against the heat, I took another two paces closer to the box. This must have been where the fire had started. I poked one end of the stick inside. A rectangular shape emerged from the debris, scattering ashes and sparks.

"David—?"

The object slithered down the stick and settled on the base of the box again, sending up another puff of ash. I retreated quickly to Toby.

"What is it? What did you find?"

In the space of a few seconds, the possibilities chased through my mind. I could say I did not know what it was. I could let someone else make the connection. I could say nothing to Toby but go and find Vanessa. Or I could say nothing to Toby or Vanessa, but instead phone the police. Or I could go back to the Vicarage and see if there was any damage there. Most of all, I wished that it was not I who had to deal with this.

"I'm pretty sure that's the tin box that contained the Youlgreave papers. It was in our house. If I'm right, someone must have broken in and stolen it. James left a can of petrol in the garage this afternoon, and I think they must have stolen that as well."

Toby whistled. "Vanessa—what's she going to say?"

"It depends if the papers were still in the box."

"No point if they weren't. Anyway, *something* was inside. What a mess."

He was right. Less than half an hour earlier, Joanna and I had been in bed together, and everything had seemed so simple. Not easy, but simple. Now, standing beside a burning tree with rain falling steadily on my head and shoulders, I felt as though nothing would ever be simple and straightforward again.

"We'd better phone the police."

"Come this way." Toby pointed the torch beam across the field to another part of the fence between it and the garden. "We can go through the stables. Less chance of meeting people, and we'll get less wet."

He took me through the darkened stables and into a yard

in the shadow of the back of the house. Soon we were in the kitchen where I had last seen Joanna. He led me along the corridor to the office by the front door. The room was empty. On the table was a wooden box, with its lid open. I saw books inside, neatly stacked. Toby shut the door behind us and put the torch on the table.

"You'd better phone. They'll take more notice of you."

He found me the number of the police station. When I got through, I talked to a desk sergeant who was reluctant to believe that anything was seriously amiss. We argued to and fro for several minutes.

"Look," the man said at last. "It's Saturday night and we're already overstretched. From what you've told me, it sounds like a bit of fun that got out of hand. But there's no real damage done, is there? Still, I'll make sure someone's round first thing in the morning."

"Isn't burglary and the destruction of property serious any longer?"

"Of course they are, sir." The policeman's good humor seemed unruffled. "I tell you what: why don't you go home and see if there's any evidence of a break-in? Maybe it wasn't your box, after all. No harm in checking. If you have had a break-in, of course, you give us a ring. I'll make a note of your call."

That was the end of my attempt to fetch the police. Toby, who had been leaning against the door smoking a cigarette, straightened up and smiled at me.

"The boys in blue not being too helpful?"

"You probably gathered what they said."

"I'll drive you down to the Vicarage if you want."

"I'd better have a word with Vanessa first. Break the news."
I hesitated. "Perhaps we shouldn't mention the box to anyone
else until we've told her."

We left the office and walked along the corridor toward the
sitting room. Little had changed in our absence. The Potter
women were still beside the head of the family, as he snored
quietly in the armchair. James and Mary, supported by a
dedicated band of helpers, were working their way methodi-
cally through the remaining contents of the bar. Rosemary
had returned and was surrounded by three youths who were
vying for her attention by the fireplace. Joanna wasn't there;
nor were Vanessa and Audrey.

"Seen Vanessa?" Toby asked.

"Thought she went out with you and David," James said.
"Did you catch our arsonist?"

"No sign of anyone. Just a burning tree."

"Sounds like your province, David. Isn't there something
in the Bible about a burning bush and the angel of the Lord?"

"Exodus. Chapter three."

I went to the nearest French window, with Toby behind
me. The rain was no longer a shower but a downpour. Reflected
light from the sitting room sparkled in the puddles on the
terrace.

"Maybe she's sheltering by the pool," Toby suggested.
"Shall I fetch an umbrella? There's one in the Jag."

"One of the boys will get it," James said. "Brian! Toby's got
a job for you."

Brian slipped through the crowd. For once Michael was
not with him. I felt a stirring of unease. If he was still outside, he would be soaked.

Toby gave Brian the car key. "The car's just outside the front door, under the canopy. There's a brolly on the back seat."

The boy ran off, glad to have a job to do, wanting to show off his speed and efficiency. Too late, I wished I had asked him where Michael was.

"Vanessa?" I called. "Vanessa?"

I waited for an answer. Beside me, Toby was silent. I stared across the lawn, a pale-gray smudge in the darkness.

Suddenly Brian was in the doorway of the sitting room. "There are two men outside," he gasped. "They've broken into your car."

There was a moment's silence.

Then Toby said, "*Shit!*" and ran past Brian, pushing him out of the way. Brian and I followed, with at least a dozen others trailing behind us. Rosemary was just behind me.

"Are you all right?" I asked in a low voice.

She did not answer. The current of people carried us side by side down the corridor into the hall. The front door was standing open. Rain gusted into the house, and a pool of water covered the tiles near the door. Framed in the doorway were two men in sodden raincoats, their bare heads wet with rain. Behind them was Toby's car under the shelter of the canopy. The driver's door was hanging open, and the panel shielding the door and window mechanisms had been removed.

"Mr. Clifford?" said the taller of the two, a man with a broad face and eyes that slanted down at the outer corners. "Mr. Toby Clifford?"

"Yes," Toby said. "Who are you?"

"Police." For an instant the man held out what might have

been a warrant card. "I'm Detective Sergeant Field, and this is Detective Constable Ingram. We'd like to ask you some questions, sir."

"What are you doing with my car? Have you broken into it?"

"It was unlocked. We—"

"You're lying. It was locked."

"Perhaps in the circumstances it would be better if you accompanied us to the station, sir. We wouldn't want to upset your guests, would we?"

Toby didn't answer. He was staring at the other man, who was holding what looked like a small brown parcel.

"I should tell you that you're not obliged to say anything unless you wish to do so," Field was saying, "but what you say may be put into writing and given in evidence."

Someone behind me gasped.

Toby swung around, turning his back on the police officers. His face was so pale it was almost green. His eyes searched the little crowd of his guests.

"You," he said, pointing at Rosemary. "You tight-arsed, screwed-up little bitch, you frigid little fucked-up cow."

He lunged at her. Automatically I stepped in front of Rosemary and he cannoned against me. Then the two policemen grabbed his arms from behind.

"Party's over," Field said.

But it was not over. Toby was handcuffed and led to the car. While Field radioed for assistance, Ingram began to take our names and addresses. He began with me. When he realized I was a clergyman, his eyebrows rose, making me feel like a naughty child caught out.

"What about Miss Clifford?" he asked me. "Where's she?"

"I don't know."

He moved on to James, who was looking almost sober again. I glanced around the crowded hall. Almost everyone was there, apart from the Potters, Joanna, Audrey, Vanessa and Michael.

And Rosemary, too, I suddenly realized: she had been there a moment ago, but now she had slipped away.

There was a light under the office door. Perhaps Vanessa had returned to pore over Francis Youlgreave's books, oblivious of the commotion. I opened the door. No one was there. The books and the torch were still on the table. So was the telephone.

"Officer?" I called to Ingram. "Do you mind if I try phoning the Vicarage to see if my family's gone back home?"

Ingram nodded, and went back to Mary Vintner, who was still nursing a large gin.

I dialed the Vicarage number. The phone rang on and on.

"I bet they're all down at the pool," James said at my shoulder. "Probably sheltering in that little hut. I expect Joanna's there as well."

"We'd better go and see. If the police let us."

Ingram raised no objection, so James and I walked back to the sitting room; James brought the torch. We went out on the terrace.

"Vanessa?" I shouted. "Audrey? Michael?"

"Joanna!" yelled James a few inches away from my left ear.

There was no reply. Just the steady rustle of the rain.

"Damn it," James said. "We'll have to go down there and get soaked."

Then someone began to scream.

It was a high, gasping sound in two parts, with the stress on the first. It sounded completely inhuman, like the cry of a seabird. But the screams made a word, repeated over and over again.

*David. David. David.*

I ran down the steps to the lawn toward the source of the scream. James flicked on the torch and followed. We pounded in the direction of the pool. My feet skidded on the wet grass. Rain ran down my cheeks and filled my eyes. The beam danced like a will-o'-the-wisp in front of us. I stumbled and almost fell down the short flight of steps from the lawn.

Rain speckled the surface of the water. The torchlight swooped from one side of the pool to another. It picked out Audrey in the shallow end, her hair hanging wet and loose on her shoulders, and the skirt of her dress floating around her on the water. She was standing with her arms upraised, her mouth wide open and her head thrown back as if she were addressing a deity only she could see.

*David. David. David.*

The beam danced on. It showed a woman in Vanessa's dress, lying on her belly in the water, with Vanessa's hair floating like black seaweed beside Audrey's ballooning skirt.

The light skipped onward. The water was no longer merely blue: reds and pinks swirled like clouds on a dawn sky. Its surface was pockmarked with a shifting pattern of raindrops.

*David. David. David.*

The wind soughed in the branches of the trees beyond the pool, and the leaves of the copper beech rustled. The beam danced back, light as a feather, first to Audrey and then to Vanessa. All the while the baying continued.

*David. David. David.*

# Chapter Thirty-Six

ONLY ONE THING could have been worse than Vanessa dead.

I had few memories of the rest of the night after we found her floating in the swimming pool, and they were little better than a succession of snapshots. Even their sequence was uncertain. In my mind I shuffled them to and fro, trying to put them into order, trying to make sense out of nonsense. Coherence is a weapon against chaos, against fear, against evil. I made myself believe that.

First in the sequence came the stench of chlorine filling my nostrils. The water was cold, almost icy. It slapped and patted me like a hostile masseuse. It did not want me to reach Vanessa.

*David. David. David.*

I was aware of an obstacle, of something clinging to me, hindering me from reaching Vanessa. I made an effort and threw it aside. Did I hit it? Not *it*: her. Audrey.

Vanessa lay in the water like a log—a thing not a person. I pawed at her, trying to get a grip. Her dress ripped. Tendrils of hair coiled around my wrist. I thought again: yes, *how like seaweed*. I hooked my arms under her armpits and pulled the top half of her body out of the water. Even with the water partly supporting her lower half, she was so heavy I could hardly raise her. She might have been made of iron. *A dead weight.*

I hauled her up. Her head lolled against my shoulder. I held her, squeezing her against my chest as, less than an hour earlier, I had held Joanna. Slowly I staggered toward the side of the pool. It was as if I were fighting my way through chilly treacle. A torch flashed like a spotlight across my face. A man was shouting but I did not have the energy to listen to the words.

*David. David. David.*

There was a splash. The water rocked in the pool and drops of it spattered on my face. James was beside me.

"Give her to me," he ordered.

I shook my head. She was my burden.

He took no notice. He pried one of my arms free and between us we half carried, half dragged Vanessa toward the ladder at the shallow end.

A little later, she lay on her back beside the pool and around her spread dark stains of blood and water. James crouched over her like an animal over its prey. Was he hitting her? Kissing her? I tried to stop him but someone held me back. Later still, perhaps, James issued orders. Blankets, bandages, hot-water bottles, ambulances. He sent people here, demanded things from there. How odd, I thought—a moment ago he was drunk, but now he seems perfectly sober.

Around us in the darkness people gathered. I heard a siren. I saw a flashing light, barely visible through the bushes of the shrubbery.

"No, no, no," someone was saying; and I did not realize it was myself until Mary Vintner wrapped a blanket around my shoulders and told me to be quiet.

"The boys," I muttered to her. "The boys mustn't see this. Where are they?"

"Don't worry," Mary said. "They're safe. We'll look after them."

"And Rosemary?"

"Don't worry."

There were police cars in the drive as well as an ambulance. In the ambulance, they made me lie down. I could not see what they were doing to Vanessa. The ride was very bumpy.

"Drive more carefully," I said. "You mustn't shake her up."

Nobody heard me; I was not even sure that I had spoken aloud.

At the hospital, they put me in a chair. Somebody gave me a cup of tea. People talked to me and I talked back to them. What I remember most clearly, however, was a cracked tile above a washbasin in a room where they took Vanessa. The crack had a curve to it. I stared at it for what seemed like hours. The longer I stared, the more I was convinced that the line the crack described was identical to the curve of Joanna's cheek from eye socket to chin. It was clearly a sign. But I could not interpret its significance.

I saw two hands before me: one palm upward, holding two white tablets, and the other with a glass of water between forefinger and thumb.

"Not heroin," I said, perhaps aloud. "Not heroin."

"These will help you relax," a woman's voice said with such authority that I knew that she was telling the truth. "Swallow them."

There was also a policeman. Before or afterward? Or

both? He wore a uniform. As he talked, he turned his cap around and around in his hands. His fingernails were chewed to the quick, and there were bright orange nicotine stains on the fingers. His voice was ugly. I did not hear what he said.

I must have slept because I remember waking. When I woke, it was as though I had climbed out of a pit of darkness into a world I had never seen before, into a bleak, featureless landscape that stretched, flat as a table, all around for as far as I could see; and above my head was the vast hemisphere of the sky; a Fen landscape, such as had surrounded me at Rosington. It was silent, apart from a faint beating of wings which might have been no more than the pulsing of my own heart.

*Janet—oh Janet*. Something was wrong, worse than wrong. *Not Janet. Wrong place, wrong time, wrong woman. Vanessa? Joanna?*

I remembered the pills on the woman's hand—barbiturates?—before I remembered what had happened to Vanessa. I turned my head on the pillow. The first thing I saw was another uniformed policeman. This one had the face of a child. His scared eyes met mine. Why was he afraid of me? I stared at him.

"How—how are you feeling?"

He didn't wait for an answer. He stood up, opened the door and murmured something to a person I could not see.

"My wife," I said; my voice sounded weak and strained. "How is she?"

"Detective Inspector Jeevons will be here in a moment," the constable said. "He'll probably be able to tell you."

"Surely you know?"

"Me? No one tells me anything."

"But is she alive?"

"I'm sorry, sir," he said, his hand on the door, eager to be gone. "I just don't know."

It was nearly an hour before I saw the inspector. In the meantime a nurse brought me tea.

"My wife?"

"Still unconscious. But she's pulled through the night."

While I drank the tea, I sat in a pair of borrowed pajamas in an armchair by the window, looking down on a hospital car park where people with sad, intent faces passed to and fro. I assumed that someone had taken away the clothes I had been wearing last night to dry them—and possibly for examination, as well. I found blood encrusted under my fingernails and washed my hands over and over again. I tried to pray but I could not find words. After a while I simply sat there and watched the car park. At last there was a tap on the door.

Sergeant Clough sidled into the room after Detective Inspector Jeevons. Clough was more subdued than I had seen him before. He kept his brown, bald head bowed and did not speak unless Jeevons asked him to. Jeevons was younger—a man in his early forties with a dark, cadaverous face, coarse skin and black hair; he had long sideburns that reached to the bottom of his ears.

"My wife. How is she?"

"She's alive, sir," Jeevons said. "But her condition's very serious."

"I can't remember properly. What happened to her? How was she hurt?"

"She was stabbed in the left shoulder and hit over the head, probably with an ashtray. Then she fell or was pushed into the swimming pool at Roth Park. By that time she was probably unconscious."

*A woman in Vanessa's dress, lying on her belly in the water, with Vanessa's hair floating black and glistening around the head . . .*

"But she was face downward. She wouldn't have been able to breathe." I swallowed. "Will she live?"

"I don't know. The *doctors* don't know. I'm sorry, sir—but there it is." He looked peeved, as though the uncertainty irritated him. "We've arrested her attacker."

My eyes were open but they saw only the swimming pool, the dark stains on the clear water. *Pink clouds in a dawn sky. Red in the morning, shepherd's warning.*

"Are you well enough for a little chat?"

I nodded. Clough had already opened his notebook.

"I understand there'd been bad feeling between your wife and Audrey Oliphant for some time?"

"I knew they didn't get on. But surely you're not implying—"

"Just asking a few questions, sir. Sorry to have to trouble you at a time like this, but it has to be done. Now—several witnesses have told us that Mrs. Byfield and Miss Oliphant were having words near the swimming pool just before the attack. Heated words, it seems. There had been another exchange of views, too, but that was in the house, and much earlier in the evening. This one was while you and Mr. Clifford were looking at the fire. Do you remember the fire?"

"The burning bush—tree, I mean?"

He frowned at me. "The one on that bit of waste ground near the garden."

"I rang the police."

"That's right. You were going to see if there had been a break-in at the Vicarage. Remember?"

"Yes. But then—"

"Your daughter says she saw Miss Oliphant starting the fire. I gather she was burning some valuable papers which belonged to your wife. Or rather which had been loaned to her."

"*Audrey* did that?"

"So it seems. Dr. Vintner tells me that Audrey Oliphant is going through the menopause. Women can do funny things at that stage in their lives. Spiteful. A little unbalanced, even." Jeevons stared out of the window. "We've seen her diary."

I thought of the red exercise book I had seen in Audrey's sitting room.

"Did you realize that Audrey Oliphant was in love with you, sir?"

"Surely that's putting it a bit strongly, Inspector? She's a devout churchgoer and I suppose as her priest I—"

"She wasn't interested in you just as a priest, sir. Take it from me. We got something else from that diary. She thought your wife was responsible for cutting up her cat."

"But that's absolutely ridiculous."

"So it seems," he said again, baring his teeth in an unpleasant smile. "But people do make themselves believe ridiculous things. It's human nature." He sighed. "And then they go and act out the consequences."

"Are you suggesting that Audrey Oliphant attacked my wife?"

"Mr. Clifford tells us there was a knife down there. He'd been cutting up cheese earlier in the evening in that little changing hut. We found the knife in the bottom of the pool. There was an ashtray in there as well—a heavy, cut-glass thing, with sharp corners. According to Mr. Clifford, it was on the verandah of the changing hut. No prints on either of them, I'm afraid."

"You're telling me that Miss Oliphant went for my wife with a knife and an ashtray? In a homicidal frenzy?"

"For what it's worth, I think she was trying to help your wife afterward. So it seems. We think she was trying to pull her out. I dare say they'll take that into account."

My mind grappled with his words. "Who will?"

"The court. Miss Oliphant's in custody, now. She'll be charged later this morning."

"It—it doesn't seem possible."

"It never does, sir, until it happens. But there's very little doubt about it. You see, your daughter saw them fighting on the edge of the pool. She saw Miss Oliphant with the knife. And then she scooped something up from the verandah."

The room was silent. Engines revved in the car park below.

"Where is my daughter?"

Jeevons glanced at his notebook. "She's with friends. Mr. and Mrs. Potter. We had a word with her earlier this morning."

"And Michael? My godson—what's happened to him?"

"He spent the night with Dr. and Mrs. Vintner. We've not talked to him yet. I'm told he's been asking after you."

"I must see Vanessa." I said Vanessa's name but I saw Joanna's face in my mind: it was as if a screen slid back in my memory: Joanna reminded me of Toby, his attack on Rosemary and the two men dripping in the doorway of Roth Park. "What happened about the drugs?"

Jeevons stared down his long nose at me. "What do you mean, exactly?"

"There were two plain-clothes policemen already at the house," I went on, trying to conceal my irritation. "They had found something—drugs?—in Toby Clifford's car. They were arresting him."

"It's a separate inquiry," said Jeevons, his voice suddenly formal and precise as though he were in a witness box. "The officers were from the drug squad. They discovered a considerable amount of heroin concealed in Mr. Clifford's car, and also some cannabis in the house."

"Someone must have told them where to look."

Jeevons said nothing.

"Toby accused Rosemary—my daughter."

"So I understand, sir."

It was typical of Toby to store his heroin in the Jaguar, typical of him to allow Michael to play in the car. But the fact that Toby had accused Rosemary could only mean that she knew about the location of the cache. Had he tried to introduce her to heroin, as he had introduced others? I remembered the day Rosemary had run upstairs into the bathroom.

"Can heroin make you sick? Physically vomit, I mean?"

Jeevons frowned. "Why do you ask?"

"Because there was one time that Rosemary came back in quite a state after seeing Toby. She acted very oddly. She was sick."

"First-time users often are sick."

"So that's how she knew where he kept the stuff." I stared at Jeevons, and suddenly I knew that I was only partly right. "But it wasn't Rosemary who tipped you off, was it? It was Joanna Clifford."

"I'm afraid I can't comment on that."

He didn't need to comment. His face confirmed what I had thought. Joanna must have phoned the police soon after we parted. Probably she had also unlocked the car to make it easy for the police. Joy stabbed me, just for an instant, and I winced with the pain of it: the pain of knowing that she did care for me, that she had been prepared to fight her addiction and face up to her brother; the pain of knowing that she believed we might have a future.

"What's happened to her? Joanna, I mean?"

Jeevons looked at me, and I sensed that he was puzzled. "Miss Clifford? She's gone to London to stay with an aunt. We drove her there last night. Why?"

"I—I'm glad she's with her family. This must be a very terrible time for her."

He was still staring at me. "Quite so."

"I must see my wife. And then I must see the children."

"That's all right, sir. We'll need to talk to you again, later. We've got a suitcase with some clothes for you in the car. Your daughter packed it."

"My daughter . . ." I echoed.

Jeevons stood up. "I'll make sure someone brings up the case. Then you can see your wife and go home. We'll give you a lift back to Roth."

I stood up as well. *I don't want to see my wife, I don't want to go home. All I want is Joanna, you stupid man.* Aloud I said, "Thank you, Inspector."

# Chapter Thirty-Seven

VANESSA WAS STILL UNCONSCIOUS when I left the hospital early in the afternoon. Before I saw her, I had an interview with the consultant.

"She's still in a coma," he said. "But that's hardly surprising. You have to remember that your wife's survived a drowning, and that's more than most people do."

"Surely she should have come out of the coma by now?"

"It's early days yet. We're hoping she'll wake up soon. Could be any time."

"But if she does wake up, will there be brain damage?"

He looked at me, his face professionally wary. "I'm afraid we couldn't possibly say. Not at this point."

As the car drew up in the Vicarage drive, the front door opened and Rosemary ran out. I kissed her, and she clung to me in a way she had not done since she was a little girl.

"How's Michael?"

She pulled herself away from me. "He's still at the Vintners'. He spent the night there."

"They told me."

"I stayed with the Potters. Mrs. Potter's here now."

I looked past Rosemary. Doris was standing in the doorway. She had an expression on her face which I had never seen before. Concern? Shock? Sadness? It was none of those things. As I was walking toward her I realized suddenly what it was: Doris was scared.

. . .

Later that afternoon, I went to collect Michael from the Vintners. James was working. Mary asked us all to supper, but I declined. Brian and Michael were playing Monopoly in the sitting room and barely seemed to notice my arrival.

"He can stay if he likes," Mary murmured. "He's no trouble."

Perhaps Michael heard. He looked up at me. "Are we going now?"

"You can stay here with the Vintners if you want. They've very kindly invited you."

He got to his feet and hauled up his jeans, which had slithered down his narrow hips. "I'll come with you, if that's OK." He looked at Mary, his face serious. "Thank you for having me."

When he and I were walking back to the Vicarage, I tried to talk to him but he answered in monosyllables. We crossed the main road and came to the gate to the churchyard. A few yards farther on would bring us to the Vicarage.

"Uncle David?"

I stopped. "What?"

Michael looked up at me and began to speak. Then three trucks trundled by, nose to tail, their engines so loud I could not hear what he was saying. I took him by the arm and led him into the churchyard. We walked around to the bench by the south porch. I sat down and Michael followed suit. It was only then that I remembered that Audrey had presented the church with this bench in memory of her parents. I wanted to stand up and run away from it, but I could not for Michael's sake.

"I haven't told the police," he said in a voice so low I could hardly hear. "I thought I should tell you first."

"Tell me what?"

"I was playing near the garden fence. The fence near Carter's Meadow. Brian had gone to the lavatory . . . I saw her, when she lit the match and dropped it in the box. There was a huge flame . . . I saw her face."

"Whose face?"

He stared up at me and there were tears in his eyes. "Rosemary's."

I said nothing. The tears were rolling down his cheeks now and his lips trembled. I put my arm around his shoulders, which seemed very small and fragile.

"I looked for you," he went on. "But you weren't there."

*I was with Joanna.* I touched Michael's hand, which was gripping the edge of the seat. "I'm sorry."

"There's more. Worse."

"Go on."

He began to shiver. "I didn't see what happened to Aunt Vanessa. But I heard it. I heard her falling in." He had stopped crying now, but his whole body was trembling.

I felt a spasm of pure anger—directed at myself, at God—that Michael should have had to witness this. I said, "Where were you?"

"Near the pool—behind that little hut thing. We were playing detectives, you see. Shadowing people. Brian was following you and Toby. I was watching Miss Oliphant."

"*Miss Oliphant.* Where was she?"

"Under the copper beech. It was raining. I think everyone else was inside. She—she was . . . sort of snuffling."

"Crying?"

"I don't know." He wriggled: the idea of adults crying made him uncomfortable in a way that arson and assault did not.

"Maybe. I didn't dare move or she'd see me. And then Aunt Vanessa came out of the house with an umbrella. She came down to the pool and started calling Audrey's name. Miss Oliphant went all quiet. I think Aunt Vanessa went to look for her in the hut. I couldn't see. But then Rosemary came running over the lawn and down the steps to the pool."

I gave him my handkerchief. He blew his nose.

"Michael?" My voice emerged as a whisper. "What happened next? Did you see?"

"No. I *heard*."

For a moment we sat in silence. I did not want him to go on. The church clock began to chime. It was six o'clock.

"There were voices near the pool," Michael said slowly. "No, just one. Aunt Vanessa's. 'No, don't be so stupid.' That's what she said. And then there was a sort of gasp, and a splash."

"But Audrey—"

"I *told* you—*she* was under the tree. I couldn't see her well, but I know it was her. And then she ran off *toward* the swimming pool."

"After the splash? After you heard the voices near the pool? Are you sure?"

"Yes."

"And you?"

"I—I went off." His face was chalk-white, except for his eyes, which were red-rimmed and huge. "She started screaming . . . I—I thought I'd look for you. I went down to Carter's Meadow but you weren't there."

"Toby and I had come back to the house a different way."

"And then . . . she was still screaming. And you came with Brian's dad."

"You did well."

With the arm that was around his small body, I pulled him gently toward me and he laid his head against my chest. He started to cry again.

Not for long, though. For a while, we sat there side by side on the bench, not moving, not speaking; and I stared into the porch at the notice board to the left of the door where Rosemary had displayed the mutilated corpse of Lord Peter.

*Epilogue*

ON THE NIGHT VANESSA DIED, the world turned white outside the hospital window. I sat and prayed until it was light enough to see the broad lawn and the black tangle of the trees along the main road. I looked out of the window at the view that Vanessa had never seen: at a landscape that belonged in a fairy tale. I was still there when Peter Hudson came to fetch me.

The sister understood hierarchy and enjoyed having a bishop on the premises. She fluttered around him, trying to anticipate wishes that did not exist. When at last she left us alone with Vanessa, Peter patted my shoulder. The amethyst in his episcopal ring caught the light: a stab of purple fire.

"Are you all right?"

"I don't know."

"Pneumonia?"

I nodded. "It was always the danger. If you're in a coma you can't cough, you see, you can't get rid of the phlegm. Apparently that's what usually carries them off. Broncho-pneumonia."

All meaningless. Words to ward off the evil spirits. How could I tell Peter what really mattered? That Vanessa's breath had rattled and wheezed. That it sounded like a mechanical contrivance, not human at all: like a clockwork toy winding down almost imperceptibly.

"The sister tells me you've been here for nearly forty-eight hours."

"She lasted longer than everyone thought she would." My eyes filled with tears and shamefully they were for myself. "Do you know, I thought perhaps she might wake up before she died? Say something. Or even just move. But she didn't, of course. She just stopped breathing."

Suddenly there had been the shock of silence. The machine had stopped. What mattered most of all was the emptiness: the sense of departure. While Vanessa had been in a coma, I had thought of her as being effectively dead; but now I knew that I had been wrong.

Peter turned and stared at the figure on the bed. His lips moved. Neither of us spoke for a moment. Her skin was pale and waxen. Her mouth was open. I hoped desperately that part of her somewhere, somehow, was still alive.

"Come along," he said. "It's time to leave now. Say good-bye."

I stooped and kissed my wife's forehead.


The hotel was a Tudor mansion near Egham. At the end of its truncated garden, the ground rose to a snow-covered ramp. Beyond the ramp was a motorway, the one which cut through my former parish a few miles to the east.

In the dining room, we had a table by the window over-looking the garden. Because of the snow, the room was lit by a clear light, so cool it was almost blue. Peter ordered cooked breakfast for both of us.

"I'm not hungry," I said when the waitress had gone.

"I am. Coffee?"

When the food came I ate ravenously. I had not eaten a proper meal since two days before. We did not talk. Afterward the waitress cleared the table and brought more coffee.

"What next?" Peter said.

"The funeral. I must see to the funeral. She—"

"After the funeral. What will you do then?"

"I can't think about that now."

"I think you can. It's time to begin letting go."

There was a silence. Peter struck a match and held it over his pipe. In the light reflected off the snow, the flame was drained of color, almost invisible. No secrets in this light. No place for darkness.

"While she was dying," I said, "I couldn't stop thinking of Joanna."

Peter dropped the match in the ashtray.

"It seems so unfair to Vanessa. As if I can't even mourn her properly."

"You've been mourning her for nearly eighteen months."

"No, I haven't. For all that time it was as if she wasn't a real person. As if I'd cheated her even of that."

"You did what you could."

"It wasn't enough. After all, what happened was my fault."

He shook his head. "Sloppy thinking. Not like you. *You* didn't attack Vanessa and put her in a coma. Rosemary did. Just as she cut up that poor cat and killed Lady Youlgreave to shut her mouth. Just as she tried to blame Michael and the teenagers for what happened to the cat, and Audrey for what she did to Vanessa. *Rosemary*. Not you."

"I made Rosemary what she is."

"Don't be so arrogant," Peter said. "She's shown sociopathic tendencies since she was a toddler. We both know that. It wasn't your fault that events conspired to tip her over the edge." He held up his hand and ticked off his points one by one on stubby fingers: "First she was furious because Vanessa took part of you away from her. Then she was jealous of Michael and your obvious liking for him. Then her exam results weren't up to the ridiculously high standards she'd set herself: that was the catalyst for what she did to that wretched cat. Then she fell in love with Toby Clifford and he paid her back by raping her. And finally Toby twisted the knife by pretending to flirt with Vanessa."

There was a silence. It was not easy to allow others to share responsibility. I wanted to keep it all for myself.

"And then of course," Peter said, "there was Francis Youlgreave."

I shrugged.

"You can't dismiss him." He sipped his coffee, then added, "Much as you'd like to. If nothing else, he gave Rosemary exactly the example she needed."

"This is all very well, but it doesn't change anything. The point is, if I hadn't been with Joanna—"

"Exactly the same thing might have happened. In a sense, Joanna's got nothing to do with this. Has it occurred to you that you're hiding behind your guilt? It means you don't have to engage with the world again. With people. With God."

"Rubbish."

"Is it?" Shrouded in pipe smoke, he studied my face. "Vanessa's dead. This is finished."

I stared back. "Rosemary's alive. So are Michael, and Audrey, and Toby. Not to mention Joanna."

"There's a limit to what you can do for them. They won't let Toby out of jail until nineteen-eighty at the earliest. And you've been advised not to see Audrey. You know what happened last time."

I had visited Audrey in the nursing home that James Vintner had found for her. Though heavily sedated, she had flung herself at me, covered my face with moist kisses, and begged me to take her home with me. She was suffering from the delusion that she was my wife.

"But Michael?" It was Michael's evidence which had clinched the case against Rosemary, and both of them had known it. "The stress of it all, and then the way Rosemary threatened him . . ."

The memory of that summer evening was as vivid as the memory of Vanessa's lifeless face this morning. I had tried to talk to Rosemary while we waited in the Vicarage study for Inspector Jeevons. But you cannot talk to someone who is disintegrating in front of you. It was as if another person now inhabited the shell of my daughter and stared at me through her eyes and spoke to me through her mouth.

*"How could you do this to me? I hate you, hate you, hate you. And God damn Michael, send him down to hell. I'll punish him if it takes me all my life. You wait and see . . . He's ruined everything, the little bastard. But he'll suffer for it, Father, I swear to God he will, and so will you . . ."*

As the thick, barely recognizable voice was stumbling through its commination, I had looked up to see Michael in the doorway. His mouth was open but he said nothing. Through the open window came the distant sound of wings. I heard the wings at Roth, and I heard them now in the dining room of this hotel almost a year and a half later. Once again despair rolled toward me, gray and inexorable like a bore streaming down a tidal estuary.

"David? Stop that. Now."

A hand gripped my arm. I opened my eyes and blinked across the table at Peter.

"Now listen to me. I know you're tired but you mustn't let your defenses down."

"But Michael heard—"

"Michael has his parents to care for him, as well as you. He's young. He'll manage perfectly well without you fussing over him."

Peter released my arm, sat back and began to prod the contents of his pipe bowl with a spent match. Tension drained away from me. This time the wave had thrown me exhausted but alive on to the river bank.

"And as for Joanna," he continued in a gentler voice, "I had a letter from her last week. She's pregnant."

Another silence stretched between us. I had not seen Joanna for nearly a year and a half. Peter had insisted on that. When he came back from Crete that summer, he had reinstated himself as my spiritual director and imposed several conditions on me. One of them was that I should not see Joanna again. It had been Peter who had arranged for her to go to the treatment center, and he who made sure that she stayed.

There she had met a medical student in his final year. After he had qualified, they had married and moved up to Northumberland, where he had been offered a partnership.

Peter had told me that Joanna was thinking of training as a nurse. I thought that the child would probably force her to postpone that. I found it hard to think of her married to another man, to think of her having another man's child.

"You need a change," Peter went on remorselessly. "Have you thought of doing some teaching again?"

"But my job—"

"You can't spend the rest of your life acting as someone else's curate in northwest London. You'd do far more good as a teacher."

I shook my head.

"There comes a point when punishing yourself becomes a purely self-indulgent exercise. The real question is how you can put your talents to best use. Let's face it, they don't lie in the pastoral direction. You're a teacher, perhaps a scholar. The last time I saw you baptizing a baby you held it as if it was going to explode."

I looked at him and saw the glimmer of a smile on his face. "In a manner of speaking, it did explode."

"I heard of a teaching job in America the other day. It's an Episcopalian theological college in the Midwest. The chap who runs it trained at Pusey House. I used to know him quite well when I was up at Oxford. If you want I can put in a word. No need to decide now. But think about it."

"I don't know. I really don't know."

"You've done enough brooding. It would do you good to get out of this country."

"There's Rosemary."

"I'll keep an eye on her. I'll visit, and I'll see that other people do."

"She was a victim too. For God's sake, Toby gave her a taste of heroin and *raped* her . . . She was so shocked and ashamed she couldn't even tell us what happened. And to make matters even worse he managed to wriggle out of that charge."

"Rape's notoriously difficult to prove. I know Rosemary has suffered—and still does. But there's absolutely no point in your making her into another rod to beat yourself with."

"I can't just run off and leave her."

"You can—and in the circumstances I think you should." Peter put his elbows on the table and leaned toward me. "You're using Rosemary as just one more excuse not to make a fresh start. Besides, if you take this job, you'd have a decent salary and plenty of opportunities to fly over and see her. If that's possible."

"What do you mean by that?"

"You know very well that she doesn't want to see you. You have to accept that."

I looked at him. Very good people can be as ruthless as very bad people.

"Come on, David," he said softly. "You can't go on drifting. You've got to leave all this behind you. You're carrying the past around like a dead weight."

I sat back and stared out of the window. It had begun to snow again. The flakes were almost invisible against the pale gray of the sky. I thought of the little girl whom Toby had seen crying in the crystal ball. I did not think he had made it up.

He had sounded so surprised—at what he saw? At his ability to see it?

When Joanna took me up to Francis Youlgreave's room in the tower, she had heard a child crying too. The same one? Had the child been merely the product of a drugged imagination? In that case, why had Toby seen it? Did that mean that the child was somewhere in the past or the future or another part of the present?

"There's so much I don't understand," I said. "The trouble is, I don't know whether a fresh start is possible. I don't know if all this is finished yet."

"It is always possible to begin again. And even if it weren't, we should try."

I stood up and smiled down at Peter, a round little man like Father Christmas without the beard. "I wonder," I said. "I wonder."

ANDREW TAYLOR is the award-winning author of numerous novels. His first novel won the John Creasey Award, and he has also been shortlisted for the Gold Dagger and the Edgar. The only author to receive the CWA Ellis Peters Historical Dagger Award twice, Taylor lives in England.

CPSIA information can be obtained
at www.ICGtesting.com
Printed in the USA
FFHW021959080319
50930515-56358FF

31192021654700